PRAISE FOR

"A litera"

—*The Daily Telegraph*

"Absolutely brilliant."

—*The Daily Mail*

"Atticus Priest will be the star of many future novels."

—*Richard Madeley*

"Nerve-shreddingly tense. Utterly addictive."

— *MJ Arlidge*

"Dawson writes the kind of thrillers I love. Non-stop, grab-you-by-the-throat tales of doing the right thing no matter the odds. Simply excellent."

—*Brett Battles*

"A terrific, fast-paced read. Mark Dawson knows how to tell a great story."

—*Scott Mariani*

"Mark Dawson has all the skills. A great thriller writer on the top of his game."

—*Steve Cavanagh*

MORE THAN 18,000 FIVE STAR AMAZON REVIEWS

THE
INHERITANCE

MARK DAWSON
THE INHERITANCE

First published in 2023 by Unputdownable Limite

Copyright © Unputdownable Limited, 2020

A CIP catalogue of record for this book is
available from the British Library.

Paperback ISBN: 978-1-0687754-4-4

Typeset by Riverside Publishing Solutions Ltd (UK)
Printed and bound by CPI Group (UK), Ltd., Croydon, CR0 4YY.

MIX
Paper | Supporting
responsible forestry
FSC
www.fsc.org
FSC® C013604

ALSO BY MARK DAWSON

To my family (especially my long-distance companion Scout),
and to the booksellers in Salisbury who have
made this series such fun to work on.

PROLOGUE

Salisbury, November 1830

Thomas Farebrother braced himself as the cart lurched over the rutted track, the iron-rimmed wheels jarring against the hardened earth pitted deep with the marks of wains that had hauled the harvest to market two months past. It had been warm then, the air thick with dust and the drone of flies, but now late autumn's chill had settled in. The damp air carried the scent of woodsmoke and rotting leaves, blown into small heaps beneath the hedgerows by the wind.

The horse huffed, its breath misting in the morning air. Samuel Larke flicked the reins, urging it forward. The three of them had been on the road for an hour, and the cold had worked its way through their coats, stiffening their fingers even where they kept them tucked inside their sleeves. Just one last rise now, then the gentle descent into Laverstock, where they would leave the cart at George Embley's farm before making the rest of the journey into Salisbury afoot.

It was four miles from Pitton to the city, and Samuel had borrowed the horse and cart from Edward Farley for the day. A rare kindness, though Farley would no doubt expect some favour in return. Samuel held the reins while Thomas and Robert Ayres sat in the back, hunched against the cold, perched atop a bed of scratchy hay that pricked their calves through their stockings.

Samuel shifted, glancing over his shoulder. "What do you think it'll be like?"

Thomas rubbed his hands together, blowing on his fingers before answering, "There'll be anger. And I don't think men will be slow in showing it."

Samuel's brow furrowed. "And trouble?"

Thomas hesitated. "Perhaps. William Turnbury told me there was a rising in Fordingbridge last week. A hundred men gathered to smash the threshing machines. The squire called in the yeomanry."

"I heard there was mischief at Longford, too," Robert said. "They sent a letter to the steward, demanding he lower the rents and raise the wages. When he refused, a mob came to his door with torches."

Samuel's grip on the reins tightened. "I don't know if I wish to be there if it turns ugly."

Thomas set his jaw, trying to reassure him. "Nothing will turn ugly. We'll hear the speeches, take an ale, and be back for the horse before dusk. You'll be home before cook sets out the pottage."

Samuel nodded, though his shoulders remained stiff, and Thomas knew he was still uneasy. He was just twenty-five, the youngest of the three of them, and though he was broad in the shoulders, he was not yet seasoned like Thomas or Robert. He had recently taken a bed in the Farley poorhouse, although he was looking for work to get out.

Samuel's parents had been taken by the pox ten years ago, one after the other, and Thomas's father had brought him into their house. There had never been much bread to go around, but the boy had been given his share, and he had grown alongside the rest of them. Now, Thomas's parents were gone too, and it was left to him to bear the burden. He was nine-and-twenty and the head of the family: him, his wife Elizabeth, their first-born child, and his ten brothers and sisters.

Money had been harder to come by these past months. Lord Brookmere had raised the rents again and, worse, the threshing machine had come to the village, threatening to take the winter work away. Where last winter there had been coin enough for flour, meat, and ale, now there was scarcely enough for bread alone. Elizabeth had been forced to stretch what little they had; she'd cut the ale thinner and boiled bones for soup instead of proper cuts of meat. Last night, she'd made a thick pottage of barley and turnips, flavoured with a scrap of salted pork saved from last week's market. The scent of it had filled the cottage, rich and hearty, but there'd been little enough to share. The last of the bread had been stale, its crust tough from age, but they had softened it with broth and eaten in silence.

And this morning, before they set off for the city, Elizabeth had made sure his belly was full. She awoke before dawn, stoked the fire, and made him a bowl of oat gruel, sweetened with a little honey and dried apples. She cracked one of their few remaining eggs into the pot, stirring it through to make it richer, and set out a wedge of hard cheese beside it. Henry had tottered out of bed and, still in his underclothes, had tried to steal a bite; Elizabeth had swatted the boy's hand away with a mock scolding.

Keeping them all fed was becoming harder and harder, especially with what Brookmere seemed intent on doing.

Something had to be done.

Thomas hoped he might find an answer in the city.

* * *

They walked toward the market square, where the clamour of voices and the sharp ring of hobnailed boots upon the cobblestones filled the air. The city smelled as it always did: damp wool, roasting chestnuts from vendors hunched over their braziers, and the ever-present stink of horse shit left by the carts that rattled through the streets.

Ordinarily, the marketplace would have been bustling with traders, their stalls heaped with sacks of wheat and barley, baskets of apples, and barrels of salted fish from Christchurch. But not today. The square was thick with people, pressed close, their faces set with hard purpose, all eyes turned toward the guildhall, where the speakers had gathered.

Thomas drew his coat tighter, shifting his weight as he craned his neck to see. He'd never seen so many people assembled here before. There must have been two hundred, maybe three, standing shoulder to shoulder, their breath misting before their faces. Farmers in threadbare coats, their hands callused and raw from years in the fields, stood beside smiths with soot-blackened faces. Women wrapped in thick woollen shawls clutched their children close. Younger men—like Thomas—stood tense and restless, fists clenched at their sides.

Samuel nudged him. "Look you there."

He gestured toward the edge of the square. Thomas turned, his gaze falling upon a group of constables loitering beneath the eaves of the Market Hall. They wore dark coats and stovepipe hats, and truncheons were tucked into their belts. One of them—a thickset man with a pockmarked face—shifted his stance, his fingers tightening around the wooden shaft of his staff as though already weighing when he might need to use it.

Thomas turned back. A cart had been dragged into the square and overturned to serve as a makeshift platform for the speakers. Three men had already addressed the crowd—a cloth merchant from Wilton, bitter over falling wages; a parish curate, railing against the Poor Law and the workhouses; and a farmer, newly turned off his land. But none had drawn the people as tight with anticipation as the man who now stepped up onto the cart.

Edward Layton.

The word was that he had once been a tenant farmer, but that was years ago. Now he was a wanderer, a speaker, a radical; and, if you were to ask the magistrates, a dangerous agitator. Thomas had heard of him before. Layton had worked common land outside Winchester, it was said, until his landlord enclosed the fields and turned him out. Now he walked from county to county, speaking at gatherings like this, urging people to rise up and resist.

And the people had come to listen.

"Brothers!" Layton's voice rang out over the heads of the crowd. "I see before me no beggars, no criminals, no rogues, as the gentry would have you believe—but honest men. Men who have laboured upon this land, who have broken their backs and bloodied their hands to feed their families, only to be told they have no right to the very soil beneath their feet."

A murmur rippled through the gathering, swelling into a chorus of voices. Thomas clenched his jaw.

"I tell you, the law is not made for men like us. It is made for *them*." Layton's arm shot out, pointing toward the grand houses that lined the square: the homes of magistrates and landowners, men who sat on the bench and ruled in favour of their own. "It's made for those who grow fat while we starve, who sit in their grand houses with bellies full and pockets heavy, while we scour for scraps in the fields they've stolen. They enclose the land, drive us from our cottages, and now they've the gall to replace our honest labour with machines and dare to call it progress."

A shout came from somewhere in the crowd. "It is not progress—it is theft!"

The words struck like a flint. A surge of energy ran through the gathering. A man beside Thomas—someone he recognised from the market—shook his fist. "Smash their machines!"

Thomas's fists tightened at his sides. He thought of Elizabeth and Henry, of their dwindling stores of flour, of the way Elizabeth had fought back tears last week when she had scraped the last of the lard from the pot.

The crowd stamped their feet against the cobblestones, the rhythmic clatter echoing off the buildings. Some clapped their hands, not in applause, but in slow, deliberate time, their voices rising, an angry tide swelling beneath Layton's words.

He raised his hands for quiet, and after a moment, the roar subsided to a low mutter.

"Friends," he said, "I've just come from Kent, where I've seen with my own eyes what men of stout heart and firm purpose may accomplish when they stand together. In Elham, in Maidstone, in Canterbury—the people have risen. They've marched to the great houses and demanded justice. Captain Swing has sent letters to warn the landowners that if they will not listen, then the people will act. They've put torch to the threshing machines that steal their bread; they've broken down the enclosures that have robbed them of their birthright."

A new stir ran through the crowd. "And what happened to them?" a voice called out.

Layton's jaw was tight. "Some were arrested. Some were tried. Some were transported, and some, it's true, have been hanged. But none of them regret what they have done. And I ask you—what other choice do we have? The magistrates will not aid us. The gentry will not listen. The parsons tell us to endure, to bear our suffering meekly—to pay their tithes—but I say no! I say we've borne enough. And if those good men of Kent, labourers and ploughmen—no different from we who stand here—if *they* can rise and make their voices heard, then I ask you—why not us?"

A roar erupted from the crowd, and men raised their fists.

Layton's voice cut through the din. "They'll call us lawless men, as they called *them* lawless. They'll send their watchmen, their magistrates, their soldiers. But I tell you this—no law, no army, no king can stand against a people who will no longer be bound in chains. And so I ask you—will you stand with me? Will you take back what is yours? Will you be free men?"

The answering cry was deafening.

"They will not give us justice," Layton roared, his voice nearly lost amid the clamour. "We must take it for ourselves!"

* * *

The protest had lingered for another hour, but with the speeches done and the late afternoon air turning even sharper, the crowd had begun to thin, men drifting away in twos and threes. Some had taken themselves to the city hostelries, seeking warmth and solace in tankards of ale, murmuring their discontent in low voices over the scrape of stools and the crackle of hearth fires.

Thomas and the others had found themselves in the India Arms on Culver Street, its low-beamed ceiling thick with pipe smoke, the fire casting flickering shadows across the lime-washed walls. The place was crowded with men from the square; the air still crackled with heat, though the edge of it had been blunted by drink.

The three of them had pooled what few coins they had and bought three flagons of ale, thick and bitter on the tongue. They drank slowly, making it last, letting the warmth seep into their bones, loosening their stiffness if not their worries.

At length, their thirsts slaked, they set off once more through the city. The streets were quieter now save for two constables beneath a flickering lantern, their truncheons hanging at their sides as they watched the last stragglers with barely concealed suspicion. They walked eastward, their footsteps echoing through the narrowing streets. The grand stone houses of the gentry gave way to meaner dwellings and then to the country lanes that led toward Laverstock.

They reached George Embley's farm and collected the cart, pressing a few pennies into Embley's hand in thanks for the hay and water he had given the horse. They clambered aboard. Samuel took the reins and urged the horse onwards, through the villages on the eastern side of the city and then into the countryside beyond.

Thomas shifted his weight, rolling his shoulders against the stiffness that had settled there. The hard bench of the cart pressed into his legs and backside, and the chill had crept deep into his muscles. His fingers ached from the cold, the skin cracked and raw, though not as badly as Robert's; his friend was rubbing his hands together, breathing on his knuckles, trying to coax warmth back into them. The wind had picked up a mile out of the city, and when Thomas looked up, he saw the first dark clouds massing on the horizon. Rain was coming.

"Well," Thomas said at last, breaking the silence, "what think you?"

Robert shrugged, pulling his coat tighter about his shoulders. "I think talk like that is like to get a man transported."

"The constables were there," Thomas said. "You saw them. They did naught."

"They couldn't well arrest the whole square."

"They could have taken Layton."

"When we were all watching?" Robert shook his head. "No. That would've set the whole crowd ablaze."

"Do you know Edmund Smith?" Thomas asked.

"Tobias's brother?"

"Aye. Did you know he's with the special constables now?"

"I did not."

Thomas nodded. "Has been this past year. I saw him in The Goat last week, after I took the sheep to market, and he told me plenty of the men are with us. They say Brookmere's wrong to do as he's done, and they'd turn a blind eye to a gathering like today no matter what was said."

The last light of day was bleeding into dusk, the sky streaked red and gold, as if it had been scored open by a blade.

Thomas hesitated, then looked between the two men beside him.

"Lads," he said, lowering his voice, "if I tell you something, will you swear to keep it to yourselves?"

"That depends on what it is," Samuel said, his fingers worrying at the reins.

"Don't be a fool," Robert said. "Of course we'd keep it to ourselves."

Thomas took a breath. He had been watching them both at the gathering, measuring them, weighing whether to speak his mind. He'd seen the anger in their eyes and heard the fervour in their voices, and the way they'd embraced Layton's words had settled his mind.

"I've been thinking on something. Things are getting worse, not better—aye?"

"Aye," they murmured.

"And are you content to let Brookmere do as he has done?"

"No," Robert said, "of course not. But there's naught that can be done to stop him."

"There is," Thomas insisted. "There *is*. Did you not hear what Layton said of Kent? Those were common men, no different from us, and they destroyed hundreds of the machines and tore down the fences. They forced the gentry to heed them."

"Aye, I heard," Robert said, "and I mind him saying there were hundreds of them." He cast a look around, the corner of his mouth twisting in wry amusement. "If you're thinking what

I think you're thinking, then you might want to reconsider your reckoning. I count only three of us."

"Do you think they *started* with hundreds?" Thomas said. "No. It would have been a handful. Men who had suffered for too long—men who would suffer no more. Maybe they started with three, like us, and maybe those three struck the spark."

Samuel exhaled. "And what spark do you mean to strike?"

"Brookmere delivered a threshing machine to the farm last week, did he not? He bought it from Taskers in Andover."

"He did," Robert said. "I saw it in the barn—it is an infernal thing."

"It is," Thomas said. "It is the Devil's work—and I say we go up there tonight and wreck it."

* * *

The rains came as they finished their supper, a fierce downpour hammering against the roof so hard that, for a moment, Thomas considered calling off what they had agreed to do. The thought was dismissed almost as swiftly as it came. Robert and Samuel had agreed to wait for him on the track north of Pitton, and he would have to go out to tell them so; given that and given that he'd be soaked through the moment he stepped beyond the threshold, they might as well go through with it.

And, he thought, the weather might serve them well. No soul would be abroad on a night like this. The downpour would shroud them, their movements lost in the rain, and any noise they made as they had their way with the machine would be swallowed by the storm.

Thomas waited until Elizabeth and the child were asleep before stirring, moving as quietly as he could so as not to wake them. It was better that Elizabeth did not know. She would beg him to stay. She would plead for patience. In years past, he might have listened. But three poor harvests, the dwindling work, and Brookmere's clear intent to drive more men to ruin had pushed him beyond patience. He'd listened to Layton that afternoon and had seen that Wiltshire's troubles were no different from those in Kent.

He dressed in his thickest woollen tunic beneath his leather jerkin and pulled on his boots. His heavy cloak would do little to keep him dry, but he fastened it about his shoulders all the same. He stepped outside, feeling the weight of the rain upon him. He lifted his face to the sky, but the storm had swallowed the stars. Had it been clear, he would have known the hour by the moon's climb beyond St. Peter's bell tower. As it was, he counted forward from supper and reckoned it near to midnight.

Robert was waiting for him at the edge of the village, standing in the dripping shadow of a thatched eave to shelter from the worst of the rain. His cloak was drawn close, the hood pulled low, but Thomas could still see the gleam of water beading on the wool. He'd come prepared and had brought the tools they would need: a heavy maul and an iron digging bar for prising apart the gears.

"Samuel?"

"I do not know," Robert said, shifting his grip on the sledgehammer's haft.

A moment later, the sound of hurried footsteps splashing through the waterlogged track made them both turn. Samuel emerged from the dark, his boots sucking at the mud with every step. He, too, was cloaked against the rain, and carried a chisel wrapped in rags to silence the sharp ring of metal upon metal.

"Sorry I'm late," he said.

Thomas nodded. "Let's get going. The sooner we're done, the sooner we're home."

They followed the track up and out of the village. At the crest of the hill, Thomas turned and looked back. Pitton lay in the hollow of the land, a huddle of thatched cottages turned grey by years of rain and smoke. The largest house in the village belonged to the steward of Lord Brookmere's estate: a two-storey timber-framed building with a slate roof, sitting apart from the rest. Across the valley, the blacksmith's forge still glowed faintly, the embers banked down for the night, the scent of scorched iron and coal lingering even in the rain.

They pressed on, their boots sinking deep into the sodden track, until they reached the fringe of woodland that separated the village from the fields. The trees gave them some respite, but not for long. The cover thinned, and then they were out into the open, the farm buildings rising before them in the dark.

The barn was a simple structure, nothing more than a timber frame with brick at the base and thick wooden doors bolted shut against the night. The machine stored away inside meant to put men like them out of work. The grain had been threshed by hand for generations, men working through winter to strip the wheat from the chaff with flails. It was long and aching work, but it was honest, and it kept bread on the table. Then the landlords had brought in the machines, and everything had changed. What had once taken twenty men a season could now be done in a matter of weeks by one or two with a machine and two willing horses. Those men who'd once laboured in the barns and the fields would be cast out, left to beg for parish relief or take to the road in search of work that did not exist.

Thomas glanced at Robert and Samuel and nodded.

This was the right thing to do.

Robert stepped up to the doors, set the digging bar against the lock and wrenched. The metal groaned but held fast. Thomas joined him, gripping the bar, and together they heaved. The lock snapped with a sharp crack, and the doors swung open.

The barn was dark, and Thomas smelled the dust and grain in the air. There was enough dim moonlight for him to see the stub of a tallow candle left by the workers. He struck flint to steel, and the spark caught.

The weak flame flickered, casting long shadows across the hulking shape of the machine that dominated the barn. It was a monstrous thing, all iron and wood, with its great drum and flailing arms, waiting for the belts to be turned by the animals that would be harnessed to it. The landlord's men had yet to bring it into use, but it was only a matter of time.

Thomas drew a slow breath. He took the bar from Robert and stepped forward. He struck the machine, the blow ringing out against the iron, swallowed at once by the rain hammering against the roof.

"Wait," Samuel said.

He went forward and crouched by the machine. His fingers found the flywheel, slick with oil, and worked their way to the key: an iron wedge set tight against the shaft. He wiggled it loose with his clasp knife, the blade slipping once and nicking his thumb. He hissed, then gripped it tighter and pulled. The key came free with a metallic squeal.

He held it up. "There," he said. "A memento."

Robert stepped up, driving the hammer down upon the wooden frame. There was a splintering crack as it buckled

14

and then another as a large chunk broke away. Samuel moved to the side of the machine, using the hammer and chisel to strike at the gears and cogs. They worked quickly, their breath coming in sharp bursts. Thomas splintered the oak beams that supported the machine's weight. Robert drove the maul down upon the iron gears, and Samuel worked at the joints, wedging the digging bar between the cogs, wrenching and twisting until the metal bent.

They moved methodically, working as fast as they dared, but even so, every crash of wood or screech of metal set Thomas's nerves on edge.

Then he saw it.

A flicker of movement beyond the barn doors.

He froze, his breath misting in the cold air.

A pinprick of light swayed in the dark, moving toward them from the far edge of the fields.

"Stop," he hissed.

It was a lantern. He lost sight of it and thought it had moved away, but then it brightened—slowly, deliberately—as if its bearer had drawn back the cloth that had hidden it.

He wiped a hand against his cloak, smearing mud across the wool, and stared.

Then came another light.

And another.

They were not alone.

He grabbed Samuel's shoulder. "We need to go."

Samuel saw the lanterns, and then Robert did too.

"Out the back," Thomas said. "Now."

They turned, skirting the wreckage of the machine, and slipped through to the rear of the barn. The door was locked, but Thomas took the bar and prised it open, opening the door and hurrying outside. The rain lashed at them as they ran, their feet sliding through puddles of water. The mud sucked at their boots, but they pushed on, heading for the cover of the trees.

Then, from the right, another lantern flared.

And another.

And another.

A shout rang through the storm.

"Halt!"

Thomas came to a stop, his boots sliding in the mud; Samuel lost his footing and fell, landing on his back. The lights swayed closer, bobbing in the hands of the men who carried them. There were at least ten and maybe more, their shapes half-hidden by the rain.

They were armed with cudgels.

The leader stepped forward, levelling a flintlock squarely at Thomas's chest. "Hands."

Thomas exhaled, lifting his arms above his head.

"Do as he says," he told the others.

Slowly, reluctantly, Robert and Samuel did the same.

The rain poured down around them as the men closed in.

* * *

The dining hall of Brookmere House blazed with candlelight, the flames of a hundred tapers flickering in their silver sconces, casting shifting shadows upon the high-plastered ceiling. The chamber had been designed to impress; its newly panelled walls bore oil paintings of Brookmere's ancestors, their austere faces peering down upon the assembled guests. Beneath them, a fine tapestry depicting the Battle of Blenheim softened the cold expanse of stone. The air was thick with the mingled scents of roasted meats, game pies laced with nutmeg, and the aroma of claret decanted into crystal goblets.

Edmund Ainsley, Lord of Brookmere, sat at the head of the long elm table, his goblet cradled in his ring-laden fingers. His valet had seen to it that he was dressed with particular care for this evening's gathering: his black tailcoat was cut from the finest wool, his waistcoat embroidered in gold thread, and the crisp white folds of his cravat framed his hawkish features. His boots, newly polished, rested on the Turkish rug beneath the table as he sat, one leg crossed over the other, and surveyed his guests.

Tonight was a triumph: a celebration of his ascendance, the completion of his grand estate, and the solidification of his influence over Wiltshire. Brookmere House, with its soaring columns and vast parklands, was built to endure, a symbol of wealth and legacy. His name would be carried back to London, murmured in drawing rooms and whispered in the corridors of power.

To his left sat Sir Richard Beaufort, a cousin to the Duke of Wellington, his grey beard neatly trimmed, his coat of deep navy adorned with gilded buttons. To his right was Lord Thomas Ludlow of Hampshire, dressed in the dark green of his family crest, lifting his goblet to signal for more wine. At the far end of the table, His Grace, the Bishop of Winchester, resplendent in silk and lace, conversed with an envoy from the Home Office.

"So," Beaufort said, raising his glass, "it seems your labourers have been busy of late."

A ripple of amusement passed through the gathered lords.

Brookmere exhaled sharply through his nose. "If you mean that rabble in Salisbury, they were hardly mine. Discontented tenants, stirred up by radicals." He waved a dismissive hand. "It will come to nothing."

"The same was said of Kent," Ludlow remarked, swirling the wine in his goblet. "Yet the riots spread, and now the courts are drowning in trials."

The bishop set his glass aside. "It is a troubling thing when men forget their place. I am told they demand the destruction of threshing machines. They claim that mechanisation robs them of honest labour."

A scoff from one of the guests. "Progress is progress. A man cannot halt the turning of the wheel."

Brookmere smiled thinly. "And should they try, there are those of us who will remind them of their folly."

Laughter rippled along the table. A silver platter of roasted pheasant was set before them, the skin crisp and glistening, while further down, a footman carved open a steaming venison pie. The scent of cinnamon and cloves drifted through the air.

"The real concern," said Beaufort, leaning in, "is how widespread this sentiment becomes. It is not merely the farmhands who complain—merchants in Salisbury grumble at the rising cost of grain, townsmen resent the price of meat. When men feel their purses emptied, they grow bold."

Brookmere arched a brow but said nothing. The truth was, he cared little for the plight of merchants or townsfolk. What mattered was control. And he had it.

The great doors of the hall swung open, the hinges groaning, and the room fell momentarily silent. A man strode in, his boots wet from the rain, his heavy cloak dripping onto the polished floor. It was William Harcourt, one of Brookmere's retainers: a broad-shouldered man with a face carved from granite and a scar running from jaw to temple.

Harcourt halted near the head of the table and bowed low. "My lord. A word, if I might."

Brookmere sighed, annoyed at the interruption. He excused himself with a murmur and stepped away from the table, leading Harcourt to a quieter alcove.

"What is it?"

"Three men, found in the barn, wrecking the threshing machine."

Brookmere's expression darkened. "Who?"

"Labourers from Pitton. One of them, a man called Farebrother, is said to have led them."

Brookmere exhaled through his nose. "Impudence. Do they have any idea how much the machine costs?"

"I should imagine not, my lord."

"One hundred pounds," he said. "And what did they think? That I would *ignore* the damage they have wrought?"

"What would you have me do?"

"Punish them."

"As you wish, my lord."

* * *

They had been kept in the barn for what must have been three or four hours. Thomas tried to speak to the men, but they wouldn't respond, and when he tried to step closer to them, the man with the flintlock, now holstered on his belt, laid his hand on the butt and shook his head. The warning was obvious, and Thomas knew it would be foolish to ignore it.

"What are we going to do?" Samuel hissed.

"We wait," Robert said. "There will be an opportunity to run. Be ready."

"Who are they?"

"His Lordship's men," Thomas said. "They must have suspected someone would try to get to the machine. How badly did we damage it?"

"Enough," Robert said.

Samuel held up the flywheel key. "And we have this."

Thomas heard hoofbeats, the rattle of tack and then a snort. The door opened, and a man came inside. He was tall and broad shouldered, with a cavalry coat slung carelessly over his shoulders, raindrops heavy on its woollen folds. His boots were muddied to the shin, and he held his riding crop in a gloved hand. His face was lean, with sharp cheekbones and eyes that glittered coldly beneath the brim of his hat.

Thomas recognised him: his name was Harcourt, and he was the lord's bailiff. He had a reputation for cruelty. Thomas had heard tell of Harcourt ordering an old cottager flogged in front of his family for gathering firewood from the estate woods; he said it was poaching, though the man had no other means to keep warm.

Harcourt spoke with the man with the flintlock and then came over to them.

"You will be delivered to the yeomanry in Salisbury, and it will be their decision what to do with you." He gestured to the door with his crop. "Walk."

They were taken in silence, cudgels pressed into the smalls of their backs, the ring of lantern light bobbing across the sodden ground. Robert asked a question—Thomas didn't catch it—but no answer was given. One man jabbed him hard enough in the ribs that he staggered, catching himself on Thomas's shoulder. Samuel said nothing at all. He was limping; he'd fallen awkwardly back by the barn and hadn't recovered.

They crossed the fields by a route Thomas didn't recognise.

"Where are we going?" He turned his head. "Where are the yeomanry?"

His question was rewarded with a clubbing blow from a cudgel on his shoulder; he gasped at the sudden pain but turned his head forward again and kept walking.

Beyond the hedgerow, far from the road and the village, they came to a clearing edged with trees and sodden thorn. It was a quiet spot, if there was such a thing that night, with the rasp of wind and the steady lash of rain.

They were given spades.

"Dig," Harcourt said.

Not a word of explanation, but the implication was clear. Thomas's stomach churned. He glanced to Robert, who held his head high, and to Samuel, who looked too stunned to speak.

"Please," Thomas said. "This is unnecessary."

One of the men lashed out with his cudgel, catching Thomas on the side of his mouth. His tongue was forced against his teeth, and he tasted blood.

"Dig!"

Thomas spat blood. "Please," he said around the pain in his mouth. "We are sorry."

The man with the flintlock took it from its holster, pulled back the hammer and levelled it at Thomas's head.

"Dig—*now*."

Thomas and the others took their spades and set to work without another word.

The earth was thick and claggy, sucking at the blades, heavy with water. They dug until their backs ached and their hands were raw. Thomas had lost track of time, but the holes were deep enough when the order came.

"Down."

Robert went first. He laid aside his spade and stepped carefully down into the grave he'd made.

He turned to face them. "You should be ashamed."

The man with a flintlock stepped forward and, without a word, raised the pistol and shot him. The crack rang across the field. Robert's body collapsed into the mud with a wet slap.

Samuel screamed. He tried to run, slipped, scrambled in the muck. Two men caught him and dragged him back. Thomas looked away as they forced him down. The man who had killed Robert was given a fresh flintlock. The second shot was louder, closer.

Thomas was next. He stood at the edge of the last grave and looked down into it. His hands trembled. He wanted to speak, to say something—anything—but there was nothing left.

One of the men behind him cleared his throat.

"Down."

Thomas swallowed hard. He stepped down. The muck came up to his ankles. He knelt.

He heard the splash of boots in the puddle behind him.

Then the hammer clicked back.

PART 1

Monday

1

Jack Turnbull jumped down from the cab of the tractor, his boots sinking up to the ankles in the sodden ground by the gate. The mud sucked at his feet, clinging thickly to the rubber, and he swore. It'd been a wet winter, one of the wettest he could remember, and even though the farm was on high ground, the water table was still up enough that the lower sections were a quagmire.

He thumbed in the combination to the padlock, pushed the button to open the clasp, and heaved the heavy iron gate back on its hinges. The top rail was slick with rain, and as he pulled it, the whole thing shuddered in protest, the posts shifting slightly in the sodden earth.

At least this field was in decent shape. It had been grazing pasture for decades, coarse fescue and ryegrass, but this year he was turning it under. Clarendon Hill Farm was a mixed operation—half arable, half livestock—and covered seven hundred acres all told, bought up piecemeal after the current Earl of Brookmere's father had been forced to sell off some of his vast estate to settle death duties in the sixties. Jack's father had scraped and borrowed to buy as much as he could, securing the family's future in a single move.

Farming had been difficult for years, but the last three or four had been particularly hard. Prices for crops had fallen, squeezed by cheap imports and supermarket contracts that left little room for profit. Barley, wheat, and oilseed rape had once been reliable, but margins had narrowed to the point where breaking even was a victory. Cattle were the same. Costs, meanwhile, had done the opposite: diesel, fertiliser, feed… everything had gone up. Brexit made seasonal labour harder to come by, and the new environmental schemes, designed to replace the old EU subsidies, were an unworkable tangle of bureaucracy.

Those problems had left farmers on the ropes, but the new inheritance tax rules felt like the final blow. The farm was in Jack's father's name, and the plan had always been for it to be passed on to Jack when the old man died. The new rules made that impossibly expensive, and if they wanted it to pass on so that it could stay as a farm—without selling chunks of it to cover the tax he'd have to pay—they'd need a plan.

And right now, he didn't have one.

Jack clambered back into the cab, wiping mud from his gloves onto the faded denim of his jeans, and settled into the well-worn seat, the foam beneath him cracked and sagging from years of use. From up here, he had a commanding view of the field: a rectangle of rough grassland bordered by woodland on three sides—Carverel Copse, Fairoak Copse and Pitton Copse—the tree line dark and tangled at the edges. The Clarendon Way ran along the southern boundary, a popular route for dog walkers and ramblers, though it was quiet today. The wind had picked up, a fresh westerly rolling in, stirring the tops of the beeches and oaks, rippling through the tufts of last season's growth.

He'd debated leaving the field for grazing, at least for another month or two, letting the cows strip it down before ploughing it under. But, while the price of wheat was still low, it *was* climbing. He'd spent hours wrestling with the farm accounts and had decided it was better to drill sooner rather than later. If the forecasts held, he'd make a small profit. That all depended upon it being dry long enough for him to get a clean seedbed.

Jack eased the tractor into gear, rolling forward in a slow, deliberate crawl toward the northwest corner, where he'd start the first pass. Some farmers ran fully automated rigs these days, GPS-guided monsters that ploughed, seeded, and fertilised without a human hand on the wheel. Jack had no time for any of that nonsense. He liked to feel the land, to work it himself, to learn its humps and hollows, its dry patches and waterlogged dips. You could let a satellite drive the machine and the job would be perfect—every furrow dead straight, every row aligned to the millimetre—but where was the craft in that? Where was the skill?

No thanks.

Not for him.

He flicked the switch to lower the six-furrow plough, feeling the hydraulics hum beneath him, and then nudged the throttle. The blades bit deep, rolling the earth in heavy, wet slabs, the rich smell of damp soil rising as he cut the first clean line through the pasture in decades. He glanced over his shoulder, watching the furrows turn neat and even, the grasses swallowed beneath the churned-up loam.

Jack smiled. This was the part of farming he loved most. He reached down for the radio and switched it on, tapping through the stations until he found Salisbury Radio. They were playing an old Blur song that he liked. He sang along with the chorus. It didn't matter; there was no one to overhear him.

He adjusted his grip on the wheel and turned it as he approached the fence, the tractor's tyres sinking slightly in the softer earth at the edge of the field. The woods were close now, their overhanging branches clawing at the cab, bare twigs scratching against the glass. It was dark beneath the canopy, the gloom thickened by a tangle of bramble and blackthorn that had grown unchecked along the boundary.

He was about to swing the tractor around for another pass when he noticed something in the ploughed earth behind him. The ground was a dark brown, with patches of green where the grass was still visible, but there, around twenty-five metres back, he saw a flash of white. It was picked out by a shaft of sunlight that shone down through a break in the trees.

He switched off the engine, opened the door, and jumped down, his boots sinking into the freshly turned soil. He walked back along the furrows, his eyes fixed on the pale curve protruding from the soil. Probably a lump of chalk, he told himself. There was plenty of that around here; the land was threaded with seams just beneath the topsoil. The plough turned it up now and again, the same way it dredged up old bits of pottery or rusted nails from God-knows-when.

But as he got closer, his certainty wavered.

It was too smooth, too curved.

It stood out starkly against the loam; not the rough, pitted surface of a chalk deposit, but something more solid.

He crouched down, brushing a layer of dirt away with the back of his glove, revealing an orb of weathered bone, its surface cracked and worn by time.

He rocked back on his heels.

Bone.

And not animal bone, either; he knew that straight away.

It was a human skull.

A gust of wind stirred the hedgerow, rattling through the tangle of blackthorn and ivy, sending a scatter of dried beech leaves tumbling across the field.

Jack wiped his face, suddenly aware of how cold his hands had become.

He turned back to the skull. His fingers brushed against something soft beneath the soil: a scrap of material, half-rotted. He pinched it between his fingers and lifted it gently.

Leather, cracked and fragile, the colour darkened with age.

He stayed where he was for thirty seconds before exhaling and reaching for his phone.

He dialled and put the phone to his ear.

"Hello, 999. What service do you need?"

"Police," Jack said. "I think I've dug up some human remains."

2

Francine Patterson took the A30 out of Salisbury and slowed as she reached the junction for Pitton. There was a protest camp in the field next to the turning. Franny had heard about it from Bob Carver: there'd been a complaint about the protestors from the villagers, and Bob had been out to have a look. He'd been typically brusque in his summation—'soap-dodging tree-huggers' was his considered analysis—but he'd concluded that since they had permission to be on the field and weren't causing a nuisance, there was nothing to be done.

Franny looked out at them as she waited for the opposite lane to clear so she could continue; there were perhaps twenty men and women, half of them standing by the side of the road, holding up their banners and placards, while the other half congregated around a fire that was sending a plume of grey smoke straight up into the air. Bob had said they were protesting against the enormous solar farm that was planned for the fields to the west of the village.

Franny had read about it in the *Journal*; Lord Brookmere was leasing nearly three hundred acres to a company who wanted to install tens of thousands of panels that would make it the biggest facility of its kind in the country. The planning process had been contentious, splitting locals into two seemingly equal-sized camps: those who welcomed the development for the cheaper electricity promised to those near the park and those—NIMBYs, Robbie had said to her when they discussed it—who lamented the loss of the fields and the change to the historic landscape. Franny erred more towards those who opposed it than those who supported it; she loved the natural landscape around the city and worried that her favourite view—seeing the spire reaching up whenever she drove back into the city from this direction—would be spoilt.

Franny left them behind her and continued south. She turned onto Slate Way and parked behind the patrol car that had been slotted into the space next to the old wastewater pumping station. The Clarendon Way continued west from here, leading into the fields and, eventually, picking up the trail through the woods that would end with Clarendon Palace and then the city.

Pete Britten and John Fulbright had responded to the call and radioed the control room to say that they needed someone from CID and that that person would need boots. Franny had been out walking with Robbie in the New Forest at the weekend and still had her Craghoppers in the car; she put them on and took a few tentative steps into the mud and wished she had her Hunters instead.

The track ran in a straight line, with open fields to the left and wire-mesh fence to the right. The ground was harder near the fence, and Franny tried to stick to that, using it to balance whenever footing became more treacherous.

This was her first call-out as a detective sergeant, and the last thing she wanted was to go arse over tit and coat herself in mud. She'd only received the official notification of her promotion last week, and Robbie had taken her out to celebrate on Saturday. They'd had dinner in Tinga and then moved on to the Everyman for cocktails and a film. She'd told him she'd be nervous when she got her first call-out for a possible suspicious death, and he'd told her to get over herself, that she'd be fine, that Mack wouldn't have put her up for promotion if she didn't think she was ready. He'd added, with a wink, that—seeing as he outranked her—he'd also had a say in whether she was pushed up to DS and hadn't had a moment's hesitation in saying she was ready. It'd do her good to get the call and get her first stiff out of the way.

He was right, but she was still nervous.

It took her five minutes to reach the field. She saw the top of the tractor cab first, and then, as she came around a bend, she saw Fulbright and Britten.

"Morning."

Britten looked up. "Morning."

She nodded over to the parked tractor. "That the farmer?"

Fulbright nodded. "Said he came out to plough the field and looked back and saw he'd dug something up."

"You've had a look?"

He nodded. "Definitely a human skull. Bits of leather in there, as well. Might be a boot."

"How old?"

"We'll need the pathologist for that."

"Rough guess?"

"Really wouldn't like to say. Probably old, but I wouldn't put much on it."

"Better go and have a look, hadn't I?"

"I think you'd better."

Franny tramped over to the tractor. It looked as if the morning's plan had been to plough the field, but the farmer had only managed a couple of passes before turning up the remains. The rest of the field was grassy and, save for a few boggy patches, in much better condition than the churned track from the road.

The farmer noticed her. He opened the cab door, and with the sound of music audible before he reached down to turn off the radio, he jumped down to meet her.

"I'm DS Patterson."

"Jack Turnbull."

He put out a callused hand, and Franny shook it.

"This your field, Mr. Turnbull?"

"My family's—we own Clarendon Hill Farm."

"Where's that?"

"Northwest of here," he said, pointing.

"Why don't you tell me what happened."

"I was ploughing the field when I saw something behind me. Went and had a look and called the police straight away when I realised what it was. Couldn't believe it. *Massive* pain in the arse."

"Why's that?"

"Wanted to get the seed drilled before the weather changes. Just my luck." He shrugged. "What happens next?"

"We'll dig it up and see whether that's it or whether there's more. And then we have to work out how old it is."

"How long will that take?"

"Depends on what we find. I'll need to get a pathologist out. I wouldn't be surprised if we need a forensic archaeologist."

Turnbull muttered a curse.

"If it's straightforward, it might only be a day or two. If it's more involved, or if we're looking at something recent, it might be longer. We'll only know more once we've had a proper look. But I promise we'll be as quick as we can."

Franny told Turnbull to wait at the cab and went to join Fulbright at the remains. At least the procedure she'd have to follow was fresh in her head from the exam: establish the scene, secure the perimeter, document everything, escalate as needed.

She glanced around as she approached the spot where the skull lay exposed.

First priority: secure the scene.

Turnbull had been sensible enough not to trample over the find, and Britten and Fulbright had already set a rough perimeter using crime scene tape and hazard markers. It wasn't a full forensic cordon, but it was enough to keep any curious dog walkers at bay.

She squatted down next to Fulbright. The ground was softer here, damp from the recent rain, and the ploughed earth was churned up in heavy clumps.

She looked at the skull. Definitely human. No question. It was pale and weathered, the surface slightly rough. The soil around it had fallen away, revealing not just the bone, but something else tangled beside it: a bit of leather, half-buried in the mud. It was blackened with age, but she could still make out the rough stitching along one side.

Franny straightened up and brushed the dirt from her hands. "Let's do this by the book. We need a proper cordon. You'll get dog walkers from the village coming out this way, and then you've got anyone doing the Clarendon Way. The path runs just over there."

He nodded, already moving back towards the gate. "I'll get the cones and tape from the car."

Franny took out her work phone and snapped a series of photos, starting wide before moving in closer. The skull, the surrounding soil, the leather fragment—everything in situ before anyone put a spade in the ground. The lighting was patchy, shifting as the sun broke through the tree line, and she made a mental note to request a full forensic photography set once the experts arrived.

Britten crossed the field to her. "What do you need me to do?"

"Give John a hand. I'll call the coroner."

Franny wasn't expecting it to be a modern burial, but they needed to be sure. If it turned out to be more recent than it appeared, they'd be looking at a full-scale investigation. If not—and she really, *really* hoped not—it'd be passed over to the archaeologists and they could forget all about it.

But that wasn't her call to make.

She turned back towards the tractor. Turnbull was waiting as instructed, leaning against the cab, arms folded, watching her with the weary patience of a man who could see his plans going up in smoke. Franny felt for him. She had a few friends who worked on farms, and they had it hard enough at the best of times; something like this—something out of the blue, impossible to foresee and outside of his control—was going to mess up his bottom line something rotten.

3

Atticus Priest had closed the window to muffle the sound of the traffic as it queued to get into the multi-storey car park outside his office.

"Mr. Priest?" the researcher said. "Are you there?"

"I am."

"Just checking you're still ready to go ahead with the interview."

"I'm ready."

"That's great. You're going to be interviewed by Nick this morning. We're just finishing up with the minister, and then he'll cut straight across to you."

"Understood."

"Can I just make sure you're in a quiet room?"

"I am."

"Can I hear the radio on in the background?"

"I was just listening to make sure he didn't come to me unexpectedly."

"Could you turn it off? We'll get feedback otherwise."

Atticus reached for the mouse and clicked to stop the feed. "Done."

"That's great."

"Can I just double-check what he'll want to talk about?"

"Your book," she said. "That'll be the main focus, and I think he'll want to talk to you about the case with the murder of the family and then how you helped the police with what happened on Salisbury Plain. I spoke to your publicist about that—I hope it's all still all right."

"Totally fine."

There was a pause. "They're just winding up. The next voice you hear will be Nick's."

The researcher stopped talking, leaving Atticus to listen to the conversation between the presenter and the government health minister who was currently being lambasted for lengthening waiting lists.

Bandit was lying in his basket, his head on his paws, gazing up at Atticus.

"We're going to be on the radio," Atticus whispered.

Bandit slapped his tail against the bed three times, then closed his eyes and went back to sleep.

"Well, *I'm* excited even if you're not."

The last two months had been a blur. Atticus had been approached by a literary agent from London who said she thought there was scope for him to write about his experience after leaving the police and setting up his business and asked whether he would allow her to take him on as a client and then pitch to publishers. He'd said yes and then had sat back in astonishment as publishers responded with offer after offer after offer. His agent, Lydia, said that she'd expected an enthusiastic response but admitted that she'd been taken aback by just *how* keen they'd been. She explained that publishing was an incestuous business, and that once one big offer had been received, it was possible to parlay that into others. Lydia put together a shortlist and recommended one over the others, Atticus had accepted her advice, pocketed the advance and started to write.

"Joining us now is Atticus Priest, a private investigator from Salisbury in Wiltshire who's about to release a memoir telling of how he solved a series of mysteries that gained national notoriety. Atticus—welcome to *Today*."

"Good morning."

"Now, then—your new book deals with a series of cases that I think it would be fair to say *baffled* the local police in Salisbury."

Atticus winced. He knew that Mack and the others from the nick might be listening, and the last thing he wanted to do was to have them traduced on national radio. "I wouldn't say they were 'baffled.' I was just able to bring a different perspective."

"Really? That's not what I read in your book. Let's take the Mallender case. It made the national news, didn't it? The murder of an entire family in an isolated house outside Salisbury."

"That's right."

"The police had charged a man and had taken him to trial before you became involved."

"Yes, but—"

"And you demolished the case. Isn't that right?"

"Well, again, I wouldn't say I 'demolished' it."

"But he was acquitted based on the evidence you found?"

"Yes."

The presenter laughed. "You demolished it."

Atticus looked over at Bandit; he cocked his head, then closed his eyes again.

"Your book—*Inference: A Life in Observation*—will be released next week. I've had the pleasure of reading a copy, and you take readers through the first eighteen months after setting up your business. Your background before that is the police. You say that you left under a bit of a cloud."

"Yes, that would be fair to say."

"I understand you were accused of taking drugs at work."

"I, er…" This wasn't supposed to be the direction that the conversation would take, and Atticus fumbled for the right response. "That's what they said, but it wasn't quite like that."

"You resigned and set up a private investigation business in Salisbury. I must say, a small city like that does seem to have suffered from an awful lot of crime. There was the Mallender case; then you were involved with the bodies dug up at the abandoned village on Salisbury Plain; then there was the man who was pushed to his death from the top of the cathedral tower; and then there were the locals importing drugs from Ireland, hidden in horse boxes. Listeners will be forgiven for thinking that it all sounds a little like *Midsomer*."

"We've had a run of bad luck."

"Bad luck? I'll say. The book goes through these investigations in some depth, but you also have advice for readers who might be looking to solve mysteries in their own lives."

Atticus felt as if the conversation had veered off the course his publicist had suggested, but now, at least, he was on firmer ground. "I do. I talk about the mindset you need to bring certainty to uncertain situations. A good investigator—whether they're a professional or just someone trying to make sense of something in their own life—needs to approach problems in a structured way. The first thing is to take emotion out of it. People jump to conclusions, especially when something feels personal, but if you want the truth, you have to deal in facts."

"And how do you do that?"

"Start with observation. Most people think they see what's in front of them, but they don't. They notice what they expect to see, or what fits the story they already have in their head. A good investigator looks at everything with fresh eyes."

"So don't assume—look at what's actually there."

"Exactly."

"The second thing?"

"Logic. Once you have your facts, you have to test them. Sometimes people hold onto an idea just because it feels right. But real investigation means constantly questioning your own assumptions. If A and B don't fit together, then something is wrong with your information. Either you've got the wrong facts, or you're interpreting them the wrong way."

"Like the police in the Mallender case?"

Atticus skirted over that. "The third thing is understanding people. People lie; they omit details; they misremember things. Sometimes they lie to deceive, sometimes they lie to protect themselves, and sometimes they lie because they don't even realise they're lying. If you can understand what's motivating someone, you can figure out what's really going on."

"And the last thing?"

"Patience. Most people give up too soon. Police have limited time and resources, and that means a lot of cases go cold. But if you keep pulling at the right thread, eventually something will unravel."

"Well," the presenter said, "if you're interested in learning more, *Inference: A Life in Observation* by Atticus Priest is out next week, and it's a fascinating look into the mind of an investigator. Mr. Priest, thank you for joining us."

"Thank you."

The line went quiet for a moment, and then the researcher's voice came back through his headset. "That was great, Atticus—thanks for your time."

Atticus leaned back in his chair, letting out a slow breath.

Bandit lifted his head lazily from his basket and gave him a look.

"What do you think?"

Bandit yawned.

"Mack's going to be mad, isn't she?"

The dog stretched and flopped back down.

"You're no help."

Bandit's tail thumped once against the floor, noncommittal.

"Walk?"

The dog leapt up and arrowed across the room for his harness and lead.

"I'll take that as a yes."

4

Rupert Ainsley sat at the head of the long, scrubbed-pine kitchen table, his fingers drumming against the wood. A pot of coffee sat untouched in front of him. His wife, Emelia, had just made it, but Rupert didn't have the stomach to drink. Emelia had taken the seat beside him, her hands folded in her lap, expression carefully neutral.

Rupert was sometimes able to put his diagnosis out of mind, especially when he was busy out on the estate, but it was always there, niggling away, never far from the surface. Nighttimes were the worst; he'd lie in bed, unable to sleep, powerless to stop himself from reaching for his phone and Googling everything he'd been told so that he could anticipate what might come next. He'd go from website to website, and it'd always be the same: he faced the slow and inexorable erosion of the self. Short-term memory loss would become disorientation and difficulty navigating even familiar places; then speech and reasoning would start to falter; and eventually, even the people closest to him—Emelia, his children—might become strangers in his mind. He'd lose the ability to dress, to eat, to recognise his own reflection. He'd read a clinical phrase that stuck with him like a barb: it was 'a progressive and irreversible decline in cognitive function.'

There'd been a lot of denial, too, and he'd spent the last week convincing himself that he'd been misdiagnosed, that the absentmindedness he couldn't dispute was just normal ageing, and the second set of scans would prove there was nothing wrong with him at all.

The doctor—Daniel Kershaw—was a picture of calm reassurance, although that wasn't enough to ameliorate the nervous tension bubbling in Rupert's gut. Kershaw had the air of a man who'd delivered bad news so often that he'd perfected the balance of authority and sympathy.

He took a folder from his bag, put it on the table, opened it, and removed a series of printouts. "I appreciate you making time for this, Rupert. Especially today—I'm sure there's a lot of work to do before the weekend."

"It's all in hand," Emelia said.

"It's seventy-five, isn't it?"

Rupert nodded. His birthday was on Saturday, and Emelia had persuaded him that he should have a party to celebrate. They were erecting a big marquee on one of the lawns, there would be music, and she'd arranged for a local firm to cater it. They were expecting five hundred guests, and Rupert had decided that it'd be the perfect opportunity to announce his decision about the future of the estate and the establishment of the Brookmere Trust. He had a speech to write, but he needed to get through this morning's meeting so he could attend to it with a clear head.

"I know this isn't an easy conversation to have," Kershaw said, "but I wanted to go through the results with you."

"Let's get on with it, then."

Kershaw angled the printouts so Rupert could see them. It was a set of monochrome images showing a series of cross-sectional slices of a human brain, arranged in a grid pattern. The scans were grainy, full of shadowy folds and ridges. Each image was marked with tiny alphanumeric codes in the corners, dates and medical data Rupert didn't understand.

"These are what we call axial slices," Kershaw said, tapping the top row. "Think of it like cutting through a loaf of bread —each image is a different layer, moving from the base of your skull up to the top of your head." He moved his pen to the bottom row. "And these are sagittal views—slices taken from the side, so we can see the brain's structure from a different perspective."

Rupert nodded slowly. "And?"

"I've reviewed the scans, and I'm afraid it confirms what we thought after the first set."

Rupert's stomach twisted. "Bollocks."

Kershaw's expression softened. "I know this isn't what you wanted to hear. But I want to take you through what we're seeing here, just so you understand why I'm confident in the diagnosis."

Rupert leaned forward, squinting at the images. To his untrained eye, they were nothing more than a sea of greys and blacks, a maze of folds and shadows.

Kershaw tapped his pen against the leftmost image. "This was your first scan from six months ago. Pay attention to this region here." He traced a small section near the back of the brain. "That's the occipital lobe—the area responsible for visual processing and spatial awareness. Now, here"—he pointed to the newer scan—"this is the latest image. You'll notice the sulci—the grooves in the brain—are slightly more pronounced, and the gyri—the ridges between them—have shrunk slightly. That's what we call cortical atrophy. It's subtle, but measurable."

Rupert frowned. The images looked almost identical to him. "I don't see much of a difference."

"Here—let me highlight it." Kershaw reached for a red pen and circled a darkened area near the back of the brain. "These areas show measurable shrinkage compared to the previous scan. It might not seem like much now, but it's an indicator of progression. This pattern—particularly in the posterior cortex—is consistent with posterior cortical atrophy."

"And you're sure? There's no chance that this is just natural ageing? My father started losing his memory when he was in his mid-seventies."

Kershaw shook his head. "Age-related cognitive decline tends to be more generalised. What we're seeing here is specific, targeted atrophy in the areas most associated with PCA. That aligns with the symptoms we've discussed—losing track of conversations, misplacing things, struggling with coordination."

Emelia laid a hand on his wrist.

Rupert jerked his hand away. "I don't feel any different than I did six months ago. I felt fine then, and I feel fine now."

"And that's a *good* thing," Kershaw said. "We want to catch this early so we can be proactive rather than reactive. But I need to be honest with you, Rupert—this is a progressive condition. It *will* get worse."

Rupert looked away.

"I know this is difficult," Emelia said, reaching for his hand again.

He moved it away again.

"At this stage, the focus is on management," Kershaw said. "There's no cure, but there are treatments that can help slow things down and improve cognitive function in the short term. I'd like you to start on donepezil. It won't stop the decline, but it can help with clarity and memory retention."

"And beyond that?"

Kershaw hesitated for the briefest moment before answering, "There are some interesting drugs in development. I keep an eye on these things, and if there's anything I think will help, you can be sure I'll recommend it."

"Thank you, Dr. Kershaw." Rupert stood. "Emelia will see you out."

5

Atticus waited for Jez to open the door to the Winchester office and then unclipped Bandit's lead so that the dog could follow Treacle inside. He and Jez had taken the dogs for a walk, taking the opportunity to catch up on the files that Jez was working on. He had half a dozen on the go; the main one was an investigation into a local businessman suspected of falsifying insurance claims, running a string of high-end vehicles through a network of chop shops and reporting them as stolen.

Jez had been tailing the man for the last three days, gathering evidence that suggested he wasn't just fabricating claims but was also running a sideline in laundering money through fake shell companies. It was tedious, meticulous work, the kind Jez said he enjoyed: long hours of financial analysis, cross-referencing company registrations, and digging into patterns that most people would miss. He liked the numbers, the neatness of it. Atticus, on the other hand, preferred being in the thick of a case; talking to people, reading their tells, coaxing out the truth one careful question at a time. Conversation didn't always come easily to him, but the structure of an investigation gave it purpose, a script he could follow, and in that he found clarity.

The decision to open a second office here had been a good one. It had looked promising early on, but the good sense of it was undeniable now. Atticus had been able to refer some of the cases that came to him in Salisbury to Jez, and Jez had been able to find plenty of additional work himself. His salary had quickly been covered, so much so that Atticus—after diplomatic prompting from Mack—had increased it by thirty per cent. Jez was still green, and Atticus occasionally had to bite his tongue when it took him too long to make a deductive leap that ought to have been obvious—at least it was obvious to *him*—but Jez seemed to have formed a decent idea of Atticus's character and foibles, and the two of them had settled into a comfortable routine.

Atticus had always thought that he preferred to work alone, but he'd started to doubt that. There had been times, in the first few months after setting up the practice, that he had gone days at a time without speaking to anyone. Bandit had kept him company, but he saw now that he had been lonely. Things were better now: he spoke to Jez several times a day, and he saw Mack most nights. It almost passed for a social life.

They'd found an office on the High Street to begin with, but Jez had been made aware of space nearer the cathedral, and they'd moved. It was a better spot, much quieter and with a good deal more prestige. They had three rooms above P&G Wells, the bookseller's and stationer's on College Street, and the view from the windows looked out on the Pilgrims' School.

Bandit immediately flopped onto his favourite spot near the radiator, while Treacle did a quick circle of the room before settling in his bed in the corner.

Jez dropped the carrier bag with his supplies onto the desk and turned to Atticus. "Coffee?"

Atticus nodded.

Jez took the jar of instant coffee and the milk from the bag and went to the kitchenette. "That was a good walk," he called back over the burble of the boiling kettle. "I needed to get out."

Atticus pulled off his coat and draped it on the back of one of the chairs. "You're spending too much time buried in receipts."

"It's got to be done. And I enjoy it."

"So you keep saying."

Atticus looked around the office. It still had that new smell: fresh paint and carpet adhesive. Jez had done a good job setting it up. The space was bright, a sharp contrast to the shabbiness of the Salisbury office. White walls and tall windows let in plenty of light, making the space feel open rather than oppressive. A sleek wooden desk sat at the centre, already bearing the signs of Jez's habit of spreading out: an open file, a coffee mug, and a half-eaten protein bar left beside his keyboard. A glass-topped coffee table sat between two low-backed chairs that Jez used for client meetings, with a neat stack of business cards and a small dish of mints. The rucksack in the corner of the room was in the process of being filled: a compact but sturdy tent, its poles neatly strapped to the side; a rolled-up sleeping mat and a lightweight sleeping bag compressed into a waterproof sack. A small camping stove was tucked into the main compartment, and a water bottle and a collapsible filter sat in one of the side pouches, while the other held a first-aid kit and a head torch.

Jez came back inside and handed Atticus his coffee.

Atticus pointed at the rucksack. "You're serious about doing it?"

"I am."

"Twenty-six miles?"

"Twenty-six miles. I've been meaning to get out there for months, and I've just been procrastinating. The weather's great for the next couple of days. And work can do without me—right?"

"I'm sure we'll survive."

"So if I don't do it now, I never will."

"And you're going to *camp?*"

"That's the plan. I'll get to Broughton and start thinking about finding somewhere."

He shrugged. "You could divert up to Stockbridge and find a hotel. I could suggest something very nice. The Greyhound on the Test—they take dogs, too. Excellent food."

Jez smiled. "That's cheating. Were you never in the Scouts?"

"Not really my thing."

"Well, *I* was. And there's something special about going to sleep under canvas."

"I'll take your word for it."

"It'll be fun."

"Call me when you're nearer to Salisbury, and I'll buy you a pint."

Atticus sipped his coffee and looked out of the window; a delivery truck rumbled by the building, rattling the panes of glass in the window frames.

"I was thinking," Atticus said, "about the radio this morning."

"What about it?"

"What do you think I should say to Mack?"

"Would she have been listening?"

49

"Probably."

"Did you remind her?"

"I forgot."

Jez shrugged. "Nothing was said that she'd have any reason to be annoyed about."

"What about the stuff about the Mallender case? She wasn't happy about all that at the time. The chief super gave her a hard time over it." He looked out of the window again. "I'm worried she'll be annoyed."

"Talk to her, then. There's no point stewing on it. I bet she'll say it's water under the bridge."

"You don't know her as well as I do."

Atticus watched a man with a dog as they ambled along the pavement. He'd always found it hard to navigate personal relationships, and his feelings for Mack made it so much more difficult. She'd been worried about her reputation in the aftermath of the Mallender case, and Atticus would rather have left his commentary on it out of the book. His editor had made it plain that that wasn't an option; his readers would expect to have Atticus's thoughts on what had happened, and he'd sent back his first draft with notes asking Atticus to include more strident criticism of the police case. Atticus had refused, and, after a week of back and forth, they'd settled on a chapter that contained an analysis of what the police had got wrong without any direct criticism. The chapter was measured and made no mention by name of any of the officers, but Atticus still found it awkward to read.

"It'll be fine," Jez said. "Talk to her tonight if you're worried, but it'll be a fuss about nothing. You'll see."

6

Franny had called the coroner's office and explained that human remains had been found that needed to be assessed. She'd been surprised when Professor Fyfe himself had called her straight back and said that he was already in Salisbury— she remembered a misper had turned up dead in a field near the hospital—and that he'd be with her in forty-five minutes.

Fyfe was as good as his word, and Franny was almost back at the road when she saw him getting out of his car. He had a reputation for irascibility, and his expression was already sour as he slammed the door and took a cautious step forward, glaring at the muddy expanse in front of him.

"For Christ's sake," he muttered, lifting a foot and eyeing the splatter of mud on his brogues. "Why do I always find myself up to my knees in mud when I come out to one of your cases?"

Franny folded her arms, biting back a smile. He'd been the same on the investigation into the bodies at Imber: sharp, impatient, and unsuited for anything outside of a controlled lab environment. He was wearing a long overcoat today that would be filthy in no time, and his navy trousers were already streaked with dirt.

She stepped forward. "Thanks for coming so quickly."

He shot her a look. "Patterson, is it?"

"DS Francine Patterson. But Franny's fine."

"What have we got?"

"A skull in a field five minutes in that direction," she said, pointing. "Farmer disturbed it while he was ploughing."

"Historic?"

"If I had to bet—yes. But I'd appreciate you confirming it."

"I'm sure you would. I'll get my kit, and we can go and have a look."

He went to the back of his car, opened the boot and took out a medium-sized box with a strap. He arranged the strap over his shoulder and moved the box so it hung down by his side. Franny led the way along the track, doing her best to tactfully ignore Fyfe's frequent imprecations at the terrain and what it was doing to his shoes.

* * *

Fulbright and Britten had taken the opportunity to put a more secure cordon in place, and the blue-and-white police tape was fluttering in the wind.

Fyfe made his way over to the skull, crouched down and looked at it.

Franny watched over his shoulder. "What do you think?"

"Obviously human. And, yes, I suspect it *is* old."

"How old?"

"That's the sixty-four-thousand-dollar question, isn't it?"

He lowered his case onto the firmer ground just outside the disturbed soil, unclipped the metal fastenings and snapped on a pair of nitrile gloves. Franny watched as he stepped closer to the skull. He crouched down, reached for a small brush from his case and used it to clear away the loose dirt around the bone. He reached into his pocket and took out a digital voice recorder, then started a recording.

"This is Professor Fyfe, attending a potential historical burial site to the west of Pitton, Wiltshire, at the request of Detective Sergeant Francine Patterson of Salisbury CID. We have a partially exposed human skull, frontal and parietal bones visible, with the occipital and mandible still embedded in the surrounding soil." He adjusted his position, the brush moving in small, precise strokes as he worked around the exposed cranium. "The bone surface is weathered but intact. No visible signs of modern decomposition. Discoloration is consistent with long-term burial in damp soil— light brown to dark grey mineral staining. No remaining soft tissue, which, of course, strongly indicates historical origin."

Franny shifted her weight slightly, watching as Fyfe reached for a small magnifier from his case, tilting his head as he examined the skull's contours.

"No significant post-mortem scavenging visible—no rodent gnawing, no animal bite marks. However, there *is* evidence of perimortem trauma."

He adjusted the magnifier.

Franny stepped closer.

"Circular defect in the left temple region, approximately half an inch in diameter, with well-defined edges. The outward bevelling of the exit wound suggests the trajectory of a projectile impact."

He stopped the recording.

Franny felt a prickle of unease creep along the back of her neck. "Gunshot?"

Fyfe nodded. "The entry wound is small and clean, consistent with a low-velocity projectile fired at close range. The exit wound is larger and more irregular. I'd like to take a closer look in the lab, but it was likely a fatal shot."

He adjusted his position, leaning toward the skull, and then paused, tilting his head and smiling. "Well, well... Will you look at that."

Franny stepped closer. "What is it?"

Fyfe used the tip of his gloved finger to nudge away more soil, revealing a small, darkened sphere embedded in the dirt near the skull. "Lead shot," he murmured.

Franny squinted at it. "From what?"

"I know a little history, Detective Sergeant, but you'd have to speak to an expert to confirm it. But if you *forced* me to make a guess, I'd say that whoever this poor fellow was, he was shot in the head at reasonably close range with a musket or a flintlock."

7

Fyfe told Franny that he was confident that this was a historical case. The lead shot would put the burial all the way back to the 1700s or 1800s, meaning that the skull had likely been in the ground for more than two hundred years. Fyfe was evidently happy to be able to wash his hands of the matter—literally and figuratively—and said that they'd need to bring in a forensic archaeologist to take over.

He said he'd send over the details of someone he knew who'd taken a referral from him for this type of work before. He was true to his word, and fifteen minutes after he left, he forwarded over a contact card for Dr. Eleanor Sawyer, a member of staff in the Department of Archaeology at the University of Southampton.

Franny Googled her and skimmed her profile: she was a senior lecturer with a particular interest in forensic excavation and early burial practices; her research focused primarily on the medieval and early modern periods, with an emphasis on burial rites, funerary customs, and the movement of populations; she'd recently published an article in *Antiquity* on the exhumation of a fourteenth-century plague burial site in Hampshire, exploring how skeletal remains and associated grave goods could offer insight into the treatment of the dead during times of crisis.

She seemed like a good fit.

Franny called, explained who she was and why she was calling. Eleanor listened without interruption, then asked a few precise questions: was the skull fully exposed or partially buried; were there any artefacts visible besides the leather fragment; had there been any prior recorded burials on the land?

Franny answered as best she could, quickly forming the impression that Eleanor knew her stuff.

"Well?"

"I'd be happy to help," Eleanor said.

"Great," Franny said. "But we're a little pressed for time. The farmer is concerned that he won't be able to—"

"Give me a couple of hours," she said. "Would that be okay?"

"A couple of hours? As soon as that?"

"It's important to get started quickly once something has been found."

"That'd certainly be helpful from my perspective."

"I'll be there as soon as I can."

* * *

Eleanor had evidently put her foot down on her journey west on the A36, because it was only ninety minutes later when she called to say she'd just arrived in Pitton. Franny said she'd walk back to meet her so she could help with any equipment she'd brought.

Britten went with her, and they found a woman at the rear of a mud-splattered Land Rover Defender. She'd parked directly behind Franny's car, practically kissing the bumper, and now she'd opened the doors at the back and was pulling on a forensic suit and boots with the kind of businesslike efficiency that suggested she'd done this a hundred times before.

Franny went over to her. "I'm DS Patterson. You're Dr. Sawyer?"

"I am. But please—call me Ellie."

"I'm Franny."

They shook hands, and Franny gave Sawyer the once-over: mid-thirties, with a sharp, intelligent face, dark brown hair pulled into a low ponytail, and the practical air of someone used to kneeling in mud.

Ellie zipped up the front of her suit, adjusting the hood before tucking a loose strand of hair behind her ear. "Right, then—what are we looking at?"

"The farmer turned up a skull. There's a fragment of leather with it—possibly a boot. The bone is weathered, but I need confirmation on how old we're talking."

"Anything else?"

"It looks like whoever the skull belonged to was shot. Professor Fyfe found a lead ball, and there's a pretty obvious entry wound."

"And you want confirmation that this is definitely historic?"

"That would save everyone a lot of trouble."

"And it'll give me an interesting project at the same time," Ellie said. "A win-win." She stepped forward, boots squelching in the mud. "Lead the way, Detective Sergeant. Let's take a look and see what we can find out."

8

Francine watched as Ellie went to work. She crouched by the exposed skull, balancing on the balls of her feet, and without touching anything, began a deliberate inspection. She bit her lip and said nothing, just tilting her head slightly, her gaze sweeping across the disturbed soil, pausing to note the angle of the exposed bone and the surrounding clumps of earth.

Franny stood behind her. "What do you think?"

"Well," Ellie said, "the condition's consistent with long-term burial."

She reached into her bag and pulled out a small digital camera. She started snapping high-resolution photographs: first the whole area, then a close-up of the skull, the soil layers around it, and the fragment of leather lying nearby.

"This is the in-situ assessment," she explained. "Once we start shifting things, we lose some of the story. The soil, the alignment, the way the remains were deposited—it all matters."

Franny nodded, watching as Ellie leaned in closer, brushing her gloved fingers across the surrounding soil without disturbing the bone itself. She pulled a soft-bristled brush from her kit and began lightly dusting away some of the loose earth around the bone. Every motion was delicate and precise. Franny had seen plenty of SOCOs at crime scenes, but Ellie's work felt different; it was less about gathering evidence and more about piecing together the elements of a story.

Ellie revealed more of the bone. "I see what you mean."

Franny saw the hole where the shot had punched through more clearly. "He was shot?"

"Looks like it, doesn't it? I'll need to take a closer look."

She turned her attention to the leather fragment nearby. It was stiff with age, dark and crumbling at the edges. Ellie let out a hum of interest and gently lifted part of the fragment, holding it carefully between her gloved fingers.

"This is vegetable-tanned leather—common in the early nineteenth century. You see the stitching? Hand-sewn, with waxed linen thread. This was a handmade item, and you're right—possibly a boot."

"So it's definitely old."

"I think your initial estimate was about right. Two hundred years feels like it might be close." She stood, brushing a loose strand of hair away with the back of her wrist. "I'll need to excavate. I'll call the coroner and tell them that we need approval for an archaeological dig rather than a forensic one. I doubt that'll take long, especially since Fyfe's already been out and the remains are already exposed. I'll ask for it to be fast-tracked so we can get ahead of further deterioration."

"When?" Franny looked at her watch. "It's six now. Too late tonight?"

She nodded. "I'll need help, too. I'll call the university and get them to send a couple of my students. We'll get a drone up so we can get a better idea of what we might find, put together an excavation strategy, and then we'll start the dig. I'll take care of all that—hopefully get started tomorrow morning."

9

Franny reported back to Bourne Hill and negotiated with the duty sergeant—a grumbling Neil Blyford—to arrange overnight security. Three uniformed officers would attend on rotating shifts to ensure that the remains were not disturbed by animals or anyone who might be interested in what had been uncovered. Franny logged the site as an active investigation area with an official case number and asked Turnbull not to tell anyone what had been found until they had a better idea of what they were dealing with. The farmer had driven away after lunch and was glum when he returned to see that Ellie was evidently setting up for an extended stay. The delay he feared was going to be longer than he might've hoped; nevertheless, he agreed not to tell anyone about the remains.

Dusk fell at just before seven, and Ellie put away her tools so they could make the site safe for the night. The skull was covered with a breathable tarpaulin to prevent moisture loss while also avoiding the buildup of condensation, the tarpaulin was secured in place with wooden stakes, and the small items—

additional bone fragments that had been uncovered together with the scrap of leather—were collected.

Franny was finally able to leave at seven thirty. She called Robbie as she trudged back to the car.

"Long day?"

"Very long. Knackered."

"Found anything interesting?"

"Looks like someone was shot and buried here two hundred years ago."

"There you go, then. You can leave it to the archaeologists."

"I've still got to come back tomorrow morning. I've already been out here for hours."

"That's what comes with promotion."

"Thank you, Robbie," she said, with no effort to conceal her sarcasm. "I'm cold and filthy."

"Want me to run you a bath?"

"Yes, please."

"How long will you be?"

"Half an hour. I'm not going to hang around."

"I'll have it ready for you," he said. "I've got a nice bottle of white in the fridge as well. I'll pour you a glass."

10

Rupert had thrown himself into his work after the meeting with Kershaw to distract himself from the confirmation of his diagnosis. The most important of his day-to-day responsibilities at the moment was his work with Azure Renewables to build the solar farm on the fields to the north of Carverel Copse. The initial lease granted Azure permission to use two hundred and ninety acres, with the Whiteway as the eastern boundary. That amount of land would make the project the largest in the country, and Rupert was interested in offering more land for them to expand further. After that, he'd driven into Salisbury for an appointment with his lawyer to discuss the formation of the Brookmere Trust.

It was gone six when he finally drove up to the house. The marquee for the party had been erected on the lawn, and Rupert pulled over into one of the passing bays to allow a van from the catering company to drive on to the gate. He would have been happy enough with a smaller event, but Emelia had insisted. It was a milestone birthday, she said, and it deserved to be celebrated. Rupert had reluctantly agreed. There was a lot to do, and Emelia had been busy: putting the seating plan together, choosing a caterer from a shortlist of three, hiring a band from London that she'd seen at a wedding in Kensington, and micromanaging the florist with a mood board she'd made on her iPad. There had been tastings, site visits, deliveries, and endless WhatsApp groups. Rupert had barely been involved—just the way he liked it—but even he had to admit the operation was being run with an exacting precision. He expected nothing less from his wife.

Emelia loved these kinds of big events, and, for her, it was a chance to show off to the London crowd she'd invited. She was thirty years younger than Rupert, and he'd seen the way her vapid friends looked around the house with wide eyes when they came to visit, assuming, no doubt, that it would all eventually be hers and imagining the weekend visits they'd be able to enjoy once he was out of the way. He'd told her and the kids what he was intending to do with the trust, but he sometimes wondered if she had her head in the sand as to what it all meant.

He reached the parking area. Emelia's car was there, together with the cars for all the children. He closed his eyes and leaned forward, resting his forehead on the wheel. There was a family meal in advance of his birthday, and it was tonight. He'd forgotten all about it. That reminded him of Kershaw and the scans and the bitter fact of it: he *was* forgetting things more often these days. Last week, he'd sworn he'd signed the paperwork for the insurance renewal, only to be told by Emelia it had never even been printed; he'd missed a meeting with the planning officer despite having a calendar reminder set on his phone, which, apparently, he'd deleted; Celeste had said she was surprised he hadn't called her back after their long chat about the gallery she wanted to buy, but Rupert couldn't remember the conversation at all and would've sworn it never happened.

He climbed out of the car and made his way to the house. He went inside and down the hall, unbuttoning his coat as he went, then stopped short as he reached the open dining room door.

Emelia was seated at one end of the table, her expression composed but with something unreadable in her eyes; his middle son, Sebastian, lounged back in his chair, arms folded; Henry was upright and stiff-backed, his jaw set in the way that usually meant he was bracing for an argument; his oldest child, Celeste, had her hands folded in front of her, and her husband, Julian, was looking at his phone; Alexander, his youngest, still had the irritating habit of glancing between everyone like he was trying to work out which side he should take before committing.

The Ainsleys were the definition of what Rupert had read in the newspapers as a 'blended family': Celeste and Henry were the children from his first marriage to Claudette; Sebastian and Alexander were born during his second marriage to Elizabeth. The children rarely agreed on anything save their disdain for Emelia and their suspicion that, at thirty years Rupert's junior, she had only agreed to be with him for the money.

Rupert had started to wonder about that himself, too.

The table had been set for dinner: a vast expanse of polished oak, waxed to a mirror shine, and lined with high-backed Georgian chairs upholstered in a deep burgundy velvet. An antique damask cloth—ivory, with embroidered Ainsley family crests—ran down the centre, overlaid by a series of placemats. Each place was laid with heavy silver cutlery, polished to a shine, and white linen napkins folded into intricate fans stood upright in the crystal-stemmed wine glasses. There were five-armed silver candelabras spaced evenly down the length of the table, wax tapers already lit, casting a warm, flickering glow across the fine china plates and decanters of claret. Polished water jugs and two silver champagne coolers—one already wet with condensation— stood beside freshly cut arrangements of flowers from the gardens. A small menu card printed on thick cream card stock had been placed at each setting, embossed with the Ainsley crest and the evening's three courses typed neatly beneath: wild mushroom soup, roast sirloin of beef, dark chocolate tart with clotted cream from the estate dairy. The fire in the hearth crackled behind the wrought-iron fender, and Emma, who worked in the kitchen with the chef, placed a basket of warm bread on the sideboard.

"Sorry I'm late," Rupert said, stopping himself before admitting that the meal had slipped his mind.

"It's fine," Celeste said.

"Happy birthday, Father," Henry said.

"Not quite. Not until Saturday."

"I think we can start the celebrations now," Emelia said.

Henry stood and reached for the champagne bottle in the nearest silver cooler, its neck beaded with condensation. He twisted the wire cage and eased out the cork with a soft pop that echoed off the high ceiling. The fizz whispered at the lip of the bottle. He made his way around the table, filling each crystal flute with a measured pour. The champagne was pale gold, catching the candlelight with every tilt of the glass.

He raised his glass. "To Father," he said. "And to the beginning of another year."

"To Father," the children repeated.

Rupert sipped the champagne and then set the flute down.

Alexander did the same, then looked at Sebastian and then at Celeste. Rupert could tell they'd been talking about him and could guess what it was about.

"Something on your mind?"

"There *is* something," Alexander said.

"Better get it off your chest, then," he said. "Let's have it."

11

Rupert looked around the table; none of his children could hold his eye. That was typical; they could only find the courage to broach difficult subjects when they had strength of numbers, but when it came to actually putting their heads above the parapet, none of them had the guts.

"Let me start you off. This is your latest attempt to persuade me that now's the time to let you have what you think you're entitled to."

Alexander took a breath. "We heard about what the doctor said this morning, and we're worried."

Celeste nodded her agreement. "We are. And we want—"

"Your money," he finished for her. "Please don't insult my intelligence. I *know* what you want—it's transparent."

The atmosphere, already taut, tightened even more.

Rupert took a big sip of the champagne. "I'll bring you all up to speed," he said. "The news this morning wasn't good. The scans show I have exactly what the doctor thought I had. But that doesn't mean I'm losing my mind. I'm still as sharp today as I was five years ago. I'm going to slow down—a little faster than I'd like, perhaps—but I've got years left, so nothing changes."

"I've been looking into it," Sebastian said. "You're right—you've probably still got years, thank God, but that doesn't mean you won't start to notice things getting worse."

"Been looking into what the doctor said? Have you been Googling?"

"There are lots of excellent websites," Sebastian said defensively. "You can scoff all you want, but there's a common theme of slow but steady decline, and when you accept that, it puts things into perspective. All of this." He gestured around him. "The house. The estate. We need to start thinking about what we're going to do about it."

Henry leaned back in his chair with a look of distaste on his face. "I just want to say, for the record, that I *don't* agree. With any of it. I don't think we *do* have to talk about it."

Alexander rolled his eyes at his brother. "Yes—you made that very clear."

"What about you?" Rupert turned to Emelia. "Do *you* think we have to talk about the estate?"

She bit down on her lip. "I think we have to at least think about the future, darling."

"We can pretend that nothing has changed and carry on," Alexander said, "just as we have until now, but I'm worried—we're *all* worried—that if we just do that, it'll make things more difficult later on."

"Please don't put words in my mouth," Henry said. "I'm not worried."

Alexander waved a dismissive hand. "Isn't it better that we sit down and make a plan now?"

Alexander was picking his words carefully, but that just made Rupert angrier. "This isn't about me. It's not even about the estate—not really. It's about *you*. Succession. You want me to promise that everything is going to happen just the way you want. Right? You want me to tell you that I haven't changed my mind, that I'm not going to change the will. You want me to tell you I don't care that you'll just sell whatever I give you and that I don't care if it means the end of five hundred years' worth of family history. Who cares about things like that if you get your money to go and fritter away on whatever today's foolish obsession is?"

"You wouldn't have to sell *everything*."

"I wouldn't? Well, *that's* a relief," he said sarcastically.

"I've taken tax advice," Alexander said. "If you give us what you said you'd give us now and live for seven years, then we don't pay tax."

"But what if the doctor *is* right?" Rupert said. "What if I do have something wrong in here?" He tapped a finger against the side of his head. "I might not last seven years."

"The tax relief tapers," Alexander said, much too quickly. "If you give a gift and you live three years afterwards, then it's only forty per cent. But if you die within three years, then we get taxed in full."

It would've been difficult to provide a colder and more heartless assessment of the situation, but Alexander was too caught up in what he was saying to realise his insensitivity.

Henry, though, wasn't. "You should be *ashamed*," he said to his stepbrother. "I had no idea you'd become so mercenary."

Alexander glared at Henry. "If you don't have anything constructive to say, then—"

Henry slapped his palm against the table. "That's *enough*. We're here to celebrate Father's birthday. He doesn't want to talk about this, and I don't think he has to."

Rupert felt his anger bubbling to the boil. "I thought I was clear with you the last time you ungrateful little shits ambushed me like this. I don't think I could've been any *clearer*. There is no way—and I mean *absolutely* no way—that I am going to sell this estate while I'm still breathing. I'm not selling anything. Not even a square inch."

"Darling," Emelia said, trying to mollify him, but it was too late.

"Let's all be completely honest. Alexander, you first—why is this so important all of a sudden?"

"Because you're not going to get any better."

"Rubbish. This is about you wanting your money now so you can waste it on stupid pipe dreams that I've told you won't come to anything."

Alexander couldn't hold Rupert's gaze.

"Shall we have some *more* honesty?" He turned his glare onto Celeste. "Why are *you* so eager to have this conversation? Still desperate for the gallery. How much was it again? Two million?"

Celeste's face reddened. "Three."

Rupert turned to Julian. "What do you think?"

Her husband shrank back. "I think this is something for the family to decide."

"But you must have an opinion?"

He turned to glance at his wife. "I think the gallery is a great opportunity for Celeste."

Rupert turned to Sebastian. "What about you?"

"It's about securing the future of the estate. If you'd actually listen—"

Rupert laughed. "You want to turn our home—the house that's been in our family for five hundred years—into a hotel. No way. Never. *Never.* This estate has survived wars, recessions, and every other bloody crisis that's come before this one, and I'll be damned if *I'm* the one to let it fall apart. The land stays in the family, and the estate stays whole—end of story."

"So we just do nothing?" Alexander said. "Pretend this isn't happening?"

"No—not nothing. I've told you what I'm going to do."

"You mean it, then? About changing the will?"

"I mean it. The land, the assets, everything—it stays together. It can't be sold off in pieces. The estate will be held in a trust. Any income generated will be shared, but none of you will be able to sell off your shares or force a sale."

Alexander folded his arms. "Who'll be the trustee?"

"Henry will," Rupert said. "He'll manage it as a whole, just as I did, just like my father did, just like his father before him."

Alexander shook his head. "This is madness."

"It's what has to be done—I didn't need to be persuaded, but if I did, tonight would've been enough. I won't have my life's work dismantled because some of you can't see further than your own bank balances."

Sebastian exhaled sharply and slumped back in his chair. "Christ."

Alexander was still shaking his head, and Celeste said nothing. Rupert watched them carefully. He knew this wouldn't go down well, but he didn't care. The estate was bigger than all of them.

"I saw my solicitor this afternoon to start the ball rolling on the Brookmere Trust and a new draft of my will. I'm seeing him tomorrow to finalise it. The changes will be made immediately."

"You're being impossible," Sebastian said.

Rupert stood. "And I'll be giving a speech on Saturday afternoon. It's the perfect opportunity to tell everyone what's going to happen." He pointed to Henry. "We'll need to find time for a chat beforehand. I'd like you to say a few words, too."

"Of course, Father," Henry said.

"'Of course, Father,'" Alexander mimicked.

For a moment, it looked as though Sebastian might argue, but then Celeste placed a hand on his arm. He took a breath, pressed his lips together, and sat back.

Emma appeared in the doorway. "Shall I serve?"

"I'll have my dinner in the drawing room," Rupert said. "Could you bring it through?"

"Of course, Your Lordship."

He stood. "Now," he said, "if you've all finished trying to put me out to pasture, I'd like to enjoy the rest of my evening in peace."

12

Atticus found he was anxious as he walked from the office to Mack's house. He'd listened to the morning's interview on the BBC website, and although he didn't *think* he'd said anything that would cause her any discomfort, it was evident that the interviewer had been interested in trying to get him to criticise the police's work in the Mallender case. It would certainly have made for a good sound bite—the increasingly renowned private investigator demonstrating how he'd outsmarted the professionals—and Atticus was relieved that he'd seen through it and politely demurred. It could have been worse. He was a junkie for praise, and he'd said things before that he shouldn't have, knowing that they were what the other person wanted to hear.

But the more he sweated on it, the more he worried that there'd be something in the book itself to which Mack might take offence. He had taken the proof copy from his desk drawer and flipped through it, sure that he'd find something negative that he'd missed or simply overlooked. At the same time, he knew he was worrying and overthinking—Mack was *always* telling him that he was prone to doing that—but he couldn't help it. She'd told him she'd read an early draft and had enjoyed it, but now he worried that she might've just said that to keep him happy. Maybe she hadn't read it at all. Maybe she was going to find out what he'd said about Mallender for the first time when the book was released.

He looked down at Bandit trotting alongside him. "She's going to be mad at me."

Bandit looked up at him and cocked his head to the side, then carried on, seemingly unconcerned.

He stopped at the off-licence on Catherine Street and bought a bottle of white wine and a tub of Mack's favourite ice cream and then continued on until he reached the Greencroft. Mack's rented house was opposite the park. She'd chosen it for its proximity to the station—it was a three-minute walk from door to door—but had also ensured that it was large enough to give each of her kids their own room when they came to stay. The place had been a bit of a mess when she moved in, but Atticus had helped with making it more appealing; they'd done a deep clean, painted the walls that were in the direst need of refreshing, and spent the better part of a month buying and assembling flatpack furniture from IKEA. Her ex-husband, Andy, had a more impressive place, but at least this house was pleasant now, and from what Atticus had been able to ascertain, the kids didn't care in the slightest.

He unlocked the door with his key and stepped inside. The door opened right onto the kitchen, and Mack was busy at the stove.

"Evening," Atticus said.

She turned and smiled at him. "Evening. Making chilli. That okay?"

"Perfect."

"Go and find something shit on the telly. Two minutes and I'll be serving up."

Atticus held up the bottle. "Fancy a glass?"

"Yes, please."

He put the ice cream in the freezer, filled a bowl of water for Bandit, took a couple of glasses from the cupboard and went through into the sitting room. It wasn't a large space, and it too had been a mess, but now it was warm and cosy. Atticus found the remote control and switched on the television, looking for something suitably banal—*Britain's Got Talent* was perfect— and dropped down onto the sofa. He uncapped the bottle of wine and poured out two glasses.

Mack brought two bowls of chilli into the lounge. She eyed the television; Ant and Dec were interviewing someone who had just juggled three small chainsaws.

"Perfect," she said, sitting down next to him. "I'm not in the mood for anything more challenging than this."

Atticus gave her one of the glasses of wine. "Cheers."

She held the glass up, and they touched.

Atticus sipped the wine and winced. "Sorry—this isn't very good."

"It's fine."

"No, it isn't. It's like antifreeze."

"Anything to take the edge off."

She prised her right shoe off with her left foot and then her left with her right.

"How was work?" he asked.

She put the glass down and picked up her bowl. "Same as ever. Endless paperwork, a pointless briefing about 'enhancing

public trust'—I still don't really know what that means—
and then two hours chasing down CCTV footage that we
hoped might give us something to go on for the hit-and-run
in Churchfields last week, but it turned out that one camera
was switched off, and the other was pointed at a brick wall."
She paused, holding up a finger. "One other thing, though,
that'll be right up your street. We got a call this morning from
a farmer near Pitton. He was ploughing a field for the first time
in years and turned up a skull."

Atticus's attention snapped into focus. "Recent or historic?"

"Historic," Mack said. "Fyfe went out and had a look, and
the consensus seems to be that it's a couple of hundred years
old, maybe more."

"So what was it doing there?"

"No idea." She took a mouthful of chilli and washed it
down with the rest of the wine in her glass. "Franny took the
call. She says the skull looked like it'd been shot—entry and
exit—and they found what they think might be a lead ball. The
early thinking is that this is a two-hundred-year-old murder."

Atticus refilled Mack's glass. "Can I go and have a look?"

She shrugged. "Maybe—"

"Why'd you tell me if I can't go?"

"You *probably* can," she said, smiling at his predictable
reaction. "I'm going out tomorrow morning to see what
they've found. Franny said they've got a forensic archaeologist
having a look. I'll have a word, and if they don't mind
sticking your nose in, I'll give you a call and tell you where to
find them."

Atticus grinned. "That's better."

Mack rolled her eyes.

She was in a good mood, so Atticus decided to broach the subject that had been worrying him. "Did you listen to the interview?"

"Shit. That was this morning, wasn't it? Sorry—got pulled into a meeting. How was it?"

"Didn't miss much."

"I'll listen to it on the iPlayer. They must have it?"

"They do," he said, finding that he'd be happy were she *not* to listen. "It was very short, though. Three minutes and then they dumped me for the weather."

"I'm proud of you."

She held up her glass, and Atticus reached over to touch his against it for a second time.

"When's the book out?" she asked.

"Monday."

"Can I get a signed copy?"

"I don't know about that," he said, only half-teasing.

She was distracted as the next act came out onto the stage.

"But you *have* read it, haven't you?" he said. "I gave you a proof copy weeks ago."

"Bits of it," she said vaguely.

Bandit padded over and rested his head on Atticus's knee. He scratched behind the dog's ears and tried not to worry. It was obvious that she *hadn't* read it, whatever she told him now. He knew, thinking rationally, that he'd done what he ought to have done—told her she should read it and given her a copy weeks ahead of publication. He'd written it carefully, too, and had reviewed it to make sure that he hadn't said something that would cause her problems. But then he remembered how insistent his editor had been about criticising the police's case, and then he worried anew about his instinct to give people what they wanted and began to fret again that maybe there was something—a sentence, a phrase—that had escaped his cautious edit. And the police *had* messed up…

It was much too late to do anything about it now.

That horse hadn't just bolted; it was out of the stable, over the fence and in the neighbouring field.

He looked over at Mack as she finished her chilli and reached for the wine; she'd had a difficult day, and now she was off the clock and relaxed, and he didn't want to spoil the mood.

"What do you think, then?" she said as she finished her second glass.

"What do I think about what? Another bottle of wine?"

"No wine," she said. "But there's beer in the fridge."

He got up.

"I meant," she called after him, "what do you think about a two-hundred-year-old cold case? Up your street?"

"I think you know me too well."

Atticus opened the fridge and took out two bottles of Moretti. He popped the lids and took them back into the sitting room.

"Could be something for your next book."

"Let's see how this one does first," he said.

PART 2

Tuesday

13

Jez Hardwicke hoisted his pack onto his shoulders and stepped out of his front door, giving Treacle a quick pat before locking up behind him. He adjusted the straps, rolling his shoulders against the weight, and ran through a mental checklist—for the third and final time—that he had everything he'd need for the next couple of days. The Clarendon Way between Winchester and Salisbury was twenty-six miles, and most people who followed the route covered the distance in two days. There were Airbnbs along the way, but he was taking Treacle, and it had been a little more difficult to find somewhere that would have them both.

Jez had taken that as a sign. It was just as he'd said to Atticus: he'd do it properly and camp.

He had a medium-sized rucksack, and by the time he'd finished packing, it was full. He had a spare set of clothes, a waterproof jacket, and a thermal fleece in case the temperature dropped. A small camping stove and a tin mug nestled alongside two packets of dehydrated meals, a flask filled with hot coffee, and a couple of protein bars in case he needed energy boosts. He had a collapsible water bowl, a small bag of dog food, and a spare lead. He'd also thrown in a first-aid kit, a head torch, a power bank for his phone, and an OS map of the stretch of Hampshire and Wiltshire that contained the trail. The pack wasn't light, but it was manageable.

He glanced over at Treacle, who was watching him with expectant brown eyes, his tail thumping against the ground.

"Ready?"

The dog bounced up and trotted over, nudging his head into Jez's legs until his lead was attached, then tugged him to get moving.

Jez had been meaning to do the walk for months but had always found excuses to procrastinate: he had his girlfriend to think about, then Treacle was too young to manage the distance, then there was how busy he'd been as he'd started to work with Atticus and set up the Winchester office, then there was the move from the High Street to College Street. None of those excuses worked anymore: he'd split up with his girlfriend, Treacle was a year old and had more than enough stamina for miles-long yomps, and the new office was established.

Jez had made the arrangements.

And he'd been looking forward to it. The trail cut through sleepy villages with thatched cottages and Norman churches, past farms that had worked the land for centuries, and along droves where shepherds had once guided their flocks across the downs. Jez had read that on a clear day, from the higher ridges, you could see for miles, the fields stretching out like a patchwork of green and gold. The thought of losing himself in the landscape, away from the noise and pace of modern life, was exhilarating; it was exactly what he needed. It was why he'd chosen to do this the *right* way: on foot, with nothing but the rhythm of his own steps and the company of his dog.

He walked to the cathedral and laid his hand against the cool stone; he'd do the same when he reached Salisbury Cathedral. He found the first marker for the trail and, after checking his map, set off toward the River Itchen and the start of the path.

14

Rupert had left the bedroom window open overnight, and he could hear the distant sound of wood pigeons cooing and the gentle lowing of cattle in the fields beyond the gardens. He looked over: Emelia was still sleeping. He reached for his watch on the nightstand. It was six thirty.

Time to start the day. Lots to do.

He swung his legs over the side of the bed. The fire in the grate had burned out, but the room was still comfortable. He stretched, stood, and went into his en suite. He parted the curtains and gazed out onto the grounds of the estate: manicured lawns, sculpted topiary, and beyond them, the rolling expanse of fields that had been in his family for centuries. He saw the huge marquee and remembered that he was going to need to write his speech in time for the party on Saturday. He'd do it tomorrow. He had a lot on his plate today.

He opened the medicine cabinet, took down the bottle with the pills for his hypertension and opened the lid. He tapped two of the pills into his palm and swallowed them, washing them down with a handful of water. He opened the cupboard and took out his blood pressure monitor and the notebook he was using to record his results. He put the sleeve around his arm and sat down, levelling out his breathing before he pressed the button to start the machine. The sleeve tightened around his arm, and then, after a couple of minutes, it bleeped that it had finished. He looked at the display and noted down the results—161/98—depressingly similar to the last months' readings. He flicked back to before Christmas and traced his finger up a column of much more encouraging numbers: 124/76, 122/80, 126/78. He'd been meaning to go back to the doctor to see whether he needed to change his medicine because, for whatever reason, the amlodipine had stopped working.

Rupert pulled on his robe and went through into his dressing room. Emma had already left the silver tray with a cafetière of coffee, a cup and a neatly folded copy of the *Times*. He poured himself a cup, reached for the paper and saw the lead story: the government taking another swing at inheritance tax loopholes.

He checked the time again. He'd arranged to meet the site manager from the team installing the solar panels after breakfast, and he was going to have to get a move on. The ink had barely been dry on the contract with Azure before the fences were erected, the trenches dug, and the rows of steel racking planted in the field. He'd seen it before, of course, during visits to similar projects, but there was something unsettling about watching his own land change so radically. Centuries of agrarian use were giving way to the sterile geometry of energy production.

Progress, he told himself.

He dressed, finished his coffee and went back into the bedroom.

Emelia was awake. "Morning, darling," she said.

"Morning."

"Did you sleep well?"

"Not great."

"Thinking about last night?"

He grunted.

"I'm sorry if you felt…"

"Ambushed?"

"The children knew you would've preferred to put it off and pretend nothing's wrong. Their view is we need to get ahead of it."

"They made that very clear."

"Did you mean what you said about the trust?"

He felt a twinge of pain in his forehead and recognised the beginning of one of his headaches. "Of course. I'm going to go and see the lawyers today. The thought of the estate being split up and sold off… I just can't bear it. They can all say what they like about how they'd respect it and what it means to me, but they've said too much now for me to believe it. Henry will respect my wishes."

"Whatever you think is right."

"I need to go. The protestors were making a nuisance of themselves at the solar farm yesterday. I said I'd look at bringing in security if they keep it up."

"Love you," she said.

He grunted again and left the room.

15

Rupert went out to the estate office to look for his car keys. He'd misplaced them and thought they were most likely to be on the desk. Part of what they said about him was true: he *had* been losing things more often recently.

The door to the office was open, and Henry was already there. He was at the desk, a pile of correspondence set out in front of him.

"Father," he said, looking up.

"You're in early."

Henry gestured to the paperwork. "Lots to do." He pushed away from the desk and stood. "And I was hoping I'd catch you. I wanted to apologise about what happened last night. It wasn't fair—everyone jumping you like that."

"I'm used to it by now."

"I would've called you to let you know, but they only told me when I got there. They know I don't agree."

"It's not your fault."

"Look, Father—I just want you to know that I don't care about money and the estate and any of that. I want you to run it for as long as you can. I want to make sure you have everything you need. And when you're ready, *I'll* be ready."

"I know."

"Did you mean what you said? About going to see the lawyers this afternoon?"

"I've made my mind up—that's what's going to happen. Are you still okay with it?"

"Running the trust? Of course."

"Good. I'm going to speak to them about the acquisitions, too."

"The others will *hate* that—buying more land when they'd rather we were selling."

"I'm past caring about what they think. We're going to put the estate back into the position it was before the land was sold off. We have an unusual opportunity—we won't be able to buy land as cheaply as this again."

"I won't let you down."

"I know you won't," he said. "Anyway—this is all bloody morbid. Can we change the subject? What are you doing today?"

Henry looked down at the piece of paper he'd been scribbling on. "Got a meeting with Tom about the pheasant shoot on Saturday; Bill Sissons wants to have a word about the results of the TB tests for the cows in Long Mead; then I want to check the northern boundary and make sure the fencing repairs were done properly."

"You heard from Azure?"

"They emailed last night. They *definitely* want more land. As much as we can spare."

Rupert nodded. The solar company was hungry, and Rupert was going to see his property lawyer this afternoon about the ongoing negotiations to buy up the neighbouring farms.

"What about Turnbull?"

"I'm meeting Danny Peart this morning in the Plough," Henry said. "He said Turnbull had to take out a loan to buy his fertiliser this year. Health and Safety are already involved in the accident, so if we can get him to push the button and take Turnbull to court… that'll be the straw that breaks the camel's back."

"How much are we offering?"

"I said we'd cover the first fifteen of his legal fees and give him ten now." Henry gestured over to the bag on the armchair near the window. "I took it out of the bank yesterday."

"Good." Rupert put his hands together and smiled. "Turnbull's going to sell his farm, he's going to sell it cheap, and then we'll lease it to Azure."

"Do I have any leeway with Peart?"

"Whatever you need," Rupert said. "Just make sure you get him on board."

"I'm on it."

Rupert swiped his keys. "I'm going to go to the farm now. The tree-huggers were making a fuss last night. I'd rather not have to hire in security, but we might not have a choice."

16

Mack checked her boots were in the back of the car, got inside and backed out of her space in the car park. She'd been into the station to take care of the usual administration—signing off on the previous day's reports, reviewing the morning's intelligence briefing, going through the shift allocation with the duty sergeant—and had called Franny after seeing that she'd gone straight to the site in Pitton after coming on shift.

It was a pleasant morning: crisp and bright and with barely a cloud in the sky. An hour in the fresh air was appealing. She reached down to the radio and skipped channels, leaving Radio One—the station her kids preferred when she ran them into school—and settling on the slightly more sedate breakfast show on Salisbury Radio. The DJ was running through the local traffic situation and, forewarned about a crash on London Road near the crematorium, she diverted through Laverstock instead.

The DJ played the new Ed Sheeran track and then cut across to the news. It was the same as ever—another political scandal, more bleak news from the Middle East, a pop star checking into rehab—and Mack found herself tuning out. Her thoughts ran back to the conversation she and Atticus had had before going to bed last night. They'd been a semi-official item for three months now, and he'd suggested, again, that they ought to think about getting somewhere together. They were with each other most nights, he argued, and it'd be more convenient for them both. It wasn't a question of saving money; he still slept in the office when he wasn't with her, and he was busy enough that he was going to need that space whatever happened.

She could see the temptation in moving their relationship onto a more official footing, but, on the other hand, she'd only just left her marriage with Andy and wasn't sure she was ready to make that kind of commitment. It wasn't that she didn't love Atticus—she did—but she wanted to be completely sure that they were right for each other for the long term before committing to something more permanent. She'd been the one who'd ended the relationship before, and she knew it'd hurt Atticus more than he admitted; she wanted to avoid that happening again.

She drove by the environmental protestors gathered at the turning for Pitton and continued until she reached the deli near Firsdown. There, she ordered four coffees to go and took them in a cardboard carrier back to the car. She headed back in the opposite direction, turned off the main road and drove south into the village. Franny had given her directions to the field, and she found it without too much bother, pulling into the space behind the squad car, Franny's Mini and two other cars that she didn't recognise.

She got out and peered through the windows of a muddy Volvo that had been jammed up against the three-bar gate, a staff parking badge with the insignia of the University of

Southampton was fixed to the inside of the glass, and a high-visibility vest with ARCHAEOLOGY FIELD TEAM printed on the back was draped over the passenger seat headrest. She could make out a canvas kit bag, a clipboard thick with notes, and a pair of dirty trowels resting beside a plastic finds tray.

She went around to the back of her own car and, sitting on the lip of the boot, changed her shoes for her Wellingtons. The sun was shining, but there was a chill in the air, and the forecast was for more of the same for the next few days. At least it wasn't raining; she looked at the muddy track that led out into the fields and was grateful that it wasn't going to get any worse. She remembered the mess they'd made of the graveyard in Imber after discovering the bodies there; it'd felt as if she had been scrubbing the mud off her skin for weeks.

She collected the tray of coffees and walked to the field. It was busy: Ryan Yaxley was standing by the gate—he'd been rota'd to secure the site until lunch or Franny had dismissed him, whatever came first—and four women, including Franny, were on the other side of the field next to the tree line that marked the boundary.

"Morning, Ryan."

"Morning, boss."

"How long have you been out here?"

"Since I came on turn."

"Here," she said, handing him one of the coffees. "Warm yourself up."

"Legend," he said, taking the coffee and taking a sip.

"How's it all going?"

Ryan glanced over his shoulder at the dig site. "Slow and steady. They've bagged everything they pulled yesterday."

Mack nodded, shielding her eyes from the low sun with her free hand as she looked across the field. "Anything new?"

"They were all very excited twenty minutes ago, but I've no idea what for."

Mack went through the open gate and walked across the field. Most of it had been left to grass, but a section near the boundary had been ploughed up. The remains looked to have been discovered six or seven metres from the fence and the trees. The excavation area had been carefully demarcated, with stakes and string marking a loose boundary. The ground had been disturbed beyond the furrows cut by the plough and then widened where the archaeologists had begun to clear more of the topsoil away.

Three women were kneeling on the ground, examining something they'd unearthed; Franny was standing behind them, looking down over their shoulders. She noticed Mack approaching and disengaged from the group, meeting her halfway.

"Morning, ma'am."

Mack held out the tray. "Here."

"You didn't have to do that."

"No, but it's cold, and I thought you could do with it."

Franny held up the cup in salute and took a sip.

Mack pointed to the others. "I'm one coffee short. Who are they?"

"That's Ellie Sawyer," Franny said, pointing to the oldest of the three women. "She's the archaeologist from the university."

"Fyfe's recommendation?"

"Yes. And the other two are students—Ellie brought them with her this morning."

"Have they found anything?"

"You'd better come and have a look."

Mack followed her to where the three women were kneeling. She'd expected the excavation to be modest, but it appeared that they'd been busy. Their tools—spades, smaller trowels, and wooden picks used to clear away compacted soil around fragile remains—had been set down to the side. They'd removed a decent amount of damp earth and, after sifting it, had dumped it in a pile.

They had dug down fifty or sixty centimetres, and Mack saw with surprise that there was more than just a single set of remains.

One skull—perhaps the one that had been discovered initially—was now fully exposed, its hollow sockets turned skyward. One of the students was working to excavate the dirt around it, and had uncovered a ribcage, shoulders, and the bones of one arm.

To the left of the first set of remains, another skull had begun to emerge from the earth, the curve of its dome unmistakable even beneath the layer of soil still clinging to it.

And farther along to the right, a third skull was partially visible, its jaw missing, the vertebrae of the neck lost beneath the remaining layers of soil.

Mack let out a breath. "Three."

"Yep."

Mack's stomach tightened. "Please say these are definitely historic."

"They are. We won't need to be involved. Ellie thinks we'll be able to ask the coroner to hand the site over to her by the end of the day."

That was a relief. Mack was busy, and the last thing she needed was a multiple murder investigation. The archaeologist—Ellie—turned back to look for Franny and saw that she was talking to Mack.

She got up and came across to join them.

"Morning," she said.

"Morning. DCI Mack Jones."

Ellie put out a hand, then, remembering that she was wearing dirt-smeared gloves, smiled and pulled it away. "Sorry. Bit mucky. Ellie Sawyer."

Mack watched as Ellie wiped her brow with the back of her wrist, leaving a faint streak of mud across her forehead. Her dark hair was pulled into a loose bun, though several strands had escaped to frame her face, and her green field jacket was streaked with dirt from the morning's work.

Mack held out the tray. "Afraid I didn't get enough."

"It's fine," Ellie said. "Joanne was sensible enough to bring a flask with her. These"—she held up the two remaining coffees—"will go down very well indeed. Thank you." She turned to the two students. "This is Joanne," she said, gesturing to a tall, freckled woman in her early twenties, with her hair tied back in a messy ponytail. "She's a postgrad student specialising in historical burials."

"DCI Mackenzie Jones. But you can call me Mack."

"Nice to meet you."

"And this is Katie," Ellie continued, nodding toward a shorter woman with auburn hair tucked beneath a woollen beanie. "She's studying forensic archaeology, but she's more interested in crime scenes than medieval churches, which makes today a bit of a bonus for her."

Katie grinned. "You don't find three skeletons on your average dig, that's for sure."

Ellie sipped her coffee. "Want to know what we've found?"

"Yes, please."

Ellie stepped far enough away from the dig to be able to describe it for Mack's benefit. She gestured to the remains on the far left. "This is the first one—the remains the farmer turned up yesterday. We started work on him first—"

"'Him'? You're sure it's male?"

Ellie nodded. "We can tell from the shape of the pelvis and the rigidity of the bone structure—the skull itself is larger, with a more pronounced brow ridge, and the jawline is more square than rounded. There are a few other indicators we'll check once we have the full skeleton exposed, but I'd be surprised if I was wrong. We're calling him Alan."

Mack crouched slightly to get a better look. "And the others?"

Ellie pointed to the second set of remains. "Bert. Too early to say for sure, but ninety-nine per cent sure he's male, too. Same skull shape, and from what we've uncovered so far, the build looks consistent. The third skeleton—Charlie—isn't fully exposed yet, but it's smaller. Could be a younger male or possibly a female."

"So at least three bodies, buried together."

Ellie nodded. "That's right. Which brings us to the real question."

"Why are they here?"

"Yep." Ellie dusted off her gloves and crossed her arms. "There are a few things we know already. They weren't buried with care—no sign of coffins, and the placement is irregular, as if they were dumped in haste. They were almost certainly buried together, which obviously leads us to the conclusion that they died at the same time. I would've suggested paupers' graves, but did Franny tell you about the wound to the first skull?"

"She did."

Joanne pointed. "Second and third skulls both have the same damage. They were all shot in the head."

Mack blew out a breath.

Franny smiled. "At least it's not our problem to worry about."

"No," Ellie said. "It's definitely ours."

Mack stared down at the skeletons, the morning sun casting long shadows over the churned-up earth. She thought of Atticus and how he would practically explode at the thought of an investigation as difficult—and potentially juicy—as this.

She looked at Ellie. "How long do you think you'll need?"

"She's asking because the farmer wants his field back," Franny added.

"Three days?" Ellie said. "Depends on what we find, but I doubt it'll be much more than that."

"Would you mind if I introduced you to someone?" Mack said. "I have a friend who'd be very interested to see what you've found."

"Atticus Priest?"

Mack turned to Franny.

She shrugged. "I told her this'd be right up his street."

"Yes," Mack said. "I spoke to him last night, and he said he'd love to come down. You could show him what you've found."

"Fine by me," Ellie said. "I heard him on the radio yesterday morning. He's an interesting character."

Mack found, to her surprise, that she suddenly felt defensive and more than a bit possessive.

"That's one way of describing him," she said.

17

Rupert drove his old Land Rover toward Pitton, passing through the village and then continuing along Whiteway to the access road for the solar farm. He crested the hill and, as he looked down from the top, saw it all laid out beneath him. The work was already well advanced: half of the panels had been installed, and they stood in neat, reflective rows, their dark surfaces angled south to maximise the amount of time they faced the sun. Metal frames glinted as work crews moved between them, some installing additional supports, others running thick cables into newly dug trenches. A cluster of vehicles—vans, a digger, and two flatbed trucks—were parked along the edge of the field, alongside stacks of yet-to-be-installed panels wrapped in protective plastic.

Rupert slowed to a stop and took it all in. It was a far cry from the wheat that had once grown here, but that was the point; this was the *future*. The Brookmere estate couldn't survive on tradition alone, and this addition to the portfolio had the potential to be very lucrative indeed.

He drove down towards the field, the wheels kicking up loose soil. He could see the site manager, Henshaw, in a high-vis jacket near one of the trenches. Rupert pulled up and cut the engine.

Henshaw turned at the sound. "Morning, Your Lordship," he called, wiping his hands on his trousers. "Thanks for coming out."

Rupert got out of the car. "Good morning, Henshaw. How's it all going?"

"Weather's held up nicely, so we're still well ahead of schedule. We'll have the first section wired in by next week. Should be fully operational before the end of the month, and then we'll move on to the second half."

"I got your message. The protestors have made nuisances of themselves?"

"More than usual. Some bastard's been tampering with the fencing. Found the eastern boundary undone, like someone wanted to make it easier to get in. Could be kids, but I think we know who it is."

"We do."

"Might need to think about security."

"I was hoping to avoid that, but never mind. I'll get Henry to deal with it. If you see anything else, let me know."

Henshaw nodded.

Rupert waited while Henshaw gave him the rest of the update, but his mind was already wandering. The protestors had arrived a month ago, and now it looked as if they were settling in for the long haul. They'd set up their camp at the junction of the A30, a prime location where they could make their case to the hundreds of drivers who went into and out of Salisbury every day. The field they were using was Jack Turnbull's land, and Rupert knew he'd given them permission to be there precisely because he knew it'd be annoying. Turnbull could bleat about the environment and how arable land shouldn't be used for solar panels all he liked, but Rupert knew it was virtue-signalling nonsense.

Didn't matter. The Turnbulls were only able to farm the land because of a historical injustice, and Rupert's plan would soon set that right. Their farm was struggling, and Rupert would make it even worse before making them an offer that they wouldn't be able to refuse. The farm would be returned to the Brookmere estate, everything put back together again, and then Rupert would lease it to Azure. Rupert would pay very good money to see Turnbull's face when he realised just how badly he'd been outsmarted.

They weren't quite ready for that yet, but they were making progress. Henry would ratchet up the pressure a little when he met the injured farmhand today. Turnbull was close to the edge, and it wouldn't need too much more to tip him over.

Rupert looked at his watch. "I need to be making a move."

"Right you are."

The meeting with the lawyers was this afternoon, but he had an appointment to keep before then, and he didn't want to be late.

He took out his phone and called Henry.

"Everything okay?" he said.

"Just seen Henshaw. The fence *was* tampered with last night."

"Want me to go and have a word with them?"

"Would you? I'd do it myself, but I've got a lot on."

"It's fine. I'll do it."

"Tell them to back off, or we'll get the police involved."

He put the phone away and went back to the car. It was a busy day, but he felt good. Surely this kind of productivity wasn't what you'd expect to find from someone with dementia, no matter how early in the progression of the disease it was. He felt a buzz of his usual contrariness: maybe Kershaw was wrong. The scans could be wrong. Rupert was fit and well and in full possession of his faculties, and he was going to stay that way for years. The children could forget all about getting their hands on the estate. He'd change the will and set up the trust to make sure his wishes were followed so the Ainsley name would forever be associated with the land.

And if they didn't like that?

Tough.

18

Henry took the bag of cash and went out to the second of the estate's two Land Rovers. He put the bag on the passenger seat and then whistled for Brutus and Cassius. The two dogs—big and energetic Rottweilers—bounded out and happily leapt into the back, anticipating a walk. He'd had both boys since they were puppies, and they'd proven to be useful on more than one occasion; he often had cause to move people off the estate, and he was taken much more seriously with them alongside.

He started the engine and headed down the drive. He had a busy morning: he'd arranged to see Danny Peart in the Lord Nelson in Winterslow, and then he had a long list of estate-management tasks that he needed to get done, including doing what his father had asked and going out to speak to the protestors.

He thought of his siblings and how they'd ganged up on his father last night, and found he was as irritated about it now as he had been then. It wasn't just the way they treated him as a glorified cash machine, although that certainly grated; it was the sense of *entitlement* that they all had, the expectation that they would eventually receive huge endowments simply because they were their father's children. None of them did anything to help with the estate. Henry, on the other hand, had been involved for years, learning from his father and the staff so that he'd be able to take over when the time came. He'd always known, in the back of his mind, that when his father died, there was going to be a struggle over the succession. He hadn't known then what provisions his father had made in his will, but had known there was a chance—probably a good chance—that the estate would have to be split and then sold off in order for them all to get their pound of flesh. The news that his father was going to change the will so that the estate was put into a trust had been a shock. He'd never suggested it before, much less that Henry would be a trustee; the legal battles that might eventually be unleashed would be brutal. Henry wondered if he should bring that up with his father now; if he did have dementia, any changes to his existing will might be vulnerable to an argument that he didn't have the mental capacity to make them.

But that would mean bringing the subject up again, and his father had made it very plain that he had no interest in discussing it. The last thing Henry wanted to do was to sour their relationship, especially now when there was so much at stake.

* * *

Henry drove up Whiteway to the junction and saw the makeshift camp ahead: a dozen tents, several ramshackle tarpaulin shelters, and a fire-pit ringed by a handful of protestors in mismatched outdoor gear. A battered old Volvo Estate sat at the edge of the field, mud caked up its sides, doors open to reveal stacks of food supplies and camping equipment.

Hand-painted placards were propped against the hawthorn hedges that faced the main road, their messages predictable:

STOP THE GREENWASH
WHAT WE STAND FOR IS WHAT WE STAND ON
GRASS NOT GLASS

The occasional driver gave them a blast of their horn in support as they went by.

Henry pulled over and parked, the left-hand wheels atop the verge. He jumped down and went back to the gap in the hedge that the protestors had used to drive in. A woman in her twenties—dreadlocks, nose ring, wearing a threadbare fleece—looked up from where she was crouched by the fire and nudged the man beside her. A ripple of murmured conversation went around the group.

Both the woman and the man got up and ambled across to intercept him.

"Hello," she said. "Come to join the protest?"

"No," he said.

"No," the man said. "You don't look the part."

Clean clothes and recently bathed, Henry thought, but kept it to himself. The man was wearing a T-shirt with a suitably twee slogan: 'There Is No Planet B.'

The woman stepped closer. "Who are you, then?"

"Viscount Brookmere."

"Ooh," she said scornfully. She turned to the man. "Did you hear that? *Viscount* Brookmere."

Henry ignored her and scanned the faces he could see. There must have been twenty of them, all dressed as if straight out of central casting for environmental activists: weather-beaten wax jackets and dirty fleeces, hiking trousers with frayed hems, boots caked in mud. Some wore knitted beanies while others sported dreadlocks or long, tangled ponytails. A dozen were standing or sitting around the fire while the others were up at the road, banging drums and chanting the same inane slogans as the ones on their placards.

Henry wanted the leader of the group.

"Where's Phillip Van Etting?"

The woman shrugged theatrically. "Who?"

"He's in charge."

"This is a communal protest. *No one's* in charge."

Henry was about to tell her he had no time for student politics, but before he could, he saw a second man make his way toward them. He was tall and wiry, in his late forties, with a tangled mop of greying hair that looked as if it had been cut with a penknife, if it'd been cut at all. A scraggly beard covered most of his face, the streaks of dirt on his cheeks suggesting he hadn't been properly acquainted with soap and water in some time. His patchwork jacket—a faded Barbour that had seen better days—was frayed at the cuffs and spattered with mud.

"This is Viscount Brookmere," the woman told him.

Van Etting came right up to Henry. "How can we help you?"

Henry folded his arms. "You've been messing around with the fencing at the solar farm."

Van Etting's mouth twitched with something that wasn't quite a smile. "What happened?"

"It was damaged in the night."

"You think *we* had something to do with that?"

"I know you did."

Van Etting shook his head. "No, we didn't."

"You think you own all this," the woman said, gesturing around her. "You think you can do whatever you want with it. But it doesn't belong to you."

"It does, actually. And it's been ours for five hundred years."

"This is our home, too. All of ours."

Henry let out a short laugh. "The *hypocrisy* of you people. You come here and complain about solar power—*clean* energy—yet you're getting your power from a petrol generator." He pointed to the unit chugging away behind the tents.

"This land should be feeding people, not lining your pockets."

Henry smiled with as much forbearance as he could muster. "I don't care what you think. The project's good for the area, and it's good for the environment. Houses in local villages will benefit with reductions in their electricity bills—have you asked them what they think? The Parish Council supported the planning application, and there were only a handful of objections."

Van Etting snorted his derision. "That's not support— you're buying them off."

The woman stepped up. "I don't know how you can sleep at night."

Henry knew there was nothing to be gained from trying to reason with people like them. They weren't interested in a conversation; they wanted to berate him, to badger him, to make life difficult until Rupert or Azure decided the whole thing wasn't worth the trouble.

But that wasn't going to happen.

"Touch the fence again, and I'll have the police here faster than you can blink."

Henry turned and made his way back to the entrance to the field.

Van Etting followed.

Henry went to the Land Rover, got inside and turned the key in the ignition.

"We're not going to stop," Van Etting shouted over the noise of the engine.

Henry kept the engine idling as Van Etting stood his ground, hands planted on his hips, as if sheer stubbornness might change the course of events. He lingered for a few moments, perhaps hoping for a parting shot, but when Henry didn't respond, he finally shook his head and stepped aside.

19

Atticus put Bandit in the back of the car and drove out to Pitton. The environmental protestors who had set up camp next to the turning were still there. Atticus had driven past them two days earlier, and, if anything, there were more now. He waited for a gap in the oncoming traffic and then turned right. A Land Rover with two large dogs in the back was trying to pull away from the verge, its progress blocked by a man standing in front of it. Atticus slowly drove by and then put the camp behind him as he continued south.

Mack had forwarded him the location of the dig. He drove through the village and continued until he reached the spot she'd marked: a track extended west, blocked by a metal gate, which was, in turn, blocked by a collection of cars. Atticus got out and opened the boot so that Bandit could disembark; the dog bounded down and started turning ever tighter circles until Atticus was ready to set off.

He followed the path. A tractor was busy in the adjacent field, running backward and forward as it ploughed the soil in readiness for crops to be drilled. Mack had told him that the farmer who'd discovered the remains was anxious that the work be concluded as quickly as possible so he could return to the field; every additional day lost increased the risk that he wouldn't be able to get the crop in the ground in time for it to grow. Atticus didn't know if the man driving the tractor was the farmer, but, when he raised his hand, the man did not return his greeting.

He reached the field and saw that Ryan Yaxley was guarding the way ahead.

"Afternoon," he said.

"All right, Atticus? Come for a look around?"

"I have—that all right?"

"The gaffer said you might be here. Go through." He pointed. "Straight ahead—can't miss them."

Atticus thanked him and made his way to the site.

The dig looked to be advanced. The remains had been almost completely uncovered, pale bones standing out against the loamy brown soil. Francine Patterson was standing at the side, her arms clasped across her chest; three more women, dressed in overalls, were crouched down with tools as they continued to uncover the bodies.

Franny saw Atticus coming over. "Afternoon."

"Afternoon."

"This is Atticus Priest," Franny said to one of the archaeologists. "Atticus—this is Ellie Sawyer. She's in charge."

Ellie straightened and wiped her gloved hands on the thighs of her work trousers. Her face was lightly freckled, her skin tanned from long days spent outside, and her eyes were a sharp, intelligent green.

"Nice to meet you," he said.

She reached up and shook his hand. "And you. I heard you on the radio yesterday."

He made a show of rolling his eyes. "Hope it wasn't too boring."

"Not at all. It was interesting. I ordered your book afterwards—can't wait to read it."

Atticus found it difficult to accept praise, Mack had tried to teach him just to be grateful, but the trick—often beyond him when it came to understanding how others saw him—was working out when he was being praised and when it was something else.

The rest of the introductions were made: Ellie introduced Joanne and Katie, and Atticus introduced Bandit. The dog was very interested in investigating the bones, tugging on his lead until he realised he wasn't going to be allowed to get any closer.

"You've come for a look at our little discovery," Ellie said.

"DCI Jones thought it might be up my street."

"It's a good one. Very interesting."

Atticus looked from skeleton to skeleton: the skulls, stark and empty-eyed, looked up at them.

"Three," Atticus said. "That's it?"

"We think so," Ellie said. "I'm waiting to see if I can get radar here to look for others, but it doesn't *look* like there are any more. The question we're looking at now is how long they've been there."

"I could probably chance a guess at that."

She folded her arms and smiled. "Go on, then."

He lowered himself to his haunches. "The wounds are interesting," he said, pointing to the skulls one after the other.

"Definitely not caused by a modern bullet. Mack told me what you found. Could I have a look?"

"This?"

She reached down to the box where the smaller pieces of evidence were being collected and took out a clear plastic bag, identified with a handwritten label. Atticus looked into the bag and saw a dull, misshapen lead sphere.

"That makes it obvious," Atticus said, "but even if you hadn't found it, you'd still be able to discount anything contemporary. A modern bullet leaves a different kind of hole—a clean, circular puncture with a bevel on the outer edges, with radiating fracture lines because of the velocity of the shot. Shotgun pellets would have looked like a scattered pattern of tiny entry wounds, each spreading outward. But those wounds are different: blunter; more irregular. The entry wounds are small and circular, but the edges aren't as sharp—I'd love to take a closer look under a microscope, but even without that, you can see they're slightly crushed inward, where the lead ball deformed on impact."

"Okay," Ellie said. "Agreed. What else?"

Atticus rolled up his sleeves and, with a quick, "Do you mind?"—and not waiting for an answer—he picked up the nearest skull. He turned it so he could look down at the bone at the top. "So—the entry wound is here." He pointed to a small, round hole on the top of the skull, slightly off-centre. "The edges of the hole are crushed inwards, which tells us the force was coming from above." He nodded to the lead ball in the bag. "If it had struck from the front or side, we'd see asymmetry in the wound pattern. Instead, the damage is uniform, meaning the ball travelled straight down into the skull." He turned the skull so that it was pointing upwards and back, opening up the angle. "The projectile passes out here, through the maxilla." He tapped a jagged hole just above where the upper jaw would have once held teeth. "See the way the bone has exploded outward? Classic sign of a low-velocity projectile leaving the body. The force builds up as the ball passes through the skull, shattering the thinner facial bones as it exits. There are secondary fractures along the maxilla where the force shattered the surrounding structure."

"The others both show the same pattern," Ellie said.

"Did you find more shot?"

"We've found two," she said. "The third hasn't shown up yet. We're going to send them to a ballistics expert for analysis."

"They would've been fired from a smoothbore flintlock."

Franny frowned. "If they were shot in the top of the head, that means—"

"That one of three things must be true." Atticus spoke over her. "One, the person or persons who fired the shots were very tall; two, the victims were very short, and we can see from their remains that they're not; or three, they were on their knees. I think we can assume the latter is the most likely."

Franny raised an eyebrow. "So that means they were executed."

"That would be my guess," Atticus said.

20

Henry drove west to Winterslow. He reached the Lord Nelson and saw there were just a couple of cars in the car park; he let the dogs out, put them on their leads and took them into the pub.

Jack Turnbull's farmhand was a man from Winterslow named Danny Peart. He was sitting at a table near the bar. He was in his late twenties, although Henry had always found him a little immature for his years. He was a big man, broad shouldered and thick necked. His right eye socket was hidden beneath a black leather patch secured with a thin strap that disappeared into his blond hair. Peart had lost the eye after the tractor tyre he was inflating had exploded, and now the Ainsleys were paying his legal bills to make things as sticky for Turnbull as he could.

"Hello, Danny."

"Mr. Ainsley."

"How are you?"

"Doing okay."

"And the eye?"

Peart laughed bitterly and pointed to the patch. "How'd you think?"

Peart was touchy about what had happened, and Henry reminded himself that he was going to have to tread carefully. Peart finished his pint and pushed the glass across the table. Henry took the hint and went to get him another. He wouldn't have stood for that kind of presumption from a pleb like Peart under normal circumstances, but Peart had the potential to be useful, and that made it worth biting his tongue.

He brought the drinks and two packets of crisps and put them down on the table.

Peart didn't thank him. "Did you hear the news?"

"What's that?"

"Jack was out ploughing on Monday. Dug up human remains."

"Really?"

"Went out there yesterday and saw it for myself. Old bones, they say. The police turned up when he found them, but it's an archaeologist there now. Jack's spitting feathers. He wanted to drill the field, and now he can't."

Another annoyance for Turnbull, and one that had the potential to cost money he probably couldn't spare.

"How long do they think they'll be digging?"

"He says he doesn't know. I got the impression he thought they'd be done soon, but we've got shitty weather coming in tomorrow. He wanted it ploughed and ready to be drilled already, and this has put him back a week, maybe two if the rain doesn't piss off." He took a sip. "Like I said—spitting feathers."

Brutus growled as a man entered the pub and went to the bar.

Henry opened one of the packets of crisps and changed the subject. "Have you spoken to the lawyer?"

Peart nodded. "Says I have a good case. Says she thinks I'll end up getting a decent pay-off."

"That's good. I think she's right."

"Says I have to put down money now if I want them to pull the trigger."

"Fifteen, wasn't it?"

"She spoke to you?"

"In general terms," Henry said. "And I'm happy to take care of it for you, like I said we would. I just wanted to be sure you definitely wanted to go ahead with it."

Peart sighed and glanced away. "I don't know."

"What's wrong?"

He shrugged.

"You were keen before."

"Jack's been good to me over the years. And I know what his lawyer will say—it was my fault."

Henry knew that was right, and from what he'd been able to discern, Peart had been at fault. He had overinflated the tyre past its recommended pressure, ignoring the safety warnings printed on the sidewall. When the rubber finally gave way, the explosion had been violent enough to take out his eye and leave him unconscious on the barn floor. There'd been talk in the village that Peart had been drinking, though there was no way to prove it after the fact. Turnbull had denied responsibility, but he *was* responsible for safety on the farm, and the case would cause him a headache even if it never made it to court.

Peart stared into his pint, his thick fingers drumming absently on the glass.

"Look," Henry said, "I get that you feel bad. But what's loyalty really worth when you've lost an eye and can't work anymore? You're not insured. What happens in ten years? In twenty? You've got to think about that."

Peart shook his head. "Don't know."

Henry leaned in slightly. "You *do* know. You just don't like the way it feels. But Jack's not going to do you any favours. He hasn't offered you anything, has he?"

Peart hesitated. "He's still giving me work."

"For now. What about in six months? What happens when he doesn't need you anymore? You really think he's going to keep paying you out of the goodness of his heart?"

Peart clenched his jaw but said nothing.

"You need to look after yourself. This isn't about revenge. It's about making sure you're not struggling when Jack doesn't have use for you anymore."

Peart took another long sip of his pint. Henry could see the wheels turning.

"How are you going to put food on the table?"

"My wife asked me that this morning."

"And she's right. If you take this to court and win—and you *will* win—you'll make enough money that you won't have to worry about work for years. Your legal fees are covered, so you don't need to worry about that. And I'll give you ten thousand now to make sure you're covered for the next few months." He thought on his feet and decided to add another sweetener. "And I'll tell you what—there's an empty cottage on the estate. Nice place—three bedrooms and a big garden for your little one to run around in. How about I let you and your family have it? Rent-free. That's worth another fifteen a year."

Peart sighed; Henry could see he was almost there.

"I still feel bad about Jack. You know how close he is to chucking it all in. This'll be it. It'll finish him off."

Peart knew the Ainsleys were trying to force Turnbull to sell up. Henry hadn't said it explicitly, but Peart was no fool; why else would they be helping him?

"Jack's been thinking of selling up for years," Henry said. "You know it, and I know it. It'll be for the best. We'll give him a good price for the land, and he can take the money and do something else. We both know how hard farming is at the moment, and it's not getting easier."

Peart supped his pint. "You're right about that."

Henry knew he had him on the hook. "So, what are you going to do?"

"I'll do it."

"Good man." Henry stood and pointed to the bag of cash. "I'll leave that with you. Call the lawyers and get the ball rolling. Sooner you get the case started, the sooner you'll get the money you're owed."

21

Henry finished his pint, told Peart to keep in touch once he'd spoken to the lawyers and, happy that he'd done what he had come to do, went outside with the dogs trotting obediently after him. He was deciding whether to take them for a walk now or drive back to the estate and take them into the woods when he noticed a car coming down the road. It was an old Suzuki four-by-four, and as it slowed and then reversed back into the car park, Henry saw the bumper stickers: a picture of Keir Starmer next to the words 'Farmer Harmer' and a yellow badge with a tractor and 'No Farmers, No Food.'

He heard the door open behind him. "Henry."

He turned. It was Peart.

"I counted the money. You're a grand short. You said…"

Peart stopped mid-sentence, his eyes passing from Henry to the Suzuki; he muttered a curse.

The dogs tugged at their leads.

Henry turned back to the car.

The driver's door was open, and Jack Turnbull had stepped out.

"Danny?" Turnbull said. "What's going on?"

"Just having a pint," he mumbled unconvincingly.

"With *him*?" The word was practically spat out of his mouth, heavy with derision.

"No," Peart said. "He was just…"

The words trailed away; Peart knew he'd been found out.

"You said you were a grand short. What did that mean?"

"Nothing, Jack. It was nothing."

Turnbull looked from Peart to Henry. His expression, already dark, became even bleaker as he joined the dots and realised what must have been happening.

"My God," he said. He turned to face Henry. "You sneaky bastards…" He shook his head, his expression mixing disgust with disbelief. "You've been putting ideas in his head, haven't you?"

"It's not that…" Peart started.

Turnbull didn't turn away from Henry, just waved a hand in Peart's direction. "Shut it, Danny. I've heard enough. Don't insult my intelligence."

Turnbull was a big man—he must've had three or four inches on Henry and outweighed him by fifty pounds—and working in the fields all his life had made him solid and strong. He took a step toward Henry; Cassius and Brutus started to growl as they sensed the change in the atmosphere and began tugging on their leads.

"How much are you paying him?"

Henry held up his hands. "I've got nothing to say to you."

"You think you can just wave your money around and get what you want? Give him enough cash, tell him what happened was my fault rather than because he was stupid enough to try to pump up the wheel without checking the tyre wall for damage first, without bleeding off the pressure like I told him to. But no—he was in a rush, wasn't he? Half cut, as usual. Didn't listen. Jammed the air line straight on, and boom."

"Jack—"

"Shut up, Danny," Turnbull snapped.

The dogs growled, their hackles standing up straight.

Henry heard the sound of hooves on the road and glanced back to see three horses and riders coming from the direction of the recreation ground.

"I've got a message for you and your dad," Turnbull said, raising his voice. "You tell him to keep his nose out of my business."

Henry's temper flashed. "Keep out of your business? Are you serious? Who gave those bloody protestors permission to go onto your land?"

"That field's fallow," Turnbull said. "And who I let onto it is up to me. And the fact is, I think they're right. You shouldn't be taking perfectly good arable land and sticking solar panels on it. Good land like that should be used to grow food."

Cassius started to bark, and egged on by his brother, Brutus joined in.

Turnbull glanced down at them, evidently unconcerned.

"Fine," Henry said. "Let them use your field. Whatever."

"I know it's you who's been sniffing around my farm, and I'll tell you this now for nothing—selling to you or your dad or any of your stuck-up brothers or sisters? Over my dead body."

"Keep telling yourself that," Henry said. "Like you have a *choice*. We'll see what the bank says when they decide they're not going to waste more money keeping you afloat."

Turnbull took another step, and Henry had to wrap the leads more tightly around his hands to keep the dogs from going for him.

"Keep your nose out of my business," Turnbull said, "or I'll do something about it."

"Are you threatening me?"

Turnbull shrugged and gave him a cold smile. "Take it however you want. But things aren't going so well for us at the moment—maybe I'll decide I haven't got anything to lose and come over to your house, and we can have a good old chat about the good sense in trying to make things worse for me and my family than they already are."

He jerked his shoulder in Henry's direction, feigning contact, and Henry flinched. He tripped over Brutus and knocked over the sandwich board advertising the week's guest ales. The dogs lunged for Turnbull, but Henry desperately held onto their leads, and they got no farther, both barking angrily as Turnbull sidestepped them and went up to Peart.

Henry craned his neck around.

"Don't bother coming back this afternoon," Turnbull said. "You're fired."

"You can't—"

"I just did," he said. "You want to sue me? Fine. I'll see you in court."

22

Atticus asked if he could stay out in the field to help with the dig. Ellie had said that he'd be welcome, provided he followed her instructions. Atticus wondered whether Mack had warned her to keep an eye on him, but promised he'd do exactly as he was told. Bandit seemed happy with the arrangement and, once he realised he was not to approach the remains, was content to trot along the perimeter of the field until he'd tired himself out, at which point he found a spot near the gate and curled up to sleep.

Atticus had been involved with forensic excavations before, most recently in the graveyard at Imber, and was interested to see the differences between what had happened then and the more archaeologically focused approach Ellie was taking here. She handed Atticus a spare pair of gloves and gestured toward the shallow trench where the others were working.

"We're focusing on careful exposure rather than rapid retrieval," she explained. "This isn't a crime scene, at least not in the usual sense. There's no urgency for evidence preservation, so we can take our time."

Atticus nodded. "But you're still working systematically."

"Of course. Each layer of soil tells us something. If we rush, we'll just end up losing context."

Atticus crouched at the edge of the trench, watching as Joanne carefully brushed loose soil away from the exposed femur of the first skeleton. The bones were surprisingly intact despite their age, the earth having preserved them well.

Atticus reached for a trowel and, under Ellie's direction, began helping to clear the soil around what appeared to be the second skeleton's ribcage. The bones here were in worse condition, the sternum fractured and partially collapsed. As he worked, he kept an eye out for anything else: a button, a scrap of fabric, anything that might tell them more about who these men had been.

Joanne let out a quiet exclamation. "Ellie… there's something here."

Ellie moved over, Atticus following just behind. Joanne was pointing to a small, corroded object lodged in the soil near the hip bone of the first skeleton.

Ellie reached for a brush and carefully flicked away the dirt.

"What is that?" Atticus asked, peering closer.

Ellie shook her head. "No idea."

She carefully extracted the object, turning it over in her gloved hand. The metal was heavily corroded but solid, with a distinctive shape: a small, rectangular iron piece with a tapered end.

Atticus reached for his phone and snapped a few quick photos of the object as Ellie examined it.

"Any ideas?" Ellie asked, using a brush to sweep away the last of the clinging dirt.

Atticus shook his head. "None." He took another picture, adjusting his angle for better lighting. "Not something that would be found on clothing. Too thick for a tag or a nameplate. It looks mechanical. Solid iron, I think, and doesn't look decorative. And the edges look too uniform to be a natural break. I think it was made to fit *into* something." He frowned, studying the object more closely. "It was near his hip, right?"

"Yes," Joanne said.

"So maybe in a pocket."

Ellie nodded. "The fabric would have disintegrated years ago, but something like this is going to last." She handed the piece to him.

Atticus nodded his agreement, turning the object in his fingers. "It'll be contemporaneous with the bodies."

"We'll still need to get it dated," Ellie said.

Atticus took a final photograph before passing it back to her. "I'll do some research tonight. Maybe I can work out what it is and where it might've come from."

23

Henry set the empty wine glass down on the table and glanced at his watch. Nine thirty. He and Sophie had met in Chesil Rectory in Winchester. Henry had brought his dates to the restaurant before and had always had a good meal; more often than not, the evenings ended just the way he wanted, too. He had profiles on several dating apps and had always found it easy to hook up with women on them; his profile pictures included one of him standing in front of Brookmere House and another leaning against the vintage Ferrari GTO he'd bought to race around the south of France in the year before coming back to work on the estate. Celeste said the photos were crass and that women would see through him straight away, but his sister had been wrong; it hadn't been like that at all. There were plenty of good-looking girls who'd fall over themselves to go out with someone so self-evidently wealthy, and he was happy to take advantage of their avarice. They got what they wanted; he got what he wanted; it was a mutually beneficial arrangement.

Tonight's date had messaged him last week, and after a few flirtatious messages, Henry had suggested they meet for dinner.

He'd pretended to listen as she regaled him with her life story: lived in Winchester, worked in a local coffee shop, fed up with singleton life and looking for a relationship, adding that she wasn't averse to a little fun when she saw the flicker of unease he couldn't suppress. She was ten years younger than him and couldn't really have been more removed from his status, but he didn't care; she was gorgeous, and it wasn't as if he was after anything more than no-strings fun, although he might have to let her think more was on offer if he was to have his way.

The waiter arrived with the bill, and Henry paid it, making sure Sophie noticed his heavy black metal credit card as he thunked it down on the table.

"How far is it to your place?"

"Ten minutes," she said. "Where's your car?"

"Colebrook Street."

He'd brought his 911 and was confident that driving her home in it would seal the deal. He'd banked on staying with her tonight and getting back to the house tomorrow morning to pick up his father for a meeting in Salisbury with the CEO of Azure. Henry was going to report that they would soon— three months, he thought—be in a position to offer them all the land they'd be purchasing from Jack Turnbull. He hadn't cleared it with his father yet, but the thought had occurred to him that he might be able to get Azure to make a payment up front and then use *that* to buy the farm. His father would be impressed; they'd have Turnbull's land and a lucrative extension to their deal with Azure, all without having to spend a penny of their own money. The run-in with Turnbull at the pub had been embarrassing and annoying, but it hadn't changed anything other than making Henry even more determined to get the land; they were going to crank up the pressure until he had no choice *but* to sell.

Sophie said she just needed to visit the bathroom. He pulled out his phone to check for messages and frowned when he saw a missed call from Emelia. That was strange; she rarely called him, and certainly not at this hour.

He pressed redial, and she picked up almost immediately.

"Where are you?" There was an edge to her voice: tight, uncertain.

"Winchester. Why—what is it?"

"Your father."

"What do you mean?"

"He didn't come back this evening."

"He was in Salisbury—he was seeing the lawyers."

"I know," she said, "but that was this afternoon."

"Have you called him?"

"He's not answering his phone. Have you spoken to him?"

"Not since this morning."

"Something's wrong."

Henry rubbed a hand over his jaw. "Where are the others?"

"They're all here."

Sophie reappeared and smiled hesitantly as she noticed he was on the phone. He held up a hand and angled his head away from her. He closed his eyes and took a breath. His sense of anticipation had vanished, replaced with a gnawing unease. He couldn't help but think of the diagnosis. Had something happened to him?

"I'll be there as soon as I can," he said. "I'll call when I'm in the car."

He ended the call.

Sophie had taken her seat again and looked at him with concern. "What is it?"

"Something's come up."

"Doesn't sound good."

"It's not. It's…" He stopped; he wasn't about to share sensitive family business with her. "Never mind. I need to go home."

She did a bad job of hiding her disappointment. "Can you still give me a lift?"

"Sorry—can't." He took out his roll of money, peeled out a twenty and gave it to her. "Get yourself a taxi."

She stared at the note and then at him. Her expression changed; the enthusiasm drained away to be replaced with something that looked very much like contempt.

He stood. "What is it?"

"*Thanks*," she muttered with sarcasm she didn't bother trying to hide. "I've had a lovely evening."

Henry put his wallet back into his pocket. "Why are you being like this?"

"Paying me off with a twenty? Seriously?"

"It wasn't a problem when I paid the bill."

She shook her head, lips pressed into a thin line. "Whatever. Don't call me again."

Henry didn't bother responding. He turned on his heel and strode out of the restaurant, already pulling his car keys from his pocket.

24

Jez finished his meal, set the empty pot aside and stretched, feeling the pleasant ache in his muscles from the day's hike. The fire flickered, casting shifting shadows against the trees, and beyond the glow of the flames, the darkness pressed in, thick and absolute. Treacle was curled up near his feet, his belly full, his ears twitching at the occasional rustle in the undergrowth. The dog let out a contented sigh. Jez reached down and scratched behind his ears.

"Good day, wasn't it?"

Treacle's tail gave a lazy thump against the ground in agreement.

They'd reached the halfway point at Broughton as the sun was ending its slow descent, casting long shadows across the fields. His legs ached a little, but he felt good, better than he'd expected after covering thirteen miles. The place he'd earmarked for camping was just beyond the village, tucked away in a wooded copse near a bend in the Test. He'd set up camp while there was still enough light to gather firewood and make a cup of tea before the evening chill set in. Dinner had been simple:

a packet of dehydrated pasta with a creamy mushroom sauce for him and a bowl of biscuits for Treacle. The dog had stared at him with hopeful eyes until Jez relented and let him lick the sauce from his bowl, too.

Jez took a final sip of water from his flask and leaned back against his pack, letting his gaze drift upward. The stars were emerging now, brilliant pinpricks in the inky sky, unspoiled out here by artificial lights. It had been too long since he'd seen them like this, stretching vast and endless above him. The copse of trees provided just enough shelter from the breeze, and there was no sign of anyone, no hum of traffic, just the rustle of leaves in the breeze and the occasional hoot of an owl awakening for the night.

He stretched his legs toward the fire. The flames flickered orange and gold, the scent of woodsmoke curling into the cool night air. He let out a slow breath. Out here, with nothing but the sky above, the fire before him, and the sounds of nature all around, the world felt distant. His worries about how to navigate the end of his relationship felt like they belonged to someone else.

He had been with Eva for eighteen months. They'd met online and had quickly become serious. Within a month they were spending most nights together, and by the third, she'd brought her toothbrush and a drawer of clothes to his flat in Winchester. Jez had liked her immediately: her dry sense of humour, her sharpness, the way she seemed to find everything so easy. She was an A&E nurse at the hospital, and he was quietly awed by her ability to stay calm in the face of things that would have shaken him.

But over time, the cracks showed. Her shifts were long and exhausting, and Jez's schedule—irregular hours, unexpected call-outs—made things harder. They'd bickered about small things that somehow felt bigger: missed messages, forgotten plans, mistakes made when he placed the online shopping order. The final argument had been over nothing, yet it had ended with Eva taking her things and walking out. That had been six weeks ago. She'd texted him to say it was over, and that was that; no chance to talk about it, to understand what had happened other than that she'd had second thoughts.

It had knocked Jez's confidence, and he'd thrown himself into his work with Atticus to compensate. That, though, was just papering over the cracks; this walk, with hours of time to think, was exactly what he needed.

25

Henry drove the 911 through the wrought-iron gates, the headlights sweeping across the gravel of the drive. The house loomed ahead, its honeyed stone catching the faint glow of the security lights. It was impressive, but there was something about its scale—the rows of tall, shuttered windows and the looming turrets—that made it feel cold, as if it was never truly lived in, just maintained, a relic from an age ago.

Henry cut the engine, sat for a moment in the silence, then pushed open the door. He grabbed his coat from the passenger seat and made his way inside. The warmth hit him immediately. He hung his coat on the old oak stand in the hallway and moved through the warren of corridors that led to the private side of the house. The state rooms—the soaring ceilings, the oil paintings of long-dead Ainsleys, the gilded furniture— were for guests and film crews, not them. The family gathered in a cluster of smaller rooms tucked away at the back, places that actually felt lived in.

As he neared the breakfast room, he could hear voices: low and urgent. The long oak table was littered with abandoned cups of coffee. Emelia sat at the head, staring at her phone. Celeste was opposite her, swirling a teaspoon through an untouched drink, with her awful husband, Julian, alongside. Alexander leaned back in his chair, arms folded. Sebastian paced near the window.

"Anything?" he asked.

Emelia looked up and shook her head. "Nothing. I've tried calling him. It just goes straight to voicemail. Have you tried?"

"In the car," he said.

"And?"

"Same."

"It's the dementia," Sebastian said. "It's worse than we were told."

"It's *not*," Henry said. "He's been absent-minded lately, but…"

"There's no reason for him to be out this late," Emelia said.

"I said the same thing," Alexander said.

Sebastian clapped his hands. "Wake up! It's the *dementia*! We've all seen it."

"He's only just been diagnosed," Henry said.

"Six months ago," Emelia said. "Yesterday was just confirmation. The doctor said he could see steady progression. I think Sebastian's right."

"Can you think of anywhere he might have gone?" Alexander said. "Anywhere else he might've planned to visit?"

"No," Emelia said.

Celeste turned to Henry. "When did you last see him?"

"This morning," Henry said. "He said he was going out to see the solar farm."

"That was it?"

"He called me afterwards. There was a problem with the fence—he thought it was the protestors."

"And he went to see them?" Alexander asked.

"No, I did. He had an appointment with the lawyers this afternoon."

"He missed it," Emelia said. "I called the partner he was supposed to be seeing half an hour ago. He didn't go."

Alexander rubbed a hand over his face. "What do we do? Call the police?"

Henry bit his lip. "No. Not yet. The last thing we want is for this to leak out. You know what Father would say if this got into the papers. He won't want the estate's business interests to be affected. And if word gets out about his... his diagnosis... it could compromise everything."

"That wouldn't happen," Celeste said.

"Don't be naïve," Henry snapped. "If Azure catches wind that Father isn't the full ticket, they'll start second-guessing the deals we're working on."

"But he's *missing*, Henry," Emelia said. "We've got to do something."

Henry went to the bookcase, returned with a map of the estate, and spread it on the table. He traced a finger along the roads and paths. "I'll go and see the protestors; then I'll drive out to the west side." He stabbed his finger against Home Copse.

Emelia frowned. "That far?"

"There's been a peregrine from the cathedral hunting over in that direction. Father's been talking about trying to get a photo of it. He might've gone out there afterwards and maybe..."

"Hurt himself?"

"I don't know. It's possible."

"I'll come with you," Celeste said.

"No. You and Julian go up to the lodge and look there."

Julian nodded. "Okay."

"Alexander," Henry said, "take the quad bike and go into the village. Go to the Plough and ask if anyone knows where he is—discreetly, for God's sake—and then, if you don't get anything, follow the track until you get to Winterslow. Just in case."

Sebastian stopped pacing. "And me?"

"Fairoak Copse and Warner's Copse. We can meet at the cottage and then go south, follow the track through Beechy Dean and Great Netley and back again."

"What about me?" Emelia asked.

"Stay here in case he comes back." Henry folded the map away.

"And if he doesn't? If we can't find him?"

"It's ten thirty now. If we haven't found him by midnight, we call the police."

26

Atticus went to Nole in the Market Square to get a pizza and brought it back to the office. He was flying solo tonight—Mack was taking her kids to the cinema—and she'd reminded him that it was important to eat, knowing that he'd probably forget otherwise. It was a fair point; she knew him too well. He sat down on the sofa, cleared the top of the packing crate he used as a coffee table, and, after ducking back out to the little kitchen on the landing to get a bottle of beer, he opened the box and took out a slice. Bandit trotted over and stared at him, his head tilted to the side.

"What?"

The dog's eyes went wide, and as Atticus looked at him, he very deliberately licked his lips.

"Seriously?"

Bandit wagged his tail, and, with a helpless chuckle, Atticus tore off the crust and tossed it to him. The dog caught it deftly and, happy with his spoils, trotted back into the bedroom.

Atticus finished the first slice and washed it down with a mouthful of beer. He was restless. He knew Mack had to spend time with the kids, but it was a reminder that there would always be something they couldn't share. She'd told him that she didn't want any more kids, and truthfully, Atticus didn't know if he wanted any, either. But they were a tie that existed between Mack and Andy, and a reminder that Mack had once shared things with her ex-husband that she'd never be able to share with him. He knew he was being unduly sensitive, and that Andy and Mack's relationship was beyond repair, but it still niggled at him.

He took another slice of pizza and tried to think of a way to distract himself before he became too maudlin. He had a couple of games of online chess on the go, but, as he got up and went to his desk, he found he wasn't in the mood. His literary agent had successfully pitched a follow-up book, and he had started work on two chapters—'The Art of the Interview: Reading Between the Lies' and 'The Forensic Mind: How to See What Others Miss'—but as he tapped his keyboard to wake the screen, he found he didn't have the motivation for that, either.

He took another mouthful of beer, found his phone and navigated to the photographs that he had taken at the dig that afternoon. He AirDropped all of them to his Mac, imported them into Photoshop and then clicked through the images of the skeletons, zooming in and out in the vain hope that he might find something of interest that had otherwise been missed. He didn't expect to find anything useful and didn't.

He was curious as to whom the remains might once have belonged to, but he knew that the odds of identifying any of them were long. At least they ought to be able to find out how long the bones had been in the ground; Ellie had told him that they would be moved to the forensic anthropology lab at the

University of Southampton, and that a reasonably accurate estimate would be discerned by way of radiocarbon dating.

He wondered whether they would be able to extract DNA. It was possible, but far from guaranteed. Soil composition and moisture levels played a role in how well genetic material was preserved, and, given the likely age of the remains, any usable DNA would be degraded. If they could recover it, though, it might be possible to compare it against modern genealogical databases. Perhaps a descendant of one of the men was still alive, a distant relative whose DNA might confirm a connection.

There was nothing he could do about that now.

He clicked through to the photographs of the object that had been unearthed. It was rusted, pitted with age, its edges corroded but still intact enough to hold its original shape. He zoomed in on the rectangular shaft and the slightly tapered ends, measuring its dimensions roughly against the scale of the nearby evidence tags. It was small—about two inches long and half an inch wide—just the right size to fit in a pocket.

The first step was to determine whether it had been cast or forged.

The irregularities in the surface, the grainy texture, and the faint traces of what might once have been a stamped manufacturer's mark suggested that the object had been cast rather than machined. That pointed to an early method of manufacture, likely before the widespread industrial standardisation of parts. He considered that for a minute, and after referring to a website on nineteenth-century agricultural engineering and historical metalwork fabrication, settled on a range between 1820 and 1840.

Atticus opened a new browser tab and began searching for historic metal components, keeping his terms broad at first—'nineteenth-century agricultural machinery parts,' 'cast-iron machine components'—before refining his queries based on the shape and estimated size of the object. He ran a reverse image search using Google Lens, knowing it was a long shot but hoping for a reference that might steer him in the right direction.

Most of the results were irrelevant: modern machine keys, miscellaneous industrial parts, rusted bolts. He scrolled past page after page of useless hits until something caught his eye.

A partial match.

Not identical, but close.

The image linked to a historical archive of early farm equipment, specifically a collection of mechanical fittings from agricultural steam engines and belt-driven machines. One of the objects—a small, worn metal piece—had a similar size and general shape, though its exact function wasn't immediately clear. The caption mentioned that it had been found among the remains of a destroyed threshing machine from the early 1800s.

Atticus switched to the Museum of English Rural Life's digital collection and began searching for images of preserved nineteenth-century threshing machines and steam-powered equipment. Within minutes, he found a comparable object: a small cast-iron component listed as part of the locking mechanism for a piece of heavy machinery.

He returned to the close-up picture he'd taken of the object and zoomed in on the partially legible text. The rust had eaten away at much of the surface, but faint indentations suggested something had once been stamped into the metal.

He adjusted the contrast, increasing the sharpness and tweaking the exposure to bring out any variation in texture. The letters darkened slightly against the corroded background, but they were still frustratingly unclear.

Atticus tried another technique—false colour imaging—that was often used in forensic analysis to enhance faint markings on deteriorated surfaces. Converting the image to grayscale, he applied an edge-detection filter to highlight any raised or recessed details.

The faint remnants of letters began to emerge.

Not bad.

But not enough.

He layered multiple photographs taken at slightly different angles and adjusted the lighting in Photoshop. He played with the highlights and shadows, emphasising the variations in depth.

Slowly, the characters started to take shape.

A faint *T*.

Maybe an *A* next to it.

And a *K* in the middle.

Atticus ran a search for 'nineteenth-century agricultural equipment manufacturers' and narrowed it to those known for producing threshing machines in the south of England.

Then he saw it.

TASKER.

He clicked the link and went to the website of the Hampshire Cultural Trust. He read:

For 170 years, Taskers of Andover were a leading manufacturer of a wide range of agricultural implements and machinery.

He scrolled down and saw a list of the machinery the company produced: portable mills for grinding corn, cake crushers, threshing machines.

Atticus leaned back in his chair, chewing the inside of his cheek. He opened another window and navigated to Wikipedia. There was a long entry dealing with threshing machines. They'd been at the centre of some of the fiercest periods of unrest in rural England after landowners had introduced them to replace farmhands, cutting the need for manual threshing and putting labourers out of work during the winter months.

Mechanisation had been the catalyst for widespread rebellion: attacks on farms, riots and arson. Things had come to a head in the early 1830s with a period of unrest that had become known as the Swing Riots, named after the fictitious Captain Swing, the figurehead of the movement and supposed sender of threatening letters to the landowners, parsons and magistrates who had attracted the ire of the rioters.

Atticus felt like he was getting somewhere, and encouraged by his progress, he went to grab another slice of pizza and a fresh bottle of beer. He took down an empty notebook from the shelf next to his desk, opened it to the first page, started a new search into the unrest, and started to write.

27

Henry pulled his coat tighter against the evening chill as he stepped outside. The wind had picked up, stirring the branches of the trees that lined the driveway. An owl called from the boughs of the great yew, a mournful, drawn-out note that sent a shiver down his spine. He looked over at the lawns and saw the outline of the marquee that they meant to use for the party on Saturday. Something was most definitely wrong; his father might have said he didn't want a fuss, but he enjoyed showing off the house to the great and the good and wouldn't have wanted to miss the opportunity that the party would provide.

He got into one of the estate's Land Rovers, started the engine and reversed, leaving a spray of gravel as he raced back to the gate and the road beyond. He could see the glow of the protestors' fire as he approached on Whiteway, once again gritting his teeth in irritation that Turnbull had let them camp on his field.

He parked the car, got out, and made his way through the open gate into the field. The camp took on a different character at night. The glow of the fire cast flickering shadows across the tents and tarpaulin shelters, the smoke curling lazily into the cold night air. A dozen figures were gathered in a loose circle around the flames, some perched on logs, others cross-legged on the ground, wrapped in second-hand fleeces and patchwork blankets. The acrid scent of woodsmoke mingled with the sweet tang of dope, and a bottle of something that looked as if it might be homemade was being passed around. Someone strummed an acoustic guitar, the chords loose and meandering, accompanied by a half-hearted attempt at singing that drifted in and out of tune. Others murmured, their words punctuated by occasional bursts of raucous laughter. A couple sat closer to the fire, their heads bent together in quiet conversation, while another group stared into the flames, their faces blank with the dazed, slow contentment of the very stoned. Beyond the firelight, the darkness pressed in, the outlines of banners and signs barely visible, fluttering slightly in the breeze, the lights of passing cars illuminating them before rushing away into the darkened countryside.

Henry walked to the fire and looked for Van Etting.

"You're back."

Henry turned to see the woman he had spoken to that morning.

"Are you sure you don't want to join the camp?"

"Of course I don't."

"You're here a lot for someone who says he isn't interested."

She drawled her sentences and was unsteady on her feet.

"My father's missing."

"And?"

"And I wanted to know if he's been up here today."

Her eyes drifted in and out of focus. "What?"

"Has my father been to the camp at all today?"

She stumbled to one side, reaching out for Henry's arm to steady herself. "Who's your father?"

He swore. It was intolerable. "Where's Van Etting?"

"Don't know."

The man who had been with the woman during Henry's earlier visit got up from the fire and came over. "You're back again."

"Where's Van Etting?"

The man was a little more sober than the woman, and Henry thought he saw a glimmer of discomfort pass across his face. "Don't know where he is."

"Yes, you do," Henry said. "Where is he?"

The man shrugged. "No, man, I don't. No clue. What's it about? Why do you want him?"

Henry knew he was being lied to. "Has he gone to the solar farm?"

"How many times do you want me to say it? I have no idea where he is."

"My father is missing. If anything's happened to him—*anything*—and you know about it, I'll see to it myself that you are *destroyed*."

He spun and walked away, hurrying back to the car.

28

Henry drove down to the start of the access road the team was using to get the equipment into the field and parked up. He found a torch in the glovebox, got out and set off at a trot. The estate stretched out before him, a vast expanse of fifteen thousand acres that went to the borders of Salisbury in the west and all the way out to Broughton and East Tytherly in the east.

Henry had tried to persuade himself that his father was fine, that there was a reasonable explanation for all of this, but the cold gnawing in his gut said otherwise. What if the dementia *was* more advanced than they'd thought? He'd Googled it as soon as the diagnosis had been received. It was a cruel, creeping disease, the websites said, starting at the back of the brain where it would affect vision and spatial awareness. But it wouldn't stay there. It would spread, and things would get worse. Had Rupert been able to hide the worst effects of it? Henry suddenly had a vision of his father wandering the fields, lost and desperate, and pushed on even more quickly.

The wind carried the rustle of dry leaves and the occasional snap of a twig from the undergrowth. A fox darted across the path ahead, a flash of reddish-brown fur vanishing into the hedge.

He stopped and cupped his hands around his mouth. "Dad!"

Nothing.

He tried again. "Dad!"

Only the wind answered, rustling through the fields.

Henry walked on, following the dirt track that led to the site, scanning the hedgerows and gaps between the trees. The temporary fencing was ahead of him, and the panels loomed behind that, black rectangles catching the little moonlight filtering through the clouds.

He reached the edge of the site and hesitated, listening.

Silence.

He walked the perimeter, shining the torch between the rows of panels, peering down the narrow tracks where the construction crews drove their vehicles during the day. His breath misted in the cold air as he moved, the beam of his torch sweeping back and forth.

Nothing.

He switched the torch off and let out a slow exhale. He wasn't here.

He pulled out his phone and checked the time: 11.25 p.m.

He was about to call Emelia to check whether she had heard anything from the others, when he saw movement.

A silhouette passed between two of the panels.

A second shadow followed the first.

Henry watched, agog, as the two shadows stayed in the cover of a line of panels and headed north. He followed, his heart racing and with an empty feeling in his stomach. He stayed close to the temporary fence, and as the boundary bent around to the right, he saw that one of the wire sections had been lifted out of its concrete blocks and pushed back to make an opening.

The two figures left the cover of the panels and crossed the field in the direction of the opening.

Henry gripped his torch tightly and moved his thumb up to cover the on-off switch. He crept forward. The wind was picking up now, rustling the hedgerows and masking the sound of his footsteps. The two figures were moving quickly with their heads down. One of them was carrying something over his shoulder.

Henry stepped over the loosened section of fencing and followed them into the field. His breath was coming harder now, a mix of nerves and adrenaline spiking in his blood. He wasn't stupid—he knew approaching two unknown trespassers in the middle of the night wasn't a good idea—but his father was missing, and what if these two knew something?

What if they'd been involved?

He picked up his pace, closing the gap between them.

"Hey!" he called.

The two figures stopped dead.

Henry took another step forward, raising his torch and flicking it on. The beam cut through the darkness, landing squarely on them. They turned in unison, faces obscured by scarves wrapped high over their noses. One was taller, lean, his frame all angles beneath an oversized coat. The other was shorter and stockier.

"What the hell are you doing here?"

The shorter man took a step back, his eyes darting left and right, looking for an escape.

The taller man found his voice. "Back off."

Henry wasn't in the mood for games. "You're trespassing."

The shorter man lunged. Henry grabbed a fistful of his jacket and pulled. The man twisted, trying to wrench free, but Henry held on. The man swung wildly, landing a glancing blow to Henry's ribs. Henry grunted but kept his hold on the man's jacket. The tall one stepped up, knocking them off balance. They crashed to the ground, rolling in the damp grass. Henry fought to pin one of them, but a knee caught him in the stomach and drove the wind from his lungs.

He gasped, struggling to recover. The end of the man's scarf brushed his hand, and Henry yanked at it, pulling it free.

Henry stared up at a face he recognised.

Van Etting.

Henry coughed, still winded. "*You.*"

Van Etting stood, helped up the shorter man, and, without another word, they ran.

Henry pushed himself up, still clutching the scarf.

"Bastards."

Henry flicked on the torch and swept it after them. They were gone. He turned, sweeping the beam of the torch over the site, and his stomach twisted at what he saw. One of the central inverter units had been vandalised, its metal casing pried open, wires ripped out in tangled loops, and the control panel smashed to pieces. Nearby, several solar panels had been cracked, their surfaces spiderwebbed with fractures: the work of crowbars or heavy boots.

"Dad!"

Nothing.

"Dad!"

He closed his eyes, straining to hear anything that might tell him his father was nearby.

Still nothing.

There was no point waiting until midnight.

He took out his phone and dialled 999.

PART 3

Wednesday

29

Henry made the call to the police at 11.40 p.m., and the first patrol car pulled up outside the house just after midnight. Henry wasn't surprised by the prompt response; even the most basic risk assessment on the information that Henry had provided—his father's age, recent medical diagnosis, and the fact he'd been missing for fourteen hours—would have flagged him as high risk. Add in the fact that Rupert was a prominent landowner and a public figure, and it was inevitable that the police would take it seriously.

Henry stepped out onto the gravel and waited by the front door as the car rolled to a stop beside his 911. Two uniformed officers got out: a man and a woman. Henry glanced at the male constable first: stocky, early thirties, tired eyes. The woman looked sharper and more alert and, judging by the way she spoke to her colleague, seemed to be in charge.

"Good evening, sir," she said. "Understand you've got a missing person."

"That's right—my father."

"And are you the one who made the call?"

"I am."

"Your name?"

"Henry Ainsley."

"I'm Constable Coverdale," she said. "And this is Constable Betts."

"You'd better come in."

Henry led the way to the family sitting room, where the others had gathered. He made the introductions: Emelia was deathly pale and struggled to stop her hands from trembling; Alexander was sitting on one of the fuchsia-coloured sofas, one leg crossed over the other with his foot bouncing up and down; Sebastian was standing near the middle window, occasionally turning to look out over the grounds; Celeste was on the second sofa with Julian next to her. Henry went to the fireplace to warm up.

Coverdale and Betts asked a series of questions to build up a timeline of Rupert's last known movements. They started by speaking to Emelia, and still clutching the same cold cup of tea she'd been nursing for the past hour, she explained that her husband had left the house that morning and had been in good spirits. She'd heard nothing from him all day and had started to be concerned when he still hadn't returned in time for dinner. She said that she'd been calling his phone every ten minutes, with each attempt going to voicemail.

"How did he seem this morning?"

"A little distracted," she said.

Coverdale looked up from her notebook. "How?"

"He had some bad news yesterday from the doctor."

"That was mentioned when you called the control room," Coverdale said. "He was recently diagnosed with dementia?"

"Yes," Emelia said. "There was a family discussion about it yesterday evening."

Sebastian chuckled. "Discussion? That's a laugh."

"How do you mean?" Coverdale asked.

"Father hasn't really accepted it," Sebastian said. "We wanted to talk to him about estate planning—you know, while he still has the mental capacity to do things—and it got heated."

"He won't talk about it," Celeste said.

Coverdale scribbled in her notebook and then looked up again. "You said the family meeting was difficult."

"I think he felt we were ganging up on him," Celeste suggested.

"And do you think it might have upset him?"

"Are you asking whether he might be depressed?" Henry said.

"Yes," she said. "What do you think? Was he?"

"I wouldn't have said so. He came to see me at the estate office after breakfast, and he was his normal self. He had a busy day with a lot to do—he seemed enthusiastic to get started on it."

Coverdale turned to the others. "What do you think?"

Everyone agreed that it was possible the argument had upset him.

Emelia dabbed at her eyes. "Are you asking whether he might be depressed because…"

Alexander finished the sentence for her. "Because they're worried he might have done something to himself."

Coverdale nodded sympathetically. "It's something that has to be considered as a possibility." She turned to Henry. "Where was he going after seeing you?"

"The solar farm. We've licensed land to a company who are going to use it to generate electricity. The contractors installing the equipment said there'd been someone tampering with the fence. There's a camp of protestors up by the A30."

"We saw them when we came in," Betts said.

Coverdale looked up from her notebook again. "Had they been trespassing?"

"Yes," Henry said. "I went out there tonight when I was looking for Father, and there were two of them in the field. One of the inverters has been vandalised, and a whole row of panels has been damaged. One of the trespassers was Phillip Van Etting. He's in charge. You should definitely go and speak to him."

Betts frowned, tapping his pen against the edge of his notebook. "Roughly what time did this happen?"

"An hour ago."

"We'll go and have a chat."

Coverdale looked from one to the other. "Is there anything else you think might be relevant?"

"There *is* something," Henry said. "Father has been trying to buy one of the neighbouring farms, and the negotiations have been… difficult."

"What farm?" Sebastian said.

"Jack Turnbull's."

Sebastian's mouth fell open. "Buying *more* land? That's the first I've heard of it. Why didn't he tell us?"

"Because he knew you'd be annoyed."

"Why would you be annoyed?" Coverdale said.

"Some of us think Rupert should be thinking of *selling* land," Celeste added.

"Certainly not buying *more*," Sebastian said. He turned to Henry. "You knew?"

"I've been working on the deal with him. And I don't think the fact that there is a difference of opinion on how the family business is run has anything to do with what's happened." He turned back to Coverdale. "The farmer's name is Jack Turnbull, as I said, and he's not happy that we've been trying to buy his farm. It's become quite contentious. I saw Turnbull today, and he was aggressive. He said there'd be consequences unless we accepted he wasn't going to sell."

"Aggressive? How?"

"Verbally," Henry said. "And then he got up into my face and…" He shrugged.

"He attacked you?"

"No," Henry said. "Not like that. But he has a temper."

"Do you think he might have something to do with what's happened?"

"No idea. But I don't think it'd be a bad idea to go and speak to him."

"We will," Coverdale said.

Emelia shifted on the sofa, then put the cold cup of tea on the table and got up. "Shouldn't we be out looking for him now?"

"Absolutely," Betts said. "But we need to establish everything we can before we do. Do you have CCTV here?"

Henry shook his head. "Not much. A couple of cameras at the main gate and near the stables. Father never wanted them installed all over the house."

"We'll take a look."

Henry went and sat down next to Emelia as Betts walked into the hallway to radio in a missing person report. Henry could hear him as he described Rupert as high risk and vulnerable due to recent medical concerns. He asked for additional officers to begin a detailed search.

"A disappearance like this usually falls into one of three possibilities," Coverdale explained. "An accident, a deliberate decision to disappear, or foul play. Is there *any* reason Rupert might have left on his own? Could he have gone to a second property, a friend's house, anything like that?"

"No," Celeste said.

"What about an accident?"

"That's what I'm most worried about," Emelia said.

"The estate is huge," Alexander added. "If he got disoriented or lost track of time, he could be *anywhere*."

Betts returned. "Control room is issuing a welfare alert with his description and checking the hospital. I've called for backup, and when that arrives, we'll begin a coordinated search. We'll start from the house and work outward, focusing on the areas he was most likely to have gone—paths, tracks, open fields."

"And if you don't find him tonight?" Emelia asked.

"We'll bring in search dogs and, if necessary, drones. Maybe the helicopter."

Henry had heard enough. He grabbed his coat. "I'm going out again."

"I'd advise against that, sir," Coverdale said. "Better to keep the search coordinated."

"He's my father. I'm not just going to sit here when I could be looking."

"Be careful, then. If anything seems off, please call it in."

Henry hurried outside, opened the garage and found the keys for one of the quad bikes. He wasn't waiting for the police. If his father was out there, lost or hurt, he'd find him himself.

30

It was seven in the morning when Detective Inspector Robbie Best went outside to make his phone call. He'd been on duty last night when Elaine Coverdale had called in and explained that the Earl of Brookmere was missing and that, in her opinion, the situation had the potential to become grim. He'd arrived at Brookmere House shortly after and had been here ever since. The lack of progress suggested he wouldn't be able to leave for hours.

He called Mack.

"Robbie," she said, "how is it?"

"Not much to report. We've had officers out all night, ground search mainly. Started from the house, radiated outwards. No sign of him anywhere. We've got dogs sweeping the wooded areas now. Nothing so far. The drone team's been up twice—nothing."

"CCTV?"

"Not much, but we've checked the footage they do have. Only people in or out last night were family or staff."

"What's the family saying?"

Robbie ambled over towards the huge marquee that had been erected on the lawn, a loose canvas flap fluttering in the gentle breeze. "They're worried," he said. "His son reported him missing around eleven thirty last night—said he'd been gone since the morning."

"And the last confirmed sighting?"

"A contractor working on the solar farm spoke to him in the morning. Says Rupert seemed fine. The protestors have been messing around with the fence, and Rupert spoke to his son to ask him to go up there and warn them off. Betts went to the camp and spoke to them, and they confirmed it. They say they don't know where Rupert is—they haven't seen him. The camp's chaotic, but the man in charge is"—he looked down at his notebook—"a Mr. Phillip Van Etting from Andover. It'd be helpful if we could pull his record."

"I'll do it."

"There is one other thing about him. Henry saw him at the solar park they're building last night. Some of the gear was vandalised. I've had a chat with him about it, and he denies it was him. Says he was at the camp all night and has people who'll back him up."

"What do you think?"

"I think it's concerning. Weather was clear, visibility good, no reason Rupert wouldn't have made it back. He's just been diagnosed with dementia, and the wife is saying he wasn't quite himself yesterday morning. It feels like something's off."

"Suicide?"

"That was my thought."

"You want me to come out?"

"No need yet. If he doesn't turn up by lunchtime, I think we need to broaden this out. One thing you could do, though—his wife said that he knows Chief Superintendent Beckton. There's a party for his seventy-fifth on Saturday, and Beckton's been invited. You should probably give him the heads-up that she might call to get him involved, especially if we can't find anything."

Mack groaned. "I'll do it now. I'll come down after lunch. Keep me posted if anything breaks before then."

"Will do."

Robbie hung up and looked across the misty field. The early sun had just started to cut through the haze, and he saw a family of deer emerging from a thick band of trees in the distance. The estate was huge, and there was no way of knowing where Rupert might have gone. He turned his attention back to the house and saw Henry Ainsley and his two dogs as they came outside and set off towards the east. Robbie raised his hand in acknowledgement, but Henry either ignored him or was too distracted to notice; he continued on his way, the dogs racing away as the three of them left the formal grounds and made for the start of the fields.

He texted Franny.

>> Morning. <<

She texted back almost at once.

>> OK? <<

>> Wonderful! <<

>> Still at Brookmere House? <<

>> Going to be here all day at this rate. <<

>> No sign? <<

>> None. <<

They continued the conversation for a couple of minutes until Franny said she needed to get ready to go to the station. Robbie said he wouldn't be surprised if she ended up out at the house with him later; she responded with a thoughtful emoji, told him to let her know if there was anything she could do in the meantime, and then signed off with a kiss.

Robbie was still getting used to the idea that he and Franny were an item. The first couple of months had been tricky. There was an age gap between them—Franny was ten years younger than him—and Robbie had been worried that people might make something out of it. Franny wasn't the slightest bit worried about it, though, and told Robbie it was his issue and that he needed to get over it. Robbie knew it reflected his own insecurity, and after a little time had passed, he'd managed to deal with it. Franny had moved things along, pointing to what had happened to the last inter-office romance—Mack and Atticus—and how their secrecy had contributed to Atticus having to leave. Robbie drew the obvious distinction—Mack had been married during the affair and had her own reasons for discretion—but Franny had been insistent, suggesting that openness was necessary to defuse any suggestion of bias that might have arisen after her recent promotion to DS.

Robbie had reluctantly agreed, even though it still made him uncomfortable. He wasn't the sort to broadcast his private life, but if people *were* going to talk, best to give them as little ammunition as possible. And truthfully, once the initial awkwardness had passed, nobody had seemed that bothered. There had been a few raised eyebrows and one or two quiet comments from the old guard, but nothing malicious. Everyone liked Franny, and most liked him, too—he thought—so it had faded quickly into the background. Besides, they weren't flaunting it.

Still, the odd moment caught him off guard. Like just now: her message with the kiss at the end. It made him smile, made him feel momentarily lighter, even in the middle of something grim, like this had the potential to be. He hadn't expected to feel that way. He hadn't expected any of it, really. Franny was sharp, quick-witted, and tenacious; someone who challenged him just enough to keep him on his toes, but not so much that he ever felt he was being mocked or belittled. She made him feel younger, not foolish.

And it felt like they had a decent chance at making the relationship a long-term thing.

He tucked his phone back into his coat pocket and turned to look out over the fields beyond the ha-ha at the edge of the lawn. Still no movement. Still no sign. The Earl of Brookmere had vanished without a trace, and Robbie had a bad feeling that he wasn't coming back.

31

Jez woke with the dawn. He lay still, taking a moment to remember where he was: the sounds of birdsong and the glow of the sunlight through canvas reminded him, together with the stiffness in his back, that he was in the tent. Treacle had fitted himself into the hollows of his body, and as Jez sat up and stretched, the dog stirred.

He reached for the zipper and opened the door, letting the morning light spill in. The air was crisp, carrying the earthy scent of damp grass and smoke from last night's fire. A low mist clung to the hedgerows, softening the landscape beyond his small clearing. He took a deep breath, feeling the coolness of it fill his lungs, then exhaled slowly.

Treacle yawned, his tongue curling as he stretched out his front legs, then wriggled free from the sleeping bag. He padded to the opening and sniffed the air, his tail giving a lazy wag. Jez smiled and reached out to stroke him before crawling over the threshold.

The morning sun had barely risen above the trees, golden light filtering through the branches, casting long shadows across the dewy grass. He could hear the gentle rush of the river nearby, birds calling to one another from the hedgerows, and, somewhere distant, the bleating of sheep.

Jez rubbed the sleep from his face and ran a hand through his hair. He pulled on his boots, then stepped over to the remains of last night's fire. The embers still smouldered, sending up the occasional curl of smoke. He crouched down and poked at the ash with a stick, coaxing the fire back to life. He collected his cooking kit and balanced the battered old kettle over the fire, filling it with water. He went into his pack for a small tin of coffee, measuring out a scoop into his collapsible mug.

Treacle was watching him intently now, ears pricked. Jez pulled out the collapsible water bowl, filling it from his flask before adding a handful of biscuits. The dog wasted no time and dug in with enthusiasm.

The kettle began to steam. Jez poured the hot water over the coffee, inhaling deeply as the aroma filled the cool morning air. He wrapped his hands around the mug and took a careful sip, letting the warmth seep into his fingers. He glanced at his watch. Plenty of time. He planned to break camp within the hour and get back on the move, aiming to reach the western edge of the trail by the afternoon. Another long day's walk lay out before him, but that was part of the appeal.

32

Atticus had worked on the problem until one in the morning and emailed Mack and Ellie before realising that he probably ought to have waited until daylight. He'd suggested a meeting at the field first thing so he could discuss what he thought was likely to be an interesting discovery and awoke at seven to find replies from both women. Ellie had said she would be happy to meet and that she was intrigued; Mack had somewhat grumpily reminded him that not everyone was still awake in the early morning but that, subject to being needed on a missing persons enquiry that she said had the potential to be delicate, she'd do her best to be there.

Atticus had a quick breakfast and then printed out the results of his work from last night and slipped the pages into his inside pocket. He waited for Bandit to finish his bowl before putting the dog into his harness and attaching the lead, swiping his keys from the table and leading Bandit out onto the street and into the close where he'd left his car.

* * *

Atticus drove out to Pitton and parked in the same place as before. He was walking around the back to open the boot for Bandit when he saw Mack's car approaching. Atticus attached the lead and held Bandit back as he struggled to get over to her to say hello.

She parked and got out, kneeling down so she could stroke the dog.

"Careful of his paws," Atticus said. "He's already dirty."

Mack gestured down to her boots. "Probably won't make much difference today. I'm going to be tramping around a lot of muddy paths."

"The missing person?"

She nodded. "It's not good."

"Who is it?"

"It stays between us?"

"Of course."

"The Earl of Brookmere."

Atticus's eyes went wide with surprise. "Really?"

"We got a call last night from his son. He didn't come home last night, and he's not answering his phone."

"How long has he been missing for?"

"A day."

"So not *that* long."

"No," she said. "But he's old, and the family said he's just…" She paused. "No further?"

"Mack—come on. You know I'd never—"

She eyed him sternly. "I mean it this time."

"Promise."

"He's just been diagnosed with dementia. It'd be difficult for him to be much higher risk. Plus, it turns out Beckton used to play golf with him, so we've been told this is high priority."

Atticus opened the gate for Mack and then followed her into the field. "Anything I can do to help?"

"We've got it under control. Robbie came out last night after uniform called for help. We've got the dogs out this morning. Drones, too. We'll find him, one way or another."

They walked toward the field. Atticus glanced over at her. "How was it with the kids?"

"Good."

Atticus noticed her stiffen a little. "Cinema?"

She nodded. "And McDonald's for tea."

He could see she didn't want to talk about it, and realised it was probably for his benefit; she knew he found it tricky to talk about a part of her life that she couldn't easily share.

She changed the subject. "Are you going to tell me what this is about?"

"Let's get to the dig—don't want to spoil the surprise."

"Please tell me this isn't going to be more work for us."

"I can guarantee you it isn't," he said. "I think I know when they were killed—pretty much to the day."

"And?"

He winked. "Just wait. I'll tell you when we get there."

33

Ellie Sawyer and the two students were already in the field, but the intensity of yesterday's work was gone. They were standing away from the excavation, looking down at the remains while they drank from a Thermos. Joanne saw Atticus and Mack and tapped Ellie on the arm; she turned and raised a hand in greeting.

"Morning," she said.

"Morning," they both replied.

Ellie held up the flask. "We've come prepared today," she said. "Coffee?"

"That would be lovely," Mack said.

Ellie found two clean paper cups and poured out drinks for both of them. Atticus took up a position where he could survey the remains: the three skeletons had been completely uncovered now, their empty eye sockets facing up at the powder-blue sky.

"Looks like you're finished," he said.

"We are," Ellie said. "Just waiting for some bags to get here; then we'll bring them out and send them off for testing. I've got a colleague who specialises in forensic anthropology at Oxford. She's happy to take a look at them for us."

Mack nodded. "Looking for what?"

"Lots of things," she said. "Osteological examination to confirm sex and age at death and to take a better look at those holes. And radiocarbon dating. Would be good to know when they were buried."

"No need for that," Atticus said.

"Really? That's the thing I'd want to know most of all."

"They were killed sometime around the end of November 1830."

She stopped and stared at him. "Sorry?"

He pointed down to the skeletons. "Most likely between Saturday the twentieth and Tuesday the twenty-third."

"Right," she said, drawing the word out. "You're going to have to tell me how you can *possibly* be so precise."

"I was bored last night, so I thought I'd see if I could find out a little more about the artefact you dug up yesterday."

"That's what you do when you're bored?"

"He doesn't have any hobbies," Mack said. "He lives a very sheltered life."

"That's right, laugh it up." Atticus grinned at her. "You'll be impressed in a minute."

"I'm all ears," Ellie said.

"Can I have the artefact?"

She collected a small box, removed the lid and took out the metal object that had been uncovered. Atticus took it from her and held it up to the sunlight, turning it over in his hands.

"I was curious about what this might be," he said, "so I concentrated on that."

"How?"

"Photoshop. I cleaned up the photographs I took and tweaked the contrast to bring out any markings that might still be visible. The corrosion had obscured most of the surface, but there were faint traces of lettering—something stamped into the metal."

She took the item and squinted at it. "I can't see anything."

"It's not easy." Atticus turned the object so that they could see it more clearly and pointed. "There—see the raised edges?"

Mack leaned in. "Yes, but I can't see any shape to them."

"I used digital sharpening tools and edge detection to isolate the most prominent features. There wasn't much—just enough to make out part of a manufacturer's name."

He pulled his phone from his pocket, and a few taps later, he had the enhanced image on the screen. He zoomed in on the barely legible letters.

"*T* and *A*," Ellie said.

Mack squinted. "And is that a *K*?"

"It is," Atticus said. "I searched for historical manufacturers with those letters in the name in that order. That led me to Taskers of Andover. One of the biggest manufacturers of agricultural machinery in the early nineteenth century and close to here. This"—he held up the object—"must've been part of something they made."

Mack held the object up. "But what is it?"

"It's a flywheel key. A small but very important component used to secure the flywheel to the shaft of a threshing machine."

Ellie frowned. "And how does that give you a date?"

"That's where we have to speculate a little. I hoped I might be able to speak to someone at Taskers—I thought maybe they might even have kept old catalogues—but the business was sold in 1983, so I stopped looking and changed tack. I thought about the context, instead, added in what we know and then extrapolated from there. We have three men, evidently executed and buried. Right?"

They nodded.

"One of them was found near to a part of a threshing machine. Might've been in his pocket. What's your early nineteenth-century history like?"

"My specialism's Early Elizabethan," Ellie said, "but I know enough to be dangerous. You're thinking it's to do with the Swing Riots?"

"I'm sure of it."

"Hold on," Mack said. "I know about them—or I know as much about them as my daughter learned in history. Farm labourers destroying machines because they were taking away their jobs?"

"Exactly that," Atticus said. "It's been largely forgotten, but it was big—especially in Salisbury. The government thought it might lead to a revolution—they were terrified it'd be like France. The riots in Wiltshire happened in November 1830. The worst was on Tuesday the twenty-third, but there were sporadic outbreaks before and after. I've been able to find references to trouble in villages all around Salisbury—Britford, Coombe Bisset, Odstock, Nunton—and it seems likely that something would've happened in Pitton, too."

"But these men were shot and dumped," Ellie said. "The men who were arrested were all tried—most of them were transported to Australia."

"A thousand of them," Atticus said. "I think what happened here was extrajudicial. We'll need to speak to a historian who knows more about this than I've been able to find out, but I think these three men went to sabotage a threshing machine, took the flywheel key to put it out of action, or as a souvenir after they destroyed it, but were caught before they could get away. I think they were brought here, then shot in the back of the head at close range with a flintlock. They were buried, and they've stayed hidden ever since."

34

Jez was nearing Winterslow when he saw a man coming in the opposite direction. That wasn't unusual—the Clarendon Way was popular for walkers and cyclists, especially near to the villages along the route—but Jez noticed the man had a large dog, and it wasn't on a lead.

Treacle was young and still nervous around other dogs. Jez had tried to socialise him as a puppy, but there'd been an incident when a larger dog had nipped him, and it had affected his confidence. These days, he usually stayed close to Jez whenever he saw another dog, but there had been a couple of occasions when he'd bared his teeth and growled and might have done more if he wasn't on his lead. The prospect of a confrontation with another dog and its owner made Jez tighten up, and he knew—his ex-girlfriend had told him again and again—that Treacle would pick up on it, and that would just make things worse.

Jez took the dog's lead out of his pocket and clipped it to his collar, bringing him in nice and tight to make sure he had close control. Jez looked up and saw that the man approaching him didn't have just one dog, but two: a second dog bounded out of the trees and tussled with the first. They were both Rottweilers.

Jez raised his hand and called out, "Could you put them on a lead, please?"

The man heard him, but he appeared to be on his phone. He did nothing and kept walking.

Jez raised his hand with the lead and pointed to it. "My dog's a bit reactive."

The man was close enough now for Jez to see him shrug.

"Please," Jez said. "Lead."

The man put his phone away. "My dogs are under control. Make sure yours is, and there won't be anything to worry about."

Jez considered himself to be level-headed, although he was prone to anger when he felt that he'd been treated unjustly, or when someone was behaving in a way that was selfish when it would have been easier to adopt a more conciliatory position.

He tightened Treacle's lead and looked for somewhere he could get off the path, but it had narrowed between two thick tangles of bramble, and there was nowhere for him to go.

The two Rottweilers, both still running loose, came closer.

Jez felt the adrenaline starting to throb, and he felt cold sweat up and down his back. The anticipation of a confrontation made it worse.

The Rottweilers might have carried on, but they didn't; they trotted over and started to sniff Treacle. Jez tried to shield him behind his legs, but the Rottweilers split up: one went around to the left and the other to the right. Treacle growled, and then, as one of the Rottweilers came in too close, he lurched ahead and tried to bite.

The other man was close now. "*Jesus*. Keep that bloody dog under control."

"He *is* under control. Yours aren't. I told you to put them on a lead, and you ignored me."

The Rottweilers were growling now, but Treacle's blood was up. He might've been smaller, and he was outnumbered, but he was younger and seemed intent on foolishly trying to show the Rottweilers who was in charge. He lurched ahead again, his teeth latching around one of the other dog's ears. The Rottweiler yelped in pain and shot back, behind his owner.

"Look what your shitty little dog did. He shouldn't be out if you can't control him."

It wasn't that Jez saw the red mist; he *felt* it.

A wave of pure, stupid anger surged through him.

The rational part of his brain knew it was ridiculous. He should've just picked Treacle up and walked away. Getting into a fight over dog etiquette was absurd. But the rational part of his brain was overruled; it was the *unfairness* of it, the smug way the man had dismissed him, and now this: blaming *him* for what had just happened?

Jez squared up to him.

"You're the one who couldn't follow a simple request—"

The man punched him in the face.

Jez staggered back, the world briefly spinning. He tasted blood—his own—sharp and metallic in his mouth. Without thinking, he lunged forward, grabbed the man by the front of his jacket and shoved him backward.

The man lost his footing on the uneven track, his boots skidding on the dirt and leaf litter, and he crashed sideways into the undergrowth. His arm flailed, catching Jez's collar, and they both went down in a ridiculous, undignified heap. Jez's knee landed hard in the man's stomach, eliciting a pained grunt. The man thrashed, trying to push him off, but Jez clung on; the two of them grappled like a pair of schoolboys scuffling in a playground.

Somewhere in the mess of limbs and curses, the man's fist clipped Jez's nose, sending another spray of blood down onto the man's jacket. At the same time, Jez's hands scrabbled at the man's arms and shoulders, trying to gain control, his nails raking across the man's skin.

Treacle, barking wildly, darted in and nipped at the man's sleeve, yanking at the fabric before retreating again. One of the Rottweilers jumped in excitedly, sending up a flurry of dirt and leaves, as if it thought this was all an elaborate game. They rolled once more, Jez's knee digging into something sharp, and then, finally, it was over.

Jez pushed himself away, his breath coming fast, his hands raw from the scuffle. His chest heaved, his face stung, and his nose was still bleeding.

The man sat up slowly, his own face streaked with mud, a long, red scratch visible across his cheek where Jez had caught him. He swore under his breath, touching his now blood-speckled jacket where Jez's nose had dripped onto him.

For a moment, neither of them spoke.

Then the man gave him a disbelieving glare.

"You got your blood all over me, you prick."

Jez wiped his nose with the back of his hand, smearing red across his knuckles.

"Yeah? Well, maybe next time you'll put your dogs on a lead."

Jez grabbed Treacle's lead and walked away, his pulse still hammering in his ears.

35

The rest of the walk had been spoiled. Jez had been looking forward to seeing the ruins of Clarendon Palace, then the spire of the cathedral, and then the city itself, but it had taken half an hour for him to calm down. His hands had been shaking from the adrenaline that was coursing around his veins, his heart felt tight, and he was sweaty from between his shoulder blades all the way down to the small of his back. He kept replaying what had happened: had it been his fault, could he have done anything differently, and would anything come of it? He allowed himself a little grace; he'd asked the man to put his dogs on their leads politely, never raising his voice or insulting him. It'd been the man who had ignored Jez's perfectly reasonable request; *he'd* been aggressive, and *he'd* thrown the first punch.

And would anything come of it?

Probably not. The other guy had no way of knowing who Jez was, and there'd been no sign that he'd followed him. He might have called the police, Jez concluded, and it'd be easy enough for them to conclude that he was walking the route and be waiting for him when he reached Laverstock, but that seemed unlikely, and as he crossed the Milford Mill Bridge, there had been no one there.

It had been an unsettling few minutes, and Jez was still embarrassed to have played a part in something so juvenile, but it was over now, and there would be no consequences. He'd just forget about it.

He walked into the city and made his way to New Street. Atticus had said he should come by the New Inn for a drink when he was done, and Jez found the prospect appealing. A beer and a chat—even with someone as unempathetic as Atticus—would help him to put things in perspective.

He went into the pub, ducking his head to pass through the low doorway, and turned left to the tables near the fireplace that Atticus had favoured whenever they had been in the pub before. He was sitting there, his laptop open on the table with a half-finished pint on the left and a splayed-open packet of crisps on the right.

"Hello," he said.

Atticus looked up at him; his expression flashed with confusion. He pointed. "What happened to your face?"

Jez exhaled and pulled out a chair, dropping into it heavily. "I had a bit of a… disagreement."

Atticus arched an eyebrow.

Jez gestured vaguely at his face. "Some idiot refused to put his dogs on a lead. Treacle got upset, things escalated, and… well, here we are."

Atticus leaned back, studying him. "Let me see."

Jez tilted his head slightly. His nose was still red, and there was a dried smear of blood near his upper lip. A bruise had started to bloom along his cheekbone. Atticus regarded it with clinical detachment.

"You got hit on the left side," he said.

Jez frowned. "What?"

Atticus tapped the side of his own face. "Bruise on your left cheek. Which means whoever hit you was probably right-handed."

Jez blinked at him. "That's your grand deduction? That he was right-handed?"

Atticus shrugged and took a sip of his beer. "He was wearing something dark—a jacket, maybe?"

Jez narrowed his eyes. "How'd you know that?"

"There's a small smear of fabric dye on your shirt collar. Faint, but it's there. Probably rubbed off when you two were— what? Rolling around in the dirt? Who was he?"

"I have no idea," Jez said. "He hit me. I tried to hit him back and didn't do a very good job. I had to settle for bleeding all over him." He gestured to his nose. "Made quite a mess."

"Then perhaps that'll be his lesson." Atticus got up. "You don't want to report it?"

"What'd be the point of that? His word against mine."

"True." Atticus reached down for his empty pint glass and held it up. "Want one? They've got a guest ale on—Portland Poster. Goes down very well."

Jez watched Atticus as he went to the bar, idly reaching down to rub Treacle's head. The dog had managed the walk without bother, but now that they were finished, he looked ready for sleep.

Atticus returned with the drinks.

"So," he said, handing one over, "I've had fun since you've been away."

"Really?"

Atticus set his own drink down and pulled out his chair. "A farmer near Pitton turned up something unexpected in one of his fields. He was ploughing, and he dug up three skeletons, buried together, no markers, no coffins. Just dumped in a shallow grave."

"What—murder victims?"

"That's what it looks like," Atticus said. "But not recent. The police were called, obviously, but when they saw the state of the bones, they decided it wasn't a modern crime. They brought in an archaeologist. I went down to take a look."

Jez leaned forward. "And?"

"One of the men had an iron object buried with him. A piece of a threshing machine from the 1830s."

Jez frowned. "And that matters because…?"

"Because *that* was the time of the Swing Riots. Violent protests all over the south. Hundreds arrested. Dozens executed. Others were transported. But these three were killed unofficially. Shot and buried." He took out his phone. "The archaeologist just messaged me. She had a call from someone at the BBC. They've heard what we've found and want to send a team down to interview her. She's asking if I want to be involved."

Jez supped his pint. "And?"

"Why not? I'm not doing anything, and it'll be good publicity for the book."

Jez took another sip of the ale. "You were right. Goes down very easily."

"What do you think? Should I do it? It'll be on the way if I drive you home."

"Of course."

36

Atticus drove them out to Pitton and parked in the same place as before. A van bearing the logo of BBC South had been slotted up against the gate. They got out, and while Jez sorted out Treacle's lead, Atticus looked inside; it was empty. He checked his watch: it was seven, and Ellie had said that the film crew had said they'd be there at seven thirty. They must have been early. They both climbed over the gate and hurried along the track.

The crew were in the field and already setting up their equipment. The cameraman was adjusting his tripod, angling the camera toward the dig, while the sound recorder tested the boom mic, holding it high above his head as he listened through a set of headphones. A woman in a puffer jacket and scarf—Atticus guessed she must've been the reporter—stood to one side, reviewing her notes while the cameraman checked the portable lights positioned behind the camera.

Ellie spotted Atticus as he approached and came over. "Evening," she said.

"They're early."

"They're keen."

Atticus gestured to Jez. "This is my colleague, Jez."

"Nice to meet you," she said.

"And you."

"I've got something to show you," Ellie said. "We excavated a little farther from the bodies this afternoon and found this."

She held up a clear plastic evidence bag. Inside was a small, rusted clasp knife. The blade was folded in, its iron surface mottled with corrosion, and the wooden handle—dark with age and soil—was chipped along one edge.

"It's a workman's knife," she said.

"Where was it?"

"Half a metre from the burial cut, just within the fill."

Jez squinted at the handle. "What's that? Marking?"

Ellie nodded and turned the bag slightly. Scratched faintly into the wood—just above a brass pin—were two initials: S.L.

Atticus took the bag from her and studied the knife through the plastic. The initials were rough, uneven, as if carved with the point of another blade. Not done for show, just for possession.

Atticus handed the bag back, thoughtful, and then nodded to the crew. "What have they said?"

"They want a short segment for the late bulletin and then something longer for breakfast tomorrow," she said.

The reporter glanced up from her notes, spotted them, and walked over with a warm, professional smile.

"Mr. Priest?"

"Atticus is fine."

"I'm Rebecca," she said. "Thanks so much for agreeing to do this."

Atticus shook her hand. "What do you need?"

"We'll start with Ellie—just a bit about the excavation and what's been found. Then we'll move on to you—we thought you could talk about how you became involved and what you think happened here."

"Sounds good."

She turned back to the crew. "Are we ready?"

The cameraman gave her a thumbs-up. "Good to go."

Rebecca made her way over to the excavation and gestured that Atticus and Ellie should follow. The cameraman indicated that they should stand side by side with Rebecca away to the right in a one-shot.

The camera light blinked red, and Rebecca launched into her introduction.

"We're here on the outskirts of Pitton, where archaeologists have uncovered three sets of human remains in what appears to be an unmarked grave dating back nearly two centuries. Experts believe the discovery may be linked to one of the most turbulent periods of rural unrest in British history—the Swing Riots of 1830."

The camera tracked her as she walked over to Ellie and Atticus. "I'm joined by Dr. Eleanor Sawyer from the University of Southampton and Atticus Priest, a private investigator from Salisbury. Dr. Sawyer—can you tell us a little about what you and your team have found here?"

"We found three skeletons, all buried in close proximity, with evidence suggesting they met violent deaths. We've found gunshot wounds in the skulls, and their placement in the trench suggests a hurried burial rather than something more formal."

"And what makes you think this might be linked to the Swing Riots?"

Ellie gestured toward the trench. "The dating is key. We're still awaiting confirmation through radiocarbon analysis, but based on initial assessments, the skeletal remains and the associated artefacts strongly indicate an early nineteenth-century timeframe. One of the most significant finds was an iron object buried alongside one of the individuals, which could be linked to agricultural machinery of the period."

Rebecca turned. "That brings me to you, Atticus. You're a private investigator—how did you become involved in this?"

"The police were called in when the remains were discovered, but once they realised it wasn't a modern case, it became a historical rather than a criminal investigation. I have a background in solving puzzles, and this is an unusual one. They knew this would be up my street."

"Dr. Sawyer mentioned an artefact. Can you tell us about that?"

"An iron object, possibly a component from a piece of machinery. I researched it, and I believe it's what's called a flywheel key from a threshing machine that came here from Andover. If that's right, it's significant—because threshing machines were at the heart of the Swing Riots. Agricultural workers saw them as a threat to their livelihoods and destroyed them in protest."

"So you believe these men were rioters who were executed and buried in secret?"

"That's the working theory," Atticus said.

Atticus continued, explaining in broad terms how he had reached the conclusions that he'd reached. The reporter brought

Ellie in again, asking her to describe what would happen to the remains and what they hoped to find.

Rebecca checked her notes and turned to Atticus. "And do you think the remains will ever be identified?"

"It's possible," Atticus said. "Three men might have disappeared from Pitton or one of the nearby villages, and even though it's two hundred years ago, it's likely that there'll be something that might refer to that. The trick will be to find out what that might be."

"And also," she said, "I suppose it's possible that there might be local folklore about what happened?"

"Absolutely," he said, "or perhaps someone watching will remember a story from their own family that's been passed down the generations."

"And how would viewers get in touch with you?"

"My email is on my website," he said. "I'd be very interested to hear from anyone who thinks they might have something that would help us to learn more about what happened here. We could be looking at one of the last remnants of a hidden chapter of history—something that was deliberately erased and forgotten."

Rebecca turned back to the camera. "A mysterious grave, a buried past, and the chance to rewrite history—this dig outside Pitton is proving to be far more than just an archaeological curiosity. If you know anything, please do get in touch with Mr. Priest—and in the meantime, we'll bring you updates as the excavation continues."

Rebecca paused for a count of three.

"And we're out," the cameraman said.

Rebecca exhaled. "Did you get it?"

"Looked great," the cameraman said.

Rebecca smiled and turned back to Ellie and Atticus. "Excellent. Thank you both."

Ellie nodded. "Happy to help."

The crew began packing up.

"Did Ellie tell you when this will go out?"

"Tonight and then tomorrow."

Rebecca nodded. "It'll be on the website, too. I think people will be interested to find out what happened—will you let me know?"

"Of course," Atticus said.

She took a card from her pocket and gave it to him. "This is me. Give me a call if you get anything else."

Atticus held the card up and tapped his finger against it. "I will."

Rebecca turned to Ellie, thanked her, and then went to help the crew as they finished packing away their gear.

"What are you doing now?" Ellie asked.

"Driving Jez back to Winchester."

"Have you eaten yet?"

"I had some crisps earlier," he said.

"That's it?"

He shrugged. "That's better than some days. It's not unusual for me to be distracted by something and then forget."

Jez joined them.

"I was going to go to the Lord Nelson for dinner," Ellie said. "You should both come. I've been speaking to a historian who specialises in the late Georgian to early Victorian eras. He published a book on the riots last year. He lives in Winterslow and said he'd come for a drink and a chat. You never know—might be interesting."

Atticus had been meaning to call Mack to see if she'd be around later, but he could do that after dinner, and there was nothing to stop her getting in touch with him earlier if she wanted to.

He turned to Jez. "Is that okay? I'll drive you back afterwards."

"Why not. It'll save me cooking."

"I'll drive you home," Ellie said. "I'm in Chandler's Ford—not much farther to go on to Winchester. Makes more sense than you going to and from here."

"Suits me," Atticus said.

37

Mack had picked the kids up from school and taken them back to hers for their tea. It was Andy's turn to have them, but he'd texted and said something had come up at work and asked whether she could look after them until he was done. Mack had been out at Brookmere House all day, but she was coming off shift and didn't have anything else that she needed to do, so she said yes; it didn't do any harm to try and keep cordial relations with Andy, and, more importantly, it would give her a few extra hours with the children.

She'd spent a lovely time with them. She'd looked inside Daisy's bag and found an English assignment where she'd been asked to write a paragraph about what her parents did for a living: Andy had received a single sentence ('my daddy makes websites') while Mack had received much more attention, with Daisy noting that her mummy helped keep Salisbury safe and that she was 'so brave that nothing scared her.' Sebastian had been playing touch rugby, and his PE kit was filthy; Mack put it on a quick wash and then dried it, folding it and putting it back in his bag so that he'd be ready for tomorrow.

She fed them both, and when Andy texted to say that he was done, she got them ready for him to pick them up.

He pulled up outside her house at just after seven.

She told the kids to put their shoes and coats on and met Andy at the door.

"Thanks for doing this," he said.

"It's fine. It was nice."

"How are they?"

"Good. They've eaten, and they've done their homework. Sebastian's PE kit was dirty, so I've sorted that out. It's in his bag."

"I would've done that."

"I know—but it was no problem."

"Thanks."

He smiled, and they paused awkwardly. It was probably the most civil conversation they'd had for months, and Mack would've told him to come inside while they waited for the kids to get ready, but she remembered how he'd been during the divorce, and the invitation died on her lips. Their relationship had detonated in the aftermath of Mack's first dalliance with Atticus, but that had been just a symptom of the malaise that had already set in. They'd been drifting apart for years, and Mack knew now that allowing herself to fall for Atticus the first time had been her way of sabotaging what was left of her marriage, a cowardly way to prove to herself that it was dead. Andy's behaviour in the aftermath had been despicable, but Mack knew she bore responsibility for the poison between them just as much as he did.

"Come on, kids," she shouted back into the house. "Get a move on. Your father's waiting."

The kids grumbled about wanting to stay longer, and Mack told them she'd see them at the weekend and reminded them that they were going to go to Paulton's Park to ride the new rollercoaster. Daisy asked if Mack would buy them doughnuts afterwards, and she said she would.

"Say thanks to your mummy," Andy said.

Daisy and then Sebastian hugged and kissed her, and she tousled their hair and shooed them down the path to Andy's waiting car. She watched them drive away with a catch in her throat and wondered, just as always, how much damage their parents' failures would inflict on their lives.

Her phone buzzed with an incoming call, and she found herself hoping it was Atticus.

But it wasn't. It was Robbie Best.

"Robbie," she said, "what's up?"

"Big problem, boss."

"Brookmere? You found him?"

"No," he said. "Not him. His son—Henry."

Robbie had explained that Henry Ainsley had been impatient and had made noises about going straight to Beckton if the investigation didn't bring in more officers.

"What's he done?"

"He's been murdered, Mack."

38

The Lord Nelson was warm and low-lit, with a fire in the grate and half of the tables occupied. Atticus and Ellie had parked their cars on the car park outside, and Atticus had chosen a corner table, away from the bar. Jez was to his right, and Ellie was to his left.

"You look confused," she said.

"I'm bad at choosing," Jez said, holding up the menu helplessly.

"Get the steak and ale pie."

"Why?"

"Because I've eaten here before, and it's excellent."

He considered that, then nodded. "Fine. I'll get the pie."

Atticus stood to go and place the order.

"And see if they have a bowl of water for Treacle?" Jez said.

Atticus nodded and went over to the bar. Ellie had been teasing Jez ever since they sat down. She was flirting with him. Atticus would've struggled to diagnose it if she'd been interested in him, but, when it was someone else, he could see it clearly. The way she held Jez's eye just a beat longer than necessary, the occasional touch on his arm when she made a point, the way her smile widened whenever he was slow to catch on to one of her jokes. Atticus was pleased. Jez had recently broken up with his girlfriend, and although he hadn't spoken about it much, Atticus knew he'd taken it badly. He'd seen it in the small things: Jez walking Treacle longer than usual, staying late at the office for no real reason, his determination to walk the Clarendon Way on his own. He'd stopped talking about future plans, too, like the wind had gone out of him. Seeing him now—laughing, leaning in, the spark back in his eyes—felt like a corner being turned.

Atticus caught the bartender's eye and relayed the order and then returned to the table. Ellie was stroking Treacle, and the dog, in turn, was rubbing the side of his head against her legs to encourage more.

"Ellie was telling me about her work," Jez said. "She started out in prehistoric archaeology."

Ellie leaned back, only for Treacle to butt his head against her legs. "Bronze Age and Neolithic sites. I did my PhD on burial practices in Iron Age Britain. Very interesting subject."

"I'm sure it was."

"Some of the things I studied would make your hair turn grey."

"Go on, then," Jez said. "Give us something juicy."

She leaned in. "Did you know that some Iron Age tribes practiced excarnation?"

"Instead of burying their dead," Atticus said, "they'd leave bodies exposed to the elements so birds and animals could strip the flesh away before gathering the bones for burial."

She looked impressed. "You know about that?"

"I must've read a book about it."

"And *just* before a meal," Jez said, feigning nausea.

Ellie grinned. "Isn't it fascinating? Studied it for most of my twenties; then I switched to forensic archaeology. Human remains, clandestine burials—all the good stuff."

"Why the shift?" Jez asked her.

"Digging up broken bits of pots wasn't as interesting as digging up people."

A waitress arrived with a bowl of water for Treacle. Jez thanked her.

"Worst dig?" Jez asked, turning back to Ellie.

"Worst in terms of conditions? Or worst in terms of what I found?"

"Both."

"Well, there was a site in Northumberland where we spent six weeks in a peat bog, waist-deep in freezing mud. That was *fun*. And then there was an exhumation where we had to dig through a Victorian cesspit to get to the burial layer. I couldn't get the smell out for weeks."

"Jesus," Jez said.

"I know. It was probably somewhere during that dig that I decided to make another change."

"To what?"

"Forensic pathology. It's not such a big leap—still working with human remains, just closer to the point of death."

"Less trowel, more scalpel," Atticus said.

"Exactly. I started retraining five years ago. Graduate medicine has been a tough slog as a mature student, especially with the day job, but I love it. I'm on a Home Office–backed pathology fast track now."

"How long will that take?"

"I'll be fully qualified next year. You know Professor Fyfe?"

Atticus managed a weary smile. "Our paths have crossed once or twice."

"I know he can be a pain in the arse, but his heart's in the right place. He's been helping me out."

Atticus studied her for a moment as she took another sip, the light catching in her dark eyes, a stray strand of hair falling loose from behind her ear. She had an easy confidence about her; she was sharp, articulate, and unafraid to tease. She was attractive, and it was obvious that Jez agreed.

The waitress arrived with their food, setting down three steaming plates of pie, mash, and thick gravy.

"Enough about me." She let a beat of silence pass before tilting her head, regarding Atticus more seriously. "What about you and the detective chief inspector?"

Atticus paused, his fork hovering over his plate. "What about us?"

"You're together?"

He nodded. "We are."

"And it started when you were in the police."

"How'd you know that?"

"I was talking to Franny."

"Oh," Atticus said, irritated that Franny had been discussing them. "That's when it started—yes."

"What happened?"

"It was complicated. She was my boss. In the end we decided we were better as friends."

Ellie studied him for a moment, as if deciding whether to push further. "But then you left?"

"Not because of that."

"Why?"

"I started to find it frustrating. Everything has to be done a certain way, and I felt it was inefficient. I can get faster results when I don't have a manual to follow."

She forked a piece of steak and put it in her mouth. "So you leave the police and go it alone."

He nodded at Jez. "Until recently. Now it's the two of us."

"Holmes and Watson?"

Jez smiled. "The bargain-basement version."

Ellie laid a hand on Jez's arm; Atticus pretended not to notice.

"What time are you expecting the historian?" he asked.

"That's a good point." She frowned and reached for her phone. "He ought to be here. He's running late."

"He lives in the village?"

"Five minutes away."

She was about to call him when they heard sirens from somewhere outside. They turned to the window as a patrol car raced past the pub, heading south.

"What's going on?" Ellie said.

Atticus frowned. "I have no idea."

They were still staring out of the window when a second police car, lights blazing, rushed through the village and followed the first. A third car followed immediately behind it: a dark grey unmarked Range Rover, a pulsing blue light flashing from its grille. It was Mack's car, and Atticus caught a brief glimpse of her profile before she raced away.

39

The convoy had turned onto Middleton Road, and Atticus had been able to see the flashing blue of their emergency lights as they headed southeast; he told Ellie and Jez that he was going to take a look and left Jez to explain that this was the sort of off-the-cuff impetuosity that he'd come to expect.

Atticus got into his car and followed. The cars had travelled down Middleton Road past the recreation ground to The Plantation and then onto Livery Road and The Street. They reached the church and turned onto the single-lane Back Drove. The cars had stopped there, with one of the patrol cars turned across the road to block further progress. The Clarendon Way headed west, identified by markers that had been nailed into a post. Atticus saw Mack's car at the back of the line but couldn't see her. He parked in the road that led to the church and then went back to the cordon.

Elaine Coverdale blocked the way.

"Evening," he said.

"Can't come any further, sir."

The headlights from one of the parked cars were silhouetting him, and she evidently couldn't make him out.

"It's me. Atticus."

She shielded her eyes. "Oh. Evening. Still can't come any further."

"What's going on?"

"Can't say."

"Is it the Earl of Brookmere?"

She shook her head. "No."

"Who, then?"

"Can't say."

"Come on, Elaine. What is it?"

"Looks like a murder," she said. "Body found in the field, lots of blood."

"And it's *not* Brookmere?"

"No."

"Who, then?"

"Stop asking—I'm not going to tell you."

"You know who it is, then?"

"Atticus—*shush*." She gestured to the track. "And don't go down there, okay?"

He raised his hands. "Of course."

He turned away and walked back up towards the church. He took out his phone and wondered about calling Mack, but she'd have her hands full and wouldn't have the time or inclination to speak to him. That being said, something interesting was evidently happening just a few hundred metres away, and it wasn't in his nature to ignore it. He continued back along the road for another twenty seconds, and after a quick glance back to make sure he wasn't being watched, he shoved between the branches of two straggly elm trees and approached the barbed-wire fence that marked the boundary between the road and the paddock beyond. The bottom wire was slack, and by putting his boot on it and pressing down, he was able to open enough of a gap to be able to wriggle through.

40

Mack made her way along the drove. Robbie Best had been waiting for her and said he'd take her to where the body had been found.

"You're sure it's the son?"

"Yes."

"You've seen the body?"

He nodded. "And I saw him this morning at the house. He's wearing the same clothes."

"Who found him?"

"Woman from the village who was giving her dogs a late walk. She was heading out into the fields and came across two dogs running free. Rottweilers—and Henry has Rottweilers. They were in a bit of a state—barking, running around in circles. They made her nervous, and she was going to turn back when her own dog found the body. He was off the path, in the yard, hidden behind some bags of silage—you'll see. It's just up here."

"Must be connected to the Earl of Brookmere going missing."

"You'd have to assume so. What are the odds otherwise?"

"Still nothing on him?"

"Not even a sniff."

"What a mess."

"I know," he said. "I've been certain all day that we'd find Rupert dead, but this is something else. Got to be foul play for both."

The air was damp, the kind of cold that seeped into the bones. They continued along the path for another five hundred feet. The drove ran to the north of a collection of farm buildings. There were several large storage barns, a large water bowser with a Union Jack flying from a flagpole atop it, and a double stack of black plastic-wrapped silage bales.

They approached the spot where the body had been found. Ryan Yaxley was stationed in the middle of the track, standing behind blue-and-white police tape that had been stretched between wooden stakes driven into the ground. Beyond the tape, a cluster of other officers moved with purpose, their torches flickering in the growing darkness.

Mack saw the rhythmic strobe of camera flashes from the yard to the left as the crime scene photographer documented the area. The flashes illuminated the spot where Henry Ainsley's body lay, off the track and hidden behind the bales. He was sprawled awkwardly, as if he had fallen backward. His shirt was rumpled, one arm bent at an unnatural angle. His face, pale in the bursts of white light, was frozen in an expression that looked like surprise.

The two dogs that had been found running loose—Henry's Rottweilers—had been tied up and were now secured to a post. One of them let out a low whine as Mack walked past.

"We'll need to get them somewhere out of the way," Mack said.

"I've called the dog handler."

"And get them inspected for evidence. You never know—might get lucky."

A forensic tent was being unpacked from a large bag, its metal frame clattering as officers worked to assemble it. A pair of crime scene investigators in white coveralls were already setting out evidence markers. One of them was crouched beside the body, noting details in a small notebook.

Mack stopped just outside the taped perimeter and turned to Robbie. "Who's been inside the cordon so far?"

"The woman who found him, me and the first responders. But it's not impossible other walkers might have gone by without noticing him. You can see how he was found—not easy to see him unless you know to look. We kept it as clean as we could. Forensics got here twenty minutes ago."

"The farmer?"

"Spoke to him. Hasn't been here today."

She nodded, stepping forward. A crime scene tech handed her a pair of gloves, and she pulled them on before ducking under the tape. She took in the scene from different angles, cataloguing the details in her mind.

She turned back to Robbie. "Cause of death?"

"Too early to say for sure, but I think it'll be obvious." He pointed to the side of Henry's head, just above the temple. "Pretty nasty. Blunt force."

Mack crouched down. The wound was partially obscured by his hair, but she could see where the blood had matted it together. She noted the way his shirt was twisted at the shoulder, as if someone had grabbed him, and the way one boot was half-off his foot.

"Any sign of a weapon?"

"Not yet. We're doing a sweep now—but we might have to wait until it's light."

Mack stood and exhaled, taking a moment before giving her first orders. "Full search of the immediate area—start with a fifty-metre perimeter and expand out if necessary. Look for anything that could be a weapon. We also need to check if he was killed here or if he was moved and dumped."

Robbie nodded and gestured to a group of uniformed officers. "You heard the skipper—start widening the search."

She turned to the crime scene photographer. "Make sure you get everything before we move him. Every angle. I want a proper record of the positioning."

Then she looked at the forensic team. "We'll need soil samples, footprints, anything you can get from the ground disturbance. If there's blood beyond what we see on him, I want it logged."

One of them nodded, already kneeling to swab near Henry's outstretched hand.

Mack turned back to Robbie. "Start pulling CCTV. Anything from the village, roads leading in and out, anything near the estate. Doorbell cams, and maybe there's something at the church. I also want the timeline nailed down—who last saw him, when, and what state he was in."

"Mack."

She swivelled.

"Jesus," Robbie said. "What's he doing here?"

"*Mack*—over here!"

Atticus was in the field on the other side of the cordon. A uniformed officer—Betts, Mack thought, although it was hard to see in the darkness—had gone over to make sure he didn't come any closer.

"What are you doing?" she called.

"Can I have a word?"

"Wait there." She turned back to Robbie and gave an exasperated shake of her head. "Got everything you need to be getting on with it?"

"I think so. What do you want to do about the family?"

"They don't know yet?"

"I haven't told them."

"I'll do it."

"Right you are, boss."

41

Atticus had made his way directly across the field, and in the darkness and knowing that he couldn't switch on his phone's torch without telling the police he was heading towards their crime scene, he'd blundered through two deep piles of horse manure. He reached the edge of the cordon and saw the activity going on inside: the flashes from a photographer's camera, CSIs looking for evidence, a tent erected off to the side and readied to be moved into place to cover what Atticus assumed to be the body. He couldn't see enough from where he was to be able to make any useful deductions and was thinking about ducking under the tape to get a little closer when he saw Robbie Best and then, behind him, Mack.

He called her name, heard the exasperation in her reply, and knew she was going to be cross with him. Still, he reasoned, she wouldn't be cross if he could give her something that might help her find out what had happened. He'd probably have to sweet-talk her a little in order to have her accept his assistance, but the prospect of a newly discovered body was too tantalising for him to ignore.

PC Betts came over and held up a hand. "What are you doing here?"

"I saw the lights."

"Come on. You know better—stay on that side of the tape."

Atticus held up both hands in surrender. "Absolutely."

He could see Mack speaking to Robbie and waited for the conversation to end. She clapped him on the shoulder and crossed the field to where he and Betts were standing.

"I've got this, Dave," she said.

Betts nodded and went back toward the track.

Mack waited until he was out of earshot and then turned. "What are you doing?"

"I was having dinner in the Nelson. I saw you all go by and thought I'd come and have a look."

"You can't just do that. It's a *murder*, Atticus."

"I'd gathered that."

"Not just any murder—it's Henry Ainsley."

"As in…"

"Yes, as in Viscount Ainsley, the heir to the Brookmere estate."

"Oh."

"Exactly—'Oh.' Potentially a *very* tricky investigation to manage."

"Let me have a quick look?"

"Come on," she said. "You know I can't."

He pointed to where the tent was being arranged. "The body's over there?"

"Yes."

"In the yard?"

She nodded. "The pathologist is on his way."

"Who? Fyfe?"

"I don't know."

"Fyfe's hopeless."

"Not your problem."

"Are you *sure* I can't have a look?"

"One hundred per cent."

"But I can help. I—"

"Let me get through tonight, and then I'll let you know what we've got. But not now."

He ground his teeth in frustration.

"Please," she said, "Atticus, go home. Let me do my job."

"Fine," he said huffily.

"I'm serious. Don't come inside the cordon."

"I won't."

"I'll call you later."

"Tonight?"

"Probably not. I've got to go and tell the family, and then I'll have to get back here. I've no idea when I'll be able to leave."

"Call if you need me."

He knew Mack was right, and that she needed to do everything by the book—at least to be *seen* to do everything by the book—but he'd always been able to offer her a different perspective, and there was nothing about what he'd seen here, such that it was, that made him think this would be different. Mack was a fantastic detective, but his opinion did not extend to everyone else at the station. Fyfe, for example, lacked flexibility of thinking and the intellectual curiosity that ought to have been mandatory for someone in his role. Atticus had seen him in action too many times before to regard the prospect of him blundering around with anything other than dread at what he might miss.

He paused and turned back, looking at the cordon as a battery-powered portable floodlight was switched on; the glow revealed the vague shape of a body on the ground, and, thinking of all the evidence that would be presented there, Atticus had to resist the urge to go back and plead his case again.

His phone buzzed in his pocket. He took it out and saw a message from Ellie: the historian had arrived, and she wondered whether she should ask him to wait before they started talking about the three bodies that had been dug up. He texted back to tell her that he'd be at the pub in twenty minutes and made his way back across the field toward the village.

42

There had been no news about Rupert all day. Emelia had followed the advice from the police and had stayed home, and, with nothing else to do, she'd gone up to her bathroom on the first floor and run a bath. She sat in it now, looking out of the window over the covered swimming pool to the darkened countryside beyond. She reached up for her glass of wine and, after taking a sip, swapped it for her phone. One of her friends from the tennis club had texted to say that some sort of archaeological discovery had been made in one of Jack Turnbull's fields nearby and that the BBC had visited it today to interview the archaeologist about what had been found. The report was due to run on the local news just after the national bulletin; she looked at the time and saw she had ten minutes to get out, get dry and go down to watch it.

It had been a long day. The police had been at the house since the early morning, and it had been difficult to see them going through all of Rupert's things in an attempt to find anything that might give them a clue as to where he'd gone. Emelia had shown the detectives up to the bedroom and had left them to it, retreating downstairs to the family sitting room, where the children had also gone to wait for daylight. They'd all gone out to look for him as soon as the sun was up, agreeing a plan between them for the rest of the day. The estate was enormous, but they'd divided it up so that they could cover all of the most obvious places to look: the solar farm, the paddocks with the horses, the ha-ha and the woods beyond it, the gamekeeper's cottage—which had been empty since November—and the barns at the bottom of Whistler's Field.

Sebastian took the south drive and the formal gardens, Alexander went out toward the beech copse and the old well, and Celeste and Julian had searched the edge of the estate near the footpath on the basis that it was Rupert's favourite walk. Emelia stayed in the house, partly to be available in case the police needed anything and partly because the idea of combing the estate for a man she feared might already be dead was more than she could face.

She pulled on her dressing gown and went to the drawing room. Celeste was sitting on the sofa with her legs curled up beneath her as she worked on something on her laptop.

She looked up. "Anything?"

"No," Emelia said.

Celeste was the only one of the children who was at the house at the moment. The boys were still out now looking for Rupert, but Celeste had come back a couple of hours ago to keep Emelia company.

She found the remote and switched on the TV, sitting down just as the local news started. She zoned out for most of it—listening to the top stories with half an ear and picturing how the presenter would report the story of Rupert's disappearance once it became more widely known—but then focused back in as the presenter handed over to a piece from a reporter standing in a field with a dark wood at her back.

"We're here on the outskirts of Pitton," the reporter said, "where archaeologists have uncovered three sets of human remains in what appears to be an unmarked grave dating back nearly two centuries."

"Look," Emelia said.

Celeste looked up, and the two of them watched together as the reporter interviewed the archaeologist responsible for exhuming the sets of remains, before cutting to the private investigator who, she said, had made the connection between the bones and a period of unrest some two hundred years earlier.

"I've heard about him," Celeste said, gesturing to the investigator.

His name appeared on the screen. "Atticus Priest," Emelia said. "He was on the radio on Monday. He works in Salisbury."

Priest spoke about a series of riots that had been caused by the introduction of mechanisation to agriculture and how he believed the remains that had been discovered in the field had belonged to local labourers who were murdered after trying to sabotage a machine.

Celeste frowned. "What did he call them?"

"The Swing Riots."

Celeste opened a fresh browser window on her laptop and typed into the search bar. "Here you go: 'The name "Swing Riots" was derived from Captain Swing, the name attributed to the fictitious, mythical figurehead of the movement. The name was often used to sign threatening letters sent to farmers, magistrates, parsons and others.'"

"Where's that from?"

"Wikipedia."

The report came to an end, and rather than watch the weather, Emelia hit the button to switch off the television.

They heard the door open and close.

"Hello?" It was Sebastian.

"In here."

He appeared in the doorway, his face set in a grim expression. He pulled off his wax jacket and draped it over the arm of a chair before running a hand through his already dishevelled hair.

Emelia stood. "Anything?"

Sebastian shook his head. "Nothing. We covered the woods at Fairoak and Warner's, but there's nothing. No sign of him."

Celeste closed her laptop. "What about the paddocks?"

"Alexander took a couple of the lads up there this afternoon. They didn't find anything either." He rubbed his eyes and sank down onto the opposite chair. "It's like he's vanished into thin air. Did you speak to the staff?"

Emelia folded her arms, pressing her fingers into her elbows. "Nobody's seen him."

Her phone rang. She took it out of her pocket and looked down at the screen.

"It's Robbie Best," she said.

"Answer it."

Her stomach plunged. Why would he be calling her now? It could only be bad news.

She laid the phone down and tapped the screen. "Hello, Detective Inspector. You're on the speaker—I'm with Celeste and Sebastian."

"Are you at home?"

"Yes," she said.

"Would it be all right if my senior officer came to see you?"

"What is it? What's happened?"

"It'd be much better if she could come and talk to you face to face."

"Have you found him?"

"I'd rather she talked to you about it."

"Tell her to ring the bell, and we'll let her in."

"Thank you, Emelia. She'll be there in twenty minutes."

She felt sick. "They've found him."

"We don't know that," Celeste said.

"Why is a senior officer coming, then? Why does it have to be face to face?"

"Who knows? It might be something else."

Emelia looked at Celeste and could see she was putting on a brave face. Sebastian, too; he was as white as a sheet. The only reason the police would send someone senior to see them was to deliver bad news in person. She closed her eyes and tried to think of another explanation, but she couldn't.

She was certain.

Rupert was dead.

She caught herself thinking in the abstract: they all had another few minutes where they could say they didn't know what had happened, not for sure, but those moments were running away like the grains of sand in an hourglass. She might already be a widow but just hadn't had it confirmed yet.

She got up and went to the drinks cabinet. "I need a gin."

43

Mack liked almost everything about her job. There were parts that were tedious—sifting through hours of CCTV footage in the hope of spotting something useful, filling out endless paperwork for court cases that might never go to trial—but they were easily outweighed by the pleasure she got from an intellectually challenging investigation, finding a missing person and taking them home, or catching someone in a lie and watching their story unravel in front of her.

This, though—the delivery of the most awful news imaginable—was the worst part of her job. She could have asked Robbie to take care of it. He knew the family, after all, and had spent most of the day with them looking for Rupert Ainsley. But Mack had always thought that kind of delegation was an abuse of her position. There were some tasks that she would not delegate, and this was one of them. It wouldn't be fair to pull rank and get someone else to do it; it would also, she felt, be disrespectful to the loved ones receiving the news if the most senior officer didn't attend. And so, with that in mind, she always made sure she was the one who passed on the saddest tidings.

She reached Brookmere House and stopped at the gates. She wound down the window and reached out to press the button for the intercom.

The speaker popped with a moment of static. "Drive in, please."

The gates opened, and Mack continued on, following the swoop of the drive as it passed between the trees on either side. She found her thoughts sliding back to Atticus and what she'd said to him. She'd done the right thing—it wouldn't have been right to have him on a crime scene that early—but she wondered if there might have been a better way to handle it. He was such a complicated bundle of neuroses and contradictions, and, given how he was brash and showy and often arrogant, it was easy to forget how sensitive he was.

She sighed and rubbed her forehead. She had to go back to the body when she'd finished with the family and introduced them to the liaison officer who was on the way, but she'd find the time to call Atticus and give him as much information as she could. Her motives might have been altruistic, but there was more to it than that; Atticus had the best instincts of any officer she'd ever met, and she wasn't too proud to admit that she stood a better chance of finding out what'd happened to Henry Ainsley with his assistance than without.

She turned the final corner, and the lights of her car fell upon the enormous house. She parked next to one of the new electric Mercedes and got out, taking a moment to compose herself and make sure she knew exactly what she was going to say. She breathed in deeply and then exhaled and started for the steps that led to the door.

She was only halfway there when a smaller door to the side opened, and an oblong of golden light was cast out onto the gravel.

"DCI Jones?" It was a female voice, but the speaker was silhouetted by the light.

"Hello," Mack said.

"Please—come in."

Mack stepped inside, closing the door gently behind her.

"Are you Emelia Ainsley?"

The woman stood in the entrance hall, her back straight, arms crossed as if bracing for impact. "I am. The others are in the sitting room. This way."

Mack glanced around. She was expecting something on the scale of Wilton House, but it wasn't quite as grand; the hallway and the rooms off it looked lived in and homely. The warmth of the house wrapped around her, and she picked up the faint scent of something floral; Emelia's perfume, she thought.

Three men and a woman were in the sitting room. Emelia introduced two of the men and the woman as her stepchildren—Alexander, Sebastian and Celeste—and the other man as Julian, Celeste's husband. Mack said hello to them, noting that they were as drawn as Emelia. The family had been waiting for news about Rupert all day, but now they were going to be given an even worse shock than they could have anticipated.

Mack cleared her throat. "Would you like to sit down?"

Emelia's fingers tightened around her forearms. "No. Just tell me. Have you found him?"

Mack hesitated for only a moment before giving a small nod. She kept her voice even, controlled. "I'm very sorry to have to tell you this, but it's your stepson, Henry."

"What about him?"

"He's been found dead."

Emelia gave a sharp inhale.

Celeste's hand flew to her mouth, her eyes wide and uncomprehending. "*Henry?*"

Sebastian took a step forward as if to say something, then stopped, shaking his head.

"No," Emelia said. "No, that's not…"

"I'm so sorry. His body was found this evening just outside Winterslow."

Emelia stared at her as though she hadn't heard. Then her lips parted, just slightly. "How?"

Mack hesitated. "We're treating his death as suspicious at this stage. A full forensic examination is being carried out."

Sebastian let out a low breath, running a hand through his hair. "Christ."

"Are you sure?" Celeste asked suddenly, her voice high and desperate.

Mack shook her head gently. "I'm very sorry. Robbie Best is there—he's seen him. There's no mistake."

The silence that followed was suffocating. Emelia closed her eyes, swaying slightly, and Mack instinctively reached out to steady her.

"I need to sit down," Emelia murmured.

Mack guided her towards the nearest chair. Celeste followed close behind, her face pale, her expression tight with shock. Sebastian remained by the doorway, staring at the floor, his jaw clenched. They sat. Emelia pressed her fingertips to her temples, shaking her head slightly as though trying to make sense of it all.

"What does 'suspicious' mean?" Alexander said. "You said you were treating it as suspicious."

"I can't give you specifics yet. We'll need to carry out a post-mortem. What I *can* tell you is that he was found off the track, partially hidden behind some bags of silage on a yard. A member of the public came across his dogs and followed them to where he was."

Celeste let out a quiet sob.

Sebastian's voice was flat. "Suspicious meaning what, exactly? Murdered?"

"I can't give you much more than that. The investigation is in its early stages. We have officers securing the scene now, and a forensic team is gathering evidence."

Alexander's hands curled into fists. "Murdered…"

"We don't know that for sure yet," Mack said.

"But you clearly *think* so," he said. "He wouldn't just've fallen down dead, would he?"

Julian reached for Celeste's hand. "Was it violent?" she said.

"The early indication is that he was beaten."

"That doesn't make any sense," Emelia said. "Who'd want to hurt Henry?"

Sebastian was staring at her, waiting for her to say something. Mack didn't answer. Speculation wouldn't help.

"This is connected, isn't it?" he asked.

Mack met his gaze. "With your father? We don't know that yet."

"Come *on*," he insisted. "Stop being so vague—you're making this worse!"

"Sebastian," Celeste warned.

"She *must* be thinking it. First, Father vanishes. Now Henry turns up dead. That's not a coincidence, is it?"

Mack nodded. "It's obviously something we'll be looking at closely."

Emelia looked as if she wanted to speak, but her mouth opened and closed again; she couldn't find the words.

"A family liaison officer is on her way," Mack said. "She'll be here to support you and keep you updated as the investigation progresses. In the meantime, if there's anything you think of—anyone Henry might have been in conflict with, anything unusual he mentioned—please let me know."

Sebastian let out a hollow laugh. "Henry was *always* in conflict with someone."

"What do you mean?"

He waved a hand vaguely. "Estate matters. Money. Business deals. He's like Father—he's always been ruthless."

"We'll need to speak to all of you about that. It'll probably be DI Robbie Best who comes to see you. Think about anyone who might wish Henry harm—him *and* Rupert—and we'll look into it."

Celeste's breath hitched. "Can I see him?"

Mack's expression softened. "Not yet. The coroner will need to examine him first."

She let out a strangled sob, curling forward, her shoulders shaking. Julian wrapped an arm around her.

"What about Rupert?" Emelia asked.

"We haven't found him yet. We'll be bringing in more officers to broaden the search."

"This is a nightmare," Alexander muttered. "An absolute bloody *nightmare.*"

Mack stood, giving them space. "I'm very sorry for your loss."

Sebastian stood, his face unreadable, and walked Mack to the door. "You'll find out who did this?"

"We'll do everything we can."

"And my father?"

"We'll find him, too." She took out her wallet and slid out one of her cards. "My number is on here. Please make sure everyone has it. If anyone can think of anything, just call. Doesn't matter when."

He took it. "Thank you."

PART 4

Thursday

44

Jez arrived back in Salisbury at just before eight the following morning. He had Treacle with him, and Atticus met him inside the Cathedral Close. They walked the dogs together, heading out to the cricket pitch at Harnham and watching as Bandit and then Treacle frolicked in the river.

Jez headed for one of the park benches and sat down. "Did you find out anything about what happened last night?"

"No," Atticus said.

"Mack didn't call?"

Atticus sat, too. "She didn't."

"Would've been busy," Jez said.

Atticus nodded. He'd been hopeful that she might give him an idea of what was going on, but there hadn't been anything until a text at two in the morning saying that she'd try to find the time to see him later. Atticus hoped that he might be able to help but realised that he wouldn't do himself—or Mack— any favours if he made a nuisance of himself.

Instead, he'd decided to set himself another task. They'd stayed at the Nelson until ten, speaking to the historian Ellie had asked about the case. The man—Sam Fairweather—worked at Salisbury Museum and was knowledgeable about Wiltshire in the eighteenth and nineteenth centuries. He'd invited them both to visit him at the museum, where he said he might be able to give them access to material that would help them find out what had happened in Jack Turnbull's field two hundred years earlier.

Fairweather had gone home after that, and rather than Atticus driving out of his way to take Jez back to Winchester, Ellie had offered to take him instead.

A pair of swans paddled upstream.

"Today is going to be interesting," Atticus said.

"You think so?" Jez asked.

"You don't?"

"Just feels like it might be a wild goose chase."

"Maybe," Atticus said, "but I think it's worth spending a couple of hours finding out."

"Why?"

"Why what?"

"Why do we care?" Jez said. "I don't mean to sound heartless, but it's nearly two hundred years ago. Whoever killed those men is dead."

"Of course they are. But isn't there value in delivering justice to them?"

"It'd be symbolic."

"That's the best they'll get."

Jez glanced over at him. "It's not just that, though, is it?"

"Are you saying I'm motivated by the challenge of solving a two-hundred-year-old murder?" He grinned. "There might be an element of that."

"You think it's possible?"

"I have no idea. It'll depend on what we can find in the archive. Sam said he had an idea where to start, didn't he?"

"The census."

"1821 and then 1831—not impossible there'll be something obvious. And then the *Journal*. Three men going missing might get a mention."

"We'll want to visit Pitton, too," Jez suggested. "There might be something about it in the collective memory."

"Agreed. We'll start at the museum and then split up."

They got up and continued across the field to the Old Mill.

Atticus couldn't stop his smile. "Did you think I wouldn't notice?"

"Notice what?" Jez said.

"You're wearing the same clothes as yesterday."

Jez tried to style it out, then, daunted by his knowledge of how quickly Atticus saw through deceit, flubbed his denial. "It's… er…"

"Didn't go home, did you?"

He winced awkwardly. "Maybe not."

"You sly dog."

"We got to Ellie's, and she asked if I wanted to come in for another drink. I mean, after the day I had…"

"I don't blame you at all."

"You don't mind?"

"Why would I?"

"You don't think it's unprofessional?"

"Of course I don't think that. What you do in your private time is for you."

"But she's sort of working on the same case."

"This isn't a case," he said. "You said it yourself—it's more of a challenge to see if we can identify the remains. She's not a client. And anyway, even *I* can see it'd be the height of hypocrisy to criticise you. It's not like my hands are clean, is it?"

* * *

Atticus and Jez went back to the office and, after making sure both dogs were fed and watered and comfortable for the next three or four hours, they made their way to the museum. Fairweather had said there was a lot of material they could sift through and that he'd arrange a space in the library for them.

They passed through the cathedral gate and walked along the narrow path until they reached Choristers Square. They'd just made their way by the gate to Arundells when Atticus's phone buzzed in his pocket. He took it out and glanced at the screen to see who was calling.

"It's Mack," he said, then took the call. "Morning. Long night?"

"Very long."

"What time did you get home?"

She didn't answer. "Where are you?"

"On the way to the museum. I thought it'd be interesting to see whether I could identify the dead men from the field."

She paused, and Atticus could feel the tension.

"Do you know where Jez is?"

Atticus looked over at Jez, and their eyes met. "He's with me now. Why?"

"We need to speak to him."

"About?"

She paused again, and Atticus's unease deepened. "Can you bring him to the station?"

Atticus stopped. "You need to give me an idea what about."

"I can't. All I can say is that it's serious, and we need to see him now. If he's not going to come, I'll have to send someone to go and get him."

Atticus frowned; something was very wrong. "I'll tell him."

"Bring him," she repeated. "It's important."

45

Atticus explained what Mack had said as he led the way to Bourne Hill.

"I don't understand," Jez said. "She say anything about what they want to talk to me about?"

"Just that it was important. Can you think of anything that might make her think that?"

"No," he said. "Nothing." He paused, then pointed up at his face. "Apart from this—something to do with what happened?"

"If that's the only thing you can think of, then yes. Maybe."

"You think he might've gone to the police?"

"It's possible."

"But *he* started it. *He* hit *me*."

"So you need to tell them that. No one else saw what happened?"

"We were in the middle of nowhere. I didn't see anyone else."

"Then it'd just be a case of your word against his, wouldn't it? Where did it happen?"

"Just before I reached Winterslow." He shook his head. "This is ridiculous. Just when I thought things were picking up."

"Look—for what it's worth, I believe you. There are lots of things about getting on with people that I'm not good at, but I *am* good at telling when someone's lying and when they're not, and you're not lying."

"I *know* I'm not!"

"So tell Mack that. Tell her exactly what happened, just like you told me, and that'll be that. We'll be in and out in no time at all, and then we can go back to the museum and start looking into identifying the dead men. All right?"

He swallowed. "All right."

Atticus tried to put a little confidence in his voice, but, in truth, he was perturbed. Mack had sounded sombre on the phone, and if it really was just a case of the man who had scuffled with Jez making a complaint, why was *she* involved? Mack was a detective chief inspector. Two men rolling around in the dirt would be way below her level. This kind of trivial matter would be something that would be handled by uniform, not the most senior detective at the nick.

It made Atticus uneasy, but he needed to keep his unease hidden; Jez was already anxious, and the last thing he needed now was another reason to feel worse.

46

They turned into the gravelled area at the front of the building and went into the station. The receptionist smiled as they approached, Atticus told her that they were there to see DCI Jones, and she told them to wait while she called to let her know they were here.

"Shit," Jez said. "I'm nervous."

"Normal to be nervous. But it'll be nothing."

Mack appeared from the door behind the reception desk, saw Atticus's raised hand and made her way across the open space to where they were waiting. She hadn't bothered with makeup this morning, and the dark crescents under her eyes betrayed a night without sleep; that, perhaps, was to be expected given what they'd found in the farmer's yard. As Atticus looked at her face and then at her body language, the feeling of unease got worse. Her jaw was tight, lips pressed into a thin line. Her shoulders were hunched slightly, and she rubbed one wrist with the other hand as she walked; that was one of her unconscious tells when something was weighing on her. She offered a smile, but it was strained and didn't reach her eyes.

"Morning," she said.

"Morning," he said, unsure quite how to respond.

"Morning, Mr. Hardwicke. Thanks for coming in."

"No problem," Jez said. "What do you want to talk to me about?"

"Shall we go through to somewhere a little more private?"

They followed her as she opened the door and led them to the interview suite. She found an empty room and indicated they should go through.

Jez frowned nervously. "What is this?"

Mack glanced at Atticus with a mixture of regret and apology; she looked back at Jez. "Where were you yesterday?"

"I was walking. I did the Clarendon Way."

"From Winchester?"

"That's right."

"In one day?"

"I camped overnight, and then I had another twelve miles or so to cover. I got into Salisbury in the afternoon."

"He met me in the pub," Atticus said.

"Where did you camp?"

"Just outside Broughton."

"And then?"

"Like I said—I finished the route. Broughton to Middle Winterslow, then Pitton, then Salisbury."

Mack pointed. "Can I ask what happened to your face?"

"I thought it might be that," Jez said wryly. "That's why you want to talk to me?"

"What happened?"

"I had a run-in with a man I met just before I got to Winterslow. It was to do with our dogs. Mine is nervous around bigger dogs, and he had two Rottweilers off the lead. I asked him to control them, and he didn't. There was an argument, and then we had a stupid fight and—"

Atticus put a hand on Jez's arm to stop him. He wasn't surprised that this was what Mack wanted to talk to Jez about, but her demeanour—the tension in her face, and the way she looked at Atticus—made him think that matters were much more serious than he had expected.

"Does he need a lawyer?"

Mack nodded. "I think he does."

Atticus squeezed Jez's elbow. "Don't say anything else for now. Just checking, Mack—he's not under arrest?"

"Not at the moment. This is just a voluntary interview, but it ought to be obvious that he's been questioned as a suspect and not a witness."

"As a suspect?" Jez exclaimed. "For what?"

Atticus squeezed Jez's elbow again. "So, to be clear—he's free to leave?"

"He is," Mack said. "But I don't think that'd be sensible in the circumstances. I have some questions I need to ask him."

Jez turned to Atticus. "What do I do?"

"I think Mack is right—we need to get you a lawyer."

"What about Treacle? I—"

"He's fine," Atticus said. "I'll take care of him. Don't worry about that."

"It'll only be for an hour or two—right? I'll answer their questions, and then that'll be that."

"Exactly," Atticus said, although he wasn't sure at all that that would be the case.

He glanced over at Mack and saw that she was pale and drawn, she was an excellent detective who knew what she was doing, and, for the first time, Atticus was worried.

47

Jez sat at the metal table, his hands clasped together, his fingers twisting anxiously as he watched Mack and a second officer take their seats opposite him. They'd kept him in the same room, but he noticed it more now: grey walls, a single strip light overhead, and a small red light blinking on the recorder in the centre of the table. It smelled of disinfectant and stale coffee. The second detective—Mack had introduced him as Detective Sergeant Nigel Archer—took out a folder and a pen.

Jez's solicitor sat next to him, opposite Archer, her notebook open on the table. Atticus had called her for him. Her name was Emily Partridge, and Atticus had vouched for her as one of the better criminal advocates in the southwest. Atticus had waited with him until she'd arrived and then left the two of them alone so Jez could explain what had happened. She was a sharp-featured woman with cropped dark hair and an air of quiet competence, and Jez's first impressions of her had been good. She advised him to keep his answers brief and factual, and Jez had nodded, barely able to process the fact that he was sitting in a police station waiting to be interviewed. He wasn't a criminal. He hadn't done anything wrong.

Mack took the file and flipped it open. She was calm but serious, her expression unreadable. Archer, by contrast, folded his arms and sat back, watching Jez with a weighty silence.

Mack pressed the button on the recorder.

"This is a formal interview under caution with Jeremy Hardwicke. Present are Detective Chief Inspector Mackenzie Jones, Detective Sergeant Nigel Archer, solicitor Emily Partridge, and Mr. Hardwicke." She looked at her watch and added the date and time. "Jeremy," she said, "before we start, I want to remind you that you are here voluntarily. You are not under arrest at this time." She leaned forward, her gaze steady. "Do you understand?"

Jez cleared his throat. "I understand."

Emily gave him a reassuring nod.

"I don't know *why* I'm here, though."

"We'll get to that," Mack said. She flipped a page in the file. "Jeremy, you told me earlier that you were walking the Clarendon Way yesterday and the day before yesterday. Can you tell us what time you set off?"

"Yesterday?"

"Yes, please."

"I camped in the woods near Broughton and then got going again in the morning. Around nine."

"And you were travelling from Winchester to Salisbury?"

"That's right. A two-day walk."

"What time do you think you would've reached Winterslow?"

"I don't know for sure—ten in the morning, something like that."

Mack opened the file, took out a photograph and laid it on the table so Jez could see it. "Do you recognise this man?"

Jez leaned forward, his pulse quickening as he studied the image.

The man in the photograph was in his mid-thirties, with the weathered complexion of someone who spent most of his time outdoors. His features were strong and angular— high cheekbones, a square jaw—and his skin was ruddy from sun and wind. His hair was dark blond and neatly trimmed, though the first hints of grey had started to show at the temples.

"Yes," he said.

Mack's expression remained neutral.

"How do you recognise him?"

Jez hesitated, rubbing his palms against his jeans. "I had an altercation with him yesterday. I've never seen him before that, though. Who is he?"

"His name is Henry Ainsley," Mack said.

"Like I say—never seen him before yesterday."

"That's Viscount Brookmere," Mack said.

"The heir to the Brookmere estate," Archer added.

Mack put the photograph back into the folder.

"The altercation," Archer prompted. "Why don't you tell us about that?"

Jez let out a slow breath, trying to steady himself. "I told you."

"Tell me again."

"I saw him ahead of me—he had two Rottweilers with him, both off lead. My dog gets nervous with dogs he doesn't know. I called out and asked him to put his dogs on their leads. He just laughed. He said his dogs were fine. I told him Treacle *wasn't* fine."

"And then?"

"One of his dogs came running over. Treacle backed off—he was scared. I put my hand out, trying to shoo the other dog away, and I told him again to put his dogs on a lead. That's when he lost it."

"Lost it how?"

"He got right up in my face, swore at me, and said if my dog couldn't handle being around other dogs, then I shouldn't bring him out. I told him to put his dogs on leads, again, and then he shoved me in the chest. Hard—enough to knock me backwards."

"What did you do?"

"I shoved him back! I wasn't just going to stand there and let him push me around!"

"You were angry?"

"He was being completely unreasonable with the dogs, and then he was violent. So, yes—I was angry."

"And then what?"

Jez pointed to his bruised cheek. "He punched me in the face."

Archer nodded. "And you?"

"I swung back at him. Hit him once, in the side of the head." He pointed to his own head, indicating where his punch had landed. "He grabbed me, and we rolled around on the ground. It was ridiculous—slapstick. I got off him and backed away. We shouted a bit more, and then he walked off. And that was it."

Mack studied him carefully.

"Which way did he go?"

"East."

"And you?"

"West—towards Salisbury."

"Did you follow him?"

"No," Jez said.

"How did you feel?"

"Pissed off, but I could see it was stupid. I was embarrassed. Why would I want to chase after him?"

"Because you were angry?"

"I was, but like I said, it was stupid. And what happened wasn't me at all."

Archer leaned forward now, his fingers steepled together. "Jeremy, your blood was found on Henry Ainsley's clothing. How do you explain that?"

Emily stiffened. "You don't have to answer that."

"I can answer it. I told you—he punched me in the face. There was a lot of blood. It dripped onto his jacket after he hit me."

"We'll need to check your clothing," Mack said. "Where is it?"

"I'm wearing it."

"We'll need to have a look at it."

"Fine."

Archer was eyeing him. "You're sure you didn't go after him? Didn't hit him again?"

"No," he said. "I'm *completely* sure."

Emily interrupted smoothly. "My client has given a full and honest account of what happened. I assume you've spoken to Mr. Ainsley about this. What does he say?"

"I'm afraid we can't speak to him," Mack said. "Mr. Ainsley was found dead late last night."

Jez's stomach dropped so fast he thought he was going to be sick. "What?"

"A walker found him in a farmer's yard just off the track, west of Winterslow. We're still ascertaining the cause of death, but he has extensive injuries to his head."

"That wasn't me," Jez said. "I didn't... I couldn't... He was fine the last time I saw him. It was east of Winterslow. He was..."

The words wouldn't come. He felt light-headed and reached out to grab the edge of the table before he slipped off the chair.

Mack sighed and closed the file. "Jeremy Hardwicke, I'm placing you under arrest for further questioning regarding the death of Henry Ainsley."

"No," he said. "It wasn't me. I didn't—"

"You do not have to say anything," Mack continued, "but it may harm your defence if you do not mention when questioned something you later rely on in court. Anything you do say may be given in evidence."

Jez turned to Emily, panic rising. "What's happening?"

He had hoped to see calmness in her face, but she looked flustered. "They're just following procedure. I think it's probably best if you don't say anything else until we've had a chance to digest what's happening here."

He swallowed down a mouthful of bile. "Get Atticus," he said. "Tell him what's happened."

48

Atticus didn't know how long Mack would need for the interview with Jez. He'd intended to go back to the museum so he could start looking through their archive for anything that might help him identify the three dead men, but, with an ill-defined sense of unease, he decided he'd stay closer at hand and went to get a coffee at Upshake and Brew in Victoria Park.

Mack called him after an hour and said they should meet. He told her where he was, and she said she'd come to him.

He bought her a coffee and had it waiting for her as she arrived.

"Thanks," she said, taking it.

"What's going on?"

"We've arrested Jez on suspicion of murder."

Atticus took a step back. "No way. That's impossible."

"I'm sorry, Atticus. Really sorry."

Atticus sat down. "He's not violent."

"How long have you known him?"

"Not *that* long."

"A few months?"

He nodded.

"So you can't say that, can you?"

"Of course I can. He's *not*."

"What's he told you?"

"Am I being interviewed as a witness?"

"No," she said. "Not yet, anyway." She sighed. "We have to be careful. Me and you, and you and him… it's awkward."

Atticus held up his hands and then laid them palms down on the table. "He told me he had a fight with someone. Something about dogs—the guy wouldn't put his dogs on leads, and he got aggressive about it when Jez asked."

"That's what he told us."

"The victim—it's the body from last night?"

She nodded. "It's Henry Ainsley."

"Ainsley… as in?"

"Yes—as in Viscount Brookmere."

"*Shit.*"

"Exactly," she said. "Shit. And we found his DNA on Ainsley's coat."

"Why do you have Jez's DNA?"

"That's what I was saying about you not knowing enough to say he's not violent. He was arrested three years ago for a Section Five public order offence. Got into an argument outside a pub in Winchester that got a little heated—someone felt threatened, called the police. He was charged, fined, nothing serious."

"And they took his DNA when they processed him?"

"It was a recordable offence," she said. "The six-year retention rule applies, so it's still on file. We ran the sample we found on Ainsley's coat, and it came back as a perfect match."

"What did he say?"

"He admitted there was an incident, but he says Ainsley walked away."

"How was the body when it was found?"

"Bad. Here—look. And if anyone asks, I didn't show you this."

Mack took out her phone, opened her email and picked one from near the top of the list. She tapped on an attachment, waited for a photo to open, and then handed the phone to Atticus. The image showed a man sprawled out on a patch of rough concrete, his body partially concealed beside a stack of plastic-wrapped bales of silage in what looked like the corner of a farmyard. The ground was muddy, scattered with straw and tyre tracks, and the body was tucked just enough behind the bales that it could easily have gone unnoticed. His arms were stiff and awkward, splayed out at odd angles, while his legs were bent beneath him.

But it was the head injuries that drew the eye. The man's skull was cracked open, a deep depression at the crown where something had struck with tremendous force. Blood had congealed around the wound, darkening the hair and matting it to the scalp. More blood had pooled beneath his head, though not as much as Atticus might have expected. His jaw was askew, as though broken, and his nose had been crushed, the cartilage flattened.

"He was bludgeoned to death," Mack said.

"When's the PM?"

"Scheduled for tonight. Fyfe's doing it."

"Will you let me see his report?"

"I'll do my best."

Atticus pointed to the screen. "We can say one thing for sure: *that* level of damage rules out the possibility that Jez punched him once."

"Agreed," she said.

"So someone else murdered him," Atticus said.

"Or Jez did."

Atticus shook his head again. "No. I find it hard enough to believe he'd get into a fight in the first place. But to do that? *Look* at it. Multiple blows with a blunt object? That would've been an absolute frenzy. You're looking for either a psychopath or someone with a very personal motive. But Jez? No. I'm telling you, Mack—it's not him."

"You've said it yourself—eliminate everything else, and what's left is what you're looking for."

"Not this time. He came to meet me when he finished the walk, and he was his normal self. He told me about what happened, and he was more embarrassed about it than anything else. I would've been able to tell if he was keeping something back, and he wasn't."

"Look at it from my perspective. His DNA is on the body of a murder victim, and he's admitted that they had a fight—what choice do I have?"

"I know." He stood. "I get it. Thanks for keeping me updated."

"Don't be like that."

"Like what?"

"Putting your guard up. I shouldn't even be telling you."

"I know…" He searched for the right words. "It's like before—we're on different sides. I'm going to show you it's not him, and you're going to blame me when I do, and it makes things difficult between us."

"I'm not going to blame you. He's been arrested, not charged. If you can find something that means I can eliminate him before we charge him, that'd be great. It's not personal."

"But Ralph Mallender…"

"What about him?"

"It made things difficult between us."

"In your head, maybe, but not in mine. It made things *complicated*, but at least it stopped us from convicting an innocent man. Find something to prove it's not Jez—you'd be doing him and me a favour."

49

Atticus went to the office. Bandit and Treacle were curled up together on the sofa, but didn't need much encouragement to rouse them for a walk. Bandit trotted over to the corner of the room where Atticus had left his harness and lead and stood there, pointing at it, his tail wagging steadily. Treacle took a moment to grasp what was being proposed, but once he'd realised it involved the prospect of fun, he bounced down from the sofa and found his own lead.

"Come on, then, boys," Atticus said. "We might have quite a bit of walking to do."

* * *

Atticus put the dogs in the cargo space of his Volvo and drove out to Winterslow. He went to All Saints' Church and left the car in the car park. The Clarendon Way cut through the village, heading east to Broughton and west to Pitton.

Atticus let the dogs off their leads and watched as they raced away. Bandit trotted obediently at Atticus's side, while Treacle—younger and with seemingly boundless energy—

sprinted to and fro, wriggling underneath hedges and barbed-wire fences, collecting sticks and bringing them back to be thrown.

Atticus crossed the quiet road that cut through the village and then followed the same narrow track he'd taken yesterday evening until he saw the police cordon. A police car blocked the path to the farmyard and the fields beyond. Atticus saw blue-and-white police tape across the path and an officer leaning against the side of the car while keeping an eye on the approach from Winterslow. Atticus recognised him: it was Phillip Newman, one of the more reasonable uniformed officers, who he thought might be persuaded to let him have a closer look.

He put the dogs on their leads and carried on, holding up a hand in greeting as he turned the corner and made for the car.

"Phillip," he said.

"Atticus," he said, and then his expression changed: his smile of recognition darkened as he must've realised Atticus was here with the potential to make things awkward. "I'd like to say this was a coincidence, but that would be stupid, wouldn't it?"

"It's not *entirely* coincidental," Atticus said, smiling as warmly as he could. "Thought I'd come and take a look around."

"Can't let you get any closer than this."

"Are you sure?"

"Come on," Newman said. "You know better than that. You know CID has a suspect?"

"Jeremy Hardwicke," Atticus said. "You know who he is?"

"Someone from Winchester."

"He works with me." He pointed down. "In fact, this is his dog, Treacle."

Treacle heard his name and wagged his tail enthusiastically.

wman reached down and scratched the dog's head.
.nd Hardwicke's blood on the dead man's body is what I
.eard."

"He didn't do it. I met him in Salisbury the day they're saying Ainsley was murdered, and there's no way it was him."

"How'd his blood get there if it wasn't him?"

"They had a disagreement," Atticus said.

"A fight, you mean?"

"Yes—and he isn't disputing that. But he says they just threw a couple of punches and rolled around on the ground a bit."

"That'll be for his lawyer to prove."

"You're absolutely right." Bandit wandered over to Newman and nudged his leg with his nose. Newman reached down and scratched his ears. Atticus tried a casual tone: "The body was found down there—right?"

"You're not going to go trampling around," Newman said.

"Don't want to. I'm just curious."

Newman eyed him, shrugged, took a quarter turn and pointed up the track. "Just there—just inside the yard, behind the silage. It was a mess—head caved in, blood everywhere."

"No witnesses?"

"No," Newman said. "I've had a couple of dog walkers go by from the village who walk this way every day, but they said they didn't see anything."

Atticus dearly wanted to take a look at the spot where the body was found, but Newman had obviously been given firm instructions not to let anyone through the cordon, and Atticus knew that this was an occasion where his own notoriety at Bourne Hill would stand against him; Newman would've known that Atticus could only really cause mischief, and with that in mind, he was the last person he'd want to have sniffing around on the other side of the tape.

"Fair enough," he said. "I'll go the other way."

50

Atticus retraced his steps. He knew that Jez had been following the Clarendon Way, and with nothing else to do and both dogs still full of energy, he decided to follow it himself. Jez had been walking from east to west, and Atticus would go in the opposite direction; he'd walk the mile from the church to Middle Winterslow and then return later to pick up his car.

Jez had said that the altercation with Ainsley had taken place on the other side of the village, two or three miles east of the church. Either Jez had been lying about that, or something else had happened to Ainsley.

Perhaps he would be able to find something that might shed a little light on it.

The fields were thick with mud, and Atticus's trousers were slathered with it by the time he reached Middle Winterslow. He carried on through the village and picked up the trail on the other side, with Easton Common Hill leading out into the countryside again. He could carry on, but there'd been nothing of interest yet, and he didn't see why that would change.

He turned around and set off again. The track passed outside the village's One Stop convenience store, and this time, Atticus fixed the dogs' leads to a sign advertising the lottery. A bowl of water had been left, and both dogs started to drink; Atticus took the opportunity to go inside.

The store was pleasant, the kind of business that had a little bit of everything for villagers who were looking for an excuse not to go into the city. There was a post office counter, a surprisingly wide selection of groceries, a photocopier, and a board where local businesses could offer their services. Atticus glanced at it and saw one of his own cards stuck into the felt with a drawing pin; he remembered asking Jez to visit businesses between here and Winchester and leave the cards in an attempt to drum up business.

"Afternoon," said the man behind the counter.

"Afternoon," Atticus said.

"How can I help you?"

"Bit of a strange one. You know there was a body found on the track near West Winterslow yesterday?"

He nodded. "There's been some gossip. Murdered, they said—that's what I heard, anyway."

Atticus paused, wondering how to broach the subject he needed to discuss. "My name's Atticus. I'm a private detective. You've actually got one of my cards on the board over there."

"You working out what happened?"

"Trying to. A man's been arrested, and it's someone I know. I'm convinced there's no way he did it, and I'm trying to find anything that'll help me prove it."

The shopkeeper nodded, put his elbows on the counter and leaned closer. "You think I might be able to help?"

"The Clarendon Way goes right in front of the shop."

"That's right," he said. "Turn left and you're on the way to Broughton, and turn right and you'll get to Pitton. Why?"

"My friend was walking it yesterday—might've gone past the shop."

"And you saw I have a camera on the wall outside?"

"I did."

"Got robbed a couple of years ago. Put it up then."

"I don't suppose it still works?"

"Wouldn't be no good to me if it didn't, would it? Want to have a look at what we recorded yesterday?"

"Yes, please."

The shopkeeper picked up his phone from the counter and opened the app that was connected to the camera. He played with the controls for a moment and then found the day that he was looking for.

"What time are you thinking?"

Atticus gave that a moment's reflection. Jez said that he had camped near Broughton and that he had set off again around 9 a.m. It was around four miles from there to the shop, and, if Jez walked at around three miles an hour, he ought to have been here around 10 a.m., give or take. He erred on the side of caution and asked the shopkeeper if he could scroll through the footage from 9.30 a.m. onwards.

The man handed him the phone. "Have a look yourself. Swipe left and right to go forwards and backwards."

Atticus thanked him and tapped play. The camera was set up high, and although the field of vision wasn't especially generous, it offered a good view of the road that ran through the middle of the village as well as the immediate area in front of the door. He scrolled ahead, pausing to check and discount the usual foot traffic: dog walkers, villagers going to their parked cars, customers passing directly beneath the lens as they went into the shop.

It was 10.20 a.m. when he saw Jez arriving from the east.

He tapped the screen to pause the footage, then rewound a few seconds to get a clearer look. There he was: unmistakable in the same dark walking gear he'd been wearing when he'd arrived in Salisbury, striding along the track with Treacle trotting obediently at his side. The dog's ears pricked up as they approached the shop, and Jez slowed, digging into his jacket pocket, likely checking for his wallet. Atticus let the footage play. Jez paused outside the shop, glancing around before bending down to secure Treacle's lead to the same post near the water bowl where he was now. He gave the dog a quick scratch behind the ears before stepping inside.

Atticus continued watching the footage, now skimming ahead for when Jez would leave. He reappeared after three minutes, carrying a small paper bag, probably something for breakfast. Treacle gave a hopeful wag of his tail, and Jez rewarded him with half a croissant, then ruffled his fur before untying the lead.

Jez turned west, heading towards Salisbury.

Atticus turned the phone so the shopkeeper could see the screen. "Do you remember him coming in?"

"I do. Is that your friend?"

"It is," Atticus said. "How did he seem?"

"Bit flustered."

"Did you notice anything about the way he looked?"

"Had a mark on his face," the man said, pointing. "Bit of blood."

"Did he say anything about it?"

"No, and I didn't ask. Dave had just turned up—he's the postman—and he needed me."

"Can you save this footage?"

"I'll email the clip. What's your address?"

Atticus gave it to him, watching as the man tapped on his phone. A moment later, he nodded. "Sent."

Atticus's phone buzzed with the incoming email. "Thanks."

He took the phone again and scrolled forwards once more. He watched the feed roll past customers coming and going.

10.30 a.m.

Two walkers stopped to buy a bottle of water.

11.00 a.m.

A cyclist stopped to adjust the chain on his bike.

Then, at 11.45 a.m., he saw something that made his mouth fall open.

A man came into view from the east, walking with purpose. His tweed jacket was buttoned up against the wind, and two Rottweilers flanked him, their noses occasionally dipping to the ground to sniff at something interesting.

Atticus recognised the man from a photograph he'd seen on the website for the Brookmere estate.

It was Henry Ainsley.

The two dogs confirmed it.

Ainsley's gaze was fixed ahead, and he didn't break stride as he passed the shop and headed west, toward the yard outside West Winterslow where his body would ultimately be found.

Atticus stared at the screen. Seeing Jez had been useful, but it would only have alibied him for earlier.

This, though, was something else.

"Do you have a pen and paper?"

The shopkeeper tore a scrap from a notebook and gave Atticus a biro.

Atticus let his thoughts run, noting down the key information.

10 a.m.: According to Jez, he ran into Ainsley east of Winterslow, and they fought.

10.20 a.m.: Jez was seen on the cameras outside the shop, arriving from the east. That made sense; it would take twenty minutes to cover the mile.

11.45 a.m.: Ainsley passed the shop, heading west.

Atticus extrapolated.

By 11.45 a.m., Jez ought to have been around four miles farther towards Salisbury. That would put him on the outskirts of the city, certainly beyond Pitton and possibly at or even just after the ruins of Clarendon Palace.

It would take Ainsley until 12.15 p.m. at the earliest to get to the yard where his body was found.

Atticus could alibi Jez from 1 p.m. onwards.

He stared at his scribble and double-checked it.

It wouldn't have been possible for Jez to murder Ainsley outside West Winterslow and then walk from there to Salisbury in the forty-five minutes before he met Atticus.

Jez could have driven, Atticus supposed, but that made no sense at all.

There was no question about it: there was no way Jez could have murdered Ainsley.

"Please don't delete that footage," Atticus said.

"It's helpful?"

"Very. I'll let the police know. They'll want to come and get a copy. And they'll probably want to ask you a few questions."

The shopkeeper didn't seem remotely perturbed; if anything, he was enthusiastic. "Happy to help."

Atticus thanked him again, bought a pair of Jumbones for the dogs and went outside. They greeted him happily, and even more so as he peeled open the packaging and gave them their treats.

He took out his phone and called Mack.

"Hello?"

"I have news," he said.

"About Jez?"

"Yes," he said. "Have you charged him yet?"

"No."

"Don't," he said. "He didn't do it."

"And you're basing that on what?"

Atticus explained what he had discovered.

"You can prove all this?"

"I've seen the footage. I'll forward it, but you'd better send someone to come and speak to the shopkeeper. I said he should expect a visit."

"Come to the station. I'll tell them not to do anything with Jez until we've talked."

51

Atticus drove back to the city, left his car in the Cathedral Close and then took the dogs back to the office. He fed and watered them and then went out again, walking to the station. He'd forwarded the video footage to Mack before leaving the store, and she'd called him while he was driving to deliver her own news: a door-to-door enquiry in Laverstock had produced doorbell footage showing Jez walking into the city at 12.40 p.m. Henry Ainsley had been seen alive on the store's camera at 11.45 a.m., meaning that there was insufficient time to have allowed Jez to murder him outside West Winterslow and *then* reach the city.

The remaining possibility—that Jez could have driven—was also handily disproven and, with a surfeit of exculpatory evidence, Mack agreed there was no case to answer. She promised that she'd take care of the paperwork so that Atticus could pick Jez up and take him home.

He reached the station and called her.

She brought Jez to the exit herself.

"I'm sorry," she said to Jez as he pulled on his jacket.

"I understand," he replied. "I know how it must've looked."

"That's very gracious of you."

Atticus turned to Jez. "Can I just have a word with Mack?"

"Of course." He pointed to the Greencroft. "I'll be over there."

Atticus waited until Jez was out of earshot and then turned to Mack.

"All okay?"

"Stop worrying," she said. "That was helpful."

"You would've found the evidence without me."

"Eventually. But you saved him an uncomfortable second interview and then a night in the cells."

"Good. I'm pleased. The last thing I want to do is to cause you a problem."

"You didn't," she said, laying her hand on his arm. "I mean it—stop worrying."

They both watched Jez make his way across the street toward the Greencroft.

"You got any other leads?"

Mack shook her head. "The focus was on him. We'll have to regroup now."

"What about the Earl of Brookmere?"

"Rupert?" She shook her head. "Nothing."

"Let me know if you'd like me to have a look at it—at either of them."

"Not now—Beckton's coming in for a briefing. But do you want to come over tonight?"

"That'd be nice. You want a Wagamama?"

"I'll be too tired to cook."

"I'll get the usual and a bottle of wine."

52

Atticus went over to where Jez was sitting next to the playground.

"How are you?"

Jez blew out his cheeks. "Fine. But I don't suppose you have a cigarette?"

"Didn't know you smoked."

"Now and again. Usually when I'm stressed about something."

"I don't—not a normal cigarette, anyway. I could roll you a joint at the office if that'd help."

"It might."

They set off, walking back into the city.

Jez glanced over. "Mack said you got me out."

"I was able to put together a timeline for you and Ainsley. It showed you couldn't have done what they said."

"So I was lucky," Jez said.

"Not sure I'd say that. You were very nearly charged with murder."

"Lucky in that if the camera wasn't there, or wasn't working, or you didn't find it…"

"There would've been another way."

"Well," Jez said, "thank you."

Atticus waved his gratitude away.

They reached New Street, and Atticus saw a woman waiting at the entrance to the passageway that led to the door of his office and the courtyard beyond. He eyed her as he approached: she was wearing a tailored navy cashmere coat that fell just below the knee, the collar turned up against the wind, and beneath it, a silk blouse in a shade of ivory that wouldn't have survived long on someone without a dry-cleaning budget to ensure it stayed pristine. She wore a pair of expensive suede boots that looked as if they had never encountered so much as a puddle, and a crocodile leather handbag, embossed with the insignia of a high-end French designer, was tucked into the crook of her arm.

"Appointment?" Jez said.

"No one in the diary today."

"Maybe she's waiting for one at the hair salon?"

"Her clothing's too expensive. Look at the coat and handbag—if you have the budget for them, you get your hair cut in Kensington or Chelsea, not here."

Atticus and Jez stepped into the passageway. Atticus went to the door and put his key in the lock, and then, as he prepared to open it, he saw that she had followed them.

"Are you Mr. Priest?"

"I am," Atticus said.

"The investigator?"

"That's me. But I don't think I have an appointment this afternoon."

"You don't. I was in town, and I thought... well, I was hoping you might be able to help me."

"The best way is to call and make an appointment. I'm afraid I don't usually have the time to be spontaneous."

"Do you think you might be able to make an exception?"

"I really don't think—"

"I'm Emelia Ainsley—the Countess of Brookmere."

Atticus's objection died on his lips. He paused, taking a moment to master his surprise. "I'm very sorry to hear what's happened to your stepson."

"And my husband," she said. "He's still missing, but…" She stopped.

"You'd better come inside."

53

Atticus offered to make Emelia Ainsley a cup of coffee, but she said she was fine. He told her he'd make one for himself and left the office to go to the kitchen. He boiled the kettle, preparing a mug for a drink he didn't really want. Jez came too, realising that Atticus wanted to speak to him.

"That's a turn-up," Jez said.

"It is."

"Is there any reason she'd know the police had me in for what happened to Henry Ainsley?"

"Probably not," Atticus said. "I doubt she would've been told."

"Still…"

"Yes," Atticus said. "It could be awkward."

"I'll take Treacle and go home. I wouldn't mind some time to myself, to be honest."

"Don't blame you."

Treacle wandered out at the sound of his name and looked at Jez expectantly.

"I'll call you in the morning," Jez said, picking up Treacle's lead. "Let me know if you need anything before then."

"Will do."

"And let me know what she wants."

* * *

Atticus took his coffee back into the office, pulled out his chair and turned it so that he could sit and face Emelia. He paid her more attention now: mid-thirties, a striking appearance with high cheekbones and a sharp jawline. The way she held herself suggested that she knew she was beautiful, and her flawless skin said she spent a lot of money ensuring that time did not take that away from her. Her blonde hair, touched with subtle lowlights, was pulled back into a chignon, and her makeup was understatedly professional. He'd seen her before; there was a picture of the Earl and Countess of Brookmere on the same website that he'd visited when he was researching Henry Ainsley.

"Biscuit?" Atticus said, proffering an opened packet of ginger nuts.

"I'm fine," she said with a smile that didn't quite mask her impatience.

Atticus took a sip of his coffee and then set it down on his desk. "So—how can I help you?"

"I saw you on the television last night."

"The dig at Pitton?"

"Yes. And then I remembered reading about you in the paper. I need someone to help with something very important, and it struck me that you'd be perfect—just what we need."

"I think I can guess what that might be about. Your husband and stepson?"

"How do you know that? It hasn't been made public."

"My assistant, Jeremy, had an altercation with your stepson yesterday. The police questioned him this morning."

"They didn't tell me that."

"They wouldn't. Jeremy had nothing to do with what happened."

"Was that him? Just now?"

"Yes," Atticus said. "I was able to show there was no way he could've done it. I'm telling you now because I wouldn't want you to find out later and think I hid something from you. I also know a little about what's happened." He smiled sympathetically. "I'm very sorry."

"Thank you."

"Tell me whatever you think I need to know."

"My husband went missing on Tuesday, and Henry was found last night. The police are flailing around and getting nowhere."

Atticus sipped his coffee again, trying to find the right way to nudge the conversation along without his usual bluntness. "You want me to help with that?"

"I think I need to be proactive. I was awake all night thinking about it, and I've decided that this—speaking to you, getting your help—is what I need to do."

Atticus noticed how in control of her emotions Emelia Ainsley was. There was an obvious undercurrent of concern— understandable in the circumstances—but she was able to hold it in check. Atticus remembered something he'd read about her on the Brookmere estate website when he'd been nosing around: she'd been an actress in the West End before meeting her husband, and he could see stagecraft in the way that she held herself—the measured cadence of her speech, the subtle changes of expression, her poise even when her eyes betrayed flickers of unease.

"I'm not naïve," she said. "I know Rupert is probably dead, too. I want you to find out what happened."

Atticus bit down on the inside of his cheek. *Here we go again.* There was no point in trying to pretend he wasn't interested in looking into what had happened—it was another big case, with the potential to be as notorious as the others on which he had worked—but Mack was investigating, too, and he didn't want to do anything that might put him and her on a collision course. Their aims would be the same, but what would happen if Mack favoured one suspect and Atticus another? What would happen if Emelia herself became a suspect? What would happen if Mack concluded that she had something to do with what had happened?

He winced, and she noticed.

"What is it?"

"It's…" The sentence drifted away unfinished as he realised he didn't really have a good enough reason to turn her request down.

"You're too busy? I'll pay more than you'll get from anyone else. What's your hourly rate?"

"Two hundred," he said, aware that he was allowing himself to slide into a position where the only answer he could give was yes.

"I'll give you five hundred."

"It's not really about the money."

"So what *is* it about? I'm desperate. The police have been looking for Rupert since yesterday morning, and they haven't been able to find him. More than twenty-four hours and they've got *nowhere*. That's incompetence. And now this has happened to Henry…"

Atticus glanced away and chewed his lip.

"Six hundred," she said.

"Which detectives have you met?"

"DCI Jones and DI Best."

"I know them both. They're good. Very good."

"As good as you?"

"I wouldn't like to—"

"Please," she cut across his false modesty. "I'm begging you. I don't know what else to do."

"Fine. I'll come have a look and see if there's something they've overlooked. But I don't want you to have unreasonable expectations. I'd be very surprised if they've missed anything."

"I'd just like to be sure that they're doing everything they ought to be doing. And perhaps you'll be able to suggest something—a fresh approach might be helpful."

"Maybe," he conceded.

"Could you come over to Brookmere House tonight?"

He nodded.

"I'll be completely honest with you. I want you to look at the children first. You know I'm his third wife?"

The website had been diplomatic about that. "I didn't."

"I am. They're not my kids—Henry and Celeste are from his first marriage, and Sebastian and Alexander are from his second. And I've never had the best relationship with any of them."

"They don't know that you're speaking to me?"

"No," she said.

"Who'll be my client? You or the family?"

"Me." She paused, pressing her fingers together. "I'm not saying I know anything that'd make me *think* they could be involved, but, on the other hand, they'd all benefit from Rupert's death."

"How?"

"My husband has been talking about changing his will. At the moment, his estate would be split between the children and me. But he's been talking about changing it so that the house and the land are held in trust with Henry as main trustee. The others have been badgering Rupert to sell land so they can get some of their money now, but he doesn't want that to happen. We had a family meeting the night before he disappeared, and he made it *very* clear how important it was to keep the house and the land in the family."

"And Henry?"

"He was of the same opinion."

"Sorry, but I have to ask—"

She cut across him, anticipating the question. "Would changing the will affect me? I don't know what Rupert would've decided, but yes, it's possible that it would've meant I received less. And so, in answer to what you're probably thinking— yes, you'd need to look at me, too. I have a financial motive for wanting the will to stay the way it is."

Atticus nodded. He appreciated the clarity; Emelia was sharp enough to understand how things might look, and confident enough to confront it head-on. That alone made her interesting. But it also put her on his list. He'd seen enough duplicity to know that people could admit just enough to appear transparent while keeping deeper truths buried. The financial motive was a red flag, of course, and if she was being *this* open about it, it might mean she had something worse to hide. Or it might mean she genuinely had nothing to fear. Either way, it was a thread worth pulling.

"There's one other thing you need to know," she said. "It's very sensitive—it can't go any further."

"Of course," he said.

She took a breath. "Rupert has been diagnosed with dementia. We'd all noticed changes to his behaviour. He was forgetting things. It was small things to start with—names, appointments. Then he'd repeat himself in conversations or ask questions he'd already asked. He'd lose things. He said it was nothing, but it got to a point where he couldn't ignore it anymore. He went to see a specialist, and the scans confirmed it."

"How did he take it?"

Emelia's fingers twisted around one another in her lap. Atticus said nothing, letting the silence stretch; he knew better than to interrupt.

"Badly," she said finally. "He was angry. First with the doctor, then with me, then with himself." Her voice wavered, but she steadied it quickly. "Rupert needs to feel in control. He runs the estate like a business. Everything ordered, under his thumb. The idea that his own mind might start to betray him *terrified* him."

Atticus watched her closely. He could see the effort behind her composure.

"He didn't want to believe it, but the doctor ran another set of scans, and he said it confirmed the diagnosis."

"And no one else knows?"

"No," she said quickly. "God, no. Only me, the children, and the doctor. We kept it quiet. He didn't want it getting out.

He was afraid people would think he was unfit to manage the estate. That it'd undermine him."

"How long ago was this?"

"He was diagnosed six months ago. We got the results of the second set of scans just before he disappeared. They confirmed it."

"I see," he said. "I don't think it'll be a surprise that I think that'll likely be relevant."

"It's not. It's also one of the reasons why the question of the will has been so divisive. It makes things more pressing. No one is questioning his mental capacity at the moment, but we all know this is only going to go one way. It needs to be settled before he gets any worse—the last thing we want is for one of the kids to decide that they're not getting what they're entitled to and contest the will in court. Assuming he's still alive to *change* the will, of course, and the longer he's away from home, the more likely it is that… that he's not."

Atticus sat back, absorbing what he'd been told. The stakes were significant, not just emotionally but financially, too. And that, in Atticus's experience, had a way of warping people's judgement.

He could already feel the familiar pulse of curiosity, the itch that told him there was something here worth investigating. Emelia had laid out her cards with enough candour to win his attention, but she'd also been careful; he couldn't shift the feeling that she'd given him a performance.

"I'll come to the house tonight and speak to everyone. I can't promise anything, but I'll start to look into what's happened."

"Thank you," she said.

Atticus saw something shift behind her eyes, but whether it was relief or calculation, he couldn't yet say.

54

Atticus called Jez while he was walking Bandit. He recounted the meeting with Emelia and asked him to put together pen portraits of the Ainsleys in time for his meeting with them later that evening. Jez said he would and rang off to get started; Atticus made sure Bandit was tired out before returning to the office to collect his bag and car keys. He filled the dog's bowls with biscuits and water and then went down to his car.

He called Jez again as he left the city.

"What have you got?"

"Something on all of them—mostly surface, but I'll dig deeper once we're done. Who do you want to start with?"

"Emelia."

"Okay," he said. "She's Rupert's third wife. Previously worked as an actress, with several minor roles in West End productions during her twenties and early thirties. Met Rupert at a wedding of mutual friends and gave up work soon after that. There's a decent amount of information on her from that time of her life: theatre reviews, society party photos, tabloid mentions when she married into the Ainsleys. Looks like

Rupert was still with his second wife when they started the relationship, and it was all very quick: six months from their first meeting to marriage. The age difference is a bit extreme: she was thirty-four, and he was sixty-seven."

"How old is she now?"

"Thirty-eight. She's originally from Maidenhead, but it looks like she's put down roots here. Well-connected socially. Patron of a couple of local arts charities, often seen at fundraisers and events. She was at the Playhouse last week for the first night of the new play they've just put on—there was a picture of her in the *Journal*. Rupert wasn't with her."

"Interesting," Atticus said. "Next."

"Celeste Ainsley. Eldest of the four children. Forty-two. Her mother is Claudette, Rupert's first wife. Educated privately, then went on to read history of art at Oxford. Worked for a major London auction house before setting up on her own as an independent consultant and valuer. Divorced once, now remarried to Julian Doyle."

"And him?"

"Bit of a ne'er-do-well. Used to run a nightclub in Shoreditch that got shut down after a licensing issue—drugs, mostly. Did a stint in rehab, cleaned up for a while, then rebranded himself as a creative director for an artisanal gin company that never took off. Looks very much like he's living off Celeste's money now, though he plays it like he's the ideas man behind everything she does. Fifteen years younger than her—just turned twenty-seven. There was a party at Brookmere House with a handful of models and soap stars from London. They're an odd couple. She always dresses well, goes to all the right places and says all the right things. He's still seen falling out of nightclubs, and he has a colourful criminal history: a caution for possession with intent, six months for assaulting a bouncer, a suspended sentence for fraud after skimming card payments from a pop-up bar in Ibiza, a stint on remand for handling stolen goods—though that case collapsed before trial."

"Odd choice for her."

"If you were feeling uncharitable, you might think she was slumming it."

"You might. Kids?"

"None."

"Social media?"

"Minimal but carefully put together: stylish interiors, flamboyant holidays, expensive plates of food at exclusive restaurants. Doyle's in plenty of the pictures. His own are a bit more varied: shirtless selfies in the gym, behind-the-scenes shots at parties he says he's 'hosting,' motivational quotes about success and hustle culture. Lots of designer labels, but nothing that suggests he's actually earning. A few pictures with minor celebrities—Z-listers, mostly—and photos of him 'networking' in Dubai or Mykonos. It's curated chaos, basically. All image, no substance."

"Next."

"Henry Ainsley. Eldest son, formerly heir apparent, now sadly deceased. Late thirties. Educated at Harrow, same as his father, studied land management at the Royal Agricultural College at Cirencester, came back to work under the Earl. Local councillor for a while but stepped back in recent years."

"Anything else?"

"Bit of a playboy. Fast cars. Several photos on his social media with different women, always younger than him."

"Runs in the family."

"Like father, like son. He had a reputation locally—charming, but not dependable. Dated a string of women, mostly from well-off families, though none of the relationships lasted. Got into trouble a few times: once for crashing a classic Aston near Wilton after a party, and there was a whispered story about him being banned from the golf club for an 'incident' with a member's wife. Still, he knew how to turn on the charm when it suited him. Rumours of heavy drinking, a few unpaid debts, nothing provable. Cleaned up his image a few years ago when he started taking a more active role in the estate. Gave interviews about sustainable land use, chaired a rural development board, even talked about setting up a foundation."

"Good—Sebastian?"

"The elder son from Rupert's second marriage to Elizabeth. Thirty-four and evidently something of a dilettante. Educated at Winchester College and dabbled in several careers: music, marketing, most recently poker. Lived in London on what was obviously a generous allowance. Runs a podcast called 'On the River,' mostly interviews with well-known online gamblers, but with very little substance. Social media suggests a carefully managed personal brand. No sign of financial independence."

"Does he still play poker?"

"Looks like it—I haven't had time to listen to any of his podcasts, but I skimmed the transcript for the last one, and he was talking about going up to play in a tournament in London last week."

"And Alexander?"

"The youngest child. Twenty-eight, also from the second marriage. Less visible online than the others. Studied engineering at Bristol, then went off travelling for three years—lots of photos on his Instagram from Thailand, Vietnam, Bali. Backpacker stuff, but with the kind of polish that suggests money was never far away. When he came back, he took a job with a property development firm—luxury flats, mostly, in the southeast. On paper, it's all above board. No obvious financial issues, no debts. But there's a wrinkle. I found his name on the register of a shell company based in Jersey. Holding firm. Hard to say what it does because it doesn't seem to do much of anything. No website, no filings of note—just a name, an address, and Alexander listed as a director."

"Tax evasion?"

"Could be. Or it could be something he doesn't want his family knowing about. Might be nothing."

"Check it out."

"I will."

Atticus reached the turning for Pitton. "What about general impressions?"

"The family tree's a bit of a tangle," Jez said, "what with the three wives and children by the first and second countesses. Rupert's the linchpin—the one holding the whole thing together—or at least he was."

"All useful," Atticus said. "Thanks."

"No problem. I'll grab dinner, and then I'll see what else I can find. Let me know if you need anything."

Atticus said he would and ended the call. He drove into the village and started the climb up White Hill towards Brookmere House.

55

Atticus drove up to the gates of Brookmere House and, as he waited to be buzzed in, saw that someone had defaced the statue of Charles Ainsley, the fifth Earl of Brookmere, that stood sentry on the side of the road. A message had been daubed in lime-green paint across his chest: VANDALS.

The gates opened, and Atticus continued along the drive to the house.

Emelia was waiting for him.

"The statue at the gates has been defaced."

"I saw. It'll be the protestors. Did you see them?"

"I did," he said.

"I'll get it cleaned in the morning." She gestured that he should come inside. "Thanks again for coming."

"No problem."

"Everyone's here."

"And they know I'm coming?"

"I told them."

"And?"

She smiled awkwardly. "They're not very enthusiastic."

"I expect they've been speaking to the police all day."

"And yesterday."

"So I can understand why they might think this is a bit much."

She waved that off. "I've told them it's important. They'll answer your questions—all I'm saying is that they might not give you the warmest welcome."

"That's fine," he said, taking off his jacket. "It wouldn't be the first time."

He followed her into the house. The waning light filtered in through leaded windows, catching on the polished bannisters and casting shadows up the panelled walls. He took in the portraits, the antique furniture, the quiet opulence that hadn't been curated but inherited, layered over generations. Emelia led the way down a short corridor and into the sitting room, where four people were waiting.

"This is Atticus Priest," she said.

Atticus examined the others as she introduced them: Sebastian, a young man who looked at him with an expression that suggested he was already bored; Celeste, a little older and with a blankness in her face; Julian, her husband, distracted by his phone; and Alexander, his arms crossed over his chest in a gesture of stereotypical wariness.

"Hello," Atticus said. "I'm very sorry to hear about what you've all been through over the last couple of days."

"Emelia says you'll be able to tell us what's happened," Celeste said.

"I'll certainly do my best."

"The police have been here all day," Alexander said. "We've already told them everything. What are you going to be able to do that they can't?"

"Maybe nothing. But I'll approach the investigation in a different way to them, and I don't necessarily have to follow the same rules they do. I have a little more flexibility of action."

He glanced around the room and saw the same expressions—ennui, apprehension, sadness—as before. This had the potential to be a difficult conversation.

"First of all," he said, "I'm going to ask you some questions about your father."

"You think it's linked, then?" Alexander said. "Father going missing and what happened to Henry?"

"I think it would be an enormous coincidence if it wasn't."

"That's what I said to the police," Alexander said, looking at the others.

"It's what we *all* said," Celeste said. "It's not rocket science."

"Emelia tells me you had a family discussion the night before your father disappeared. There was some disagreement about estate planning?"

Sebastian turned to Emelia. "You told him about that?"

"Of course I did."

"You aired our dirty washing with a stranger," he complained. "I can understand telling the police, but…"

"I'll be discreet," Atticus said. "I won't be able to do my job properly unless I have all the facts."

"*I* don't have a problem with that," Celeste said. "Emelia probably told you—Father said he was going to change his will so that it all went into a trust rather than to us individually. None of us were particularly happy about that." She looked at the others. "Is that fair?"

"None of us were happy apart from Henry," Sebastian said.

"He was going to be a trustee," Atticus said.

"With the power to determine when—*if*—we got what was promised to us," Alexander finished.

"But that doesn't mean we'd want anything to happen to Father," Sebastian said.

"Or Henry," Celeste added.

"Of course not," Atticus said, "but I still have to rule you all out. I have a timeline of the morning that Rupert disappeared, but it'd be helpful if you could each tell me what you were doing."

"I slept in," Alexander said. "My girlfriend is in New York, and I was up late talking to her."

"We went out for a walk," Celeste said, indicating Julian. "A peregrine falcon from the cathedral has been hunting in the fields. We were hoping we might get a glimpse of it. Father was keen, too."

"Sebastian?"

"I was on the train to London. I had business meetings all day."

"'Business,'" Celeste said, shaking her head. "Playing poker isn't business."

He ignored her dig. "I play semi-professionally," he explained.

Atticus nodded. "Let's put your father aside for the moment and talk about Henry. I understand he was last seen yesterday morning."

"He went out to look for my husband," Emelia said.

"When?"

"Early."

"On foot or in his car?"

"On foot. He had his dogs with him. He often went out for long walks, and I think he thought he'd be able to cover ground the police hadn't covered."

"Going east? Towards Winterslow?"

"Yes," she said.

"When was the last time you heard from him?"

"He called me around eleven," Celeste said.

"He called everyone," Emelia added.

"Saying what?"

"That he wanted a family meeting at lunch," Celeste said.

"Did he say what he wanted to talk about?"

"He said he'd had an idea about Father," Alexander said.

"He said that to all of you?"

They each nodded in confirmation.

"But not what he was thinking?"

"I asked," Sebastian said. "He said it had to be something we spoke about all together."

"And did you think that was strange?"

"*Everything's* been strange," Sebastian said. "I didn't really think about it until later—after… well, you know."

"After he was found."

"Exactly."

"Thank you," Atticus said. "What did the rest of you do yesterday morning?"

"I went out looking for Father," Alexander said.

"And me," Sebastian added.

"Julian went to the solar farm," Celeste said.

"Went on a bit beyond that, too," he said, "just in case."

Atticus nodded and turned back to Celeste. "And you?"

"I was here," she said. "I had a meeting on Zoom I couldn't get out of."

"I was here, too," Emelia said. "In case Rupert came back."

"With the police?"

She nodded. "They were here all morning. DI Best."

"I know Robbie. I'll have a word with him later." He looked at his watch. It was getting late, and he could see he was starting to test their patience. "Thank you for being so helpful. One more question for now, and then I'll let you get on with the rest of your evening. I think it'd be useful if you told me what you think might have happened here."

"Isn't that *your* job?" Julian said.

"You know Rupert and Henry. You'll have a better idea than anyone else."

Celeste folded her arms. "I think they've upset someone, and it's got them both into trouble."

"Who?"

She rolled her eyes. "That's a *long* list."

The family took turns with their speculations, suggesting that it might have been the environmental protestors who were upset about the solar farm or the farmer from whom Rupert and Henry were trying to force the sale of land. Emelia said that Henry had scared off protestors who had vandalised equipment at the solar farm on the day Rupert had gone missing, and Celeste added that Henry had had a physical altercation with the farmer earlier that same day.

"Who else might be upset with Henry?" Atticus asked.

"The same people who are angry with Father. Henry did his dirty work for him."

Atticus took notes, grateful for their willingness to speculate. It was like watching a tightly wound spring slowly unwind, the pressure of recent events giving them permission to vent suspicions and frustrations. Celeste mentioned a former gamekeeper who'd been dismissed under unclear circumstances and was now drinking heavily and apparently 'saying things' in the pub. Emelia added that one of the estate's tenants—a woman who ran a small dairy farm—had accused Rupert of hiking her rent unfairly and had threatened legal action before backing down. Julian, more flippant, said half the village hated Rupert for blocking an old permissive footpath through the woods. And there was a land agent who'd fallen out with Henry more than once over commission payments and had been 'on edge' for weeks.

Atticus stood. "Thank you again. I appreciate your honesty."

"What now?" Emelia said.

"I'd like to come back first thing tomorrow and look around the house."

"You can look tonight if you like."

"Tomorrow's better—when it's light."

He crossed the room toward the door.

Emelia followed. "I'll see you out."

They stepped into the hall.

"That went better than I expected," she said.

"Good."

"It's been a long day. A long *two* days. But they know we need answers."

"And I'll do my best to get some."

56

Mack drove to the hospital and parked. She pulled down the visor so she could look at her reflection in the vanity mirror. Dark circles smudged beneath her eyes, and her hair was coming loose from the ponytail she'd hastily tied that morning; a few strands stuck stubbornly to her temples. She reached up, ran her fingers through the mess, and exhaled. She felt every hour of her shift weighing down on her, and it wasn't done yet. She took out her phone and saw that Atticus had sent her a picture of a Wagamama takeaway. She texted back, said she'd be back later and told him not to wait to eat, and that she'd heat her meal up again when she got home.

She straightened in her seat, rubbing her temples. Fyfe was conducting the post-mortem, and she'd said she'd be there to observe.

* * *

Mack pulled on the disposable gown, snapping the ties at the back and then pulling on a pair of nitrile gloves, stretching them snugly over her fingers. She arranged the surgical mask to cover her nose and mouth; the scent of disinfectant was still strong, even through the material. She pushed the door open and stepped through into the post-mortem suite.

Fyfe was already in position beside the stainless-steel table. His assistant—a young forensic technician named Dani—stood by with a clipboard, ready to document his findings. The naked body of Henry Ainsley lay on the slab, a Y-shaped incision already traced on his torso in preparation for the internal examination. The overhead lights cast a stark glow over his pale skin.

Mack exhaled and stepped closer. "Evening."

Fyfe didn't look up. "Hello, Mack. Are you okay?"

"Never better."

He gestured to the dead body. "Not the most pleasant part of the job."

"Not my first time. Let's get on with it."

Fyfe nodded to Dani and turned his attention to Ainsley's head, where the worst of the injuries had been sustained. The scalp had already been peeled back, exposing the fractured skull beneath. Mack had seen her fair share of dead bodies, but something about the sheer brutality of the wounds on display made her stomach tighten.

Fyfe picked up a probe and gestured to the damage. "Cause of death is no mystery here. Blunt force trauma. Multiple impacts, sustained over a short period." He traced the outline of the fractures with his gloved fingers. "See this large depression on the crown? Likely this would've been the first blow. A heavy one. Would've stunned him, possibly even knocked him out. And then here"—he pointed to a second fracture, slightly offset from the first—"that's a follow-up. Almost identical in force and angle, suggesting the same weapon." He pointed again. "Two blows, both very significant, but the killer keeps going. Third impact here—left parietal bone, just above the ear. Then another, further down, near the occipital region." He paused, adjusting the overhead lamp. "Take a look."

Mack leaned in.

Fyfe pointed to the temple. "It suggests the weapon had a defined, weighted end—possibly something with a square or rounded striking face."

"A hammer?"

"That's what I was thinking. This kind of impression is consistent with something like that. No defensive wounds on the hands or arms. If I had to guess, I'd say he was either caught completely unaware or was already incapacitated by the first blow. No signs of a struggle—nothing. The blows were delivered with force, but also with precision. This wasn't random violence—it was intentional."

"Time of death?"

"Based on rigor and livor mortis and the ambient temperature outside when he was found, I'd estimate maybe seven or eight hours before discovery."

Mack nodded. "Anything else I should know?"

Fyfe peeled off his gloves and disposed of them. "I don't think so. No signs of restraint, no post-mortem injuries. I'll compile my full report this evening and send it over, but I think you've got what you need. The man was beaten to death with a heavy instrument, and the lack of defensive wounds suggests he didn't see it coming or was unable to resist. If you find anything that might've caused this, I ought to be able to tell you with a decent level of certainty whether it's a match."

Mack thanked him, then went outside. She pulled the mask from her face as she stepped into the corridor and dumped it in the bin, the gloves and gown following. She went outside and breathed in a lungful of fresh air.

PART 5

Friday

57

Atticus left Mack in bed just after six and made his way through the quiet streets to Queen Elizabeth Gardens. The city was only just beginning to wake: a few early joggers and someone unloading bread from the back of a van outside Reeves. The dew was still fresh on the grass, and Bandit nosed his way through the undergrowth along the river while Atticus kept one eye on the rising sun behind the cathedral spire. They went to the office via Aroma, where he ordered a flat white and two breakfast baps. He ate one and gave the other to the dog.

He'd arranged for his upstairs neighbour, Jacob, to look after Bandit for the day. Atticus knocked on the door, handed Jacob a twenty for his trouble and waited for the dog to bound up the stairs in search of treats before getting his coat and heading out to his car.

* * *

Atticus drove back out to Pitton, and, as he waited to turn right off the A30, he glanced out at the protest camp and wondered whether he ought to stop and have a word. He recalled the defaced statue outside Brookmere House and remembered what he'd been told last night about the bad blood between both Rupert and Henry and the protestors. Henry had reported that he had disturbed two trespassers at the solar farm, it seemed they were prepared to resort to criminality to make their point, but it was one thing to smash up a solar panel or deface a statue and quite another to bludgeon someone to death.

He drove through the village and continued on to the house. Emelia opened the door to his knock, and he could immediately see that something had upset her. Her face was pale and drawn, and there was a glimmer of something— fear, perhaps—in her eyes.

"Morning."

She nodded.

"Are you all right?"

She shook her head, and, for a moment, he thought she was about to cry.

"Is it Rupert?"

"No," she said. "Something else—you'd better come in."

Atticus followed her inside to the kitchen.

"Coffee?" she offered. "Might put a tot of something in it, too, or do you think it's too early for that?"

She was distracted and rambling.

"Emelia—what is it?"

She gestured to the kitchen table with a wave of her hand. "Over there."

Atticus went over to the table. It was unremarkable: a stack of newspapers, marketing circulars that had managed to avoid the bin, a copy of draft rental particulars for a cottage on the estate. The only thing that looked unusual was the opened envelope and a folded-over letter that had been taken out and left on the table. Atticus leaned down, reached for the letter and then stopped.

"When did this arrive?"

"This morning."

"Who else has touched it?"

"Just me. Why?"

"Do you have a piece of kitchen roll?"

She frowned. "Yes—but I don't understand. Why do you—"

"Please—if I could just have a piece."

She tore a square of paper from a roll on the counter and brought it across. Atticus thanked her, folded the paper in half and used it to cover the tips of his thumb and forefinger as he very carefully pinched the letter by the top edge and unfolded it.

The paper was cheap and greyish, the sort that came in multipacks from stationer's or supermarkets, coarse to the touch and thinner than standard printer paper. The letter had been written in large, block capitals with a thick black marker pen, the kind that might be used to label boxes in a garage. The strokes were heavy, the ink bleeding slightly into the fibres of the paper.

YOU TOOK OUR LAND. NOW YOU'LL PAY.

Emelia was biting her lip. "That's a threat—right?"

"It reads like one."

"What does it mean? 'You took our land'? Rupert's family have owned the Brookmere estate for five hundred years."

The letter was signed beneath with a single word, similarly capitalised:

SWING

Emelia pointed to the word. "I saw what you said on the TV. The Swing Riots. It's to do with that, isn't it?"

"Maybe," he said. "But it doesn't make much sense. I'm going to need to have a think about it."

He was also going to need to talk to Jez.

He examined the letter again. There were no identifying marks: no letterhead, no smudges, no fingerprints that he could see. The envelope was made of the same cheap paper stock, sealed with a heavy-handed swipe of Pritt Stick that had left a faint white residue along the flap.

"Where did you find it?"

"In the box with the rest of the mail from yesterday."

"Hand-delivered," Atticus mused. "No stamp or postmark. I don't suppose there's a camera there?"

"No," she said.

Atticus turned the envelope over and studied the front. It was blank.

No salutation, no sender.

"Whoever wrote this didn't want it traced. But they weren't as careful as they probably thought they were."

"What do you mean?"

He gestured toward the corner of the envelope. "See this?" he said. "There's a faint red mark—looks like oil or grease. It's been rubbed off, but not completely. I think we'll find that's a transfer from a gloved hand, maybe from handling tools or machinery." He tilted the letter toward the light streaming through the window. "And the way the marker's been used— look how uneven the pressure is. It's someone with strong hands, not used to writing neatly. And the angle of the strokes suggests someone who's left-handed."

"That's very specific."

He held the paper up. "The paper itself—see here? Faint crease down the left-hand side. That's not from folding—it's where the sheet was torn from a pad. A glued-top pad, not a spiral one."

"How does that help?"

"It tells us that the letter was written in a hurry, probably not at a desk. Someone grabbed what was to hand—a cheap pad, a fat marker, didn't even think to use a proper envelope. This wasn't planned days in advance—it was reactive. It was emotional."

"Someone got angry and wrote it on impulse?"

"Probably. This is someone local, someone who's personally invested with the family, and someone who wants to rattle the cage. They didn't bother to hide their handwriting properly— they didn't print the message or use a typewriter—and they didn't disguise the delivery. It's raw. They wanted to lash out in a way that wouldn't risk anything more than a slap on the wrist. Do you have a freezer bag?"

She fetched one from a drawer. Atticus took a photo of the letter and the envelope and then slid both items inside the bag. He picked up a pen from the table and wrote the date and time on the outside.

"You'll need to give this to the police," he said. "They can check for trace evidence. Just in case. I wouldn't be surprised if there's something useful—the sender hasn't been particularly careful."

58

Atticus told Emelia that he was going to have a look around the grounds before he searched the house. He went outside and walked out onto the lawns, making his way to the ancient yew and leaning his back against its trunk as he took out his phone and called Jez.

"Morning," he said. "How are you?"

"Slept like a baby," Jez said.

"Recovered?"

"Feels like it didn't happen. How was your evening?"

"Very interesting." He turned at the sound of a car approaching on the driveway and saw Celeste Ainsley arriving. "They've been squabbling over what'll happen to the estate when the Earl dies. He's been diagnosed with dementia, and it's brought everything into focus. There was a big argument the night before he disappeared."

"About the succession?"

"Yes. There's a lot at stake."

"And you think that's the motive?"

"It's *a* motive. The Earl's current will says that Emelia and his children will inherit, but he was going to change it so that it all went into trust with Henry as trustee. None of them were very happy about that apart from Henry."

"And then the Earl disappears, and Henry is murdered."

"I know. It's suspicious."

"Do you think it's one of them?"

"Too early to say."

Atticus paused as Celeste got out of her car and gazed over at him, he raised his hand in greeting, and she went inside.

"Still there?"

"I'm here," he said. "Something unusual happened this morning. I'm at Brookmere House now, and someone left a Swing letter in the post box."

"As in—"

"As in a threatening letter very similar to the ones that were sent to landowners in the 1830s."

"Saying what?"

"Nothing specific—a general threat. I took a photo. I'll send it to you once we're finished."

"What do you want me to do about it?"

"Go to the museum and speak to Ellie's expert. See what he thinks. I'd like to look into the possibility that there's a connection between the three dead men and this letter."

"Really?"

"I know—it's a stretch."

"A big stretch. They died two hundred years ago."

"But the land where the bodies were dug up used to be part of the Brookmere estate. George Ainsley was the landowner at the time those men were killed and buried. I know it's unlikely there's a link, but I'd still like you to look into it. If you can identify the men, maybe one of them has some kind of connection to what's happened."

"I'll try," Jez said.

"We also can't ignore the fact the bodies being dug up made the news this week, and I was talking about the riots and how they might be connected. It's more likely that it's someone trying to make a point."

Jez said he agreed.

"The Ainsleys also aren't very popular," Atticus said. "They've upset everyone with the solar farm, and I'm getting the impression that that's not the only reason people don't like them. But it'd be good to be able to strike that off as a motive."

"Anything on the Earl?"

"Nothing," Atticus said.

"He's dead, isn't he?"

"I'm almost certain of it."

"I'll set off now," Jez said. "Where's Bandit?"

"Upstairs with Jacob. He'll take Treacle too if you ask him nicely."

"What are you doing now?"

"I'm going to look around the house and see if I can find anything interesting."

"Have fun."

"Let me know if you find anything."

59

Alexander Freeman was on his way back into the city from the crematorium when he received the call. He pulled over and listened, his mood gradually curdling, as he learned that Atticus Priest had been instructed by the Ainsleys to help them understand the twin catastrophes that had befallen them. He finished the call and then stared into the middle distance as he tried to work out just how much of a threat he was facing. There'd been the odd bump on the road so far, but nothing he hadn't been able to handle.

This felt different.

The police could be an inconvenience, but Freeman could manage them.

Priest was a wildcard. He wasn't beholden to the rules that could hamper an official investigation; he was intelligent, methodical, tenacious; and, worse of all, he had a knack of making intuitive leaps that couldn't be predicted.

Freeman didn't fear anyone, but he respected problems.

And Atticus Priest was a problem.

If he was already sniffing around the Ainsleys, then it was only a matter of time before he caught Freeman's scent.

That meant decisions had to be made.

He opened his contacts and swiped down until he found the name of the man he wanted. He tapped to dial and watched the traffic heading into town as he waited for the call to connect.

"Hello?"

"It's Alexander Freeman."

"Hello, Mr. Freeman."

"I've just had some troubling news, and I think you might be able to help me deal with it. Where are you?"

"London."

"Can you get to Salisbury?"

"I can be there in two hours."

60

Atticus went back inside. Celeste and Emelia were in the kitchen, and the atmosphere was brittle: Emelia stood by the sink with her arms folded tightly across her chest, while Celeste perched on a stool at the kitchen island and looked down at the letter inside the freezer bag. Her face was pale, her jaw clenched tight, and her eyes shone with an anger barely held in check.

Celeste stabbed a finger at the letter. "It's from whoever did it... whoever it was who killed Henry. Isn't it?"

Atticus shook his head. "I'd be very surprised."

"Who, then?"

"I told Emelia—I'm going to look into it. I just spoke to my colleague, and we have some ideas. We'll be as quick as we can, but I'm afraid you'll have to be patient."

"It's the same person," Celeste said. "I know it."

Atticus turned to Emelia. "Have you told the police?"

"I called Robbie. He's coming over now."

"Good. I'll have a word with him when he gets here. In the meantime, do you think you could show me around the house?"

She unfolded her arms. "Of course. Where would you like to start?"

"The master bedroom?"

Emelia showed him through the house to a staircase and up to the first floor. They followed the landing to a large bedroom.

"This is it," she said, pausing by the door. "Shall I leave you to it?"

"If that's all right."

"I'll be downstairs if you need me."

Atticus thanked her, waited until her footsteps had faded away down the corridor and then turned back to the bedroom. It was spacious and stately, dominated by a heavy oak four-poster bed with dark green drapes, a matching antique wardrobe, and an imposing mahogany dresser. A large bay window overlooked the gardens.

He started with the wardrobe, flicking through Rupert's neatly arranged suits, running his hands through the pockets. There was nothing of note, so he went to the bedside table. He opened the top drawer and inspected the contents, again finding nothing of obvious relevance. He pulled open the lower drawer and saw a collection of books. He picked one up: a historical account of land management in the nineteenth century. He replaced it and shut the drawer.

He crossed the room to the dresser. The top was meticulously arranged; Atticus had already formed the opinion that Rupert wasn't the kind of man who left things lying around. There was a wooden valet tray holding a pair of reading glasses, a silver pen, and two business cards. Atticus picked up the first and saw it belonged to a partner at a firm of solicitors in Salisbury. The second was for a Dr. Daniel Kershaw, with a mix of medical and academic titles listed beneath his name. He was a bachelor of medicine and a bachelor of surgery with an MA and a PhD from Oxford and a Fellowship at the Royal College of Surgeons. There was a link to a website and a practice address listed in Southampton. Atticus took out his phone and visited the website. Kershaw had specialisms in multiple sclerosis, headaches, Parkinson's disease, epilepsy and dementia.

Atticus took photos of both cards.

He opened the top drawer of the dresser and saw underwear and neatly folded handkerchiefs. He checked beneath them, running his fingers along the base in case of a false bottom. There was nothing. He moved to the second drawer. More folded clothing: vests, T-shirts, all arranged with an almost military precision.

The bedroom had two en-suite bathrooms: his and hers. Atticus looked in Emelia's first, found nothing of interest, and crossed to Rupert's. It was a pleasant room, as well ordered as his side of the bedroom. The tiles were a soft, mottled grey, the fittings traditional but well maintained: polished chrome taps, a clawfoot tub beneath a frosted window, and a basin flanked by glass jars filled with cotton buds and neatly folded facecloths. A shaving kit stood to one side, the brush perfectly clean and the razor carefully dried.

Atticus opened the mirrored cabinet above the sink. The shelves inside were arranged with meticulous care. There was a bottle of cologne, a small tin of balm for razor burn, and an orange-capped prescription bottle. He picked it up and looked at the label: amlodipine, 10mg, for hypertension.

He put the bottle back and opened a drawer in the counter. He took out a blood pressure monitor and a notebook. He opened the notebook and turned to the first page. Three columns: the date, then space for Rupert to record his systolic and diastolic blood pressure. The readings started eighteen months ago and were all high: 160/98, 165/102, 158/100. He turned the pages and found a horizontal line across the page, it was a year ago, and the numbers started to level out before settling into a much more regular pattern: 125/82, 122/80, 130/85. Atticus flipped the page again until he came to the readings for the most recent months. They were higher again: 156/99, 161/103, 158/105.

He put the pills back and went back into the bedroom. Emelia was standing in the doorway.

"Anything?"

"Rupert's taking medication."

"Blood pressure. It was high, but the pills helped."

He went over to the dresser and picked up the business cards. "And I found these."

She held up the lawyer's card. "Lucinda's been doing conveyancing work for the estate."

"Buying or selling?"

"I only found this out when we had the meeting before he disappeared. Rupert's been trying to expand. His father sold off a big chunk in the sixties. Rupert says it broke him—said he was ashamed of it. He wants to put things back the way they used to be."

"Who was he seeing about getting the will changed?"

"Same firm, different partner." She screwed up her face, trying to remember. "Can't recall the name, but I could find it if it'd help. Rupert was supposed to be going in for a meeting with them on the afternoon of the day he went missing. I called to check, and he didn't turn up."

Atticus held up the second card. "Dr. Kershaw?"

"That's who he's been seeing for the dementia."

He put the cards down again. "Could I have a look in his study?"

61

They went back downstairs again, and Emelia led the way to the library. It was an impressive space: walls lined with mahogany bookcases filled with hardbacks ranging from antique leather-bound volumes to modern first editions; a rolling ladder fixed to a brass rail to allow access to the upper shelves; heavy velvet curtains hanging to the sides of the arched windows; a Persian rug covering most of the floor, the pattern worn in places. It smelled of old paper and cigar smoke.

Atticus went over to the desk. The surface was a testament to Rupert's meticulous nature and was mostly clear save for a closed laptop, a heavy silver pen, and a leather-bound notebook with a matching strap keeping it shut. A brass letter opener lay beside a neat stack of correspondence.

Atticus picked up the envelope at the top of the stack. It was large: A4 size, thick cream paper with a high cotton content, clearly expensive. The seal had been opened carefully with a blade, the tear neat and straight. He tipped the contents out onto the desk and saw a series of medical scans. They were printed on thick acetate sheets, semi-translucent with high-contrast monochrome images in rows of four.

"Those are from Rupert's MRI," Emelia said. "Dr. Kershaw came around with them on Monday."

The images showed Rupert's brain from various angles: axial, sagittal, and coronal slices. Atticus wasn't qualified to interpret them, but the annotations printed along the edges—"posterior cortical atrophy suspected" and "ventricular enlargement noted"—were suggestive.

Atticus laid the scans on the desk, took his phone and snapped photographs of each of them. He gathered them up, put them back into the envelope and then filtered through the rest of the stack. Most of it was mundane: a quarterly newsletter from Historic England, a water bill, a letter from a charity soliciting donations, a flyer for a wine-tasting event at a business in the city, a draft invoice addressed to Nathalie Elms for rent due from a livery business.

He put the envelopes down and tried the desk drawer. It was locked.

"Do you know where he'd keep the key?"

"Probably on his keyring."

"And where would that be?"

"With him."

Atticus opened the laptop and tapped the keyboard to wake it; a dialogue popped up asking for a password.

"And this?"

"Sorry—I'm afraid I'm not being very helpful."

"Could he have written it down somewhere?"

"Maybe, but I don't know where."

She hovered by the door.

Atticus glanced up. "Leave me to it again if you like. I'll shout if I need you."

She gave a nod. "I'll be in the kitchen. Can I make you a coffee?"

"That'd be nice."

She left him alone again, and Atticus turned his attention back to the room. He left the laptop and began a search of the rest of the study. He went to the filing cabinet against the far wall. It wasn't locked, but a quick scan revealed only mundane documents: bank statements, property deeds, old invoices. If there was something Rupert didn't want people finding, he'd hidden it well.

Atticus went to the door to be sure that Emelia wasn't nearby and then turned his attention back to the desk. He reached into his pocket and took out his picks, selecting a tension wrench and a hook. He inserted both into the keyhole and felt for the pins. The first two clicked easily, but the third resisted. He adjusted the tension, worked the pick with delicate precision, and, after another moment, the mechanism gave with a quiet *snick*.

He eased the drawer open and took out the contents: a bundle of papers bound with an elastic band, a small leather wallet, and a mobile phone.

The papers were financial documents: printouts from an online bank account in Henry's name detailing a series of monthly payments—modest but consistent—sent to an account in the name of Cressida Ltd. over the last eighteen months.

He turned to the wallet. It was unremarkable: brown leather, worn corners. Inside were two receipts—both for the

Grey Hound in Broughton, dated months apart—and a note written in looping handwriting:

> *See you next week. I'll leave the key like always.*
> *Please be careful.*

Atticus photographed it.

The phone was interesting, Emelia had said Rupert had taken his with him, but that its location had stopped pinging soon after he'd left the house, most likely because he'd switched it off. Why would he have a second phone? As a spare? He powered it up, waited for the screen to come alive and saw, to his surprise, that it wasn't password protected. It was an old Nokia dumb phone with only two apps: messaging and the camera.

He opened the messages.

There was one thread from a number that hadn't been linked to a contact.

Atticus scrolled through.

Two messages in the exchange.

He read.

>> Can't wait to see you again <<

>> Me too. Last night was amazing <<

Atticus frowned. So this was why the phone had been hidden, it wasn't a spare, it was a second phone for Rupert to contact someone without Emelia's knowledge.

He tapped to open the gallery and saw a dozen photographs. They were mostly of the same woman: early thirties, striking red-gold hair usually tied back in a loose ponytail, a tanned, weathered complexion, and the wiry build of someone who spent most of her time outdoors. Her features

were strong—wide mouth, angular jaw, dark green eyes—
and there was something earthy and self-assured in her
expression. In most of the photos she was wearing jeans and
boots, sometimes a padded vest over a flannel shirt. A couple
were selfies taken indoors: one in front of a mirror in what
looked like a modest kitchen, another where she lay in bed,
tousled and half-covered by a duvet, smiling up at the camera.
There was an intimacy to the shots. A few were obviously
posed, sent deliberately, while others had the grainy, hurried
look of photos taken in stolen moments.

Atticus went back to the bank statements. He opened a
browser window on his phone and navigated to the website
for Companies House. He typed the name of the company—
Cressida Ltd.—into the search bar and skimmed the half page
of results. There was a company with that name registered to an
address on Easton Common Lane, Middle Winterslow, that
offered livery for horses.

He paused and closed his eyes, thinking.

The address was familiar.

He typed it into his phone and realised why.

It was where Jez said his fight with Henry Ainsley had
taken place.

Cressida Ltd. traded under the name Orchard View Stables.
Atticus Googled it and found a simple, slightly outdated
website built on a DIY platform. The homepage featured
a banner image of a large timber-clad stable yard flanked by
paddocks with sweeping countryside in the background.
Below the image, a tagline read: 'Friendly, professional livery
in the heart of rural Wiltshire. Full, part and assisted livery
options available.' He scrolled down and saw a list of services:

daily turnout, mucking out, feeding, rug changing, exercising, and twenty-four-hour supervision. The website mentioned on-site accommodation for the manager and direct access to the Clarendon Way.

A short About Us section followed, with a single line: 'Run by Nathalie Elms, a lifelong horsewoman with over fifteen years' experience.'

There were a dozen photos: well-maintained stables, a sand arena, several horses grazing in small paddocks, and one image of a woman standing beside a bay mare, smiling toward the camera. The photo was taken at a distance, but even so, Atticus could see enough.

It was the same woman from the photographs kept on the hidden phone.

He had a face to match the name.

He had a location.

And a connection with Rupert.

Atticus checked that he had photos of everything—the receipts, the note, the text conversation, the photos—and then carefully replaced the items in the drawer and locked it again.

He went into the kitchen. Emelia had prepared two mugs of coffee and was reaching into the cupboard for additional mugs.

"Find anything?"

"Not really," Atticus said.

She nodded to the window. "The police are here."

Atticus looked out and saw Mack's car.

She was making her way to the door with Robbie Best behind her.

62

Atticus waited in the kitchen but was able to hear the conversation when Emelia opened the door and invited Mack and Robbie to come inside.

"Thank you for coming."

"Of course," Mack said. "How are you getting on?"

"Didn't sleep much last night."

"I'm not surprised."

"Do you have anything about Rupert?"

"Not yet."

"Really? *Nothing*?"

"We're bringing in more officers to help look this morning."

"How can he just disappear? How is that even *possible*?"

"I understand the frustration—I really do. We're doing everything we can."

"What about Henry?"

"We have a number of lines of enquiry, and I'm hopeful we'll make progress today. I'd like to have a talk with you about a possible change in strategy later, too, if that's all right. We've been very quiet about this so far, and I wonder whether now might be the time to go public."

"I didn't want to," Emelia said.

"I know. But things have changed."

Emelia nodded.

"I could bring in a hundred officers," Mack said, "but that's still nothing compared to having local people keeping an eye open—and they can only do that if we ask them."

"We can have a chat about it later," Robbie said, taking over. "You said you had something you wanted us to look at."

"Yes. Please—come in. It's in the kitchen."

They came through. Mack and Robbie must have seen Atticus's Volvo next to the house, so both had mastered any surprise that they might otherwise have shown upon seeing him sitting at the table.

"This is Atticus Priest," Emelia said.

"We know each other," Mack said.

"Of course. You used to work together."

"We did."

"I hired Atticus yesterday to help us. I hope that's not treading on any toes?"

"Not at all," Mack said. "We've always been able to work together without getting into each other's way."

Mack caught Atticus's eye, and he was relieved to see the little upturn of her mouth that was one of her easiest tells: she was amused to see him rather than annoyed.

Emelia invited them to sit at the table.

"The letter," Robbie said. "Could we have a look?"

Atticus took the bagged-up letter and slid it across the table. "Hand-delivered at some point between yesterday morning and this morning. No cameras covering the post box, unfortunately."

Robbie read it and frowned.

"You see?" Emelia said. "It's like I told you—it's a threat."

Mack read it and then turned to Atticus. "What do you think?"

"It ties in with something we found at the dig in Pitton."

Mack encouraged him to go on, so he explained his theory: that the three men had been executed and buried after vandalising a threshing machine during the riots of 1830. He told them that the disturbances had acquired their moniker— the Swing Riots—on account of the mythical leader of the working men, the vengeful Captain Swing who was reputed to send threatening letters to the landowners oppressing the poor.

"It's a working theory at the moment," he said. "I'd like to look into it a bit more before I put my name to it."

"Go on, then," Robbie said, tapping a finger against the letter. "Why was it sent?"

"Three possible explanations." Atticus raised his index finger. "The first explanation is that it was sent by someone who knows what happened to Rupert and Henry."

"That's the easiest conclusion to draw."

"And the laziest. It's also the easiest explanation to dismiss. We know that Henry was killed at some point on Wednesday, probably in the late morning or early afternoon."

"That's what Fyfe thought at the PM," Mack said. "Eight or nine hours before he was found."

"My interview about the excavations and the connection to Captain Swing was on TV that evening. So the only people who knew about what we'd found before Henry was killed are me and the archaeologists, and I'm sure it wasn't them. If it was sent by the person who killed Henry, it'd have to be a *staggering* coincidence—someone was inspired by the Swing Riots at almost exactly the same time as three men were dug up who had a possible connection to the riots. The odds of *both* of those things happening at the same time are miniscule. I think we can safely dismiss it."

"Agreed," Mack said.

Robbie nodded, too. "The other explanations?"

"There is an element of coincidence that we'll have to accept—that the letter, which I'll accept looks very much like a threat, was sent by someone who wanted to frighten the Ainsleys but *didn't* know about Rupert and Henry. I'm not fond of coincidences, but I think relying on coincidence as an explanation might be unavoidable in this case." He raised his forefinger. "So, number two—the letter was sent by someone who has a link going all the way back to whatever happened to the three men and wants to make the Ainsleys fearful."

Robbie looked bemused. "Seriously? What are you saying— a *descendant* sent it?"

"I said it was possible. I didn't say it was likely."

"We can dismiss that for now," Mack said.

"I agree." Atticus raised his thumb. "Number three— the letter's from someone who has a grudge against the family. They saw the TV report about the bodies being dug up and heard what I said about what might've happened in the 1830s. What do we know about the riots? They were aimed at landowners and farmers taking advantage of workers. You've already said there are local people who feel that the Ainsleys have been taking advantage of them—maybe one of them was watching the TV and saw what'd been dug up in the field, thought it'd be fun to stir things up a little and sent this. They wouldn't have known about what had happened to Rupert and Henry."

"It's *not* connected to them, then?" Emelia said.

"Not directly," Atticus said. "Like I said—I think it's a coincidence."

Mack looked over at Atticus. "A word?"

63

Mack took Atticus outside into the hallway and closed the door so they wouldn't be overheard.

"You *hate* coincidences."

"I do," he said, "but I also accept that they happen from time to time. The alternatives here are more salacious, but I don't think they're as credible."

"The ancestors?"

"Jez is going to try to identify the remains."

"And you think that's possible? You think he can?"

"Difficult, but not impossible."

"All right," Mack said. "I'll have the letter analysed."

"My guess is that'll get you something useful. Whoever sent it wasn't careful. I think it was sent impetuously by someone acting before thinking."

She nodded.

"You'll let me know if you find anything?"

"I'll think about it," she said. "It depends if you're in a reciprocal mood. You didn't think to tell me about being instructed to act for the family?"

"I didn't know she wanted me to help until late last night. She turned up at my office unannounced. I was going to tell you when you got home, but it was late, and I was tired."

"You were asleep when I got back."

"And I was out before you were awake this morning. It's not a secret—I just didn't have a chance to tell you, and I thought you probably had enough on your plate."

"That's true. Beckton's involved now. He was supposed to attend Rupert's birthday party tomorrow. Emelia's been onto him, and he's been onto me, asking why we haven't found Rupert. I told him I'm starting to get worried that we *won't* find him."

"You won't," Atticus said. "Not alive, anyway."

"You think that, too?"

"Whoever killed Henry killed Rupert."

Mack sighed. "Emelia said she was worried about suicide. The diagnosis must've been hard for him to accept, and Emelia and the children all said they'd had a big bust-up the night before he disappeared."

"Suicide would've been my guess, too, but then you found Henry."

"What do you think about the family?"

He chuckled. "All unpleasant."

"Unpleasant enough to be involved?"

"They've all got the motive—he was going to change his will, and that'd be bad for them. I don't know beyond that."

"I'm going to arrange interviews with them this afternoon."

Atticus paused, wondering whether to tell Mack about the discoveries he'd made before she arrived.

She noticed his distraction. "What is it?"

He was caught between telling her about Nathalie Elms and keeping his own counsel. He decided to tell her a little, but not everything.

"I think Rupert was having an affair."

"How do you know that?"

"I can't tell you that—not yet."

"Atticus…"

"I'm not sure," he lied. "I could be wrong. I'd like to be more confident."

"Who?"

"Don't know that yet," he said, lying again.

Mack stared at him, weighing up whether she believed him or not. Atticus found he regretted saying anything at all. He hated being dishonest with her, but he knew that if he revealed that he knew any more—the fact that he'd already identified Nathalie, that he knew where she lived, and that Jez and Henry's fight took place nearby on the day that Henry was subsequently murdered—then he would lose his chance to investigate her involvement in whatever had happened.

She eyed him. "You'll tell me as soon as you find anything out?"

"Of *course*," he said with mild indignation.

"Don't give me that," she said.

"What?"

"Pretending to be offended. It wouldn't be the first time you've kept something back."

"If I find anything, I'll tell you—I promise."

The kitchen door opened before Mack could object any further.

It was Emelia. "I've spoken to Robbie," she said. "You really think posting on social media is a good idea?"

Mack shared a final look with Atticus, then turned away from him. "I do," she said. "Shall we talk about it?"

Atticus took the opportunity to make his exit.

64

Jez's instinct was that it was going to be next to impossible to identify a trio of disappearing machine-breakers whose remains had been buried in a field for nearly two hundred years, but he had promised Atticus he would try. He went to Salisbury Museum and told the man on the desk that he was there to meet Sam Fairweather. The man said he'd call him and asked him to wait.

He went over to the side of the room and picked up a tourist leaflet with a map of Salisbury. He looked at it, vaguely interested, his thoughts turning to the task that Atticus had set him. The three men had almost certainly been killed because of their involvement in the Swing Riots, and the letter that had been sent to the Ainsleys was signed Swing; it was possible that the letter had nothing to do with what had happened to Ainsley, but the timing was suspicious. Vengeance seemed like an unlikely motive, there would be no one alive to bear a grudge, and Jez didn't think the prospect of a descendant seeking revenge for something that happened so long ago was credible.

Jez had his own motive for solving the puzzle: he wanted to impress Atticus. It was difficult not to feel daunted by him, and some of the deductive leaps that Atticus made were so impressive that Jez had often felt completely out of his league. Atticus hadn't been able to offer anything to help him with this task; Jez knew it would be difficult to put names to the dead, and knew that, if he could, it would win him admiration— grudging, perhaps, but it all counted—from Atticus.

"Hello, you."

Jez turned; Ellie was standing behind him, grinning.

He smiled back. "Hello."

She wore a navy jumper, and her jeans were tucked into a pair of well-worn boots. Her hair was pinned up in a messy bun, a pencil stuck through it, and there was a smudge of something—soil or charcoal—on her cheek. She looked like she'd come straight from the dig, and Jez found the contrast striking: intelligent, earthy, completely at ease in her skin. Her eyes crinkled when she smiled at him, and Jez felt a flush of warmth.

"I didn't know you were going to be here," he said.

"Likewise," she said. "What are you up to?"

"I've come to see Sam. Atticus asked me to try to identify the remains."

"Long shot."

"Very, but I don't mind trying. What about you?"

"Here to see Sam, too. We found something last night before we finished up at the field. I think I know what it is, but I wanted to get it confirmed before I told you and Atticus."

She reached into her pocket and took out a clear plastic evidence bag. She held it by the corner so that it dangled, and Jez could see what was inside: a small, crudely stamped copper disc, about the size of an old penny, with the faint impression of a number on the side that Jez could see.

"What is that? A coin?"

"Not sure. But Sam will know."

"He's just on the phone," the man on the desk said. "He'll be with you as soon as he can. Go inside and wait for him if you like."

They went through into the first gallery and ambled up to a glass display cabinet with objects dug up at Stonehenge and Old Sarum.

"Been here before?" Ellie asked him.

"Never."

"I used to come with my mum and dad," she said. "They took me to places like this all the time. Did I tell you about them?"

"You didn't."

"Both archaeologists. Probably inevitable I'd follow in their footsteps. They used to pick places to go on holiday after making sure there was a good selection of ruins that we could visit."

"But now you're going to be doing something different," he said.

"Eventually. Got to get my qualifications first."

They continued further into the gallery.

She reached for his hand and gave it a squeeze. "The other night was fun."

"It was."

"Did you tell Atticus?"

"Didn't need to. He knew straight away."

"Same clothes as the day before?"

Jez nodded. "He's much too observant to miss something like that."

They heard footsteps and turned to see Sam Fairweather. Ellie released Jez's hand, reaching out to offer it for Sam to shake instead.

"Morning. Didn't expect to see *both* of you."

"I came on the off chance you'd be here," Ellie said. She held out the bagged token. "Found something at the dig, and I wanted the benefit of your expertise."

He took it and gave it a quick look. "That's a workhouse token."

"I thought it might be."

"Where did you find it?"

"Near the bodies. We were just finishing up when I noticed it."

"Someone is going to have to explain that for my benefit," Jez said.

Sam nodded. "Workhouse tokens were currency issued by individual workhouses, usually stamped with its name or initials." He stopped. "You know what workhouses were?"

"I've read my Dickens," he said. "Places where the poor were sent to work in exchange for food and shelter."

"Victorian poverty prisons, basically," Ellie added.

"Close enough," Sam said. "The poor worked, and then they were paid with these. If we go back to the start of the nineteenth century, there was a shortage of real coins, so they minted these tokens out of copper instead. The workers would spend them in local shops; the shops took the tokens to the workhouse; the workhouse exchanged them for cash."

"You said they were stamped—is this one?"

He opened the bag and took the token out, turning it in his fingers. He squinted. "Looks like it, but it's hard to see."

He licked his thumb and used it to clean both surfaces of the token. "Here we go. It'll need to be cleaned up properly, but you can just make it out. See here?" He turned the token so that Jez and Ellie could see it and, specifically, the capitalised FARLEY that was just visible through the patina of grime. "There was a poorhouse in Penny's Lane in Farley until 1834—that's when they moved the poor from the parishes around the city into the new Alderbury Union workhouse."

"That's all fascinating," Jez said, "but it doesn't identify the man who had it."

"But it'll get you a little closer. We're thinking 1830 for the men—yes?"

"That's what Atticus thinks."

"So let's have a look at the Admission and Discharge Register for the poorhouse. The hard copy's kept in Swindon, but you're in luck: I digitised all the registers from the poorhouses near Salisbury last year."

65

It took Atticus ten minutes to drive from Brookmere House to Winterslow. He followed the directions on his phone to the address of the livery yard he'd Googled, parked on the road a little way down from the gate and went the rest of the way on foot.

It was an impressive facility: a wide gravel drive led past a smart timber-clad office with a slate roof, opening out onto a central courtyard framed by two long, low brick stable blocks with dark green doors. The buildings were modern but sensitively styled, with flower tubs placed at intervals and fresh hay poking from nets hung on open stable doors. Beyond the yard, the land dropped gently away to a view of neat paddocks enclosed by post-and-rail fencing, where several horses grazed, their tails flicking at flies. To one side, a large floodlit outdoor arena was bordered by a mirrored wall, and in the distance, gallops curved between lines of hedgerow and mature oak trees.

He opened the gate and followed the drive to the buildings. He could hear the sound of a radio, and as he turned the corner, he saw a woman mucking out one of the stables. She had a wheelbarrow outside the open door and was using a pitchfork to remove wet straw that smelled of ammonia.

"Hello," he said.

She turned, saw him and frowned. "Hello."

"Nathalie?"

She rested the pitchfork against the wall. "Who's asking?"

"My name's Atticus."

"Sorry—what?"

"I know," he said with a shrug and a smile. "Weird name. Blame my parents."

"How can I help you?"

"I was hoping we might be able to have a chat. I'm working for the Ainsley family."

He watched her face for a reaction and saw obvious defensiveness: her jaw tightened, and she blinked more than was natural.

"Who?"

"I'm a private investigator. You know who they are, and I'm sure you can work out why they've hired me."

Her arms crossed over her chest, and she shifted her weight onto one foot, leaning back a little.

"I know about you and Rupert. And I know you know he's missing. I'm trying to help find him. Please—could we have a talk?"

She bit the corner of her mouth. "I don't know where he is, and I don't want to get involved. That family…" She shuddered. "That family is *crazy*."

She turned, reached down for the handles of the wheelbarrow and started towards a large muck heap.

Atticus wasn't about to give up as easily as that.

"What about Henry? I know he came to see you the day before yesterday."

Atticus *didn't* know that—at least not for sure—but he was confident and thought the risk of reaching the wrong conclusion was one worth taking.

"I've got nothing to say. You're trespassing on private property. Please leave or—"

"Henry's been found dead, Nathalie. And you would've been one of the last people to see him alive."

She stopped and, after a beat to lower the wheelbarrow, turned back to face him. "*What?*"

"Murdered. The police don't know he came to see you yet, but they will. Speak to me now and I'll tell you what I know so it won't be a surprise when they get here."

The colour drained from her face, and, for a moment, Atticus thought she was going to fall. She stepped back and grabbed the top bar of a nearby gate to steady herself.

"*Murdered?*"

"Yes."

"Where?"

"His body was found in a farmer's yard on the other side of Winterslow. Not very far from here." He held up his hands in an attempt to show her he meant her no harm. "I know it has nothing to do with you. I think he came to see you to ask whether you could help find his father. Like I said—I know about you and him."

"If Henry's been murdered…" Her words petered out.

"Yes," Atticus said for her. "I'm afraid it's very likely that Rupert's been murdered, too."

Nathalie closed her eyes, and this time, her knees did buckle. She stumbled but managed to hold herself up.

"You should sit down. Could we go inside? I'll tell you what I know, and maybe you can help me understand some of the things I don't."

66

The house was as impressive as the facilities outside. It was a long, low-built Georgian farmhouse, constructed from Chilmark stone with sash windows framed in white and a slate roof that glinted in the sunlight. Nathalie led the way to the front door, opened it and went inside. The hallway had exposed wooden beams overhead and flagstone floors. A boot room off to the right was strewn with riding gear: muddy boots lined up beneath a wooden bench, jackets hanging on a row of brass hooks, a saddle slung over a rail.

"Let's go into the sitting room," she said, pointing down the hall.

The room was bright and spacious, with oak floorboards, an open hearth stacked with logs, and large windows that looked out over the paddocks.

"Please," she said. "Sit down."

Atticus did.

"Would you like a drink?"

"A coffee would be lovely."

"Just a moment."

She left the room and went down the hall; Atticus thought he could hear sniffling. He took the opportunity to look around. The furniture was a blend of vintage and modern: a deep, linen-covered sofa, a couple of mid-century armchairs, and a farmhouse-style table beneath a wrought-iron chandelier. On the walls were framed photographs of horses mid-jump, prize ribbons arranged in orderly rows, and a single, slightly faded newspaper clipping mounted behind glass. He went to the mantelpiece and looked through the framed photographs, his eye stopping on one of Nathalie with Rupert. It looked like some sort of equestrian event, with both of them in jodhpurs and riding boots and both holding colourful rosettes up to the camera.

He heard the sound of her returning footsteps and moved over to the window.

"Coffee," she said, putting a tray with a cafetière and two mugs down on a side table.

"This is very impressive," Atticus said, gesturing to include the house and the land outside the window. "Do you own it all?"

"My company rents it," she said.

"Is Rupert involved with the business?"

She poured coffee for him. "The Brookmere estate is the landlord."

She handed him the mug, and they both went to sit down.

"How did you meet?"

"I was riding an event at Larkhill, and he was there. You know he rides?"

"I didn't."

"He loves horses. He was a very good rider when he was younger. He competed at Badminton for years. Still very capable now."

Nathalie was using the present tense; Atticus's suggestion that Rupert was very likely dead hadn't been accepted yet. He didn't correct her.

"My box was parked next to his," she said. "We had a wait before the time we were due to compete and got talking. I was looking for a yard for my business, and he said he might be able to help. I didn't know who he was then—he was just another rider."

"You got on well, though?"

She nodded. "He took my number and said he'd give me a call. He did, we started to talk, and he offered me this place."

Atticus needed to nudge the conversation on to more personal subjects and trod carefully for fear of offending her or frightening her into closing down again. "The two of you became close?"

"Over time. And before you say anything, it wasn't anything to do with the money. I knew his surname was Ainsley, and obviously I Googled him and worked out who he was, but I don't care about any of that. He's a lovely man, and we bonded over horses. We got to know each other better, and over time—over *months*—we got closer and closer, and then one thing led to another."

"I'm not interested in the reasons for your relationship. It doesn't make a difference to me. I just want to find out what happened."

"You know he was having trouble at home?"

Atticus feigned ignorance. "How do you mean?"

"His family—you've met them?"

"I have."

"And?"

Atticus shrugged. "Eccentric."

"*Insane*," she corrected. "They'd been arguing about what happens to the estate when he dies. The inheritance. His kids fought over it like cats in a sack for years—the will was going to give it to them and Emelia, but none of them were happy with how long it was going to take and the tax they'd have to pay. They didn't want to wait. They wanted him to sell up and distribute the money now, and Rupert had had enough. He called me the day he disappeared. There was an argument the night before—did they tell you?"

"I know a little."

"They ganged up on him and told him they didn't want to wait—he told me it was the final straw."

"I was told he didn't want the estate to be split up."

"He didn't. He told me he was going to change the will so it was all kept in trust. That way, the estate couldn't be sold unless all of the trustees agreed."

"Do you know who he wanted as trustees?"

"Henry was one," she said, "and he was going to ask one of the partners at the law firm in the city he uses."

She bit her lip.

"And you?"

"Yes," she said. "He said he'd change the will, and then he'd tell his wife. You've met her?"

"She instructed me."

"How was she?"

"Very concerned."

She snorted derisively. "It's an act. She doesn't care about him. I doubt she ever did. It's all about the money. The marriage is a sham. He was always going to leave her."

"So the two of you could be together?"

"I told him I wasn't interested in his money. I told him I was happy here, and I wasn't going to move into the house, but he said I'd be able to move the horses to the stables they have there. There's more land, obviously. Hundreds of acres. I hadn't made my mind up about that."

"Did he tell you whether he was going to give you a bequest in the will?"

She paused, then nodded.

"I'm not asking because that gives you a motive for wanting something to happen to him. It's the opposite. The will would need to be changed for you to benefit—and if anything has happened to him, the will *won't* be changed."

"And I told you," she said firmly, "I'm not *interested* in his money. If he wants to give something to me? Fine. I won't say no. But that's not why the two of us are together. I love him, and he loves me."

Atticus knew she was going to have to work hard to persuade people of that, given that Rupert was rich and she was much younger than him, but his point about motive was well made; there was no reason for her to wish him ill.

67

Atticus watched Nathalie and saw nothing that made him think she was being deceitful. Reticence about the fact that she'd been seeing Rupert would have been understandable, but the shock of the news that Atticus had delivered had stripped all that away.

"We need to talk about Henry," he said.

"What happened to him?"

"He was beaten to death."

"Jesus," she muttered.

"When did he come to see you?"

"Around half ten. He walked up to the gate with his dogs. I'd never met him before, but I recognised him—he looks like Rupert."

"How was he?"

"Angry. He had a bruise on his face." She pointed to her right eye. "I asked if he was all right, and he said he'd had an argument with someone on the track about his dogs."

Jez didn't need anything to prove his innocence, but her account corroborated the time he'd given in his story. It was useful, too; between what Jez had said and what Nathalie was saying now, Atticus was able to fill in more of Henry's final hours.

"And Henry knew about you and Rupert?"

She nodded. "I don't *know* how he knew. Rupert never said."

"He didn't tell you how he knew?"

"No." She stared at him. "How do *you* know?"

"I found the phone he used to speak to you."

She rolled her eyes. "I was always telling him to be more careful, but he never listened."

"What did Henry want?"

"It was about Rupert—when I saw him last, did I have any idea where he was. I said I saw him at the weekend. I was riding at Tidworth, and he came to watch me. And then he called me the night before he went missing."

"To say what?"

"He told me about the argument, that he'd decided he was definitely going to change the will and that he'd arranged a meeting with the lawyers. Henry knew all that, too."

"How long was he here for?"

"Not long. Ten minutes."

"And after he left?"

"I was here with the horses. One of our mares has a keratoma—she just had surgery to take the tumour out of the hoof, and I have to change the dressing every day."

"Can you prove that? The police will ask."

"One of my grooms was here. And we've got cameras in the yard. I would've been with Apple for an hour, and then I would've taken Cohen into the yard for flatwork. That'll be on the camera, too."

"That's good."

"You mean I have an alibi."

"That's exactly what I mean."

"I don't have any reason to want to hurt Henry. And I certainly don't have a reason to want to hurt Rupert."

"I know. What about Emelia—she doesn't know about you and Rupert?"

"I don't think so. He said he wanted to tell her, but that he hadn't." She shrugged. "But then, on the other hand, he told me none of the family knew, and that wasn't right—Henry knew." She shrugged. "I *doubt* Emelia knew, but I can't say for sure."

"How was Rupert the last time you met? In himself, I mean."

"The same as always. He was always happy when he came here. Why?"

"The police were worried that Rupert's disappearance might've been to do with his dementia."

"'Dementia,'" she repeated, laughing bitterly. "That's bollocks. He didn't have dementia. There's no way."

"But he's been diagnosed. I've seen the scans."

She waved a hand.

"And Emelia and the children all said he's been forgetful."

"That's true," she admitted. "But so what? Who doesn't forget things when they get older? My dad used to forget where he parked the car—he'd swear up and down it was parked somewhere, and it'd end up somewhere else. But that wasn't dementia. He just became more absent-minded the older he got."

"The diagnosis was—"

"Dodgy." She spoke over him.

"Why do you think that?"

"Because I didn't believe it when he told me, and the more I thought about it, the more I thought the whole thing smelled *off*. They knew he was leaning towards changing his will. Emelia, his kids—all of them. They knew. He'd told them months ago he was thinking about it. They all benefited from the will as it was, and they didn't want him to change it. They'd lose everything. How could they stop him from changing his will? Why not make it look like he's lost his mind? Maybe then he *can't* change it."

She spread her hands, as if encouraging him to signal that he agreed with her thesis.

"I'm sorry, Nathalie, but that sounds tenuous."

"I know it does. I would've said that, too, but then I started to look into it, and I found proof that what they've been saying isn't right. You know the doctor who diagnosed him?"

Atticus nodded. "Kershaw."

"Daniel Kershaw. I looked up his record with the GMC." She went over to a folder on the table and opened it, rifled through the papers inside, and pulled out something she'd printed. "Look and tell me that's not *weird*."

The printout was of a search result from the registration and licensing page of the website of the General Medical Council. Daniel Brett Kershaw was listed as registered as a doctor, but there was a note to say he was suspended for twelve months.

"What did he do?"

She took out a second piece of paper and gave it to Atticus.

It was headed 'Warnings on the Registrant's Registration.'

Atticus read aloud: "'On 14 January 2025, Dr Daniel Kershaw was found to have removed prescription medicines from a hospital dispensary without authorisation, in breach of controlled substances regulations. This behaviour does not meet with the standards required of a doctor. It risks bringing the profession into disrepute and undermines public trust in the safe handling of medication. The required standards are set out in Good Medical Practice and associated guidance. In this case, paragraph 65 is particularly relevant: "You must make sure that your conduct justifies patients' trust in you and the public's trust in the profession." This failing is sufficiently serious to require a restriction on Dr Kershaw's registration. His registration is therefore suspended for a period of twelve months.'"

"See?" she said, pointing at the paper. "Rupert told me Kershaw was the best neurologist outside London. Does that look like the kind of thing you'd expect to see on the record of a doctor who's as good as he's supposed to be?"

"No," Atticus said. "It doesn't."

She took the printout back and waved it. "He shouldn't even have been practising!"

"Did Rupert know about this?"

"I only found out after he disappeared. I haven't had the chance to tell him."

"Did you tell Henry?"

"Yes. I showed him what I just showed you."

"What did he say?"

"He was shocked."

Atticus paused, a thought itching at him, an idea that he couldn't quite slot into the right place to understand it. He'd only been here fifteen minutes, and he'd learned a lot; his understanding of what had happened to Rupert and Henry had been nudged in a different direction, and he was going to have to let it marinate for a while.

He stood.

"Are you done?"

"I am. Thank you for your time."

"What happens now?"

"I'm going to have to mention what you told me to the police. They'll find out eventually, and if they do and they realise I didn't tell them... well, it wouldn't put me in their good graces. Or you. They'll send someone to talk to you."

"What do I tell them?"

"Just what you told me," Atticus said. "They'll have questions for you, but nothing that you need to worry about. You haven't done anything wrong."

68

Sam took Jez and Ellie into a room that looked as if it was used for research. There was a large bookcase along one wall, a desk with two computers and a printer. He wheeled in an additional chair from an adjoining office and arranged it and two others around one of the computers. He sat at the keyboard with Ellie on one side of him and Jez on the other and opened a database.

"They kept a register of anyone who was admitted to and discharged from the workhouse," he said. "A lot of the registers have survived. Very useful for genealogy. We digitised them so people can look at them when they're trying to put together their family trees. Here—this one is for Farley in 1830."

Jez looked at the headings across the top of the screen: Name, Age, Last Residence Before Admission, Condition, Calling and If Able-Bodied. The names and details of the poor were written in neat script beneath the headings; Jez counted to fifty and then stopped, estimating there were one hundred and fifty or so listed names.

"The only problem is how to work out which one had your token."

"I think I can do that." Ellie took out her phone and found the picture of the clasp knife. "We found this near the bodies."

Sam looked at the screen. "*S* and *L*."

Jez ran his finger down the screen until he reached Larke, Samuel.

He followed the entry to the right and saw that Larke was twenty-five when he entered the workhouse in June 1830, that he was single, that his calling was noted as farm labourer, that he was able-bodied and that his previous address was Peartree Cottage in Pitton.

"Samuel Larke," Sam said. "I think you've found one of your men."

69

Atticus left the yard and drove back to Brookmere House. He let his thoughts unspool. Meeting Nathalie had raised more questions than it had answered: about Rupert, about what kind of man he was, and about who might know the truth. The affair painted him in a new light and opened up motivations in people he hadn't previously considered might be suspects. He needed evidence to help guide him; there were hints of it now, just beginning to show through, but he needed more.

He called Jez as he turned onto the A30. "How are you getting on?"

"Got one of them," he said. "Samuel Larke. He was in the workhouse in Pitton."

"How did you find that out?"

"Ellie's here, too. She found a workhouse token, and we checked the register."

"*S* and *L*," Atticus said. "On the knife. Very good—well done. What about the others?"

"Still working on them."

"Try the newspapers."

"That's the next port of call. I'll let you know if we get anything."

Atticus turned at the junction and accelerated toward Pitton.

"I've had some luck, too," he said.

He recounted what he had discovered with Nathalie, adding that her account backed up what Jez had said about his encounter with Henry. He mentioned what he had discovered about Dr. Kershaw.

"What are you going to do about it?"

"I'm going back to the house," he said. "I have a couple of things to check."

"Do you know what happened?"

"I have a better idea than I did yesterday." Atticus pulled off the road and slowed in front of the gates to Brookmere House. "I'm here. Call me if you find anything."

* * *

Emelia opened the door to Atticus's knock.

"Anything?"

He'd already decided to delay telling her about the affair. Nathalie didn't think she knew about the relationship, and although Atticus knew he wouldn't be able to keep it from her forever, there was no benefit in revealing it now. He wasn't holding back to spare her feelings; he wanted to have the full picture before confronting anyone. When the time came to share the truth with the family, he wanted to observe their reactions with as much clarity—and leverage—as possible.

"I went to look at where they found Henry," he said instead.

"And?"

"Nothing very helpful, I'm afraid."

"What about Rupert?"

He shook his head. "No further on that, either." He followed her inside. "I'd like to have a look upstairs again."

"Where?"

"In your bedroom—is that okay?"

He would've liked to have gone alone, but Emelia led the way up the stairs again and into the master bedroom. Nothing had changed since Atticus's first visit. He went into Rupert's bathroom, opened the medicine cabinet and took out the jar of pills. He tipped out a handful, picked one up between thumb and forefinger and examined it: a small tablet, slightly scored down the middle, no distinct branding but similar in shape and colour to any number of generic drugs.

She looked at him quizzically. "What are you looking for?"

"Not sure."

He opened the drawer and took out the notebook that he'd seen before. He flipped it open and held it out so Emelia could see it.

"Have you seen this before?"

"No."

"Rupert was recording his blood pressure every morning. When did he start taking the pills? Eighteen months ago?"

"There or thereabouts."

Atticus turned back through the notebook to the first recorded readings.

"Here," he said. "This is eighteen months ago—before he started taking the pills. Look at the readings he was getting: 160 over 98, 165 over 102, 158 over 100—all consistently high." He flipped through until he was a month after the date that Rupert had started treatment. "And here, look at the difference the amlodipine made. The numbers go right back down to where we'd expect to see them: 125 over 82, 122 over 80, 130 over 85."

"He said things were getting better."

Atticus flipped forward to the most recent page of readings.

"But these are the numbers for the week before he disappeared: 148 over 96, 152 over 100, 160 over 105. Much higher again. And they've been higher for the last six months."

"That's... strange."

"He didn't say anything about it?"

"He said the readings were a little higher, but he didn't tell me how much higher."

"What do you think happened?"

"Stress? There's been a lot going on with the solar farm, then his diagnosis and the arguments about succession. Could that be it?"

"Maybe," he said, although he didn't think that was very likely at all.

He put the notebook down on the marble counter and took photographs of every page. He cupped his hand and carefully funnelled the pills so that they fell back into the vial. He held the container up so Emelia could see it.

"I'm going to borrow these for a day or two if that's all right."

"Yes—just make sure that they're here when Rupert gets back. He'll need them."

"Of course," Atticus said, although his confidence that Rupert would return was even less now than it had been before.

70

Robbie Best took Constables Fulbright and Collison with him to the protest camp on the A30. He could've gone alone, but it wasn't beyond the realm of possibility that Van Etting or the others there might take issue with the line of questioning he was going to have to pursue. Henry Ainsley had said he'd seen Van Etting and a second man vandalising the equipment at the solar farm, and that meant there was a decent chance that Robbie would need to take Van Etting back to the station for an interview under caution; he might not like that very much.

"What's he like?" Fulbright asked as they walked towards the access gate.

"Has a record. Couple of aggravated assault charges—got into a fight outside a pub in Frome, left the other bloke with a broken jaw. Then he was nicked for threatening behaviour at a housing protest in Bristol—threw a bottle at a security guard. Nothing that's seen him do serious time, but enough to suggest he's got a temper."

"Think he's in the frame for this?"

"No idea. There's been bad blood between him and the Ainsleys, and Henry said he had a run-in with him the night before he was killed." Robbie shrugged. "We'll see what he has to say. Just keep your eyes open."

Robbie opened the gate and led the way across the field to the camp. He'd pulled Van Etting's mugshot from his last arrest and recognised him standing by the smouldering fire.

"Mr. Van Etting?"

He turned to see Robbie and the two uniformed constables and took a step back. "Who's asking?"

He took out his warrant card and held it up so Van Etting could see it. "I'm Detective Inspector Best from Salisbury CID. Do you think we could have a word?"

"About?"

"You and the Ainsleys."

"What about them?"

"Just a couple of questions."

"Do I have a choice?"

"Absolutely," Robbie said calmly. "You're not under arrest. But if you'd rather not speak here, I can take you to the station, and we can have the conversation there—with a solicitor, if you'd prefer."

Van Etting clenched his jaw. "It's fine. We can talk here."

Robbie looked at him and tried to get a read. His tone was casual, but there was a tightness around his mouth and the faintest flicker of nerves in his eyes: tiny tells that he was more rattled than he wanted to let on. His arms were crossed, and his body angled slightly away, as if he was ready to walk. Robbie had seen it before: bravado covering apprehension.

"Did you know Rupert Ainsley is missing?"

"I'd heard that," he said.

"Really? Who told you?"

"His son was here on Tuesday night."

"Henry?"

"That's right."

"What did he want?"

"Asked whether we'd seen him."

Robbie nodded. "And did you speak to him?"

"No," Van Etting said. "It was Susannah."

"Who's that?"

"One of the protestors here."

"What did she tell him?"

"That we hadn't. When did he go missing?"

"Tuesday morning. He went to the solar farm, and that was the last time anyone saw him."

"It doesn't have anything to do with us."

"When did *you* last see him?"

"Never met him."

"Really?"

He shook his head. "We've tried to get a meeting with him to talk about what he's doing, but he's not interested. He sends his stooges when he wants to tell us something."

"When's the last time you saw Henry?"

Van Etting started to speak and then stopped; Robbie thought he noticed a flicker of unease pass across his face.

"Mr. Van Etting?"

"Tuesday morning. He came here to speak to us about the solar farm. He accused us of messing with the fence."

"Did you?"

Van Etting paused again.

"Answer the question, please."

"No," he said.

"You need to be *absolutely* sure about that. If I find out that you're lying to me, it won't look good for you."

"I don't understand," he said. "Has he accused us of doing something?"

"Let me just ask you again so we're completely clear—when was the last time you saw him?"

"I told you—Tuesday morning. Why do you keep asking me? What's he said?"

"Henry Ainsley was found dead on Wednesday."

Robbie eyed Van Etting carefully, watching for a reaction. He blinked, once, then again, but too slowly. His mouth opened, then closed without a word.

He swallowed. "Dead? How?"

"He was murdered."

Robbie saw the blood drain from Van Etting's face, leaving his skin pale and waxy. "That has *nothing* to do with me. I... I..."

Robbie hushed him with an upraised hand. "I'm going to ask you one more time, Mr. Van Etting. When was the last time you saw Henry Ainsley? I know it wasn't Tuesday morning."

"It was that night. Tuesday night."

"When?"

"Late—after eleven."

"Where?"

"The solar farm. I was there with Joseph."

"What were you doing?"

He started to speak and then stopped. "Do I need to speak to a lawyer?"

"I don't know, Mr. Van Etting. Do you?"

He chewed on the inside of his lip, then—evidently deciding it was better to be honest—inhaled deeply and then exhaled. "We went to damage the panels. We cut through the fence and smashed some of them with crowbars. And one of the inverters, too—we smashed it up."

"And you saw Henry?"

"He saw us as we were leaving."

"Go on."

"He tried to stop us, and there was a scuffle. All three of us ended up on our arses."

"You hit him?"

"I didn't. Joseph might've done, but it was nothing. Handbags."

"Who's Joseph?"

"Joseph Mason. He's someone I know. We've been to other protests together."

"Where can I find him?"

"London. He went back early Wednesday morning."

"But you can get in touch with him?"

"I have his phone number."

"I'll have that later, if you don't mind. But let's talk about Wednesday." Robbie eyed him again. "Where were *you*?"

"Here."

"All day?"

"I went into Salisbury in the afternoon."

"Anyone with you?"

Van Etting shook his head. "I was by myself." He bit down on his lip; he must have realised that he'd been asked to provide an alibi and couldn't. "Look—whatever happened to Ainsley, it hasn't got anything to do with me."

Robbie let the silence stretch, watching Van Etting squirm under the weight of his own words. Then he nodded, slowly and deliberately.

"You're not under arrest, Mr. Van Etting," he said. "But I'm going to need you to come with me."

Van Etting's eyes widened. "Why?"

"You've just admitted to trespass, criminal damage, and a confrontation with a man who was found dead the next day. I think you can appreciate why I'd want to take this further."

"I've told you what happened."

"And now you're going to tell it again—under caution, at the station. We'll also be collecting your clothing and shoes from that night, and we'll need your consent for DNA and prints."

Van Etting opened his mouth to object but seemed to think better of it.

Robbie turned to Fulbright. "Get transport arranged and call the custody sergeant. Tell him we're bringing one in for questioning."

71

Atticus drove back into the city and made his way to the police station. He parked in the car park, took out his phone and navigated to Facebook. He opened his feed and saw that a post had just been made from the police's account. It had a photograph of a smiling Henry Ainsley and was headed: 'Appeal for Information: Death of Henry Ainsley and Disappearance of Rupert Ainsley.'

Atticus read:

"We are appealing for information following the discovery of the body of Henry Ainsley, found near Winterslow on Wednesday morning. Henry was last seen that morning in the vicinity of the Clarendon Way, walking with his two dogs. His death is being treated as suspicious, and we are urging anyone who may have seen Henry or spoken to him that day to come forward. We are also appealing for help locating Henry's father, Rupert Ainsley, who has been reported missing. Rupert was last seen on Tuesday morning leaving Brookmere House near Pitton. He is described as a white male, approximately 6 feet tall, with thinning grey hair and a clean-shaven face. He was wearing a brown waxed jacket,

red corduroy trousers, and boots. Rupert is well known locally and may appear confused or distressed. If you have any information that may assist our enquiries—regarding either Henry or Rupert—please contact Wiltshire Police on 101, quoting incident number 63547837. Please share this appeal."

Atticus flicked down to the comments and saw that not all of them were sympathetic.

He'd texted Mack before leaving Brookmere House and said he needed to see her. She told him she was planning on getting some fresh air, and they could meet in the Greencroft. Atticus crossed the road and saw her by the children's play area; he jogged across.

"How are you?" he asked.

"Tired. Did you see the appeal?"

"Facebook? Just now."

"Radio, too, and I'm going to be on the local news tonight."

"Might help."

"Emelia didn't want to do it, but they've realised we've hit a brick wall, at least when it comes to Rupert. It's four days now, and we're no closer to finding out what's happened to him."

"I think we both know what's happened."

"Yes." She sighed. "I think we do."

They sat down on one of the park benches.

Atticus glanced over at Mack; she looked wrung out.

"What about Henry?"

"We might have an angle," she said. "Robbie went to speak to the protestors. One of them admitted to smashing up some of the solar panels on the night before Henry was killed. There were two of them—this man, Van Etting, and another one from London. Henry caught them at it. Van Etting said they came to blows."

"Henry had a fight with someone *else*?"

"We know he had a temper."

"What does Robbie think?"

"Not convinced it's him," she said, "but we'll see. He's asked for a solicitor to sit in on his interview. We're just waiting for her to get here, and then we'll see what he has to say for himself."

"Let me know if anything comes out of it."

She glanced over to him. "That's not like you."

"What's not?"

"You'd normally ask if you could watch."

"I don't need to watch."

"Because you've got something else?"

"Maybe."

"You *said* you wouldn't keep anything to yourself."

"And I won't."

She gestured for him to continue.

"I'm not sure I'm on the right track yet. That's why I wanted to see you. I need you to do something for me." He took out the jar of pills that he'd taken from Rupert's medicine cabinet and held it up.

"What's this?"

"Medication. Rupert was taking it."

She took the vial and looked at the label. "Amlodipine."

"For high blood pressure. He'd been on it for months."

"And? He's old—hypertension's not unusual, is it? My dad takes felodipine—same thing."

"I'd like you to get the pills tested."

"Why would I do that?"

"Humour me."

She raised an eyebrow. "You think it's something else?"

"I think it *might* be something else."

She stared at the vial for a moment, then gave a shrug and a nod. "All right."

"Can you expedite it?"

"I'll see what I can do."

"Thank you." He reached out for her hand and took it. "Want me to come over tonight?"

"I don't know what time I'll be able to get away. Beckton's coming in an hour—wants to know why we haven't made progress. Ten points for guessing who he blames."

"I could cook."

"I'll be too late."

"I'll leave it in the fridge. You can warm it up when you get in."

She squeezed his hand. "Warm up the bed for me, too?"

72

Atticus went back to the office, collected Bandit from Jacob and crossed the city again to Mack's house. He used his key to open up and went inside, Bandit leaping onto the sofa and immediately curling up to sleep.

He went into the kitchen, opened the fridge and looked at what he had to work with. There wasn't much: four eggs in the tray, half a red onion in a ziplock bag, some grated cheddar in a Tupperware tub, a handful of wrinkled cherry tomatoes, and a lone courgette hidden behind a bottle of wine. He took everything out and set it on the counter. He found a knob of butter and turned on the hob, setting a frying pan over a gentle heat. He diced the onion and courgette, halved the tomatoes, and beat the eggs in Mack's chipped mixing bowl. Once the butter was sizzling, he softened the onion and courgette first, then added the tomatoes until they blistered. He poured in the eggs and stirred slowly with a wooden spoon, folding in the grated cheese at the end. He plated up a portion for himself with a slice of toast from the bread bin, then transferred the rest into a clean container, letting it cool before snapping on the lid and slipping it into the fridge for Mack.

He went through to the living room, where Bandit was already snoring. He sat in Mack's spot on the sofa with the dog's weight pressed against his leg and took out his phone.

He wanted to build up a picture of the doctor who had diagnosed Rupert. Nathalie's reservations about him had been well made, and the more Atticus considered it, the more certain he became that Daniel Kershaw was central to what had happened, not just to Rupert, but—most likely—to Henry as well.

He wanted to know what kind of man he was dealing with.

He started with the obvious. A basic Google search turned up Kershaw's private clinic, a practice specialising in neurology run out of a Georgian townhouse in Southampton. The website was slick and professionally designed: pale blue accents, serif fonts, stock images of smiling families. There were glowing testimonials, a list of qualifications, and tastefully lit headshots of Kershaw himself: late thirties, wide smiles, expensive haircuts, expensive teeth.

He checked LinkedIn and found his work history. Kershaw had trained in London, undertaken research in Zurich, and had been practising privately for the last five years. The endorsements painted a picture of someone ambitious, charming, and media savvy.

But it was a slick veneer. The ruin of his reputation—and his inability to practise—wasn't mentioned. Atticus cross-checked the website's claims with the General Medical Council's online register and the disciplinary notice Nathalie had discovered. Kershaw had been suspended following a fitness-to-practise hearing. Digging further, he found reference in an archived local news report to an internal hospital investigation, followed by the police being called after Kershaw was caught attempting to remove a supply of diazepam from a secure dispensary. He hadn't been charged—only cautioned—but the GMC had acted swiftly, and the result was his suspension.

The restriction meant he wasn't permitted to treat patients independently. His clinic, Atticus now realised, operated in a legal grey area: Kershaw offered 'consultations' and 'second opinions,' but formal diagnoses or prescriptions were issued by other doctors on staff, most of whom were conveniently less qualified and less well known.

He kept digging.

Instagram was revealing. Kershaw had a public account and clearly enjoyed the limelight. There were selfies in conference lobbies, behind the wheel of a Mercedes coupe, on the deck of a yacht moored off Sandbanks. He'd tagged friends, but there were no signs of a spouse or children. It looked like he preferred his social ties to be transactional.

The latest post was from earlier that same evening: Kershaw grinning beside a branded hospitality board at Eastleigh Football Club, pint in hand, with the caption *Back to the Silverlake tomorrow—come on you Spitfires! #eastleighfc #matchday*

Atticus clicked the location tag and scrolled. Kershaw was in similar posts with other season ticket holders and was clearly a regular in the club's hospitality suite.

He jotted down the information he might be able to use. Kershaw liked football, yachts, expensive restaurants, boutique wine merchants.

It was plenty to go on.

He opened Eastleigh's website, navigated to the match-day hospitality page, and booked a table for one at tomorrow's game. He chose the same package Kershaw was likely to have: a pre-match meal, a seat in the sponsor's stand, and access to the bar.

He tucked his phone away, scratched Bandit behind the ears, and leaned back against the sofa.

He knew the type. Men like Kershaw built façades so thick they forgot what lay underneath. But everyone had weak spots: ego, insecurity, the need to be admired.

All Atticus had to do was find the seams. And then give them a pull.

PART 6

Saturday

73

Franny woke early. She'd forgotten to pull the curtains all the way across the window, and the dawn's light had fallen across her face.

She looked at the clock: half six.

She lay back and sighed; today was Saturday, and she'd been hoping for a lie-in. It'd been a long week, bookended by the discovery of the bodies in the field in Pitton and then the ongoing investigation into the murder of Henry Ainsley and the disappearance of his father. Robbie had suggested they go for a walk in the New Forest; they'd been talking about the walk from Brook to Minstead with a pitstop for a pint and something to eat at the Trusty Servant. She hadn't had nearly enough sleep and was going to need an infusion of caffeine if that was still going to be a prospect.

She reached for her phone and opened Facebook, looking for the post that had been made about the Ainsleys, but, before it could open, her phone buzzed in her hand with an incoming call.

She didn't recognise the number.

"Who is it?" Robbie grumbled.

"No idea."

"Don't answer."

"It's a Salisbury number. I'd better take it."

Robbie mumbled something about going back to sleep and turned over. Franny accepted the call and put the phone to her ear.

"Hello?"

"DS Patterson?"

It was a male voice; Franny thought she recognised it.

"It is," she said. "Who's calling?"

"It's Jack Turnbull." He paused. "From Pitton—you came out to look at the remains in my field."

Franny swung her legs out of bed, her toes sliding into her slippers. "Mr. Turnbull," she said, "it's half past six on a Saturday morning. Is everything okay?"

"I'm sorry for calling so early. I haven't slept all night. I waited for as long as I could, but I…" He trailed off.

Franny stood. She remembered him from before: gruff and taciturn. He didn't sound like that now. He sounded anxious.

"What is it, Mr. Turnbull? How can I help?"

"I think I've done something stupid—something really, really stupid."

Franny went to the window and looked out at St. Anne's Street. "What is it?"

"Could I see you?"

She blinked in the bright morning light and rubbed her eyes. "Of course. Do you want me to come to the farm?"

The relief in his voice was almost pitiable. "Would you?"

"Let me get up and get ready. I could be with you in an hour—how's that?"

"That's perfect. Thank you. I'll see you then."

He ended the call.

"Who was that?" Robbie said.

"Turnbull."

"Who?"

"The farmer who found the remains at Pitton."

"It's bloody early. What did he want?"

"Wants to talk."

"About?"

"Didn't say," she said, reaching for her dressing gown. "But he sounded frightened."

74

Robbie stopped the car and stared at the satnav. "Shit. Missed the turning."

Franny pointed. "Down there."

"I know, I know," Robbie grumbled.

He put the car into reverse and backed up beyond the junction he'd just passed. Franny hadn't visited the farmhouse before, but the map said this was the right way, and as they turned right, she saw a sign on the post-and-rail fence for Clarendon Rise Farm.

Franny had recounted the conversation with Turnbull to Robbie. He'd said she should've asked him to come to the station rather than going out to see him. She disagreed, suggesting that he'd sounded close to panic, and, after a little amiable bickering, he'd said that if she was determined to go to the farmhouse, then he was coming, too. It wasn't an unreasonable suggestion, given the context and what had been happening over the course of the last few days. Turnbull's stoic reserve had made him a difficult man to read, but his tone on the phone had put her on edge. Something had bothered him, and she was pleased to have Robbie with her to hear him out.

They drove down the unpaved track and parked in front of the farmhouse: a square, whitewashed building with a deep thatched roof. The roof's edges were crisply cut, the ridge line patterned with decorative scalloping. The house itself was modest, symmetrical and stout, with four tall sash windows on the front face and a smaller one above the front door. A small, pitched porch protruded above the entrance, supported by thin white posts and crowned with ageing zinc. A crooked flagstone path led through the lawn to the door, flanked on either side by low shrubs and flowers starting to come into bloom. Smoke curled faintly from the chimney.

Robbie pulled over, and they both got out.

"I'll do the talking," Franny said.

"He's all yours."

* * *

Turnbull looked dreadful: his eyes were red-rimmed and glassy, and the skin beneath them was puffy. His hair stuck out in clumps, he hadn't shaved, and his shirt was buttoned wrongly at the collar.

"Thanks for coming."

"Not a problem."

"And I'm sorry for disturbing you on a Saturday." He looked over her shoulder at Robbie. "I don't think we've met."

"Detective Inspector Best. I work with Francine."

Turnbull frowned, then gave a little nod. "Please—come in."

Franny went first with Robbie behind her. Turnbull led them into the kitchen at the back of the house and indicated that they should sit at the wooden table. "The kettle's on," he said, nodding to the Aga. "Coffee?"

He was procrastinating, but Franny was happy to let him move at whatever pace made him comfortable. It was obvious that he had something on his mind, and he was struggling to find the right way to approach it. There was a tremble to his hands as he found three mugs and prepared coffee for them all.

"So," Franny said, "what did you want to talk to me about?"

He hesitated. "I don't know whether I need a lawyer."

"Why? Have you done something?"

"No," he said, then, realising he wasn't making sense, added, "Not what it might look like, anyway."

She smiled reassuringly. "It's up to you. Get a lawyer if you think you need one, but we're here now, and if you think you have something important to say, you should probably just tell us."

He pursed his lips and glanced away, then turned back with a look of conviction on his face. "It's about the Ainsleys," he said.

Franny felt the hairs on the back of her neck stand up. "Okay. Go on."

He brought the mugs to the table, handed them out and then sat down. "I saw the Facebook post yesterday. The post about Henry's murder and Rupert going missing." He was paler now than he had been when he'd opened the door. "I just want to say, right at the start, before I say anything else, that I didn't do it. I had *nothing* to do with it."

"Why would you feel the need to tell us that?"

"Because what I'm about to tell you will make it *look* as if I did."

Franny risked a quick glance over at Robbie; he'd leaned forward a little, and the annoyance at being dragged out of bed on a Saturday morning was gone. He, like Franny, was taut with anticipation.

"What do you want to say?"

"Henry Ainsley and I had an argument outside the Nelson in Winterslow on Tuesday. There were witnesses. I don't know—you might've been told about it already?"

"Best if you tell us what happened," Franny suggested.

"The Ainsleys have been trying to buy my family's land for years. I don't know if you know—this all used to be part of the Brookmere estate. My grandad bought it from Rupert Ainsley's father in the sixties. They had a tax problem and had to sell off a chunk, and it was a buyer's market back then— we were able to get it at a good price. Rupert's been wanting to buy the land back for years. He makes an offer, we turn it down, he goes away telling us we're being short-sighted, that we'll sell eventually, and when we do, it'll be for less, but then he comes back a couple of years later and offers more. It's been like that for as long as I can remember. Family joke, really. Thing is, things are different now—the shoe's on the other foot."

"Because of the change to inheritance tax?"

He nodded. "My old man is on his last legs, and now it'll be the taxman coming after *us*, not them. Rupert made an offer two months ago for half of what the land's worth. I told him to clear off, but Henry came back the next week and said the offer was on the table for another week, and then they'd reduce it. And this time he did. Took two hundred thousand off."

"And do you have to sell?"

"I've looked at the books to see if there's any way we could get around it, but, if there is, I can't find it." He sipped his coffee; his hand was still shaking. "But that's not all they've done. Danny Peart—one of the lads who works on the farm—silly bugger had an accident last month. He was pumping up a tyre on one of the tractors when it exploded. It was his own fault—he's always been one for taking a shortcut, and he'd been drinking, too. He lost an eye. We've looked after him, and we would've kept looking after him, except he decided it'd be a good idea to report us to Health and Safety and then to sue us for damages." He breathed in and out, and Franny could see that he was angry. "We'd win if it went to trial, but that's not the way these things go. We can't afford a lawyer, and our insurance won't cover it. Danny's got lawyers— good ones from London—and they've made it clear they'll drag it out as long as they can, make it so expensive that we either have to settle and agree to pay him money we can't afford or try to fight and go bankrupt that way."

"How's he affording London lawyers? What is it—he's got it on no-win, no-fee?"

"No." A muscle in Turnbull's jaw pulsed as he ground his teeth. "That's what I was arguing with Henry about. I caught him and Danny in the pub. It's obvious now what they've been doing—the Ainsleys are paying for his lawyers. They're using this whole mess to turn up the pressure on us. We could go to them and take their ridiculous offer, and I reckon the legal case goes away just like that." He clicked his fingers. "I saw Henry there, and I lost my rag. I told him what I thought of him."

"And?"

"I put the shits up him, and he fell over. But there were people who would've seen what happened—Danny was there, and I saw some riders go past—and it might've looked different to them. I just thought… well, I thought I ought to get out in front of it and tell you."

Franny and Robbie shared a glance, she'd always trusted herself as a decent judge of character, and she didn't get the feeling that Turnbull was lying.

"You did the right thing."

He drew in a deep breath. "That's not all. I sent a letter to the Ainsleys yesterday. An anonymous letter. It's stupid, but I'm worried it might've looked like a threat."

"I think I've seen it," Franny said.

The letter had been photographed and logged as an exhibit, entered into the HOLMES 2 system like everything else, where it would sit among the endless notes and statements and scraps of evidence the team were pulling together.

Turnbull got up, taking his empty mug to the sink. Robbie looked across the table at Franny and cocked an eyebrow quizzically; Franny gave a minute shrug of her shoulders. The conversation had already been a surprise, and now it looked as if it was going to take an unexpected detour.

"I didn't know anything about what'd been found in the field until I saw it on the news," Turnbull said.

"The interview?"

He nodded. "I've always had a thing for history, especially local history. I let metal detectorists onto the fields when they're resting, and they've dug up all sorts of things: old coins, buckles, a Roman brooch once. I saw what they said on the TV about the bodies and how they thought they might be connected to the rioters and looked it up. The fact that they were found on our land... It's been a major pain in the arse, and the delay's cost me money I can't afford, but it's still... it's interesting."

"How do you go from that to sending the letter?"

"Because I thought it was..." Turnbull paused, looking for the right words. "Because I thought it was apt. Look at them— big landowners, more money than sense, all that influence and power. And then look at us—we've got the farm, but you know how much profit we made last year? Ten grand. I'm out in the fields ten hours a day, six days a week, and I made a ten-grand profit. We don't have a pot to piss in. I looked at what I was reading about those poor bastards that were dug up, and I started thinking about what might've happened to them. I started drinking, and I got pissed, and I thought it'd be funny to send the Ainsleys a letter—maybe it gives them something to think about, or maybe it's just a way for me to get my own shot in." He stared at Franny and then at Robbie. "But I had *no* idea that Rupert was missing. And I had no idea that Henry had been found dead. I swear on my life. I saw the post, and I could see what it'd look like when you worked out who sent it, and I knew you *would* find out."

"Because you weren't careful?"

"I was *pissed*," he repeated. "And I didn't give a shit that they'd find out it was me. My fingerprints will be all over it." He took a pad of paper from the table. "Here—this is the paper I wrote it on. And they've probably got cameras up that'll show me putting it into their bloody post box."

They didn't, but Franny didn't see any reason to mention that. "You've done the right thing by telling us."

"What's next? Do you need me to do anything?"

"I think it'd be a good idea if you could come to the station and give us a formal statement," Robbie said.

Turnbull looked apprehensive at the suggestion. "Really?" He turned to Franny. "Is that necessary?"

"I don't think it's a bad idea. It doesn't mean you're guilty of anything. You're just getting it down on paper and putting your name to it."

"But I won't get into trouble? About the letter, I mean."

"I doubt it," Robbie said. "You shouldn't have sent it, but if you didn't have anything to do with what happened to—"

"I *don't*," he interrupted.

"Then I'd be surprised if things went any further."

Franny remembered the revision for her sergeant's exam and wondered whether the letter might fall under the Malicious Communications Act. Turnbull's intent would've had to have been to cause distress or anxiety, but, even if that was proven, she couldn't see much chance that Mack would want to push things up to a formal investigation.

"You've owned up to it, too," she told him. "That'll stand in your favour."

75

Jez woke to daylight falling across his face and opened his eyes, blinking. He lay back and closed his eyes again, smiling at the memory of last night. Ellie had driven over and stayed. Jez had cooked dinner for them both, and then they'd watched a film. They had been talking about films that had made an impact on them as children, and the choice had been narrowed down to either *Labyrinth* or *The Neverending Story*. They had settled on the former after Ellie had reminded Jez about David Bowie's ridiculous costume; they watched it with the benefit of two cheap bottles of Zinfandel from Tesco and then went to bed together. He opened his eyes and turned, but the bed was empty; he was about to get up when Ellie came through the bedroom door with Treacle at her heels. She had two cups of coffee.

"Morning," she said.

"Morning."

She held up the mugs. "Black, one sugar?"

"Exactly."

Ellie was wearing one of his shirts, long enough to reach halfway down her thighs. She handed him his coffee and then went around to the other side of the bed, sat down and slid her legs beneath the sheets, shuffling up so her back was against the headboard.

She leaned across and kissed him on the lips. "I had fun last night."

"Me too. What time did you wake up?"

"Six," she said. "I always wake early."

"What time is it now?"

"Eight thirty."

He rolled his eyes. "Sorry. It's not like me to sleep in."

"You fell asleep before the end of the film, too," she said with mock disappointment. "I'd normally consider that to be sacrilege, but you have an excuse."

"Do I?"

"You're exhausted. It's not every week you're arrested for murder."

He laughed. "Thankfully."

"I took the opportunity to make myself busy. I did a little research on our mystery men."

She reached over to the bedside table and collected the laptop that she'd brought with her last night. "You know we thought we'd have to go to London to look through the newspaper archive?"

"Yes," he said.

"Well, we don't. They've all been digitised—they've got a run of the Salisbury and Winchester *Journal* that goes all the way back to the 1700s."

She opened the laptop and tapped a key to wake the screen. Jez sipped his coffee and then shuffled back so he was sitting up next to her. She'd opened a browser window filled with the scratchy, uneven type of 1830s print.

"This is the edition for Monday the twenty-ninth of November," she said. "It's the first paper published after the riots on the twenty-third. They report trouble at Sutton Scotney and Havant and a call for men to enrol as special constables. It was obviously a big deal—look, they even published a proclamation from the King." She read aloud. "'Whereas great multitudes of lawless and disorderly persons have, for some time past, assembled themselves in a riotous and tumultuous manner, for the purposes of compelling their employers to comply with certain regulations prescribed by themselves, with respect to the wages to be paid for their labour.' He says they'll pay fifty pounds to anyone who gives evidence against rioters and five *hundred* to anyone who gives information against anyone convicted of burning barns or breaking up machines."

"Five hundred? In 1830?"

"I know. It's nearly fifty thousand today."

"They must've been *shitting* themselves."

She tapped the keyboard and brought up another article. "This is from Salisbury. 'The citizens were considerably excited that a party of rioters, after destroying a threshing machine at Bishop Down's Farm, were proceeding, armed with bludgeons, iron bars and portions of machinery they had broken, towards this city.' They were going after an iron foundry, and there was a confrontation with the yeomanry on the Greencroft."

"Anything on Samuel Larke?"

She grinned, tapped to open a third page of the newspaper, and read out loud again: "'Sir, It is with the gravest concern that I write to solicit the aid of your widely read publication in drawing attention to a matter of some urgency and distress. Three men—Thomas Farebrother, Robert Ayres and Samuel

Larke—all formerly in my employ upon the Brookmere estate near Pitton, have, without warning or known cause, absented themselves and have not been seen since the evening of the 22nd instant. Their families remain in a state of considerable anxiety, and despite thorough inquiries undertaken by my steward and others in my service, no reliable information as to their whereabouts has been obtained. In these unsettled times, when unlawful assemblies and acts of riot have, I regret to say, become more frequent across the countryside, such disappearances must be taken with the utmost seriousness. I would caution against undue speculation, yet I cannot dismiss the possibility that their vanishing may be connected to the recent disturbances. Should any reader of this *Journal* possess knowledge, however slight, that may aid in the discovery of these men, I entreat them in the name of Christian charity and neighbourly duty to come forward without delay. Any information may be conveyed in confidence to my steward at Brookmere House or to the constables at Pitton. A suitable reward will be offered for such intelligence as may lead to the safe return of the said men, or to the discovery of their fate.' It's signed 'Ainsley, Brookmere House, near Pitton.'"

Jez leaned back and blew out his cheeks. "Found them. Well done."

"I wonder, though," she said. "Ainsley would probably have been the landowner. What do you think the chances are that he wrote to the newspaper to cover up the fact that he was the one who had them killed?"

"Or it was someone who worked for him," Jez said.

"I don't know how we'd ever be able to prove that. This is probably as far as we'll be able to go."

"Agreed." He reached over to the bedside table for his phone. "I'll text Atticus."

Ellie put the laptop down and then took his phone from his hand.

"Tell him later," she said.

76

The man slipped between two parked cars so he could get to the wall at the edge of the top floor of the multi-storey car park. There was a magnificent view of the cathedral from here, but he barely looked at it; his focus was on the first-floor window of the address on New Street that Mr. Freeman had given him. The building was a three-storey Georgian townhouse. A shallow bay window jutted from the first floor, painted white, its multi-pane sash windows shut against the bustle of the street below. Beneath it, the ground floor had been converted into a shopfront for a bridal studio: modern signage on the glass, the black timber plinth and inset doorway suggesting older bones beneath the contemporary face. A passageway passed through an arched entrance to the left. It was a Saturday morning, and the street bustled with vans and delivery lorries, the upper storeys of the buildings festooned with strings of coloured bunting that fluttered lazily in the breeze.

The man took out a pair of binoculars and focussed on the bay window. It was partially obscured by blinds, but he could see enough to be reasonably confident that no one was inside.

Mr. Freeman had warned him that he would need to be careful, and that the man he had been told to investigate was unusually observant. That was fine. He'd always been careful when going about his work, the value of taking his time drilled into him by his instructor at Chicksands, back when he'd first been recruited into the Intelligence Corps. He'd worked for military intelligence for ten years, sometimes at home and sometimes abroad. He'd honed his skills in the Balkans during the tail end of the Kosovo unrest, and later during quiet, deniable operations in the Middle East: gathering intelligence, trailing suspects, maintaining deep cover. Surveillance work was muscle memory by now.

After his demob, he'd set up as a private contractor and had made a decent living tailing high-net-worth individuals, occasionally assisting with corporate espionage, and high-stakes divorce cases, including the one in Monaco from which he had just returned.

He did other work, too, making problems disappear in return for a much more significant fee. He was quiet and methodical with that, too.

This job wasn't so different. Mr. Freeman had told him the man he was to watch was a private detective, but unlike most in the business, this one was apparently more impressive. He was a thinker, and someone who noticed everything. That was all right. The man didn't plan to get close. His job was to watch and report, nothing more.

He shifted his weight and checked the window again. Still no movement, but, as he lowered the binoculars, he saw a man turning into the passageway. He waited for thirty seconds until he saw a shadow in the window. He made a note of it, timestamped it, and lowered the binoculars.

Atticus Priest was at home.

* * *

The man watched Priest leave the building. He started the timer on his watch. Priest had his dog with him and looked like he was taking it for a walk; the man had noted down the last two similar occasions when he had done that and guessed he would be out for a minimum of thirty minutes.

That ought to be enough.

The man took out a pair of nitrile gloves and put them on, then picked up the small leather satchel with his equipment and hurried down the stairs of the car park, emerging opposite the office. He crossed the road and went to the door in the passageway that led inside. There was another door at the back, but that one was too overlooked for him to break in there. The passage was more private; the only risk of being observed was by people coming out of the courtyard or passing by on the street.

The man checked: both the courtyard and the street were clear.

He looked at the stopwatch: three minutes had passed.

He took out his lock picks and knelt in front of the door, selecting a tension wrench and half-diamond pick with practiced care. He inserted the wrench into the bottom of the lock and applied slight pressure, then slipped the pick above it, feeling for the pins. It was an old mortice lock, well-maintained but nothing he hadn't dealt with before. He set the pins one by one, listening for the faint clicks, eyes flicking up every few seconds to check the street.

The lock yielded with a quiet snick. He opened the door slowly, stepped inside, and closed it behind him.

The man checked his stopwatch: four minutes gone.

All good.

He'd already checked the cached particulars on the estate agent's website from when it had last been advertised and took a moment to match the floor plan with what he could see. There was a flight of stairs up to a landing, with three doors off it: a door with frosted glass to the bathroom; another glass door leading to the flat upstairs; and a pair of wooden doors offering access to the office's two rooms.

The office doors were also secured. He took a rake and the wrench, slid them into the lock, and worked them with a smooth, practiced hand. The cylinder gave way, and the man eased the door open just wide enough to slip inside, closing it carefully behind him. He looked around: two rooms, one evidently used for sleeping given the futon on the floor and the dog bed in the corner; the other, the one he'd been watching from across the road, more like an office.

He put the satchel on the floor and opened it, removing a compact black device, no larger than a matchbox. It was a data skimmer. He located the cable running from Atticus's router to his connection and clipped the skimmer in line. It would intercept traffic without interrupting the signal.

He crossed to the far wall, unscrewed a double socket plate with a stubby multi-tool and replaced it with an identical socket fitted with a GSM unit that was capable of receiving incoming calls to allow covert real-time monitoring. He screwed it into place and then added a second in the bedroom. He paused, took a step back, and looked around. Both rooms appeared exactly as they had before. Nothing out of place.

The man took out his phone and opened a secure app to test the feed. A low hum came through, followed by the sound of a passing car outside.

The bugs were working just as they should.

He checked his watch: sixteen minutes.

More than enough time to exit safely. He closed the door, reset the lock, and slipped back into the street.

Atticus Priest was almost at the archway as the man passed through it.

His dog tugged at the lead, anxious to get in close enough to be stroked.

The man reached down and obliged. "Nice dog," he said.

"Most of the time," Priest replied.

"What is he?"

"German Short-haired Pointer."

"Thought so. My sister had a GSP once. Lots of energy."

Priest smiled. "Lots of walks."

"I bet." The man reached down and scrubbed the dog behind the ears. "Nice to meet you both."

"And you."

Priest turned into the archway.

The man crossed the road and went back to the car park.

He took out his phone and sent a one-word message to Freeman:

>> *Done* <<

77

Eastleigh Football Club was near Southampton. It was a non-league outfit, but still, Atticus noted as he collected his bag and stepped out of the car, a very impressive operation. The pitch was surrounded on all four sides by stands; one end was large and modern and housed a well-stocked shop on the ground floor and an entertaining suite on the floor above. Atticus approached the nearest steward for directions and was sent into the shop, from where the cashier indicated that he should take the lift. He emerged on the first floor facing the entrance to the suite.

"Hello," he said, taking out his ticket and showing it to the man on the door.

"Just yourself?"

"Just me."

"Been before?"

"Never."

"Show your ticket to one of the girls, and they'll take you to your table. Lunch is just about to be served."

"Perfect—thanks."

Atticus did as he was instructed and was taken to a table set for one next to the wide window that looked down on one of the goals and the pitch beyond. He sat down, ordered a coffee and looked around the room. He'd continued his review of Kershaw's social media, pleased to see that his obvious self-regard had inspired him to post dozens of selfies. The match was still an hour away, and the room was only half full, but, as Atticus cast his eyes from left to right, he saw someone who looked very much like the doctor coming in through the door he had just used. He was dressed in a navy blazer over a pale blue shirt with the collar open, slim-cut jeans that looked too tight to be comfortable, and a pair of bright white trainers that gleamed like he'd wiped them down just before coming in. From the garrulous way in which he spoke to the man at the desk and the slight sway to his gait, Atticus suspected that he might already have had a pint or two.

The waitress returned with Atticus's coffee and an onion bhaji that was the starter for the three-course pre-match meal. Atticus thanked her and watched as Kershaw made his way across the room to a table only three over from where Atticus was seated.

He'd planned to wait until half-time to make his approach, but, as he watched Kershaw idly swiping through his phone, he decided there was no reason to wait. He carried his coffee across the suite, doing a slow circuit like he was stretching his legs before the game. As he neared Kershaw's table, he paused and frowned thoughtfully.

"Excuse me, but I think I know you."

Kershaw looked up from his phone, surprised. "Yes?"

"Daniel Kershaw?"

"I am."

"I *thought* that was you," Atticus said with a friendly smile. "Sorry to interrupt—my name's Ben. I was at your talk in Winchester last month—at Royal Southern Health?"

"The panel?" he said.

"That's right—on early-stage cognitive decline."

Kershaw's face immediately brightened, his ego piqued. "That was a good one. Standing room only."

"I was one of the ones who had to stand. You made quite an impression. What you were saying on posterior cortical atrophy... I hadn't heard it framed like that before."

Kershaw smiled. "It's not often covered in public forums. People still think of dementia as just memory loss. PCA is visual, spatial—and confusing as hell if you don't know what to look for."

"That's what stuck with me."

"Why are you interested? Are you in medicine?"

"Journalist."

Kershaw looked pleased to be recognised and even more pleased to be praised. Atticus had detected a neediness in some of his posts and had hoped he might be able to elicit just this kind of response.

Atticus gestured to the empty chair. "Do you mind?"

"Go ahead."

Atticus lowered himself into the seat. "Thanks. Always nice to put a face to a name. You a regular here?"

"Season ticket holder. Long-suffering. You?"

"First time," Atticus said. "I'm down here to do an interview tomorrow. I've been trying to visit as many non-league clubs as possible, and I thought I'd add it to the list."

"How many have you been to?"

"Eighty-one. Didn't expect to bump into someone off the lecture circuit."

Kershaw chuckled, pleased. "Small world."

78

The match kicked off, and Atticus went out to his seat in the stand to watch. He didn't have much time for football, so he distracted himself by keeping an eye on Kershaw. Alcoholic drinks were forbidden in the stands, but it looked as if the doctor had circumvented the restriction by way of a hipflask he kept in the inside pocket of his jacket. He took regular sips of whatever was inside, and as they all made their way back to the lounge for a half-time snack, he was a little more unsteady on his feet than he'd been when he had made his way to the stand earlier.

Atticus joined him at the bar. "Poor excuse for a half of football."

Kershaw glanced across at him. "Tell me about it. Dogshit. They need the points today, too."

Atticus gestured to the bar. "What are you having?"

"A pint if you're buying."

"I'll bring them over."

Atticus ordered the drinks, and while he was waiting for the barmaid to pour them, he reached into his pocket for his phone. He saw a missed call from Mack and tapped the screen to return it.

"Afternoon," he said.

"Where are you?"

"At the football."

"What?"

"Fancied something different."

"You don't even *like* football. Where—Salisbury?"

"Eastleigh."

"Atticus…"

"What?"

"You're up to something."

"Me? Never." The first pint was poured and put onto the bar. "What's up?"

"I've had the lab report back—the pills you gave me."

He straightened, pressing a hand against his ear to hear her better. "And?"

"Well, you were right—they're not amlodipine."

"Sure?"

"That's what the report said—I'll read it to you. 'Tablets are not amlodipine as labelled. Identified active compound: scopolamine hydrobromide.'"

Atticus opened a browser window and navigated to a pharmacological database he'd used before. He searched it.

"Atticus? You still there?"

"I'm here."

"Scopolamine is used to treat nausea."

"I'm looking it up now," he said, and read out the result. "'Scopolamine is a muscarinic antagonist commonly used in low doses to treat motion sickness and postoperative nausea.

In higher or prolonged doses, it can cause confusion, memory impairment, visual disturbances, dry mouth, tachycardia and disorientation.'"

He looked over at Kershaw.

Rupert's medication had been switched.

He'd been taking the wrong drug for months.

"Atticus?" Mack said.

"Still here."

"Why were they mislabelled?"

He ignored her question. "Can you send me the report?"

"I just did," she said.

His phone pinged with an incoming email, right on cue. "Got it."

"Why were they mislabelled?"

"Still working that out."

"You need to tell me what's going on."

"I know," he said. "I will—just give me a little longer. Are you around tonight?"

"Yes."

"I'll come over."

"And tell me?"

"I'll give you what I know. I'll see you later."

He ended the call.

The second pint was delivered. Atticus asked for a couple of bags of crisps to go with the drinks, paid, and then took it all to the table.

"Here you go," he said.

Kershaw looked up from his phone. "Thanks."

He took his pint and raised it, allowing Atticus to touch the glasses together before they both drank.

79

Atticus trailed Kershaw back into the stand, taking a seat a few rows behind and to the left. The away team scored within five minutes of the restart, prompting groans from the home fans around them. Kershaw muttered something incomprehensible under his breath and took another long pull from his hipflask, shielding it with an exaggerated discretion that only made him more conspicuous.

Atticus watched carefully.

Kershaw was struggling to sit upright now, his body slumped in his seat, his head swaying back and forth as if he was trying to keep up with the movement of the ball but couldn't quite remember why. His neighbour—a man in a club scarf and wool flat cap—glanced sideways at him with growing annoyance.

Kershaw had been drunk at half-time, but Atticus wondered whether this rapid insobriety was caused by something other than the booze he'd been chugging. The doctor had gone to the bathroom before going back to the stand, and Atticus found himself wondering whether he'd taken something else—

something pharmaceutical—while he was away. A benzo, maybe. An opiate. Both had a stronger effect when mixed with alcohol, and a man in his position ought to be able to get hold of them easily enough, even with his suspension; he had form for it, after all.

By the seventy-minute mark, Kershaw had begun muttering to himself, then laughing abruptly at nothing. He tried to stand, swaying to and fro, and nearly stumbled down the concrete step in front of him. Two stewards who had been watching him from the edge of the pitch came over.

"Sir," one of them said, "I think you've had a bit too much."

Kershaw looked annoyed. "I'm fine."

"You're not, mate," said the other steward. "We've had a couple of complaints, and we can't have you falling down the steps."

Kershaw tried to wave them off but couldn't seem to focus. "This is ridiculous."

"Come on," said the first steward. "Out we go."

Kershaw resisted, but only feebly. He was helped to his feet and escorted down the steps. Atticus followed at a distance, waited until the stewards had guided Kershaw through the door and into the car park, then hung back near the exit to the lounge, pretending to check his phone. A few moments later, the stewards re-emerged without him, chatting and chuckling as they headed back to their posts.

Atticus crossed the car park. Kershaw was standing unsteadily beside a black BMW, blinking blearily at his keys as if unsure which one opened the car.

"You all right?" Atticus asked.

Kershaw turned. He squinted, his eyes bleary and unfocused. "Oh, it's you."

Atticus stepped closer. "I saw they took you out. What's up?"

"Asked me to leave." Kershaw gave a theatrical shrug. "Apparently I've had too much to drink. Need to get home."

Atticus smiled. "Well, you're definitely not in any state to drive. Want a lift?"

Kershaw hesitated. "I'm good. I can drive."

"I saw a police car when I was coming in—you don't want to lose your licence, do you?"

He swayed. "Suppose not."

"I'll drive you. Come back and pick up the car in the morning."

Kershaw looked down at the keys, then at the car, as if weighing the effort required.

"All right," he said at last, shoving his keys into his jacket pocket. "Probably best. Good of you."

80

Atticus knew where Kershaw lived: he'd established a company to deliver his medical services, and the registered address was a residential property in Southampton. Atticus put the postcode into his satnav and followed the directions south and into the city, navigating the early evening traffic as the streetlights started to flicker on.

Kershaw slumped in the passenger seat. Whatever he'd taken had exerted a heavy toll; he was sluggish and glassy-eyed. His speech was slurred, and his eyelids drooped, blinking slowly as though it took effort to focus. Every so often he'd mumble something incoherent and sway to the side, bumping gently against the door.

The address was for the penthouse flat in Imperial Apartments, an imposing Victorian building that dominated the corner of a wide, tree-lined junction. The architecture was grand and unapologetically ornate: tall arched windows with elegant keystones, rows of wrought-iron Juliet balconies, and rust-red brickwork offset with decorative white stone. The upper floors curved around the corner like the prow of a ship.

Atticus had checked online for details of the last time the penthouse had been sold; Kershaw had paid a million for it.

Atticus pulled into a residents-only parking bay. He helped Kershaw get out of the car, offering him his hand and then tugging him up to his feet. He was unsteady and would have fallen were it not for Atticus supporting him with an arm around his waist.

"Come on. Let's get you inside."

He raised Kershaw's arm and draped it across his shoulders and then helped him across the pavement to the main entrance. The doors were set beneath a stone pediment etched with the building's original name, the lettering faded but still legible. The lobby was a slice of preserved Edwardian grandeur: a high ceiling above black-and-white marble flooring, a carved ceiling rose surrounding a crystal chandelier, brass fittings and a large oak reception desk behind which sat a uniformed concierge.

"Evening."

The man looked up. "Evening." He paused. "Dr. Kershaw?"

"Had a bit too much to drink at the football," Atticus said, adjusting Kershaw's dead weight on his shoulder.

"I'll say. And who are you?"

"A friend from university. Thought I'd better make sure he got back in one piece."

"Good for you. Better sign you in."

Atticus nodded helplessly at Kershaw. "You couldn't do it for me, could you?"

"Of course. What's your name?"

"Ben Mitchell."

The concierge wrote the name into the guest book.

"You know how to get up to the penthouse?"

"I don't."

"Lift's round the corner," he said, pointing to a wide hallway with polished brass wall lamps. "Want a hand getting him up there?"

"I'm fine," Atticus said with a grateful nod. "But thanks."

He guided Kershaw toward the lift, its polished cage door pulled halfway open. He dragged it the rest of the way, helped Kershaw inside, and closed the scissor gate behind them. The lift shuddered as it rose, groaning as it passed each floor.

"Friend from university?" Kershaw mumbled.

Atticus didn't answer, and Kershaw didn't ask again. They reached the top floor, and the gates opened. Atticus helped Kershaw out and along the corridor. The penthouse door was modern against the period hallway, fitted with a keyless entry pad and, to Atticus's annoyance, a doorbell camera.

Too late to worry about that; he'd seen cameras downstairs, too.

Atticus reached into Kershaw's inside jacket pocket and found his car keys, his phone, his wallet, a slim keycard, a folded piece of paper, and a plastic medicine bottle. He pulled them all out, turned the bottle in his hand and looked at the label: diazepam.

Atticus wasn't surprised.

He took the keycard and swiped it.

The lock clicked.

He pushed the door open, shouldered Kershaw inside, and used his foot to close it behind them.

81

Atticus stepped into the apartment and guided Kershaw into a large, open-plan living space. He took stock of the room: high windows and wide-plank wooden flooring; a sleek, modern kitchen stretching along the back wall; pale grey cabinets and reflective metro tiles offsetting the three pendant lights suspended above a marble-topped breakfast bar; a trio of bar stools, each a different colour, tucked neatly underneath; a sofa facing a discreet bar built into the corner under a floating staircase. The bar's navy-painted cabinet was stocked with neatly ordered bottles and glassware, and above it a mirror reflected the rest of the space.

A pair of wingback chairs stood at angles near the bar. Atticus manoeuvred Kershaw carefully toward one of them and helped him down, watching as he slumped back, barely conscious.

He set the items from Kershaw's jacket pocket on the bar, then picked up the little fold of paper. He opened it carefully and saw a small pile of white powder. There was no way to tell what it was, but Atticus suspected benzodiazepine. It might be

Valium or Xanax, tablets crushed into powder so it could be snorted. He folded the paper again and left it on the counter. The wallet had debit and credit cards and some cash, but nothing else of interest. He put that back on the counter, too.

He took the phone and tapped the screen: facial ID was enabled, and, after a moment, it offered a keypad for a secondary means of authentication. Atticus turned the phone around and aimed it at Kershaw. The camera scanned his face, and, satisfied, the device unlocked with a faint vibration.

Atticus checked the phone and saw that it only had a sliver of battery life left. He crossed to the breakfast bar, where he found a charger, plugged the phone in to power it up, and then navigated to the settings and switched off the auto-lock.

He left it to charge and began to explore the rest of the apartment. The first door off the hallway led to a sleek, modern bathroom; nothing of interest there.

The next room was an office, sparsely decorated but immaculate. A standing desk faced the window, and shelves lined one wall, filled with medical textbooks. He moved to the far side of the room, drawn to a brushed-steel filing cabinet. He tried the top drawer and found it was unlocked. Inside were neat folders of paperwork: insurance documents, invoices for private consultations, prescription receipts. He opened the second drawer and found a small, locked box at the back. This one gave more resistance, but the lock was basic: a flick of his pocket pick and it popped open. Inside, nestled among other pharmaceutical samples, was a white bottle without a printed label. He unscrewed the cap and tipped two tablets into his palm. They were almost identical in shape and colour to the tablets in Rupert's cabinet. He pulled out his phone and took photos of the bottle and the pills. Then he carefully replaced everything as he'd found it.

He carried on to a spare bedroom—empty, no furniture, nothing other than cardboard boxes full of bric-a-brac—and then to the master suite. The room was tidy, almost prim. Built-in wardrobes framed the windows, and the bed was neatly made with a floral throw and a regimented line of bright, plump cushions. Everything was deliberate, as if Kershaw were trying to impose order on a life that had long since slipped beyond his control. The mirrored glass bedside tables gleamed, clear on top save for matching lamps, a clock and a framed photograph. Atticus picked up the photo and examined it: it showed Kershaw—younger, healthier, his face fuller and unlined—grinning in a black hoodie with CLASS OF 2005 written across it. He stood between a man and a woman, presumably his parents, both leaning in proudly. The man was heavyset, his dark hair already thinning, while the woman wore a bright mustard-yellow jumper and clutched her son's arm with both hands, her face lit with damp-eyed joy. Kershaw himself looked slightly overwhelmed, as though he hadn't yet come to believe he'd made it. Behind them stretched a red-brick Georgian building, and farther back, the pale stone bulk of a much larger building. The three of them stood in front of a striking modern statue of a woman in an Elizabethan-style ruff collar.

Atticus took out his phone and photographed it before replacing it on the bedside table.

A wicker basket sat at the foot of the bed, a fur throw stashed inside. A small desk under the window held a few personal items: a bottle of aftershave, a silver pen, a worn green notebook.

He went to the desk and took the notebook. It felt soft at the edges, as if the leather had been smoothed down by nervous fingers. Atticus thumbed it open. The first pages were neat enough: lists of drug names, dosages, scribbled prices beside each one.

Diazepam.

Tramadol.

Zopiclone.

He took out his camera and snapped several pictures, making sure that he had captured it accurately.

He opened the drawer and struck gold. He found a sheaf of medical scans that looked very similar to the ones that he had seen at Brookmere House. He took out his phone and found the photos that he had taken of those scans and compared the annotations at the sides of both sets of images. They were identical save for a single deletion: the scans in the drawer included a name that had been removed from the scans that Rupert had been told were for him.

Nicholas Penfold.

Atticus went back down to the kitchen. Kershaw was asleep. He took the phone and flicked through the open apps. Kershaw had left WhatsApp running, and Atticus scrolled through the message list. Most were mundane, but there were exchanges with someone who had not been given named contact details.

The first message in the thread was from Kershaw.

>> The scans are ready. Send the money. <<

The reply was from the unnamed contact.

>> Sent. <<

>> Received. I'll email him and make an appointment. <<

There was silence for ten days, and then another message from the unnamed contact.

>> He's asking questions. What should I do? <<

>> Tell him to speak to me. <<

>> He wants more scans. <<

>> I'll take care of it. <<

Kershaw snorted softly in the chair, mumbling something unintelligible.

Atticus opened the phone's settings and saw that it was on the Vodafone network. He opened his bag and took out a slim pack containing a fresh, unregistered SIM card tied to the same network; it was one of several he carried for moments like this, one for all the main carriers, each registered under a false name and topped up in cash. He took Kershaw's phone, turned it over, and used an unfolded paper clip to pop open the SIM tray. With a glance to make sure Kershaw was still out cold, he removed the original SIM and slid the new one into place. He wiped the screen with the hem of his jacket before unplugging the phone from the charger and slipping it back into Kershaw's pocket.

He went back to the bedroom, collected the scans and then arranged them on the counter next to the fold of paper, the keycard, the car keys, the diazepam bottle, and the wallet.

That ought to be enough to flush Kershaw out.

Atticus took one last glance around the room and stepped quietly back toward the door.

82

Kershaw very slowly came around. The room tilted gently as he opened his eyes. It wasn't spinning—he'd woken up feeling worse than this before—but there was a lag between his brain and the world around him. The ceiling was unfamiliar. His mouth was dry. His tongue felt like sandpaper.

He blinked.

What time was it?

He pushed himself up with a groan and sat on the edge of the chair, elbows on knees, hands hanging loose. The room was in semi-darkness with the faint glow from the oven clock the only source of light.

He looked over and blinked again until his eyes focused: it was coming up to nine in the evening.

He remembered the Valium he'd snorted earlier.

How many lines?

Two?

Three?

Too much?

And how had he got home? He couldn't remember.

His jacket was hanging neatly on the back of the opposite chair. He stared at it. That wasn't right. He never left it there.

The fold of paper with the crushed Valium and his wallet were arranged in a neat line on the breakfast bar, along with his car keys, the keycard and the diazepam bottle.

What?

His heart lurched. He stood unsteadily.

The scans he'd shown to Rupert were spread out next to them.

He would never have left them out like that.

He'd left them in the drawer upstairs.

Someone had been here.

He took his phone out of his jacket pocket and tapped the doorbell camera app.

The screen loaded, the spinning wheel making his stomach twist.

Finally, the app came up.

It showed him the most recent instances where a person had been detected:

5.30 p.m.

5.50 p.m.

He tapped the first recording and saw his own glassy-eyed face. He was leaning on the shoulder of a man half a head taller, supporting him as he walked him to the door.

Kershaw didn't recognise him.

He watched the video twice, then again, rewinding and pausing on the moment the man looked straight at the camera before helping him inside.

Definitely didn't recognise him.

He closed the clip and opened the next one, watching as the same man exited, turning back to close the door.

Kershaw dropped the phone on the counter.

His stomach clenched, and a bitter taste flooded his mouth. He barely made it to the kitchen sink before he was sick, one hand gripping the edge of the basin, the other pressed against the wall as he heaved. The acid burned his throat.

He turned on the cold tap and rinsed his mouth, watching the water swirl yellow and then clear.

He wiped his face on his sleeve, breathing hard, then splashed water over his face. He ran a tea towel under the tap and pressed it against the back of his neck.

He needed to call someone.

He dropped the towel in the sink and went to the counter, unlocked his phone and scrolled, hesitating for only a second before tapping the number.

He raised the phone to his ear.

It rang once and then twice, and then it went to voicemail.

Kershaw waited for the message to play out and then cut straight to it. "There's a problem."

83

Atticus drove back to the office, collected Bandit and took him out for a late walk around the cathedral. It was a pleasant evening, and there were still little groups of people sitting around on the lawn. He walked to the Walton Canonry before turning back, sitting on one of the benches near the chapter house that offered a view of the cathedral. Bandit spotted a half-eaten sandwich near an overflowing rubbish bin and hurried across to it before Atticus could intervene. He devoured it in two bites before trotting back over to sit next to the bench.

"Anyone would think I never feed you."

The dog cocked his head as Atticus took out his phone. He opened a browser and navigated to the Vodafone website, entering his username and password, and then found the number of the SIM he'd put into Kershaw's phone. He tapped it and waited for the website to open.

"What do you think, boy? Think we'll get anything?"

Bandit turned around and lay down.

Atticus tapped the number and waited for the website to load. The signal was slow, patchy around the cathedral grounds, but eventually the usage summary came up.

Two outgoing calls had been made since he had left the flat. Atticus narrowed his eyes.

The first call: less than ten seconds.

The second was longer: almost three minutes.

He copied the outgoing numbers into his notes app.

It took him thirty seconds to cross-reference the first and a simple Google search to find the second.

"Look at that," he said, glancing down at Bandit. "*That's* interesting."

He called Mack.

"Are you in?"

"Got in half an hour ago. Where are you?"

"Just walking the dog. Can I still come over?"

"You said you'd tell me—"

"I know who did it," he cut across her.

"Did what?"

"I know who murdered Rupert and Henry Ainsley."

"Who?"

"I'll come over now, and we can run through it," he said.

"Atticus…"

"On my way," he said. "I'll bring a bottle."

"Atticus! You can't keep—"

"I'm going to need you to do a couple of things for me."

PART 7

Sunday

84

Sunday dawned bright and warm, and Atticus made the preparations for what he intended to do while he was out walking Bandit. He called Emelia and told her that he needed to speak to the whole family: her and the children. She asked him why, and he said he had made some progress, but he had some additional questions that he needed to ask. She sounded uneasy but said that everyone had stayed at the house the previous evening and that they'd planned to stay for the party, now cancelled. Atticus thanked her and said he would be over at ten.

He called Mack next and checked that she had been able to do what she'd promised. She said that she had, and that she'd make her way to the house with Robbie, Franny and two constables who could provide muscle in the event that it was needed.

Atticus walked to Harnham again, taking advantage of the peace and quiet to run through his conclusions for a final time. He'd only managed an hour or two of sleep, unable to quieten his mind, and had eventually surrendered and got up. He tested his theory from every angle, and nothing he did revealed enough of a weakness for him to worry that he was wrong. He was confident that he could answer the two most important unresolved questions: what had happened to Rupert and Henry, and who was responsible. There were details that remained unclear, but the answers would become obvious once he applied the necessary amount of pressure in the right places.

He passed the Old Mill and followed the Town Path back into the city. Jacob would look after Bandit while Atticus drove out to Brookmere House for the last time.

85

Atticus got out of the car just as Mack arrived. Robbie and Franny were with her, and he gestured that he wanted to speak to them before they went inside. They gathered outside the redundant marquee.

"Are you sure about this?" Mack said.

"I think so."

"There are other ways to go about it," Robbie said. "Take them to the station and interview them."

"It's better this way. This will be a surprise—less time to think of a way to wriggle out of it."

"And potentially more explosive," Robbie said.

"That's why we're here in numbers." He frowned. "Where's the uniform?"

"There's been an RTA near the college," Mack said. "Couldn't spare them. But there are three of us—that ought to be enough."

Atticus looked over to the house and saw a twitch of the curtains. Emelia peered out at them.

"Let's hope so," he said. "Shall we?"

* * *

The Ainsleys had gathered in the family sitting room. All of them were there: Emelia, Celeste and Julian, Sebastian and Alexander. The woman from the kitchen delivered a tray with a large cafetière of coffee and enough mugs for all of them. Emelia indicated that they should help themselves, and Atticus took his turn to pour, the delay in getting started tightening his nervousness. He was confident he was right, but he still felt the little niggle of contrariness: what if he wasn't? He was going to embarrass himself in front of everyone, including—*especially*—Mack.

He stood and waited for everyone to resume their seats.

"Shall we start?" Emelia said.

"We should," Celeste said. "I have a call in an hour, and I don't want to miss it."

"I shouldn't need as long as that," Atticus said.

"Good," Alexander said.

Atticus ignored him. "Thank you for seeing us this morning."

"Why are the police here?" Sebastian said.

"I'll get to that. I'll get to everything." He took a breath and cleared his throat. "First of all, I'm sorry to say I think Rupert is dead. That shouldn't come as a surprise—I'm sure you've all reached that conclusion yourself. It would simply be too much of a coincidence that he should go missing days before Henry was murdered. It's very likely that whoever killed Henry also killed him."

Atticus watched the room as he spoke but saw nothing that struck him as unusual: the atmosphere was grave, and his suggestion was met with sombre nods.

"Where's his body?" Alexander said.

"I'm afraid I'm not sure we'll ever have an answer to that question. I suspect the murderer or murderers had a little more time to prepare for Rupert than they did for Henry. Rupert's murder was planned, and Henry's was spontaneous. They were able to arrange for Rupert's body to be removed and disposed of—buried, most likely, or burned."

Alexander didn't look convinced. "So why was Henry's body left to be found?"

"I doubt they *wanted* it to be found. Henry's murder was an act of desperation—and my guess would be that the murderers were disturbed before they were able to move him. Henry had no reason to be in the yard where he was found. He was attacked on the path, and then, when it was obvious to the murderers that they wouldn't be able to move the body without the risk of being seen, they dragged him into the yard, probably with the intention of coming back when it was dark. But he was found before they had the chance to do that."

Alexander wrinkled his nose. "Really?"

Atticus looked over at him, disguising his irritation at being doubted. "I've read the report describing where he was found, and I've seen the crime scene photographs. There's evidence he was dragged—scuff marks in the dirt at the edge of the track, broken stems of grass, the way his jacket was bunched high around his shoulders, as if he'd been pulled by the arms or under the armpits. Someone moved him, and they did it quickly and badly."

"That's all well and good," Emelia said. "But who?"

"I'm getting to that. Just humour me a little longer. I look for three things when I'm investigating a crime: motive, means and opportunity."

"That's a cliché," Celeste said.

"Of course, but there's often truth in clichés. We can start with motive since that's the easiest to find."

"Jack Turnbull," Sebastian suggested. "He has reason."

"Robbie told us he confessed to sending the threatening letter," Emelia said.

Atticus looked over at Robbie and nodded. "That's what I heard. Doesn't change anything."

"Henry and Father were trying to buy the Turnbull farm," Celeste said. "And we all know how Father would've gone about doing that—he wouldn't have fought fairly. Same with Henry."

"That's true enough," Franny confirmed. "He was paying one of Turnbull's labourers to bring a personal injury claim against him. Danny Peart—the labourer—admitted there was an argument outside the Nelson in Winterslow about that. Turnbull spotted them together and worked out what they were up to."

"There you are," Sebastian said. "There's your motive."

Atticus nodded. "That *would* be a motive—a good one, too, money and resentment at being bullied—but it wasn't him."

Celeste folded her arms. "How can you be so sure?"

"You'll see."

"The protestors, then," Alexander suggested.

"No," Atticus said. "They might've disagreed with the solar farm, but that doesn't mean they had a reason to kill."

"They confessed to vandalising the equipment," Franny said.

"Van Etting confessed," Robbie added. "He's been charged with criminal damage."

"There you go," Celeste said.

Atticus shook his head. "No. Going from criminal damage to murder is quite a jump. It's not them, either."

"You keep saying no," Alexander said crossly, folding his arms. "So who *was* it, then?"

Atticus cast his arm around the room, taking in Emelia and Rupert's children. "It's obvious, isn't it? It's one of you."

The atmosphere changed as if at the flick of a switch. Atticus was prepared and looked from one to the other, assessing their reactions: Celeste blanched and looked away; Emelia sat still, her hand frozen against her mouth; Julian looked at her in what looked very much like alarm; Sebastian gave a short, nervous laugh that rang false; and Alexander, his face reddening, shifted his weight and folded his arms tighter across his chest.

"You all had motive. In my experience, it's either jealousy or money at the root of these things, and you all stood to lose a *lot*. His will, as it stands, benefits you all. It'll make you all very rich. Emelia—you stand to inherit as his wife. The rest of you would inherit equally as his children, and you"—he turned to Julian—"would benefit as the husband of one of the children. But Rupert had started to talk about changing his will. You told me that yourselves. He felt he was being pressured into doing something he really did *not* want to do—break up the estate and sell it so you each got your bequests early, hopefully with enough time between receiving them and his death to be exempt from tax."

"That's it?" Sebastian said. "That's your conclusion?"

"Part of the conclusion. It's motive, as I say. And it only gets us some of the way there."

Mack looked uncomfortable, he knew she'd chide him later for his theatrics, but that would be after—he hoped—he delivered her the guilty party.

"I want to concentrate on Rupert first." He looked over at Emelia. "I'm sorry for what I'm about to say. I think it might come as something of a surprise, and I would've preferred to tell you separately, but I don't think the circumstances will allow it."

He'd expected her to look confused, but she didn't. "Nathalie?"

Atticus was surprised. "You know?"

"For months."

"But you didn't mention it? Not to me or the police?"

"He said it was over. He swore it was over, and I believed him."

Atticus felt a flutter of doubt. Knowing her husband was cheating gave her a much stronger motive than he'd credited.

Celeste shook her head. "I'm lost. Who's Nathalie?"

"The latest in a long line of women your father took to his bed," Emelia said.

"Why didn't you—"

"Tell you?" She spoke over her. "Because it's *embarrassing*. Jesus—put yourself in my shoes. I suppose it shouldn't've been a surprise. He had form. It's not like I didn't know what he was like, is it? I'm his third wife, and he started seeing me before he left Elizabeth."

"I'm sorry," Alexander said. "Who are we talking about?"

"Her name is Nathalie," Emelia said. "She rides horses. Has a livery yard near Winterslow. Your father would tell me he was going somewhere else and went there instead. I don't know much more than that."

"Atticus?" Mack prompted.

"I know more than that. I found evidence he was seeing her when I went through his study. I found a second phone he used to speak to her. There were messages and photos on it. I went over and spoke to her." He pressed his fingers together. "They met while they were at a riding event. They were close— close enough that Rupert was planning to leave you, Emelia. And he told her he was going to change his will—she was going to get your share, and he was going to make her a trustee with Henry."

"She told you this?"

"She did."

Two spots of red bloomed in Emelia's cheeks; Atticus pressed on.

"You said Rupert had decided that the estate was to be kept intact. He'd arranged a meeting with his solicitors that was due to take place just after he disappeared. He was moving quickly. Making a new will would have changed everything. Emelia— you would've received nothing. The rest of you would've found your inheritances locked away inside a trust you couldn't touch without Henry's cooperation—and he was on Rupert's side. You all knew that. You were losing your grip on him, and you were running out of time. Rupert confided in Nathalie about your argument with him the night before he vanished. He told her it had been the final straw—that he wasn't going to be bullied into changing his mind and that he was more determined than ever to protect the estate. And then, the next day, he disappeared."

Alexander shifted uncomfortably.

Atticus continued, "Nathalie told me something else that I found particularly interesting. It was about Rupert's diagnosis of dementia. He told Nathalie, but she didn't believe it. She said Rupert's hypertension had returned at around the same time as she noticed his mental condition getting worse. It seemed odd to her, so she looked into it—specifically into Dr. Kershaw. And this is where it starts to get really interesting."

He paused, letting them feel the weight of what he was about to say.

"Kershaw is suspended from practising as a doctor. Professional misconduct—he was caught stealing prescription drugs. He's a man with no business diagnosing a head cold let alone a condition that'd strip Rupert of his independence and authority."

"Suspended?" Celeste exclaimed. "*What?* How were we supposed to know *that?*"

Atticus brushed that off. "There's one thing that I wasn't sure about—how did Rupert end up going to Kershaw?"

Emelia paused, thinking. "He never told me that. I assumed he'd looked online."

"That's unlikely. Kershaw *did* have a private practice, but he was taken off all of the databases the insurers use when he was suspended. Rupert would've had to find his website and then make an appointment that way, but that'd be an unusual way to go about finding a doctor."

"How, then?"

"I think Kershaw was recommended."

"By whom?"

Atticus spread his hands. "By one of you." He looked from face to face. "Whoever it was probably killed him. Anyone want to own up to it?"

He watched them again and saw confusion, indignation and impatience.

"Didn't think so," Atticus said. "Let's carry on. Detective Chief Inspector—perhaps you could tell them about Rupert's medical record?"

"We've checked his records," Mack said. "Rupert was diagnosed with hypertension two years ago. He was prescribed amlodipine to treat it, and it did exactly what it was supposed to do. His blood pressure went from being unhealthily high to almost normal."

"But then it went back up again," Atticus said. "He took readings every day and recorded them all in a notebook. It's all there—the thing I thought was strange was that it started to get worse again a month or two before the time he first saw Dr. Kershaw."

Mack reached into her pocket and took out an evidence bag with the jar of pills Atticus had taken from the medicine cabinet in Rupert's bathroom. "These are marked as Istin—that's the brand name for amlodipine. We sent them off to be tested, and it turns out that the pills are not amlodipine. They're scopolamine."

"Which is what?" Alexander said.

"It's usually prescribed to treat motion sickness and nausea."

"You find it in nightshade," Atticus said. "It's a psychoactive drug—they used to use it recreationally."

Emelia looked baffled. "So why was Rupert taking *that*?"

"In higher doses it can cause confusion, memory impairment, disorientation... You can probably see where I'm going with this."

She gaped at him. "Someone switched his medication?"

"They did."

"Because..."

Atticus finished for her. "Because the side effects of scopolamine can mimic the symptoms of dementia. His blood pressure goes up because he's off the amlodipine, and he starts to show symptoms of dementia because of the scopolamine he's taking instead. He was being gaslit."

Emelia shook her head. "But the scans…"

"The scans," Atticus said, nodding. "Yes, they certainly looked conclusive, didn't they? But they're not."

"We sent them to an expert," Mack said. "They said that for someone in the situation Rupert thought he was in—just diagnosed, early onset—you'd expect to see mild cortical atrophy, maybe some subtle changes. Early signs, nothing too dramatic. But that's not what was in those scans. They were *much* worse—*far* more advanced than you'd expect in a man with Rupert's reported symptoms."

Atticus took over. "It's almost as if Kershaw wanted Rupert to see something tangible, and a scan of a real case would be too subtle."

"There was one other thing about the scans," Mack said. "They have metadata on them: scan date and time, serial number of the scanner, the hospital where they were done. We checked the patient ID with the NHS database, and it confirmed it—the scans were for a man called Nicholas Penfold, one of Kershaw's last patients before he was suspended."

"The scans were altered," Atticus said. "Penfold's name would've been on them, but Kershaw took it off."

Emelia looked stunned. "He *switched* them?"

Atticus nodded. "Kershaw wanted Rupert to think that he had dementia. He didn't. We'd be able to prove that if we ever find his body, but, assuming that's not possible, even finding the real scans that Kershaw arranged for Rupert ought to be enough."

"But why would Kershaw do something like that?"

"Good question," Atticus said. "I thought it'd be good to have a chat, so I went to see him."

86

There was a slight shift around the room, a tightening of posture. Atticus was near to the end of what he had to say, and the prospect of what he meant to do filled him with anxious energy. Mack, too, must have sensed it; she had turned so that she could watch everyone at once.

"Kershaw was convicted of stealing drugs from the hospital he used to work at in order to satisfy his own addictions," Atticus said. "The conviction and the suspension that followed haven't prompted him to mend his ways—he was barely coherent when I found him. But that gave me the opportunity to investigate. I found messages on his phone. Conversations with someone unnamed, someone who appeared to be paying him. 'The scans are ready. Send the money.' 'He's asking questions. What should I do?' All of it suggested that a lot of effort was being expended to keep Rupert under control. And to prepare the argument that he lacked the mental capacity to change his will."

He swept his gaze across them again.

"But Rupert pushed back and made it clear he was going to revise it anyway. The murderers must've been concerned that their plan wouldn't work and changed tactics. They killed him instead."

The room had gone utterly still.

"I'll give you another chance—anyone want to own up to it now?"

There was silence.

"Doesn't matter. We're nearly there, but we need to talk about Henry first. I was trying to put together the last few hours of his life, but there was a space of an hour or two on Wednesday morning when it wasn't clear—until I went to see Nathalie, and she said that he'd come to see her. It turns out that he knew about the relationship and wanted to ask her whether she knew where Rupert might have gone. Nathalie said she didn't but shared the concerns she had with the diagnosis and, specifically, that Kershaw wasn't what he was pretending to be. You told me that Henry called each of you that morning to set up a family meeting—right?"

They all nodded.

"Did he tell you why?"

"I told you," Emelia said. "He said he had some questions about Rupert that we were going to have to deal with."

"Same," Celeste said.

"And me," Alexander added.

Sebastian nodded. "That's right."

"I can't say what Henry said to any of you," Atticus said, "but my guess is that he told one of you a little more than just that. Maybe he said what Nathalie had told him about Kershaw faking the diagnosis, and it was obvious that the game was up. Whatever it was, it caused a panic, and the decision was taken that Henry was going to have to be killed. He was intercepted just as he left Winterslow and set off towards Pitton. He was bludgeoned to death, probably like Rupert was, and then moved off the track so he could be taken away when it was dark."

Atticus looked from face to face and still saw no reaction.

"I'm sorry," Emelia said, "but this is just speculation. The stuff about Kershaw—you might be able to prove that, but how can you link it to us?" She turned to Mack and Robbie. "There's nothing that's been said that'd give you anything, is there?"

"Kershaw is almost certainly guilty of several criminal offences."

"But we're not saying he murdered Rupert and Henry, are we?"

"No," Atticus said. "But he knows who did."

"What if he won't say?"

"He doesn't have to," Atticus said. "I made sure Kershaw knew I'd found out about what he'd done. I wanted him to know. I wanted him to *panic*. People do things without thinking when they're frightened, and I thought he might contact whoever he'd been working with. And I was right. He did."

Robbie frowned. "How do you know that?"

"I switched the SIM in his phone before I left. He wouldn't know I'd done it. Phones store everything on the device these days—contact details, messages, emails, browser history, whatever—so he'd be able to make calls and send messages just like before. The only obvious difference is that the recipient would see an unknown number. Since I own the SIM, it was easy to find out which number was dialled—I just had to go online and have a look." Atticus reached into his pocket and took out a piece of paper. "It was this one."

"But you can't say who the number belongs to," Alexander protested. "They wouldn't be stupid enough to use a number registered to them, would they?"

"No," Atticus said. "And since I've got all of your numbers, it was easy to cross-reference the number he called with all of yours, and, of course, I didn't get anywhere. Not surprising. Whoever's behind this isn't stupid. Quite the contrary: they're very clever—much too clever to use their own number to speak with anyone who could incriminate them. This'll be a pay-as-you-go number, used just to contact Kershaw and anyone else who might be involved."

Atticus glanced over at Mack and nodded; she took over, just as they'd agreed when they'd discussed Atticus's proposal last night. "What they might not know," she said, "is that the police can go to the networks and get all kinds of information on that number. We can get call records—who it's contacted, when, and for how long; and we can get cell-site data—which towers it connected to, where it was when it made calls or sent texts. Even with an unregistered number, you can see patterns. We'll build up a picture of where a person has been and then look to see if the phone was used in the same places. We'll be able to link it back to them. It's just a matter of time."

Atticus took out his own phone and held it up. "But we can probably short-circuit all that. I could just call the number now."

He hadn't been sure whether to push all his chips into the middle, but he decided that he was close and that the gamble was worth the pay-off.

Alexander spread his arms. "They wouldn't be *stupid* enough to have the phone with them."

"But they wouldn't have thought this morning was a risk. All this"—Atticus gestured to himself, then Mack and Robbie and Franny—"would've come as a surprise. They'll be terrified that Kershaw has been found out, but I doubt they would've thought to leave the phone behind." He unfolded the paper with the number on it. "No, I'm confident—the phone's in the room with us now."

Atticus's attention was split between entering the number and the reactions of those around him. He knew he was taking a risk. It *was* possible that the phone Kershaw had called wasn't in the room, and that Atticus's showmanship would blow up in his face. But he'd already mitigated against that as far as he could, and, besides, this was too much *fun* for him to resist. It was as close as he'd ever get to magic; this was him pulling away the shroud to reveal the trick.

He finished tapping in the numbers and pressed call.

Sebastian surged out of his seat.

A phone rang.

Sebastian barged into Robbie, knocking him aside, and ran.

87

Sebastian had barged Robbie with enough force to knock him over and was faster than Atticus had anticipated. He set off in pursuit, hearing the sound of Sebastian's footsteps as he disappeared deeper into the house.

"Call for backup," he yelled over his shoulder.

Atticus's experience of the building was limited to the parts that Emelia had shown him, and Sebastian headed away from those areas and toward the statelier areas that were rarely used: formal rooms with locked doors and shuttered windows, corridors lined with ancestral portraits and furniture under dust sheets.

Atticus moved fast, following the echoes of Sebastian's footfalls down a wide hallway panelled in oak. The house was a maze. He turned sharply into a gallery lined with oil paintings.

Atticus heard footsteps and spun to see both Franny and Robbie.

"Where is he?" Robbie said, already panting for breath.

"Lost him," Atticus said. "Where's Mack?"

"She went out to the front."

"He won't go that way. He'll go for the woods at the back."

Franny had her phone in her hand. "Backup's coming."

"How soon?"

"They're coming from the city."

"Not soon enough," Atticus said.

A side door banged shut ahead.

Atticus opened it and found himself in the servants' passage, low-ceilinged and narrow. There was an open door ahead; Atticus jogged up to it and stepped into the side yard.

He stopped on the doorstep and scanned the grounds.

He saw it: movement near the stable block.

Sebastian.

He was sprinting across the gravel path, headed for the storage sheds.

Atticus ran full tilt in pursuit. He glanced left and saw Mack as she ran around the corner of the house.

"There!" Atticus called out.

Sebastian didn't look back.

Robbie and Franny followed them outside.

"The stables!" Atticus yelled.

Atticus heard the rasp of a metal door being dragged open.

"Stop!" Mack shouted.

He heard the sputter and cough of an engine trying to catch and pushed harder, his lungs burning and his feet pounding across the grass.

The engine roared to life.

Atticus rounded the corner as Sebastian raced a quad bike out into the courtyard. The tyres kicked up a spray of gravel and mud as the bike shot through an open gate and across the rear paddock, the engine snarling like an angry wasp. Sebastian was hunched low over the handlebars; he didn't look back.

Atticus chased him to the edge of the field, but he was too late. The quad was already halfway down the slope, heading for the narrow bridle path that joined the Clarendon Way.

He stopped, panting hard, watching the red taillight vanish into the trees.

Mack reached him. "Shit."

"Yep."

"Did you know it was him?"

"I knew it was one of them. We just had to flush him out."

"You certainly did that," she said.

The sound of the engine faded.

Franny arrived with Robbie puffing behind her.

"He's going east," Atticus said. "Away from the city."

"I'll call the control room," Franny said. "You never know—we might get lucky."

Mack took Atticus by the elbow. "Do you have any idea where he might go?"

"No," he said.

That was *largely* true.

88

Atticus took a sip of his coffee and winced; it was tepid. He'd been sitting in McDonald's all afternoon, taking a stool at the raised bench in the window. It offered an excellent vantage to observe the comings and goings on Winchester Street: the queue of people waiting to be served in Subway, the shoppers going into the entrance of the Cross Keys Arcade, the slackening weight of traffic as the city slowed down for the evening.

Atticus was particularly interested in the shop selling garish American confectionary opposite. It had only been open for six months, taking the space in the unit that had lain vacant after the previous business had failed during COVID. The store squatted beneath a garish pink sign that screamed 'American Sweets & Souvenirs,' its letters plastered with stars and stripes, flanked by grinning cartoon mascots. The shelves were stacked floor-to-ceiling with lurid, overpriced candy: bright packets of Nerds, Sour Patch Kids, and Airheads. Souvenirs cluttered the front: key rings, knock-off baseball caps, and T-shirts. The floor tiles were a harsh checkerboard, the lighting too bright, too clinical, as if trying to distract from the shop's general emptiness. A handwritten sign offered 'Currency Exchange' at implausibly good rates, while the solitary member of staff loitered near the fridge, staring at her phone.

He finished what was left of his burger and wondered whether he should get another coffee. It had been a busy few hours. Sebastian had managed to disappear. He had been spotted in Winterslow but had raced through the village and continued into the countryside. A police Facebook post appealing for help had not generated anything other than lurid interest that had started to leech into local groups. The *Journal* had picked up the story and had published a piece on its website and socials; Mack had said that the nationals had taken notice of that and that the press office had fielded calls from several hacks looking for juicy stories. Mack wasn't enthused by the prospect of being involved in another nationally reported story, but she knew the increased scrutiny would be worth the discomfort. The attention on Sebastian would increase, and the chances of him being flushed out would improve.

The same could be said for Daniel Kershaw. The doctor hadn't been at his apartment when the police went to visit, and he hadn't returned since. His family and friends had been visited, and none of them had been able to offer any insight into where he might've gone. Atticus had been concerned when Mack had relayed the news that he was missing, and now he'd become fatalistic. Kershaw had left his passport and was last seen on the building's cameras getting into a taxi on Saturday evening without any luggage or anything that might suggest he was preparing to go on the run. Atticus suspected, instead, that he was going to see someone in the hope that that person might be able to help him, but, as the hours went by, he became less and less confident that he would be found alive.

Loose ends were being snipped.

He saw movement outside the candy shop and watched as the woman started moving the merchandise inside, getting ready to close up for the night.

He looked at his watch: it was 6.30 p.m.

Fair enough. The prospect of more fast food wasn't very appealing, so he decided it was time to call it a night. He texted Jez and confirmed that he would take the first shift tomorrow— he sent back a picture of an Egg McMuffin and said he could put as many of them as he liked on expenses—and got up to dump his rubbish in the bin. He hadn't expected to get lucky on his first try and had known this was going to need patience.

Trouble was, patience wasn't one of Atticus's strengths.

PART 8

Monday

89

Jez picked at the remains of a hash brown and nursed a second coffee. He'd been in McDonald's since just after eight, a notepad open beside his tray. The morning rush had come and gone: foreign students with brightly coloured backpacks, council workers cleaning up after Sunday night, shop workers with takeaway lattes. It was a slow Monday morning, and Winchester Street had settled into a lazy rhythm.

He looked up at the sweet shop on the other side of the road and concluded that the cluttered window display must have been designed by a committee of over-caffeinated teenagers. A single staff member was on duty, head down, scrolling through her phone. Jez had watched her as she opened up, observed her adjusting the display trays, rearranging the lollipops and sour candy, and dragging a mop across the tiles. None of it looked like it needed doing.

He'd jotted a few notes: foot traffic was light, and there had been no customers in the last hour. A man in a long coat had loitered outside briefly, peering in through the glass, but moved on without entering. Two deliveries had arrived:

one small crate of drinks and another unmarked box that was wheeled straight through to the back.

Atticus had called him last night to ask him to come and watch this morning. They had taken the chance to swap notes. Atticus told Jez what had happened at Brookmere House, that Sebastian Ainsley and Daniel Kershaw were both on the run, and that he had reason to believe that the vigil at the sweet shop might provide useful information that would help find them. Jez asked what that might be, but Atticus told him he couldn't say; he was clearly not prepared to go into details, and Jez knew better than to press.

Jez told Atticus that he and Ellie were confident that they'd identified the three men from the field. Atticus had sounded impressed and had said they would be able to discuss it later, when the business with the Ainsleys was concluded.

His phone buzzed with a text. He looked and saw it was from Ellie. She said that she'd made another breakthrough: she'd pulled the census returns for Pitton for 1901 and had found reference to a Mr. Henry Farebrother. His year of birth was listed as 1823, and his occupation was retired gamekeeper. He would have been seven in 1830, and Ellie said he could have been Thomas's son. She'd checked the 1911 census and saw that Henry wasn't listed—most likely dead—although his daughter, Sarah, was still alive. Ellie said that she would try to follow the Farebrother family line to see whether any relatives were still living in the area.

Jez chewed the last bite of hash brown and took a swig of his coffee. It had gone cold.

He fired off a message to Atticus.

>> Nothing yet. Manager's still phoning it in. Anything from Mack? <<

Atticus replied at once.

>> Just spoke to her. Both men still missing. <<

Atticus added a photo of both dogs splashing around in the river.

>> They're having fun. I'll dry them off and take over at 12. <<

Jez settled back, cracked his knuckles, and resumed his watch.

90

Atticus took over a little earlier than midday. He was taut with anticipation and couldn't settle at the office, he knew he'd end up bouncing off the walls if he stayed, so he decided to go and relieve Jez instead. He and Ellie had made excellent progress in identifying the dead men in the field, and now they wanted to put together a family tree for Farebrother—or either of the other two—with the hope of finding a living relative. Atticus was trying hard to be more empathetic and could see that Jez would be happier spending the time with Ellie. Mack would've been proud of the effort he was making in being a better employer.

Atticus had spoken to Mack on the phone while he walked the dogs. The search for Sebastian Ainsley and Daniel Kershaw had continued apace overnight. Officers had combed the woods behind Brookmere House with thermal-imaging drones and dogs, but no fresh trail had been found. Patrols were stationed at all road access points east of Salisbury. Their faces had been added to the regional missing persons bulletin, and officers had begun checking CCTV footage from train stations and coach terminals. Interpol had been notified as a precaution, and a financial flag had been placed on both men's accounts in case they tried to access money.

Atticus didn't believe either man would have the wherewithal to stay off the radar without help, and that was why he was here.

* * *

Atticus was contemplating the slightly unpleasant notion of a third cheeseburger when he noticed a man coming into the restaurant. He went to the counter and lowered a heavy-looking rucksack to the floor. He placed an order, then took out his phone and scrolled through it while he waited for his food to be prepared. Atticus turned his face away and watched him through the reflection in the window.

It was Charlie Freeman.

Atticus hadn't seen him since he had been shot in Samantha Hargreaves's cottage. Charlie was lean but solid, dressed in a grey wool jumper and navy joggers that clung to his wiry frame. A beanie was pulled low over his forehead, dark sunglasses hid his eyes, and he had a pair of wireless earbuds in his ears.

Charlie had been implicated in the conspiracy with Hargreaves and the others and was facing an autumn trial on charges of conspiracy to supply Class A drugs and possession of a firearm. Mack had glumly predicted that he would be represented by the best lawyers money could buy and had been proven right. She was confident that he'd do time, but not confident at all that it would amount to anything more than a symbolic slap on the wrist. And in the meantime, his lawyers had secured him his liberty with remand on bail rather than in custody.

Atticus watched in the glass as Charlie slung the rucksack back onto his shoulder, collected the bag with his order and a milkshake and went back outside. His gait had a subtle hitch; there was a fraction of hesitation in his stride, as if he was favouring one side. He carried himself just a little tighter through the middle, protecting the spot where the bullet had punched its way inside his gut. It wasn't enough to slow him down, but it was there: a slight stiffness, a wince that flickered and was gone before most people could register it. Atticus knew to look, though; he'd been in the kitchen with him and had helped save his life.

Atticus held his breath as Charlie waited for the road to clear, then crossed over and went into the sweet shop.

Atticus dropped his empty cup and grease-smeared wrapper into the bin and went outside. Freeman was talking to the young woman at the counter. Atticus stayed on the opposite side of the street, aware that Charlie would recognise him if he made himself too obvious. Freeman slipped the rucksack off his shoulder and gave it to the woman.

Atticus wondered whether he should go over and speak to him but decided not. Charlie Freeman was a violent man, and Atticus doubted he'd get anything useful.

Atticus needed the one pulling the strings, not the puppet.

He needed to speak to his father instead.

91

Atticus parked the car and got out, going around to the back to open the boot so Bandit could jump down. He attached the dog's lead to his harness, shut the boot and looked across the road to Alexander Freeman's house. It was the kind of country property that wore its wealth lightly, not ostentatious, but quietly impressive. It was built from flint and warm red brick and sprawled across two and a half storeys under a steeply pitched, moss-dusted tile roof that looked as though it had settled comfortably over centuries. Mature wisteria curled up the walls, their blossoms trailing purple against the brick, and the window frames—tall, white-painted, multi-paned— reflected a garden in full summer bloom. There was a softness to the setting: well-pruned trees either side of the house, while a paved terrace was shaded by a white parasol over a weathered teak table and chairs. The Land Registry reported that Freeman had purchased the property three years earlier, and that it had cost him nearly four million. Freeman's businesses—respectable on the surface but hiding a whole host of illicit activity— had evidently treated him very well.

Atticus had met Freeman before on two separate occasions. The first was when Atticus was still a detective constable. Freeman had come in for a voluntary interview after one of the distributors who moved his high-grade skunk rolled over and named him as the supplier. The intelligence was solid, but Freeman had dismantled the interview with unsettling ease. He had been polite, composed, even amused; not a man on the back foot, but one able to survey the whole board while Atticus had still been arranging his pieces. Everything had a plausible explanation, all of it just the right side of unverifiable. Atticus had finished the interview knowing that Freeman was guilty and certain there wasn't a shred of evidence they could pin on him.

Their second meeting was much more recent and much more unsettling. Freeman had followed Atticus to Standlynch after the conclusion of the case against Samantha Hargreaves. The purpose of the meeting was ostensibly for Freeman to thank Atticus for saving Charlie's life, but there had been something else, too. Freeman knew things about Atticus that he should never have known, and it felt as if he was giving him a polite warning not to pull at any threads that might cause trouble.

Freeman was brilliant, cold, and methodical. He wasn't the East End thug in a suit for whom he might once have been mistaken, but someone more refined and *far* more dangerous. Atticus had a high opinion of himself, and there was only one criminal he'd come across whom he would consider his equal: Freeman.

Knowing that was the reason Atticus was sick with nerves as he walked up to the front door.

"Hello."

Atticus turned. Freeman was walking down the road towards him. He was wearing hiking boots and a fleece-lined gilet zipped halfway over a thick jumper. As Atticus watched, three big dogs bounded after him. He remembered the conversation at Standlynch. Freeman had said he kept Malinois; they were big dogs, with sleek, muscled bodies and intelligent, alert eyes. Bandit was usually a sociable dog, but, at the sight of them—several inches taller and several pounds heavier—he edged around so that Atticus was between him and them.

Atticus wondered whether it might be better to put Bandit back in the car, but one of the dogs padded over before he could.

"Well, well," Freeman said. "Atticus Priest. To what do I owe the pleasure?"

"I was hoping we might be able to have a word."

"What about?"

Freeman's dog started to growl.

"Sorry," Freeman said. "Ronnie can be a bit over-friendly." He pointed at Bandit. "GSP?"

"That's right."

"Lovely breed. What's his name?"

"Bandit." Atticus gestured to the bigger dogs. "Yours?"

"Ronnie, Reggie and Charlie."

"After the Krays?"

Freeman smiled. "Bang on. I was born the street over from them, and I know their old manor like the back of my hand. You been to Bethnal Green?"

"I don't believe I have."

"Not missing much, not these days. Swamped by ponces from the city. Wasn't like that when I was growing up. It was proper then. Tight-knit. My old man knew the twins—not well, but enough. They never touched anyone who didn't have it coming. Bit of order, bit of respect. You don't get that now."

Reggie and Charlie ambled over. Freeman could see that Bandit was uncomfortable and could easily have put them on their leads but didn't. Atticus knew what he was doing: he was friendly and affable on the surface, but he was letting Atticus know who was in control.

"I'm just going to put Bandit in the car," Atticus said.

"I'll be over there, by the tap. The boys have got muddy— the wife will kill me if I let them in the house without cleaning them off."

Atticus retreated, glad for the moment alone to consider the good sense of coming here. It had seemed like the right thing to do before, but, now that he was here, he remembered how daunting Freeman could be. He'd wanted to confront him, to mark his card so he knew Atticus was onto him, but that all seemed like empty bravado now. He gave a moment's thought to getting into the car and driving off, but knew he'd hate himself for his cowardice if he did that. And there was something else: Atticus recognised an equal in Freeman, and there was a fizz of excitement at the prospect of matching wits with him.

He opened the boot. Bandit leapt in gratefully and curled up. Atticus made sure the driver's side window was open and went back to the house.

Freeman looked up from the tap where he was cleaning the dogs' feet. "So how can I help you?"

"I wanted you to know that I know," Atticus said.

Freeman glanced up and smiled. "You know? What do you know?"

"About you and the Ainsleys."

The smile faded. Atticus looked for a reaction beyond that but couldn't get a read. Freeman was inscrutable: calm to the point of indifference, like someone who'd already weighed the situation and decided exactly how far he was willing to go.

"I know the family," Freeman said. "Very generous when it comes to charity. I have a few charitable ventures myself— did you know that?"

"I didn't."

"Smaller-scale things, mostly—supper clubs at interesting places. The Earl was kind enough to let us use the formal dining room at Brookmere House for an event. We had a shit-hot chef down from London, entertainment from a jazz quartet I heard at Ronnie Scott's. Cost a grand per person, and then we had an auction at the end. Raised fifty grand for the hospice."

"Washing your reputation?"

Freeman chuckled, showing off a mouthful of small white teeth. "Cheeky bugger, aren't you?"

Atticus had felt uncomfortable before, but Freeman's sheer lack of concern was making it difficult for him to concentrate. He was obviously curious about what Atticus had come here to say, but it was a kind of lazy curiosity, in the same way that someone might watch a spider crawl across the ceiling; mild interest, but ready to crush it if it came too close.

"Shall we talk about Sebastian Ainsley?"

"The son? What about him?"

"How did you get your hooks into him? I'm guessing it was gambling. I know he's in debt. The police pulled his bank statements, and he's in the hole for over a hundred thousand. The family said he's had a weakness for poker for years—

online, to start with, but he's been playing in London. I only bring that up because I know you run a couple of games for big spenders."

Freeman held up his hands. "That's true, but it's not illegal. The club's kosher—it's licensed. Everything's above board."

"So I wouldn't find that Sebastian owed you a lot of money?"

Freeman shrugged. "I have no idea."

"Did he play at your club?"

"No clue. I'm not involved with the day-to-day. You'd have to speak to the manager. I could set up a meeting if you think that might be helpful."

"That's all right. I can sketch it out for myself."

Freeman finished washing the paws of the last dog and stood. "I'm going to have to make tracks. I've just bought a two-year-old thoroughbred, and they're taking him up to the gallops for the first time."

Atticus eyed him. "What about Daniel Kershaw?"

Freeman's sangfroid dipped for a fraction of a second. Most people would've missed it—the slight tightening of the jaw, the blink that lingered just a moment too long, the pause before his mouth twitched back into its usual half-smile—but Atticus was watching.

"Kershaw," he repeated, buying himself another second or two to compose himself. "Don't think I know any Kershaws."

"He's a doctor. Very impressive CV until he was caught stealing prescription drugs. The police said he took so many they couldn't all have been for his own personal use. They said they were looking into reports that he had someone buying them off him in bulk."

"That doesn't sound sensible."

"I went over to his place in Southampton on Saturday evening. He was drunk out of his mind. I was able to prove he'd been gaslighting the Earl so the estate could be sold off and given to his kids, but I couldn't work out which of the kids was involved. So I swapped the SIM card in his phone for one of mine so I could see who he called when he sobered up and realised I'd been nosing about. He made two calls—the first one was to Sebastian Ainsley, no doubt to warn him that things were probably about to get tricky for them. The second was to a shop that sells sweets and chocolate on Winchester Street. Do you know the one I'm talking about?"

"Opened a few weeks ago? I've seen it."

"I've been looking into it. Funny place—hardly anyone ever in it. I'm pretty sure it's being used for money laundering."

Freeman rolled his eyes. "Do you think so?"

"I was watching it this afternoon, and you'll never guess who I saw going inside."

"Who?"

"Your son—Charlie."

"So? Perhaps he was buying chocolate."

"No, I don't think so." Atticus took out his phone. "He had a rucksack with him, and he gave it to the woman who was in charge. I recognised *her*, too. Cassie Clare. I nicked her when I was police. She was one of the girls you were running out of the flats on Fisherton Street."

"What is it they say? Smallsbury."

"You're right—I'm sure it's just a coincidence. But I just wanted to see if you had anything to say before I looked into it a little more." He felt a tremor in his fingers and hoped it wasn't too obvious. "I did a little research into Charlie last night. He went to school at Westminster, didn't he?"

"We wanted to give him the best possible education." Freeman cocked his head to the side. "You're not going to tell me that's a crime, are you?"

"No, of course not. But I saw a graduation photograph when I visited Daniel Kershaw. I didn't recognise where it was taken at first, but I've taught myself how to geolocate photographs, and this one was very easy. There was a statue behind Daniel and his family of Elizabeth I—she founded Westminster. So that tells me that Daniel *and* Charlie both went to Westminster. They're the same age, too, so the chances are good they were both there at the same time."

"I'm sure you're arriving at a point, Atticus, but you'll need to make it quick. I really do need to be off."

"Of course—I'll sum up. Here's what I think happened: Sebastian Ainsley gets into trouble with his gambling and ends up owing you a lot of money, he asks his father to advance him his inheritance, but his father says no; Sebastian comes to you and says he can't pay, and you suggest another way to get the money; Charlie and Daniel Kershaw have kept in touch, and they've built a little pharmaceutical business together; Kershaw is caught and suspended and needs to earn. How am I doing?"

"It's a remarkable story. Is that it?"

Atticus shook his head. "We're getting to the remarkable part. Someone comes up with the idea to gaslight Rupert into thinking that he has dementia. The initial plan is to get him to distribute the bequests sooner rather than later, but, when it becomes obvious that he's not going to do that—that he's actually going to change the will, so Sebastian doesn't get anything at all—you decide to adapt your strategy."

Freeman's tone remained cordial, but something had shifted. There was a new sharpness behind the eyes, not anger, but calculation. Atticus had seen it in him before. "Meaning?"

"You had the Earl killed, and when Henry Ainsley worked out what was going on, you had *him* killed, too. Kershaw was given the number of the shop to call in an emergency, and he called it on Saturday, after I left, when he realised he'd been found out."

"And where is he now?"

"I imagine he's dead—and I wouldn't be surprised if Sebastian is, too."

Atticus watched him, desperate for a reaction that would confirm his analysis, but Freeman masked it with a hearty laugh. "You really do have a vivid imagination."

"Not really."

"Have you mentioned any of this to your girlfriend?"

That was a warning dressed as a question, a way of letting Atticus know that he wasn't the only one who had done his homework. He'd made the same threat before, but it felt more immediate now.

"I don't think I've got enough to do that yet."

"That's good. You wouldn't want to waste her time with silly stories when she's busy trying to find out what really happened."

"You're right. It is just a theory. But that's not to say I won't be able to prove it in the end. That's the thing with me, Mr. Freeman—I *hate* leaving things unfinished. Everyone tells me it's one of my weaknesses."

Freeman reached out his hand; Atticus found he was incapable of shunning it.

"It's good to see you again, Atticus. Let me know if I can be of any more help."

Freeman held onto Atticus's hand for a beat too long, his eyes never once leaving Atticus's face.

Atticus's throat was dry.

"Don't worry," he said. "I will."

EPILOGUE

Freeman clocked the sign—Rainbow Bridge Pet and Equine Crematorium—and slowed down, turning off the road and onto the gravelled drive that led to the business. The facility was just outside Stockbridge, off Longstock Road, and surrounded by arable fields that lent it perfect isolation.

There had been a dairy farm here once, owned by the Bryson family for more than two hundred years. That business had failed, but Albert Bryson had performed a radical commercial pivot and set up the crematorium instead. It had been successful and would have continued that way if not for Bryson allowing himself to fall behind on the loans he'd taken out with the bank.

Bryson's children had gone to the same school as Freeman's, and the two of them had developed a loose acquaintance while on the sidelines of the weekly sports fixtures. Bryson had told Freeman about his plight, and sensing the opportunity for a deal, Freeman had offered to loan him the money to pay the bank back.

Bryson had gladly accepted and—as Freeman had anticipated—had quickly fallen behind on repaying the new loan. They'd gone for a drink, and Freeman had suggested another way to service the debt: Bryson would give Freeman fifty-one percent of the business. Bryson had laughed at that, thinking it was all one big joke and probably expecting relaxed terms for repayment that he might be able to abuse, until Freeman switched off the warmth and switched *on* the cold ruthlessness that he knew would be terrifying.

He'd repeated his terms: fifty-one percent of the business and the use of the facilities whenever necessary.

Bryson had accepted.

The office was a small brick building with the actual crematorium at the back. The rectangular building was clad in vertical wooden slats, giving it a more contemporary look. It was plain and discreet, with only the exhaust vents protruding from the roof giving any kind of clue as to what happened inside.

Freeman watched as the van backed up to the large roller door. He opened the smaller door to the side and went in. Bryson had been given the afternoon off. His naivety as to Freeman's business had been disabused, but although he might have hazarded a guess as to the reason why Freeman occasionally needed his very particular equipment, he'd never articulated it. There was really only one purpose to which it could be put, and, since Freeman obviously wasn't using it to dispose of dead animals, the alternative was so macabre as to be unspeakable.

Freeman flicked the light switch, and the overhead LEDs cast a stark white glow over the polished concrete floor and the massive industrial cremation unit that dominated the far end of the building. The room smelled of ash and disinfectant, the faint traces of past incinerations still hanging in the air.

The van's engine cut out, and the back doors swung open. Freeman's son Charlie and one of the lads—

Pete Matthews—stepped out. Matthews, burly and with thick forearms covered in tattoos, jerked his chin toward Freeman in greeting.

"Where do you want them, boss?"

"Where do you think?" He gestured toward the crematorium's loading area. "Straight in."

Matthews climbed into the van and pulled out a bundle wrapped in a heavy-duty plastic sheet and secured with thick, industrial zip ties. The weight inside was unmistakable, and it was starting to smell. Matthews and Charlie gripped it at either end and manoeuvred it onto a collapsible gurney. The wheels squeaked as they pushed the trolley past the control panel and toward the main cremation chamber. The incinerator was still warm from its last use. Freeman checked the display screen; the temperature had dropped to around 200 degrees Celsius, but it wouldn't take long to get it back up.

"On three," Matthews said.

They hoisted the wrapped body up onto the metal loading tray that extended from the incinerator's front panel. Freeman stepped forward and gripped the thick black handle that controlled the loading door. He pulled it open with a dull hiss, revealing the chamber lined with scorched firebrick. He stepped aside as Matthews guided the gurney forward, tipping it up just enough to let gravity take hold. The body slid inside with a muted thump.

"Sorry, Daniel," Charlie muttered.

Freeman frowned. "Sorry?"

"Yeah," he said. "I've known him for years. He was a mate."

"He was an idiot. This wouldn't have happened if he'd been more careful." He pointed back to the open door of the van. "And him."

They loaded Sebastian Ainsley onto the gurney and dumped him into the chamber to fall atop Kershaw. They stepped back, and Freeman closed the door, turning the handle until he felt the seal lock into place. He reached for the touchscreen and brought up the preheat sequence. The burners hummed to life, and the air around them thickened with heat. He tapped the control panel again to bring the temperature up all the way. The flames inside surged to life, rolling across the chamber with a dull roar.

"Give it ninety minutes," he said. "Then run the afterburner."

Matthews pointed to the chamber. "And the ash?"

"There's a horse booked in for tomorrow morning. Sweep whatever's left of them into the bone grinder and leave it. By the time it's all mixed together, no one will be able to tell the difference." Freeman pointed at the van. "Make sure you've cleaned that so it's spotless."

Freeman went back outside and walked over to his car. The scheme that Sebastian Ainsley had proposed had always been a bit of a punt, but the risks were manageable, and the potential rewards were outsized. It might have been a long shot, but it had been going well. The gaslighting of Rupert Ainsley had progressed just as Kershaw had predicted. Sebastian had introduced Rupert to Kershaw, and the doctor had gone to work: swapping his pills to promote symptoms that might look like dementia and then faking the scans that proved it. The scheme had been working until the Ainsley kids pushed too hard and too fast, and Rupert had changed his mind.

And now, look what had happened because they hadn't followed his instructions more carefully: Rupert was dead, his body incinerated, and now Sebastian and Kershaw would be the same.

Freeman looked up at the smoke that curled out of the chimney and found his thoughts turning to Atticus Priest. The devices in the office were operating as they should, but they hadn't been installed in time to prevent him from bringing the scheme crashing down.

Freeman had complicated thoughts about Priest. He'd saved Charlie from bleeding to death after he'd been shot, but that kind of credit only went so far. His interference with the Ainsleys might have cost Freeman hundreds of thousands of pounds—millions, even—and as he opened the door of his car and lowered himself into the seat, he wondered whether now might be the time to have a little chat, to explain to him that there were darkened corners in Salisbury into which it would be unwise for him to shine too much light.

Because it wasn't the first time Priest had interfered in Freeman's business.

The dope farm in the woods.

The drugs at the livery yard.

And now this.

Fool me once, shame on you.

Fool me twice, shame on me.

This was three times. What did that say about him? Freeman had given Priest some grace after saving Charlie's life, but that was all used up now.

He started the engine and pulled away.

Three times Atticus Priest had put his nose into business that didn't concern him.

There wouldn't be a fourth.

AFTERWORD

The seed for this story was planted on a walk.

I spend a lot of time walking the paths around Salisbury with my dogs, and it was while exploring the Clarendon Way—the ancient route linking Salisbury and Winchester—that the idea for this novel began to take shape. The countryside along that path is rich with history, and as I passed through villages, skirted fields, and paused by old farm buildings, I found myself thinking about the generations of people who had lived and worked there. The landscape is beautiful, but it hasn't always been kind.

This book is, in part, about pressure. The pressures faced by those who work the land—then and now. Starting in the seventeenth century, the Enclosure Acts swept across the country, transforming a communal way of life into a system that left many labourers dispossessed. Then came mechanisation, rendering many jobs obsolete and forcing rural communities to adapt or vanish. And today, farmers still face immense challenges: from rising costs and tighter margins to the impact of climate change and shifting agricultural policy. I wanted to explore what it means to be tied to the land in both memory and reality—and what happens when the past refuses to stay buried.

Although many of the locations in this book are inspired by real places—Pitton, Winterslow, and the sweeping fields on either side of the Clarendon Way—I've taken liberties with geography, names, and details. The Brookmere Estate doesn't exist, and neither does the Ainsley family. This is not a factual map of Wiltshire, but Atticus's version of it. The places here are fictionalised, shaped to fit the story, but they hopefully still feel real enough to walk through.

Thanks are due to my editors, my advance readers, and the booksellers who have helped readers find Atticus. Special thanks to the team in Waterstones—especially Salisbury, but across the southwest—who have been a pleasure to work with, and to whom this book is dedicated. And, as ever, thanks to my family.

And thank *you* for taking that walk with me—and with Atticus. I hope you enjoyed it. The next one isn't too far away.

Mark Dawson

Salisbury, 2025

GET EXCLUSIVE
MARK DAWSON MATERIAL

Building a relationship with my readers is the very best thing about writing. Join my Reader Club for information on new Atticus Priest books and deals plus occasional free content from all of my series.

Sign up at my website: **www.markjdawson.com**